John Bell

Bell's British Theater Consisting of the most esteemed English Plays

Volume the Thirteenth

John Bell

Bell's British Theater Consisting of the most esteemed English Plays
Volume the Thirteenth

ISBN/EAN: 9783744767040

Printed in Europe, USA, Canada, Australia, Japan

Cover: Foto ©Andreas Hilbeck / pixelio.de

More available books at **www.hansebooks.com**

B E L L's

RITISH THEATRE.

VOLUME the THIRTEENTH.

BRITISH THEATRE;

COMEDIES.

LONDON

Printed for John Bell near Exeter Exchange in the
STRAND.

BRITISH THEATRE,

Confifting of the moft efteemed

ENGLISH PLAYS.

VOLUME THE THIRTEENTH.

Being the Sixth Volume of COMEDIES.

CONTAINING

The Inconstant, by Mr. Farquhar.
The Double Dealer, by Mr. Congreve.
The Foundling, by Mr. Moore,
The Spanish Fryar, by Mr. Dryden.
The Double Gallant, by Mr. Cibber.

LONDON:

Printed for John Bell, at the Britifh Library, Strand.

M DCC LXXX.

Publish'd for Bell's British Theatre June 1st 1777.   Thornthwaite Sculp.

SINGHAM in the Character of ORLANA.

Proud of my power & am resolved to use it.

THE
INCONSTANT;
OR,
THE WAY TO WIN HIM.

A COMEDY,

As written by Mr. G. FARQUHAR.

DISTINGUISHING ALSO THE

VARIATIONS OF THE THEATRE,

AS PERFORMED AT THE

Theatre-Royal in Drury-Lane.

Regulated from the Prompt-Book,

By PERMISSION of the MANAGERS,

By Mr. HOPKINS, Prompter.

In nova fert animus mutatas dicere formas
Corpora————————————————Ovid. Met.

LONDON:

Printed for JOHN BELL, near *Exeter-Exchange*, in the *Strand.*

MDCCLXXVII.

T O

RICHARD TIGHE, Eſq.

SIR,

DEDICATIONS are the only faſhions in the world that are more diſliked for being univerſal ; and the reaſon is, that they very ſeldom fit the perſons they were made for: but I hope to avoid the common obloquy in this addreſs, by laying aſide the poet in every thing but the dramatic decorum of ſuiting my character to the perſon. From the part of Mirabel in this play, and another character in one of my former, people are willing to compliment my performance in drawing a gay, ſplendid, generous, eaſy, fine young gentleman. My genius, I muſt confeſs, has a bent to that kind of deſcription ; and my veneration for you, Sir, may paſs for unqueſtionable, ſince in all theſe happy accompliſhments you come ſo near to my darling character, abating his inconſtancy.

What an unſpeakable bleſſing is youth and fortune, when a happy underſtanding comes in, to moderate the deſires of the firſt, and to refine upon the advantages of the latter ; when a gentleman is maſter of all pleaſures, but a ſlave to none ; who has travelled, not for the curioſity of the ſight, but for the improvement of the mind's eye ; and who returns full of every thing but himſelf ? An author might ſay a great deal more, but a friend, Sir, nay, an enemy muſt allow you this.

I ſhall here, Sir, meet with two obſtacles, your modeſty and your ſenſe ; the firſt, as a cenſor upon the ſubject, the ſecond, as a critic upon the ſtile : but I am obſtinate in my purpoſe, and will maintain what I ſay to the laſt drop of my pen ; which I may the more boldly undertake, having all the world on my ſide ; nay, I have your very ſelf againſt you ; for by declining to hear your own merit, your friends are authorized the more to proclaim it.

A 2

Your

Your generosity and easiness of temper is not only obvious in your common affairs and conversation, but more plainly evident in your darling amusement, that opener and dilater of the mind, music:—from your affection for this delightful study, we may deduce the pleasing harmony that is apparent in all your actions; and be assured, Sir, that a person must be possessed of a very divine soul, who is so much in love with the entertainment of angels.

From your encouragement of music, if there be any poetry here, it has a claim, by the right of kindred, to your favour and affection. You were pleased to honour the representation of this play with your appearance at several times, which flatter'd my hopes that there might be something in it which your good-nature might excuse. With the honour I here intend for myself, I likewise consult the interest of my nation, by shewing a person that is so much a reputation and credit to my country. Besides all this, I was willing to make a handsome compliment to the place of my pupilage; by informing the world that so fine a gentleman had the seeds of his education in the same university, and at the same time with,

SIR,

Your most faithful, and

Most humble Servant,

G. FARQUHAR.

[5]

P R E F A C E.

TO give you the history of this play, would but
cause the reader and the writer a trouble to no
purpose; I shall only say, that I took the hint from
Fletcher's Wild Goose Chase; and to those who say that
I have spoiled the original, I wish no other injury but
that they would say it again.

As to the success of it, I think it but a kind of Cremona
business, I have neither lost nor won. I pushed fairly,
but the French were prepossessed, and the charms of
Gallic heels were too hard for an English brain; but I am
proud to own, that I have laid my head at the ladies feet.
The favour was unavoidable, for we are a nation so very
fond of improving our understanding, that the instruc-
tion of a play does no good, when it comes in compe-
tition with the moral of a minuet. Pliny tells us, in his
Natural History, of elephants that were taught to dance
on the ropes; if this could be made practicable now,
what a number of subscriptions might be had to bring the
Great Mogul out of Fleet-street, and make him dance
between the acts!

I remember, that about two years ago, I had a gentleman from France* that brought the play-house some
fifty audiences in five months; then why should I be
surprised to find a French lady do as much? It is the
prettiest way in the world of despising the French king,
to let him see that we can afford money to bribe away his
dancers, when he, poor man, has exhausted all his stock,
in buying some pitiful towns and principalities: *cùm mul-
tis aliis.* What can be a greater compliment to our generous nation, than to have the lady upon her re-tour to Pa-

A 3   ris,

---

* Constant Couple.

ris, boaſt of her ſplendid entertainment in England, of the complaiſance, liberty, and good-nature of a people, that thronged her houſe ſo full, that ſhe had not room to ſtick a pin; and left a poor fellow, that had the misfortune of being one of themſelves, without one farthing for half a year's pains that he had taken for their entertainment.

There were ſome gentlemen in the pit the firſt night, that took the hint from the prologue to damn the play; but they made ſuch a noiſe in the execution, that the people took the outcry for a reprieve; ſo that the darling miſchief was over-laid by their over-fondneſs of the changeling: 'tis ſomewhat hard, that gentlemen ſhould debaſe themſelves into a faction of a dozen, to ſtab a ſingle perſon, who never had the reſolution to face two men at a time; if he has had the misfortune of any miſunderſtanding with a particular perſon, he has had a particular perſon to anſwer it: but theſe ſparks would be remarkable in their reſentment; and if any body fall under their diſpleaſure, they ſcorn to call him to a particular account, but will very honourably burn his houſe, or pick his pocket.

The new-houſe has perfectly made me a convert by their civility on my ſixth night: for to be friends, and revenged at the ſame time, I muſt give them a play, that is,——when I write another. For faction runs ſo high, that I could wiſh the ſenate would ſuppreſs the houſes, or put in force the act againſt bribing elections; that houſe which has the moſt favours to beſtow, will certainly carry it, ſpight of all poetical juſtice that would ſupport t'other.

I have heard ſome people ſo extravagantly angry at this play, that one would think they had no reaſon to be diſpleaſed at all; whilſt ſome (otherwiſe men of good ſenſe) had commended it ſo much, that I was afraid they ridiculed me; ſo that between both, I am abſolutely at a loſs what to think on't: for tho' the cauſe has come on ſix days ſucceſſively, yet the trial, I fancy, is not determined. When our devotion to Lent, and our Lady, is over, the buſineſs will be brought on again, and then we ſhall have fair play for our money.

There

There is a gentleman of the firſt underſtanding, and a very good critic, who ſaid of Mr. Wilks, that in this part he out-acted himſelf, and all men that he ever ſaw. I would not rob Mr. Wilks, by a worſe expreſſion of mine, of a compliment that he ſo much deſerves.

I had almoſt forgot to tell you, that the turn of plot in the laſt act, is an adventure of Chevalier de Chaſtillon at Paris, and matter of fact; but the thing is ſo univerſally known, that I think this advice might have been ſpared, as well as the reſt of the preface, for any good it will do either to me or the play.

[9].

PROLOGUE.

LIKE hungry guests, a sitting audience looks;
Plays are like suppers: poets are the cooks.
The founders you: the table is this place:
The carvers we: the prologue is the grace.
Each act, a course; each scene a different dish:
Tho' we're in Lent, I doubt you're still for flesh.
Satire's the sauce, high-season'd, sharp and rough;
Kind masks and beaux, I hope you're pepper-proof.
Wit is the wine; but 'tis so scarce the true,
Poets, like vintners, balderdash and brew.
Your surly scenes, where rant and bloodshed join,
Are butcher's meat, a battle's a sirloin:
Your scenes of love, so flowing, soft and chaste,
Are water-gruel, without salt or taste.
Bawdy's fat venison, which, tho' stale, can please:
Your rakes love haut-goûts, like your damn'd French cheese.
Your rarity for the fair guest to gape on,
Is your nice squeaker, or Italian capon;
Or your French virgin-pullet, garnish'd round,
And dress'd with sauce of some—four hundred pound.
An opera, like an oglio, nicks the age;
Farce is the hasty-pudding of the stage.
For when you're treated with indifferent cheer,
You can dispense with slender stage-coach fare.
A pastoral's whipt cream; stage-whims, mere trash;
And tragi-comedy, half fish and flesh.
But comedy, that, that's the darling cheer;
This night we hope you'll all inconstant bear:
Wild fowl is lik'd in play-house all the year.
Yet since each mind betrays a diff'rent taste,
And every dish scarce pleases ev'ry guest,
If ought you relish, do not damn the rest:
This favour crav'd, up let the music strike:
You're welcome all——now fall to, where you like.

DRA-

DRAMATIS PERSONÆ.

MEN.

	Covent-Garden.
Old *Mirabel*, an aged gent. of an odd compound, between the peevishnefs incident to his years, and his fatherly fondnefs towards his fon,	Mr. Shuter.
Young *Mirabel*, his fon - -	Mr. Smith.
Cap. *Duretete*, an honeft good-natured fellow, that thinks himfelf a greater fool than he is, - -	Mr. Woodward.
Dugard, brother to *Oriana*, -	Mr. Gardner.
Petit, fervant to *Dugard*, afterwards to his fifter, - -	Mr. Cufhing.

WOMEN.

Oriana, a lady contracted to *Mirabel*, who would bring him to reafon.	Mrs. Leffingham.
Bifarre, a whimfical lady, friend to *Oriana*, admired by *Duretete*,	Mifs Macklin.
Lamorce, a woman of contrivance,	Mifs Ogilvie.

	Drury-Lane.
Old *Mirabel*, -	Mr. Yates.
Young *Mirabel*, - -	Mr. Smith.
Capt. *Duretete*, - -	Mr. King.
Dugard, - - -	Mr. Davies.
Petit, - - -	Mr. Wefton.
Oriana, - -	Mifs Younge.
Bifarre, - - -	Mrs. Abington.
Lamorce, - -	Mifs Platt.

Four Bravoes, two Gentlemen, and two Ladies.
Soldiers, Servants, and Attendants.

THE

ACT I.

SCENE, *The Street.*

Enter Dugard *and his Man* Petit, *in Riding Habits.*

DUGARD.

SIRRAH, what's a clock?

Pet. Turn'd of eleven, Sir.

Dug. No more! We have rid a swinging pace from Nemours since two this morning! Petit, run to Rousseau's and bespeak a dinner at a Lewis d'Or a head, to be ready by one.

Pet. How many will there be of you, Sir?

Dug. Let me see——Mirabel one, Duretete two, myself three——

Pet. And I four.

Dug. How now, Sir, at your old travelling familiarity! When abroad, you had some freedom for want of better company; but among my friends at Paris, pray remember your distance——Begone, Sir.—[*Exit* Petit.]—This fellow's wit was necessary abroad, but he's too cunning for a domestic; I must dispose of him some way else.—— Who's here? Old Mirabel and my sister! My dearest sister!

Enter

Enter Old Mirabel *and* Oriana.

Ori. My brother! Welcome.

Dug. Monſieur Mirabel! I'm heartily glad to ſee you.

Old Mir. Honeſt Mr. Dugard! By the blood of the Mirabels, I'm your moſt humble ſervant.

Dug. Why, Sir, you've caſt your ſkin ſure; you're briſk and gay, luſty health about you, no ſign of age but your ſilver hairs.

Old Mir. Silver hairs! Then they are quick ſilver hairs, Sir. Whilſt I have golden pockets, let my hairs be ſilver an they will. Adſbud, Sir, I can dance, and ſing, and drink, and——no, I can't wench. But, Mr. Dugard, no news of my ſon Bob in all your travels?

Dug. Your ſon's come home, Sir.

Old Mir. Come home! Bob come home! By the blood of the Mirabels, Mr. Dugard, what ſay ye?

Ori. Mr. Mirabel return'd, Sir!

Dug. He's certainly come, and you may ſee him within this hour or two.

Old Mir. Swear it, Mr. Dugard, preſently ſwear it.

Dug. Sir, he came to town with me this morning; I left him at the Bagnieurs, being a little diſordered after riding, and I ſhall ſee him again preſently.

Old Mir. What! And he was aſhamed to aſk a bleſſing with his boots on? A nice dog! Well, and how fares the young rogue, ha?

Dug. A fine gentleman, Sir. He'll be his own meſſenger.

Old Mir. A fine gentleman! But is the rogue like me yet?

Dug. Why, yes, Sir; he's very like his mother, and as like you as moſt modern ſons are to their fathers.

Old Mir. Why, Sir, don't you think that I begat him?

Dug. Why yes, Sir; you married his mother, and he inherits your eſtate. He's very like you, upon my word.

Ori. And pray, brother, what's become of his honeſt companion, Duretete?

Dug. Who, the Captain? The very ſame he went abroad; he's the only Frenchman I ever knew that could not change. Your ſon, Mr. Mirabel, is more obliged to

nature

Nature for that fellow's compofition, than for his own : for he's more happy in Duretete's folly than his own wit. In fhort, they are as infeparable as finger and thumb; but the firft inftance in the world, I believe, of oppofition in friendfhip.

Old Mir. Very well; will he be home to dinner, think ye?

Dug. Sir, he has ordered me to befpeak a dinner for us at Rouffeau's, at a Louis d'or a head.

Old Mir. A Louis d'or a head! Well faid, Bob; by the blood of the Mirabels, Bob's improved. But, Mr. Dugard, was it fo civil of Bob to vifit Monfieur Rouffeau before his own natural father, eh? Heark'e, Oriana, what think you, now, of a fellow that can eat and drink ye a whole Louis d'or at a fitting? He muft be as ftrong as Hercules; life and fpirit in abundance. Before Gad, I don't wonder at thefe men of quality, that their own wives can't ferve them. A Louis d'or a head! 'tis enough to ftock the whole nation with baftards, 'tis faith. Mr. Dugard, I leave you with your fifter.   [*Exit.*

Dug. Well, fifter, I need not afk you how you do, your looks refolve me; fair, tall, well-fhaped; you're almoft grown out of my remembrance.

Ori. Why, truly, brother, I look pretty well, thank nature and my toilette; I have 'fcaped the jaundice, green-ficknefs, and the fmall-pox; I eat three meals a day, am very merry when up, and fleep foundly when I'm down.

Dug. But, fifter, you remember that upon my going abroad you would chufe this old gentleman for your guardian; he's no more related to our family, than Prefter John, and I have no reafon to think you miftrufted my management of your fortune: therefore pray be fo kind as to tell me, without refervation, the true caufe of making fuch a choice.

Ori. Look'e, brother, you were going a rambling, and 'twas proper, left I fhould go a rambling too, that fomebody fhould take care of me. Old Monfieur Mirabel is an honeft gentleman, was our father's friend, and has a young lady in his houfe, whofe company I like, and who has chofen him for her guardian as well as I.

Dug. Who, Mademoifelle Bifarre?

B

Ori.

Ori. The fame; we live merrily together, without fcandal or reproach; we make much of the old gentleman between us, and he takes care of us; ' we eat what ' we like, go to bed when we pleafe, rife when we will,' all the week we dance and fing, and upon Sundays go firft to church, and then to the play.——Now, brother, befides thefe motives for chufing this gentleman for my guardian, perhaps I had fome private reafons.

Dug. Not fo private as you imagine, fifter; your love to young Mirabel's no fecret, I can affure you, but fo public that all your friends are afhamed on't.

Ori. O' my word then, my friends are very bafhful; though I am afraid, Sir, that thofe people are not afhamed enough at their own crimes, who have fo many blufhes to fpare for the faults of their neighbours.

Dug. Ay, but fifter, the people fay——

Ori. Pfhaw! hang the people, they'll talk treafon, and profane their Maker; muft we therefore infer, that our king is a tyrant, and religion a cheat? Look'e, brother, their court of enquiry is a tavern, and their informer, claret: they think as they drink, and fwallow reputations like leeches; a lady's health goes brifkly round with the glafs, but her honour is loft in the toaft.

Dug. Ay, but fifter, there is ftill fomething——

Ori. If there be fomething, brother, 'tis none of the people's fomething; marriage is my thing, and I'll ftick to't.

Dug. Marriage! Young Mirabel marry! He'll build churches fooner. Take heed, fifter, though your honour ftood proof to his home-bred affaults; you muft keep a ftricter guard for the future: he has now got the foreign air, and the Italian foftnefs; his wit's improved by converfe, his behaviour finifhed by obfervation, and his affurances confirmed by fuccefs. Sifter, I can affure you, he has made his conquefts; and 'tis a plague upon your fex, to be the fooneft deceived by thofe very men that you know have been falfe to others.

' *Ori.* Then why will you tell me of his conquefts ?
' for. I muft confefs, there is no title to a woman's fa-
' vour fo engaging as the repute of a handfome diffimu-
' lation; there is fomething of a pride to fee a fellow
' lie at our feet, that has triumphed over fo many; and

' then

' then, I don't know, we fancy he muſt have ſomething
' extraordinary about him to pleaſe us, and that we have
' ſomething engaging about us to ſecure him ; ſo we
' can't be quiet till we put ourſelves upon the lay of be-
' ing both diſappointed.

' *Dug.*' But then, ſiſter, he's as fickle——

Ori. For God's ſake, brother, tell me no more of his
faults ; for if you do, I ſhall run mad for him : ſay no
more, Sir ; let me but get him into the bands of matrimony, I'll ſpoil his wand'ring, I warrant him; I'll do his
buſineſs that way, never fear.

Dug. Well, ſiſter, I won't pretend to underſtand the
engagements between you and your lover ; I expect, when
you have need of my counſel or aſſiſtance, you will let
me know more of your affairs. Mirabel is a gentleman,
and as far as my honour and intereſt can reach, you may
command me to the furtherance of your happineſs : in
the mean time, ſiſter, I have a great mind to make you
a preſent of another humble ſervant ; a fellow that
I took up at Lyons, who has ſerved me honeſtly ever
ſince.

Ori. Then why will you part with him ?

Dug. He has gain'd ſo inſufferably on my good humour, that he's grown too familiar ; but the fellow's cunning, and may be ſerviceable to you in your affair with
Mirabel. Here he comes.

Enter Petit.

Well, Sir, have you been at Rouſſeau's ?

Pet. Yes, Sir, and who ſhould I find there but Mr.
Mirabel and the Captain, hatching as warmly over a tub
of ice, as two hen pheaſants over a brood——They
would not let me beſpeak any thing, for they had dined
before I came.

Dug. Come, Sir, you ſhall ſerve my ſiſter, I ſhall ſtill
continue kind to you ; and if your lady recommends your
diligence upon trial, I'll uſe my intereſt to advance you ;
you have ſenſe enough to expect preferment.——Here,
ſirrah, here's ten guineas for thee, get thyſelf a drugget
ſuit and a puff-wig, and ſo——I dub thee gentleman
uſher.—Siſter, I muſt put myſelf in repair, you may expect me in the evening——Wait on your lady home,
Petit. *[Exit Dug.*

                                                 Pet.

Pet. A chair, a chair, a chair!

Ori. No, no, I'll walk home, 'tis but next door. [*Ex.*

SCENE, *a Tavern, discovering young* Mirabel *and* Duretete *rising from the table.*

Mir. Welcome to Paris once more, my dear Captain, we have eat heartily, drank roundly, paid plentifully, and let it go for once. I liked every thing but our women, they looked lo lean and tawdry, poor creatures! 'Tis a sure sign the army is not paid.——Give me the plump Venetian, brisk and sanguine, that smiles upon me like the glowing sun, and meets my lips like sparkling wine, her person shining as the glass, and spirit like the foaming liquor.

Dur. Ah, Mirabel! Italy I grant you; but for our women here in France, they are such thin brawn fallen jades, a man may as well make a bed-fellow of a cane chair.

Mir. France! A light unseasoned country, nothing but feathers, foppery, and fashions: ' we're fine indeed, ' so are our coach-horses; men say we're courtiers, then ' abuse us; that we are wise and politic, *non credo seigneur:* ' that our women have wit; parrots, mere parrots, af- ' surance and a good memory, sets them up:'——There's nothing on this side the Alps worth my humble service t'ye—Ha, *Roma la santa!* Italy for my money; their customs, gardens, buildings, paintings, music, politics, wine and women! the Paradise of the world;——not pestered with a parcel of precise old gouty fellows, that would debar their children every pleasure that they them- selves are past the sense of: commend me to the Italian familiarity: here, son, there's fifty crowns, go pay your whore her week's allowance.

Dur. Ay, these are your fathers for you, that under- stand the necessities of young men; not like our musty dads, who because they cannot fish themselves, would muddy the water, and spoil the sport of them that can. But now you talk of the plump, what d'ye think of a Dutch woman?

Mir. A Dutch woman's too compact; nay, every thing among them is so; a Dutch man is thick, a Dutch

woman

woman is fquab ; a Dutch horfe is round, a Dutch dog is fhort ; a Dutch fhip is broad-bottom'd ; and, in fhort, one would fwear the whole product of the country were caft in the fame mould with their cheefes.

Dur. Ay, but Mirabel, you have forgot the Englifh ladies.

Mir. The women of England were excellent, did they not take fuch unfufferable pains to ruin what nature has made fo incomparably well ; they would be delicate creatures indeed, could they but thoroughly arrive at the French mien, or entirely let it alone ; for they only fpoil a very good air of their own, by an aukward imitation of ours ; their parliaments and our taylors give laws to three kingdoms. But come, Duretete, let us mind the bufinefs in hand ; miftreffes we muft have, and muft take up with the manufacture of the place, and upon a competent diligence we fhall find thofe in Paris fhall match the Italians from top to toe.

Dur. Ay, Mirabel, you will do well enough, but what will become of your friend ; you know I am fo plaguy bafhful, fo naturally an afs upon thefe occafions, that—

Mir. Pfhaw ! you muft be bolder, man : travel three years, and bring home fuch a baby as bafhfulnefs ! A great lufty fellow ! and a foldier ! fye upon it.

Dur. Look'e, Sir, I can vifit, and I can ogle a little, —as thus, or thus now. Then I can kifs abundantly, and make a fhift to——but if they chance to give me a forbidding look, as fome women, you know, have a devilifh caft with their eyes—or if they cry—What d'ye mean ? What d'ye take me for ? Fye, Sir, remember who I am, Sir——A perfon of quality to be ufed at this rate ! 'Egad, I'm ftruck as flat as a frying-pan.

Mir. Words of courfe ! never mind them : turn you about upon your heel with a *jantee* air ; hum out the end of an old fong ; cut a crofs caper, and at her again.

Dur. [*Imitates him.*] No, hang it, 'twill never do.—— Oons, what did my father mean by fticking me up in an univerfity, or to think that I fhould gain any thing by my head, in a nation whofe genius lies all in their heels ! ——Well, if ever I come to have children of my own, they fhall have the education of the country, they fhall

learn.

learn to dance before they can walk, and be taught to sing before they can speak.

Mir. Come, come, throw off that childish humour, put on assurance, there's no avoiding it; stand all hazards, thou'rt a stout lusty fellow, and haft a good estate; look bluff, Hector, you have a good side-box face, a pretty impudent face; so that's pretty well.—This fellow went abroad like an ox, and is returned like an afs.   [*Aside.*

Dur. Let me see now, how I look. [*Pulls out a pocket-glafs, and looks on't.*] A side-box face, say you!—'Egad, I don't like it, Mirabel.—Fye, Sir, don't abuse your friends, I could not wear such a face for the beft countefs in Chriftendom.

Mir. Why can't you, blockhead, as well as I?

Dur. Why, thou haft impudence to set a good face upon any thing, I would change half my gold for half thy brafs, with all my heart.   Who comes here?   Odfo, Mirabel, your father.

Enter Old Mirabel.

Old Mir. Where's Bob? Dear Bob!

Mir. Your blefling, Sir.

Old Mir. My blefling! Damn ye, ye young rogue; why did not you come to fee your father firft, firrah? My dear boy, I am heartily glad to fee thee, my dear child, faith—Captain Duretete, by the blood of the Mirabels, I'm yours.   Well, my lads, ye look bravely faith. —Bob, haft got any money left?

Mir. Not a farthing, Sir.

Old Mir. Why, then I won't give thee a foufe.

Mir. I did but jeft, here's ten piftoles.

Old Mir. Why, then here's ten more; I love to be charitable to thofe that don't want it——Well, and how d'ye like Italy, my boys?

Mir. Oh, the garden of the world, Sir; Rome, Naples, Venice, Milan, and a thoufand others—all fine.

Old Mir. Ay, fay you fo! And they fay, that Chiari is very fine too.

Dur. Indifferent, Sir, very indifferent; a very fcurvy air, the moft unwholefome to a French conftitution in the world.

Mir. Pfhaw, nothing on't; thefe rafcally Gazetteers have mifinformed you.

Old Mir. Misinformed me! Oons, Sir, were not we beaten there?

Mir. Beaten, Sir! the French beaten!

Old Mir. Why, how was it, pray, sweet Sir?

Mir. Sir, the Captain will tell you.

Dur. No, Sir, your son will tell you.

Mir. The Captain was in the action, Sir.

Dur. Your son saw more than I, Sir, for he was a looker on.

Old Mir. Confound you both for a brace of cowards: here are no Germans to over-hear you; why don't ye tell me how it was?

Mir. Why, then you must know, that we marched up a body of the finest, bravest, well-dressed fellows in the universe; our commanders at the head of us, all lace and feather, like so many beaux at a ball—I don't believe there was a man of them but could dance a *charmer*, Morbleau.

Old Mir. Dance! very well, pretty fellows, faith!

Mir. We capered up to their very trenches, and there saw, peeping over, a parcel of scare-crow, olive-coloured gunpowder fellows, as ugly as the devil.

Dur. 'Egad, I shall never forget the looks of them, while I have breath to fetch.

Mir. They were so civil, indeed, as to welcome us with their cannon; but for the rest, we found them such unmannerly, rude, unsociable dogs, that we grew tired of their company, and so we e'en danced back again.

Old Mir. And did ye all come back?

Mir. No, two or three thousand of us stayed behind.

Old Mir. Why, Bob, why?

Mir. Pshaw—because they could not come that night. —But come, Sir, we were talking of something else. Pray, how does your lovely charge, the fair Oriana?

Old Mir. Ripe, Sir, just ripe; you'll find it better engaging with her than the Germans, let me tell you. And what would you say, my young Mars, if I had a Venus for thee too? Come, Bob, your apartment is ready, and pray let your friend be my guest too, you shall command the house between ye, and I'll be as merry as the best of you.

' *Mir.* Bravely said, father.

' Let

' Let mifers bend their age with niggard cares,
' And ftarve themfelves to pamper hungry heirs;
' Who, living, ftint their fons what youth may crave,
' And make them revel o'er a father's grave.
' The ftock on which I grow does ftill difpenfe
' Its genial fap into the blooming branch ;
' The fruit, he knows, from his own root is grown,
' And therefore fooths thofe paffions once his own.'

 END of the FIRST ACT.

A C T   II.

SCENE, *Old* Mirabel's *Houfe.*

Oriana *and* Bifarre.

BISARRE.

AND you love this young rake, d'ye?
   Ori. Yes.

Bif. In fpight of all his ill ufage.

Ori. I can't help it.

Bif. What's the matter with ye ?

' *Ori.* I'fhaw !

Bif. Um !—before that any young, lying, fwearing, flattering, rakehelly fellow fhould play fuch tricks with me, I would wear my teeth to the ftumps with lime and chalk.—Oh, the devil take all your Caffandras and Cleopatras for me.—Pr'ythee mind your airs, modes, and fafhions; your ftays, gowns and furbelows. Hark'e, my dear, have you got home your furbelow'ed fmocks yet ?

Ori. Pr'ythee be quiet, Bifarre ; you know I can be as mad as you, when this Mirabel is out of my head.

Bif. Pfhaw ! would he were out, or in, or fome way to make you eafy.—I warrant now, you'll play the fool when he comes, and fay you love him, eh !

Ori. Moft certainly ;—I can't diffemble, Bifarre :—— befides, 'tis paft that ; we're contracted.

Bif. Contracted ! alack a-day, poor thing. What you have changed rings, or broken an old broad-piece between you ! ' Heark'e, child, han't you broke fomething elfe ' between ye ?

' Ori.

Ori. No, no, I can assure you.'

Bif. ' Then, what d'ye whine for ? Whilst I kept that
' in my power,' I would make a fool of any fellow in
France. Well, I must confess, I do love a little coquet-
ting with all my heart? my business should be to break
gold with my lover one hour, and crack my promise the
next; he should find me one day with a prayer-book in
my hand, and with a play-book another. He should have
my consent to buy the wedding-ring, and the next moment would I laugh in his face.

Ori. Oh, my dear, were there no greater tie upon my
heart, than there is upon my conscience, I would soon
throw the contract out of doors; but the mischief on't
is, I am so fond of being ty'd, that I'm forced to be just,
and the strength of my passion keeps down the inclination
of my sex. But here's the old gentleman.

Enter Old Mirabel.

Old Mir. Where's my wenches! Where's my two little girls ? Eh ! Have a care, look to yourselves, faith,
they're a coming, the travellers are a coming. Well !
which of you two will be my daughter-in-law now ?
Bisarre, Bisarre, what say you, mad-cap ? Mirabel is a
pure wild fellow.

Bif. I like him the worse.

Old Mir. You lie, hussey, you like him the better, indeed you do: what say you, my t'other little filbert ? he !

Ori. I suppose the gentleman will chuse for himself,
Sir.

Old Mir. Why, that's discreetly said ; and so he shall.

Enter Mirabel *and* Duretete, *they salute the Ladies.*

Old Mir. Bob, heark'e, you shall marry one of these
girls, sirrah.

Mir. Sir, I'll marry them both, if you please.

Bif. [*Aside.*] He'll find that one may serve his turn.

Old Mir. Both ! Why, you young dog, d'ye banter
me ?—Come, Sir, take your choice.—Duretete, you shall
have your choice too; but Robin shall chuse first. Come,
Sir, begin.

Mir. Well, I an't the first son that has made his father's dwelling a bawdy-house—let me see.

Old Mir. Well; which d'ye like ?

Mir. Both.

Old Mir. But which will you marry ?   *Mir.*

Mir. Neither.

Old Mir. Neither! Don't make me angry now, Bob; pray, don't make me angry. Look ye, firrah, if I don't dance at your wedding to-morrow, I shall be very glad to cry at your grave.

Mir. That's a bull, father.

Old Mir. A bull! Why, how now, ungrateful Sir? Did I make thee a man, that thou shouldst make me a beast?

Mir. Your pardon, Sir; I only meant your expression.

Old Mir. Hark ye, Bob, learn better manners to your father before strangers. I won't be angry this time; but, oons, if ever you do it again, you rascal—Remember what I say——

Mir. Pshaw! what does the old fellow mean by mewing me up here with a couple of green girls? Come, Duretete, will you go?

Ori. I hope, Mr. Mirabel, you han't forgot——

Mir. No, no, Madam, I han't forgot; I have brought you a thousand little Italian curiosities. I'll assure you, Madam, as far as a hundred pistoles would reach, I han't forgot the least circumstance.

Ori. Sir, you misunderstand me.

Mir. Odso, the relics, Madam, from Rome! I do remember now, you made a vow of chastity before my departure; a vow of chastity, or something like it; was it not, Madam?

Ori. Oh, Sir, I am answered at present.   [*Exit.*

Mir. She was coming full mouth upon me with her contract. Would I might dispatch t'other!

Dur. Mirabel——that lady there, observe her; she's wond'rous pretty, faith, and seems to have but few words: I like her mainly. Speak to her, man; pr'ythee, speak to her.

Mir. Madam, here's a gentleman, who declares——

Dur. Madam, don't believe him; I declare nothing— What the devil do you mean, man?

Mir. He says, Madam, that you are as beautiful as an angel.

Dur. He tells a damn'd lie, Madam; I say no such thing. Are you mad, Mirabel? Why, I shall drop down with shame.

Mir.

Mir. And so, Madam, not doubting but your Ladyship may like him as well as he does you, I think it proper to leave you together. [*Going, Duretete holds him.*

Dur. Hold, hold—Why, Mirabel, friend, sure you won't be so barbarous as to leave me alone. Pr'ythee, speak to her for yourself, as it were. Lord, Lord, that a Frenchman should want impudence!

Mir. You look mighty demure, Madam—She's deaf, Captain.

Dur. I had much rather have her dumb.

Mir. The gravity of your air, Madam, promises some extraordinary fruits from your study, which moves us with curiosity to enquire the subject of your Ladyship's contemplation. Not a word!

Dur. I hope in the lord she's speechless: if she be, she's mine this moment. Mirabel, d'ye think a woman's silence can be natural?

Bif. But the forms that logicians introduce, and which proceed from simple enumeration, are dubitable, and proceed only upon admittance——

Mir. Hoity toity! what a plague have we here? Plato in petticoats?

Dur. Ay, ay, let her go on, man; she talks in my own mother-tongue.

Bif. 'Tis exposed to invalidity from a contradictory instance; looks only upon common operations, and is infinite in its termination.

Mir. Rare pedantry!

Dur. Axioms, axioms! self-evident principles.

Bif. Then the ideas wherewith the mind is pre-occupate—Oh, gentlemen, I hope you'll pardon my cogitations! I was involved in a profound point of philosophy; but I shall discuss it somewhere else, being satisfied that the subject is not agreeable to your sparks that profess the vanity of the times. [*Exit.*

Mir. Go thy way, good wife Bias. Do you hear, Duretete? Dost hear this starch'd piece of austerity?

Dur. She's mine, man, she's mine! My own talent to a T. I'll match her in dialects, faith. I was seven years at the university, man, nursed up with *Barbara, Celarunt, Darii, Ferio, Baralipton.* Did you ever know, man, that 'twas metaphysics made me an ass? It was, faith. Had

she

she talked a word of singing, dancing, plays, fashions, or the like, I had foundered at the first step; but as she is—Mirabel, wish me joy.

Mir. You don't mean marriage, I hope.

Dur. No, no, I am a man of more honour.

Mir. Bravely resolv'd, Captain.   Now, for thy credit, warm me this frozen snow-ball; 'twill be a conquest above the Alps.

Dur. But will you promise to be always near me?

Mir. Upon all occasions, never fear.

Dur. Why, then, you shall see me in two moments make an induction from my love to her hand, from her hand to her mouth, from her mouth to her heart, and so conclude in bed, *categorematicè*.

Mir. Now the game begins, and my fool is entered—But here comes one to spoil my sport.   Now shall I be teized to death with this old fashioned contract.   I should love her too, if I might do it my own way; but she'll do nothing without witnesses, forsooth.   I wonder women can be so immodest.

Enter Oriana.

Well, Madam, why d'ye follow me?

Ori. Well, Sir, why do you shun me?

Mir. 'Tis my humour, Madam; and I'm naturally swayed by inclination.

Ori. Have you forgot our contract, Sir?

Mir. All I remember of that contract is, that it was made some three years ago; and that's enough in conscience to forget the rest on't.

Ori. 'Tis sufficient, Sir, to recollect the passing of it; for in that circumstance, I presume, lies the force of the obligation.

Mir. Obligations, Madam, that are forced upon the will, are no tie upon the conscience.   I was a slave to my passion when I passed the instrument; but the recovery of my freedom makes the contract void.

‘ *Ori.* Sir, you can't make that a compulsion which
‘ was your own choice; besides, Sir, a subjection to your
‘ own desires has not the virtue of a forcible constraint:
‘ and you will find, Sir, that to plead your passion for the
‘ killing of a man, will hardly exempt you from the
‘ justice of the punishment.

‘ *Mir.* And so, Madam, you make the sin of murder

‘ and the crime of a contract the very same, becaufe
‘ that hanging and matrimony are fo much alike,’

Ori. Come, Mr. Mirabel, thefe expreffions I expected
from the raillery of your humour; but I hope for very
different fentiments from your honour and generofity.

Mir. Look ye, Madam; as for my generofity, ’tis at
your fervice, with all my heart: I’ll keep you a coach
and fix horfes, if you pleafe, only permit me to keep my
honour to myfelf; ‘ for I can affure you, Madam, that
‘ the thing called honour, is a circumftance abfolutely
‘ unneceffary in a natural correfpondence between male
‘ and female; and he’s a madman that lays it out, confi-
‘ dering its fcarcity, upon any fuch trivial occafions.
‘ There’s honour required of us by our friends, and ho-
‘ nour due to our enemies, and they return it to us again;
‘ but I never heard of a man that left but an inch of his
‘ honour in a woman’s keeping, that could ever get the
‘ leaft account on’t.’ Confider, Madam, you have no fuch
thing among ye; and ’tis a main point of policy to keep
no faith with reprobates—Thou art a pretty little repro-
bate; and fo get thee about thy bufinefs.

Ori. Well, Sir, even all this I will allow to the gaiety
of your temper: your travels have improved your talent
of talking, but they are not of force, I hope, to impair
your morals.

Mir. Morals! Why, there ’tis again, now. ‘ I tell
‘ thee, child, there is not the leaft occafion for morals in
‘ any bufinefs between you and I.’ Don’t you know,
that of all the commerce in the world, there is no fuch co-
zenage and deceit as in the traffic between man and woman? We ftudy, all our lives long, how to put tricks upon
one another. ‘ What is your bufinefs now from the time
‘ you throw away your artificial babies, but how to get
‘ natural ones with the moft advantage? No fowler lays
‘ abroad more nets for his game, nor a hunter for his
‘ prey, than you do to catch poor innocent men.’ Why
do you fit three or four hours at your toilet in a morning?
Only with a villainous defign to make fome poor fellow a
fool before night. ‘ What are your languifhing looks,
‘ your ftudied airs and affectations, but fo many baits and
‘ devices, to delude men out of their dear liberty and
‘ freedom?’ What d’ye figh for? What d’ye weep for?
C

What

What d'ye pray for? Why, for a hufband: that is, you mplore Providence to affift you in the juft and pious dengn of making the wifeft of his creatures a fool, and the head of the creation a flave.

Ori. Sir, I am proud of my power, and am refolved to ufe it.

Mir. Hold, hold, Madam; not fo faft. As you have variety of vanities to make coxcombs of us, fo we have vows, oaths, and proteftations of all forts and fizes to make fools of you. ‘ As you are very ftrange and whim-‘ fical creatures, fo we are allowed as unaccountable ‘ ways of managing you.’ And this, in fhort, my dear creature, is our prefent condition: I have fworn and lied briſkly, to gain my ends of you; your Ladyfhip has patched and painted violently, to gain your ends of me: but fince we are both difappointed, let us make a drawn battle, and part clear on both fides.

Ori. With all my heart, Sir; give me up my contract, and I'll never fee your face again.

Mir. Indeed I won't, child.

Ori. What, Sir, neither do one nor t'other?

Mir. No, you fhall die a maid, unlefs you pleafe to be otherwife upon my terms.

Ori. What do you intend by this, Sir?

Mir. Why, to ftarve you into compliance. Look ye, you fhall never marry any man; and you'd as good let me do you a kindnefs as a ftranger.

Ori. Sir, you're a———

Mir. What am I, miftrefs?

Ori. A villain, Sir.

Mir. I'm glad on't. I never knew an honeft fellow in my life, but was a villain upon thefe occafions. Ha'n't you drawn yourfelf now into a very pretty dilemma? Ha, ha, ha! the poor lady has made a vow of virginity, when fhe thought of making a vow for the contrary. Was ever poor woman fo cheated into chaftity?

Ori. Sir, my fortune is equal to yours, my friends as powerful, and both fhall be put to the teft, to do me juftice.

Mir. What, you'll force me to marry you, will ye?

Ori. Sir, the law fhall:

Mir. But the law can't force me to do any thing elfe, can it?

Ori. Pfhaw! I defpife thee—monfter.

3   *Mir.*

Mir. Kifs and be friends then.   Don't cry, child, and you fhall have your fugar-plumb.   Come, Madam, d'ye think I could be fo unreaf nable as to make you faft all your life long? No, I did but jeft; you fhall have your liberty.   Here, take your contract, and give me mine.

Ori. No, I won't.

Mir. Eh! What, is the girl a fool?

Ori. No, Sir, you fhall find me cunning enough to do myfelf juftice; and fince I muft not depend upon your love, I'll be reveng'd, and force you to marry me out of fpite.

Mir. Then I'll beat thee out of fpite; and make a moft confounded hufband.

Ori. Oh, Sir, I fhall match ye; a good hufband makes a good wife at any time.

Mir. I'll rattle down your china about your ears.

Ori. And I'll rattle about the city to run you in debt for more.

Mir. Your face-mending toilet fhall fly out of the window.

Ori. And your face-mending periwig fhall fly after it.

Mir. I'll tear the furbelow off your clothes; and when you fwoon for vexation, you fhan't have a penny to buy a bottle of hartfhorn.

Ori. And you, Sir, fhall have hartfhorn in abundance.

Mir. I'll keep as many miftreffes as I have coach-horfes.

Ori. And I'll keep as many gallants as you have grooms.

Mir. I'll lie with your woman before your face.

Ori. Have a care of your valet behind your back.

Mir. But, fweet Madam, there is fuch a thing as a divorce.

Ori. But, fweet Sir, there is fuch a thing as alimony; fo, divorce on, and fpare not.   [*Exit.*

Mir. Ay, that feparate maintenance is the devil——there's their refuge. O' my confcience, one would take cuckoldom for a meritorious action, becaufe the women are fo handfomely rewarded for it.   [*Exit.*

SCENE *changes to a large parlour in the fame houfe.*

Enter Duretete *and* Petit.

Dur. And fhe is mighty peevifh, you fay?

C 2

Pet.

Pet. Oh, Sir, she has a tongue as long as my leg, and talks so crabbedly, you would think she always spoke Welch!

Dur. That's an odd language, methinks, for her philosophy.

Pet. But sometimes she will sit you half a day without speaking a word, and talk oracles all the while by the wrinkles of her forehead, and the motions of her eyebrows.

Dur. Nay, I shall match her in philosophical ogles, faith; that's my talent: I can talk best, you must know, when I say nothing.

Pet. But d'ye ever laugh, Sir?

Dur. Laugh! Won't she endure laughing?

Pet. Why, she's a critic, Sir; she hates a jest, for fear it should please her; and nothing keeps her in humour, but what gives her the spleen. And then for logic, and all that, you know——

Dur. Ay, ay, I'm prepared; I have been practising hard words and no sense, this hour, to entertain her.

Pet. Then place yourself behind this screen, that you may have a view of her behaviour before you begin.

Dur. I long to engage her, lest I should forget my lesson.

Pet. Here she comes, Sir; I must fly.

[*Exit* Pet. *and* Dur. *stands peeping behind the curtain.*
Enter Bisarre *and Maid.*

Bis. [*With a book.*] Pshaw, hang books! they sour our temper, spoil our eyes, and ruin our complexions.

[*Throws away the book.*

Dur. Eh! The devil such a word there is in all Aristotle.

Bis. Come, wench, let's be free; call in the fiddle; there's nobody near us.

Enter Fidler.

Dur. Would to the lord there was not!

Bis. Here, friend, a minuet—quicker time, ha!——
Would we had a man or two.

Dur. [*Stealing away.*] You shall have the devil sooner, my dear dancing philosopher.

Bis. Uds my life! here's one.

[*Runs to* Duretete, *and hauls him back.*

Dur. Is all my learned preparation come to this?

Bis. Come, Sir, don't be ashamed; that's my good boy. You're very welcome; we wanted such a one—

'Come ſtrike up—I know you dance well, Sir; you're
finely ſhap'd for it——Come, come, Sir; quick, quick,
you miſs the time elſe.

Dur. But, Madam, I come to talk with you.

Biſ. Ay, ay, talk as you dance, talk as you dance: come.

Dur. But we were talking of dialectics.

Biſ. Hang dialectics! mind the time—quicker, ſirrah.
[*To the Fidler.*]—Come——And how d'ye find yourſelf
now, Sir?

Dur. In a fine breathing ſweat, Doctor.

Biſ. All the better, patient, all the better. Come,
Sir, ſing now, ſing; I know you ſing well; I ſee you
have a ſinging face; a heavy, dull, ſonata face.

Dur. Who, I ſing?

Biſ. Oh, you're modeſt, Sir!—But come, ſit down;
cloſer, cloſer. Here, a bottle of wine——Come, Sir,
' fa, la, ley;' ſing, Sir.

Dur. But, Madam, I came to talk with you.

Biſ. Oh, Sir, you ſhall drink firſt! Come, fill me a
bumper—Here, Sir, bleſs the king.

Dur. Would I were out of his dominions——By this
light, ſhe'll make me drunk too.

Biſ. Oh, pardon me, Sir, you ſhall do me right! fill
it higher——Now, Sir, can you drink a health under
your leg?

Dur. Rare philoſophy that, faith.

Biſ Come, off with it to the bottom——Now, how
d'ye like me, Sir?

Dur. Oh, mighty well, Madam!

Biſ. You ſee how a woman's fancy varies; ſometimes
ſplenetic and heavy, then gay and frolicſome. And how
d'ye like the humour?

Dur. Good Madam, let me ſit down to anſwer you;
for I am heartily tired.

Biſ. Fie upon't! a young man, and tired! Up, for
ſhame, and walk about: action becomes us—a little faſter,
Sir—What d'ye think now of my Lady La Pale, and
Lady Coquette, the Duke's fair daughter, ha? Are they
not briſk laſſes? Then there is black Mrs. Bellair, and
brown Mrs. Bellface.

Dur. They are all ſtrangers to me, Madam.

Biſ. But let me tell you, Sir, that brown is not always
deſpicable.

C 3

defpicable. Oh, lard, Sir, if young Mrs. Bagatelle had kept herfelf fingle till this time o' day, what a beauty there had been! And then, you know the charming Mrs. Monkeylove, the fair gem of St. Germain's.

Dur. Upon my foul, I don't.

Bif. And then you muft have heard of the Englifh beau, Spleenamore; how unlike a gentleman——

Dur. Hey—not a fyllable on't, as I hope to be faved, Madam.

Bif. No! Why, then, play me a jig. Come, Sir.

Dur. By this light, I cannot; faith, Madam, I have fprained my leg.

Bif. Then fit you down, Sir; and now tell me what's your bufinefs with me? What's your errand? Quick, quick, difpatch—Odfo, may be you are fome gentleman's fervant, that has brought me a letter, or a haunch of venifon.

Dur. 'Sdeath, Madam! do I look like a carrier?

Bif. Oh, cry you mercy! I faw you juft now; I miftook you, upon my word: you are one of the travelling gentlemen. And, pray, Sir, how do all our impudent friends in Italy?

Dur. Madam, I came to wait upon you with a more ferious intention than your entertainment has anfwered.

Bif. Sir, your intention of waiting on me was the greateft affront imaginable, however your expreffions may turn it to a compliment. Your vifit, Sir, was intended as a prologue to a very fcurvy play, of which Mr. Mirabel and you fo handfomely laid the plot. Marry! No, no, I'm a man of more honour. Where's your honour? Where's your courage now? Ads my life, Sir, I have a great mind to kick you. Go, go to your fellow-rake now; rail at my fex, and get drunk for vexation, and write a lampoon. But I muft have you to know, Sir, that my reputation is above the fcandal of a libel; my virtue is fufficiently approved to thofe whofe opinion is my intereft: and for the reft, let them talk what they will; for, when I pleafe, I'll be what I pleafe, in fpite of you, and all mankind; and fo, my dear man of honour, if you be tired, con over this leffon, and fit there till I come to you.

[Runs off.

Dur. Tum ti dum. *[Sings.]* Ha, ha, ha! Ads my
life.

life, I have a great mind to kick you—Oons and confusion! [*Starts up.*] Was ever man so abused?—Ay, Mirabel set me on.

Enter Petit.

Pet. Well, Sir, how d'ye find yourself?

Dur. You son of a nine-eyed whore, d'ye come to
abuse me? I'll kick you with a vengeance, you dog.

[Petit *runs off, and* Dur. *after him.*

END of the SECOND ACT.

A C T   III.

SCENE *continues.*

Enter Old and Young Mirabel.

OLD MIRABEL.

BOB, come hither, Bob.

Mir. Your pleasure, Sir?

Old Mir. Are not you a great rogue, sirrah?

Mir. That's a little out of my comprehension, Sir;
for I've heard say, that I resemble my father.

Old Mir. Your father is your very humble slave. I
tell thee what, child, thou art a very pretty fellow, and
I love thee heartily; and a very great villain, and I hate
thee mortally.

Mir. Villain, Sir! then I must be a very impudent
one; for I can't recollect any passage of my life that I'm
ashamed of.

Old Mir. Come hither, my dear friend; dost see this
picture?   [*Shews him a little picture.*

Mir. Oriana's! Pshaw!

Old Mir. What, Sir, won't you look upon it?—Bob,
dear Bob, pr'ythee, come hither, now. Dost want any
money, child?

Mir. No, Sir.

Old Mir. Why, then, here's some for thee. Come here
now. How canst thou be so hard-hearted an unnatural,
unmannerly rascal; (don't mistake me child; I an't
angry) as to abuse this tender, lovely, good-natur'd, dear
rogue? Why, she sighs for thee, and cries for thee, pouts
for thee, and snubs for thee, the poor little heart of it is
like

like to burſt.   Come, my dear boy, be good-natured, like your own father, be now—and then ſee here, read this—the effigies of the lovely Oriana, with ten thouſand pounds to her portion; ten thouſand pounds, you dog; ten thouſand pounds, you rogue: how dare you refuſe a lady with ten thouſand pounds, you impudent raſcal?

Mir. Will you hear me ſpeak, Sir?

Old Mir. Hear you ſpeak, Sir! If you had ten thouſand tongues, you could not out-talk ten thouſand pounds, Sir.

Mir. Nay, Sir, if you won't hear me, I'll begone, Sir; I'll take poſt for Italy this moment.

Old Mir. Ah, the fellow knows I won't part with him! [*Aſide.*] Well, Sir, what have you to ſay?

Mir. The univerſal reception, Sir, that marriage has had in the world, is enough to fix it for a public good, and to draw every body into the common cauſe; but there are ſome conſtitutions like ſome inſtruments, ſo peculiarly ſingular, that they make tolerable muſic by themſelves, but never do well in a conſort.

Old Mir. Why, this is reaſon, I muſt confeſs, but yet it is nonſenſe too; for tho' you ſhould reaſon like an angel, if you argue yourſelf out of a good eſtate, you talk like a fool.

Mir. But, Sir, if you bribe me into bondage with the riches of Crœſus, you leave me but a beggar for want of my liberty.

Old Mir. Was ever ſuch a perverſe fool heard?—'Sdeath, Sir, why did I give you education? Was it to diſpute me out of my ſenſes? Of what colour, now, is the head of this cane? You'll ſay 'tis white, and, ten to one, make me believe it too.   I thought that young fellows ſtudied to get money.

Mir. No, Sir, I have ſtudied to deſpiſe it: my reading was not to make me rich, but happy, Sir.

Old Mir. There he has me again now.   But, Sir, did not I marry to oblige you? ·

Mir. To oblige me, Sir! in what reſpect, pray?

Old Mir. Why, to bring you into the world, Sir; wa'n't that an obligation?

Mir. And becauſe I would have it ſtill an obligation, I avoid marriage.

Old

Old Mir. How is that, Sir?

Mir. Becaufe I would not curfe the hour I was born. —

Old Mir. Look ye, friend, you may perfuade me out of my defigns, but I'll command you out of yours; and tho' you may convince my reafon that you are in the right, yet there is an old attendant of fixty-three, called pofitivenefs, which you nor all the wits in Italy fhall ever be able to fhake. So, Sir, you're a wit, and I'm a father; you may talk; but I'll be obeyed.

Mir. This it is to have the fon a finer gentleman than the father; they firft give us breeding that they don't underftand, then they turn us out of doors becaufe we are wifer than themfelves. But I'm a little aforehand with the old gentleman. [*Afide.*] Sir, you have been pleafed to fettle a thoufand pounds fterling a year upon me; in return of which I have a very great honour for you and your family, and fhall take care that your only and beloved fon fhall do nothing to make him hate his father, or to hang himfelf. So, dear Sir, I'm your very humble fervant. [*Runs off.*

Old Mir. Here, firrah, rogue, Bob, villain!

Enter Dugard.

Dug. Ah, Sir! 'tis but what he deferves.

Old Mir. 'Tis falfe, Sir, he don't deferve it: what have you to fay againft my boy, Sir?

Dug. I fhall only repeat your own words.

Old Mir. What have you to do with my words? I have fwallowed my words already, I have eaten them up; and how can you come at them, Sir?

Dug. Very eafily, Sir; 'tis but mentioning your injured ward, and you will throw them up again immediately.

Old Mir. Sir, your fifter was a foolifh young flirt,— truft any fuch young, deceitful, rake-helly rogue, like him.

Dug. Cry you mercy, old gentleman! I thought we fhould have the words again.

Old Mir. And what then? 'Tis the way with young fellows to flight old gentlemen's words; you never mind them when you ought. I fay, that Bob's an honeft fellow, and who dares deny it?

Enter

Enter Bifarre.

Bif. That dare I, Sir; I fay, that your fon is a wild, foppifh, whimfical, impertinent coxcomb; and were I abufed as this gentleman's fifter is, I would make it an Italian quarrel, and poifon the whole family.

Dug. Come, Sir, 'tis no time for trifling; my fifter is abufed, you are made fenfible of the affront, and your honour is concerned to fee her redreffed.

Old Mir. Look ye, Mr. Dugard, good words go fartheft. I will do your fifter juftice, but it muft be after my own rate; nobody muft abufe my fon but myfelf: for altho' Robin be a fad dog, yet he's nobody's puppy but my own.

Bif. Ay, that's my fweet-natured, kind old gentleman. [*Wheedling him.*] We will be good then, if you'll join with us in the plot.

Old Mir. Ah, you coaxing young baggage! what plot can you have to wheedle a fellow of fixty-three?

Bif. A plot that fixty-three is only good for, to bring other people together, Sir; ' a Spanifh plot, lefs dangerous ' than that of eighty-eight; and' you muft act the Spaniard, becaufe your fon will leaft fufpect you; and if he fhould, your authority protects you from a quarrel, to which Oriana is unwilling to expofe her brother.

Old Mir. And what part will you act in the bufinefs, Madam?

Bif. Myfelf, Sir; my friend is grown a perfect changeling: thefe foolifh hearts of ours fpoil our heads prefently; the fellows no fooner turn knaves, but we turn fools. But I am ftill myfelf, and he may expect the moft fevere ufage from me, becaufe I neither love him nor hate him.   [*Exit.*

Old Mir. Well faid, Mrs. Paradox; but, Sir, who muft open the matter to him?

Dug. Petit, Sir, who is our engineer-general. And here he comes.

Enter Petit.

Pet. Oh, Sir, more difcoveries! are all friends about us?

Dug. Ay, ay, fpeak freely.

Pet. You muft know, Sir——Od's my life, I'm out of breath——You muft know, Sir—you muft know——

Old Mir. What the devil muft we know, Sir?

Pet. That I have [*Pants and blows.*] bribed, Sir——
bribed——your son's secretary of state.

Old Mir. Secretary of state! who's that, for Heaven's
sake?

Pet. His valet de chambre, Sir. You must know, Sir,
that the intrigue lay folded up with his matter's cloaths;
and when he went to dust the embroidered suit, the secret flew out of the right pocket of his coat, in a whole
swarm of your crambo songs, short-footed odes, and long-
legged Pindarics.

Old Mir. Impossible!

Petit. Ah, Sir, he has loved her all along! there was
Oriana in every line; but he hates marriage. Now, Sir,
this plot will stir up his jealousy; and we shall know, by
the strength of that, how to proceed farther. Come, Sir,
let's about it with speed.

'Tis expedition gives our king the sway;
For expedition to the French give way;
Swift to attack, or swift—to run away. [*Exeunt.*

Enter Mirabel *and* Bisarre, *passing carelessly by one another.*

Bis. [*Aside.*] I wonder what she can see in this fellow,
to like him?

Mir. [*Aside.*] I wonder what my friend can see in this
girl, to admire her?

Bis. Aside.] A wild, foppish, extravagant rake-hell.

Mir. [*Aside.*] A light, whimsical, impertinent mad-cap.

Bis. Whom do you mean, Sir?

Mir. Whom do you mean, Madam?

Bis. A fellow that has nothing left to re-establish him
for a human creature, but a prudent resolution to hang
himself.

Mir. There is a way, Madam, to force me to that resolution.

Bis. I'll do't with all my heart.

Mir. Then you must marry me.

Bis. Look ye, Sir, don't think your ill manners to me
shall excuse your ill usage of my friend; nor, by fixing
a quarrel here, to divert my zeal for the absent; for I'm
resolved, nay, I come prepared to make you a panegyric,
that shall mortify your pride like any modern dedication.

Mir. And I, Madam, like a true modern patron, shall
hardly give you thanks for your trouble.

Bis.

Bif. Come, Sir, to let you fee what little foundation you have for your dear fufficiency, I'll take you to pieces.

Mir. And what piece will you chufe?

Bif. Your heart to be fure; 'caufe I would get prefently rid on't; your courage I would give to a Hector, your wit to a lewd play-maker, your honour to an attorney, your body to the phyficians, and your foul to its mafter.

Mir. I had the oddeft dream laft night of the duchefs of Burgundy; methought the furbelows of her gown were pinned up fo high behind, that I could not fee her head for her tail.

Bif. The creature don't mind me! Do you think, Sir, that your humourous impertinence can divert me? No, Sir, I'm above any pleafure that you can give, but that of feeing you miferable. And mark me, Sir, my friend, my injured friend, fhall yet be doubly happy, and you fhall be a hufband as much as the rites of marriage, and the breach of them can make you.

    [Here Mirabel *pulls out a Virgil, and reads to himfelf while fhe fpeaks.*

Mir. [Reading.] *At Regina dolos, (quis fallere poffit amantem?)*
Diffimulare etiam fperáfti, perfide tantum—Very true.—
Poffe nefas.

By your favour, friend Virgil, 'twas but a rafcally trick of your hero to forfake poor pug fo inhumanly.

Bif. I don't know what to fay to him. The devil— What's Virgil to do with us, Sir?

Mir. Very much, Madam, the moft *à-propos* in the world—for, what fhould I chop upon, but the very place where the perjured rogue of a lover and the forfaking lady are battling it tooth and nail. Come, Madam, fpend your fpirits no longer, we'll take an eafier method: I'll be Æneas now, and you fhall be Dido, and we'll rail by book. Now for you, Madam Dido.

  Nec te nofter amor, nec te data dextera quondam,
  Nec moritura tenet creduli funera Dido——

Ah, poor Dido!
                            [Looking at her.
                                  Bif.

Bif. Rudenefs, affronts, impatience! I could almoft ftart out even to manhood, and want but a weapon as long as his to fight him upon the fpot. What fhall I fay?

Mir. Now fhe rants.

Quæ quibus anteferam? jam, jam nec maxima Juno.

Bif. A man! No, the woman's birth was fpirited away.

Mir. Right, right, Madam, the very words.

Bif. And fome pernicious elf left it in the cradle with human fhape to palliate growing mifchief.

[*Both fpeak together, and raife their voices by degrees.*

Mir. Perfide, fed duris genuit te cautibus horrens Caucafus, Hyrcanæque admorunt Ubera Tigres.

Bif. Go, Sir, fly to your midnight revels.——
Mir. Excellent!

*I fequere Italiam ventis, pete regna per undas,
Spero equidem mediis, fi quid pia numina poffunt.*

[*Together again.*

Bif. Converfe with imps of darknefs of your make, your nature ftarts at juftice, and fhivers at the touch of virtue. Now the devil take his impudence, he vexes me fo, I don't know whether to cry or laugh at him.   [*Afide.*

Mir. Bravely performed, my dear Libyan; I'll write the tragedy of Dido, and you fhall act the part: but you do nothing at all, unlefs you fret yourfelf into a fit; for here the poor lady is ftifled with vapours, drops into the arms of her maids; and the cruel, barbarous, deceitful wanderer, is in the very next line called pious Æneas.—— There's authority for ye.

Sorry indeed Æneas ftood
    To fee her in a pout;
But Jove himfelf, who ne'er thought good
    To ftay a fecond bout,
Commands him off with all his crew,
    And leaves poor Dy, as I leave you.   [*Runs off.*

Bif. Go thy ways, for a dear, mad, deceitful, agreeable fellow.   O' my confcience I muft excufe Oriana.

That lover foon his angry fair difarms,
Whofe flighting pleafes, and whofe faults are charms.
[*Exit.*

Enter Petit, *runs about to every door, and knocks.*
Pet. Mr. Mirabel ! Sir, where are you ? no where to be found ?

Enter Mirabel.
Mir. What's the matter, Petit ?
Pet. Moft critically met—Ah, Sir, that one who has followed the game fo long, and brought the poor hare juft under his paws, fhould let a mungrel cur chop in, and run away with the pufs.
Mir. If your worfhip can get out of your allegories, be pleafed to tell me in three words what you mean.
Pet. Plain, plain, Sir.   Your miftrefs and mine is going to be married.
Mir. I believe you lie, Sir.
Pet. Your humble Servant, Sir.   [*Going.*
Mir. Come hither, Petit.   Married, fay you ?
Pet. No, Sir, 'tis no matter; I only thought to do you a fervice, but I fhall take care how I confer my favours for the future.
Mir. Sir, I beg ten thoufand pardons.   [*Bowing low.*
Pet. 'Tis enough, Sir—I come to tell you, Sir, that Oriana is this moment to be facrificed ; married paft redemption.
Mir. I underftand her; fhe'll take a hufband out of fpight to me, and then out of love to me fhe will make him a cuckold : ‘ 'tis ordinary with women to marry one ‘ perfon for the fake of another, and to throw themfelves ‘ into the arms of one they hate, to fecure their pleafure ‘ with the man they love.’   But who is the happy man ?
Pet. A lord, Sir.
Mir. I'm her ladyfhip's moft humble fervant. ‘ A ‘ train and a title, hey ! Room for my lady's coach ! a ‘ front row in the box for her ladyfhip ! lights, lights ‘ for her honour !’—Now muft I be a conftant attender at my lord's levee, to work my way to my lady's couchee —a countefs, I prefume, Sir.——

Pet.

Pet. A Spanish count, Sir, that Mr. Dugard knew abroad, is come to Paris, saw your mistress yesterday, marries her to-day, and whips her into Spain to-morrow.

Mir. Ay, is it so? and must I follow my cuckold over the Pyrenees? Had she married within the precincts of a billet-doux, I would be the man to lead her to church; but as it happens, I'll forbid the banns. Where is this mighty Don?

Pet. Have a care, Sir, he's a rough cross-grained piece, and there's no tampering with him; would you apply to Mr. Dugard, or the lady herself, something might be done, for it is in despight to you, that the business is carried on so hastily. Odso, Sir, here he comes. I must be gone. [*Exit.*

Enter Old Mirabel, *dressed in a Spanish habit, leading* Oriana.

Ori. Good my Lord, a nobler choice had better suited your Lordship's merit. My person, rank, and circumstance, expose me as the public theme of raillery, and subject me so to injurious usage, my Lord, that I can lay no claim to any part of your regard, except your pity.

Old Mir. Breathes he vital air, that dare presume
With rude behaviour to profane such excellence?
Shew me the man————
And you shall see how sudden my revenge
Shall fall upon the head of such presumption.
Is this thing one? [*Strutting up to* Mir.

Mir. Sir!

Ori. Good my Lord——

Old Mir. If he, or any he——

Ori. Pray, my Lord, the gentleman's a stranger.

Old Mir. O, your pardon, Sir——but if you had—remember, Sir,——the lady now is mine, her injuries are mine; therefore, Sir, you understand me.———Come, Madam. [*Leads* Oriana *to the door, she goes off,* Mir. *runs to his father, and pulls him by the sleeve.*

Mir. Ecoute, Monsieur le Count..

Old Mir. Your business, Sir?

Mir. Boh!

Old Mir. Boh! What language is that, Sir!

Mir. Spanish, my Lord.

D 2

Old Mir.

Old Mir. What d'ye mean?

Mir. This, Sir.   [*Trips up his heels.*

Old Mir. A very concise quarrel, truly——I'll bully him——*Trinidade Signeur*, give me fair play.
                                        [*Offering to rise.*

Mir. By all means, Sir. [*Takes away his sword.*] Now, Signeur, where's that bombaft look, and fuftian face your Countfhip wore juft now?   [*Strikes him.*

Old Mir. The rogue quarrels well, very well, my own fon right!——But hold, firrah, no more jefting; I'm your father, Sir, your father!

Mir. My father! Then by this light I could find in my heart to pay thee. [*Afide.*] Is the fellow mad? Why fure, Sir, I ha'n't frighted you out of your fenfes?

Old Mir. But you have, Sir.

Mir. Then I'll beat them into you again.
                                        [*Offers to ftrike him.*

Old Mir. Why, rogue——Bob, dear Bob, don't you know me, child?

Mir. Ha, ha, ha! the fellow's downright diftracted. Thou miracle of impudence! would'ft thou make me believe that fuch a grave gentlemen as my father would go a mafquerading thus? That a perfon of threefcore and three would run about in a fool's coat to difgrace himfelf and family? Why, you impudent villain, do you think I will fuffer fuch an affront to pafs upon my honoured father, my worthy father, my dear father? 'Sdeath, Sir, mention my father but once again, and I'll fend your foul to thy grandfather this minute!
                                        [*Offering to ftab him.*

Old Mir. Well, well, I am not your father.

Mir. Why then, Sir, you are the faucy, hectoring Spaniard, and I'll ufe you accordingly.

Old Mir. The devil take the Spaniards, Sir, we have all got nothing but blows fince we began to take their part.

Enter Dugard. Oriana, Maid, Petit. Dugard *runs to*
        Mirabel, *the reft to Old* Mirabel.

Dug. Fye, fye, Mirabel, murder your father!

Mir. My father! What is the whole family mad? Give me way, Sir, I won't be held.

                                        Old Mir.

Old Mir. No? nor I neither; let me be gone, pray.
[*Offering to go.*

Mir. My father!

Old Mir. Ay, you dog's face! I am your father, for I have bore as much for thee, as your mother ever did.

Mir. O ho! then this was a trick it seems, a design, a contrivance, a stratagem—Oh! how my bones ach!

Old Mir. Your bones, Sirrah, why yours?

Mir. Why, Sir, han't I been beating my own flesh and blood all this while. O, Madam, [*To* Oriana.] I wish your Ladyship joy of your new dignity. Here was a contrivance indeed!

Pet. The contrivance was well enough, Sir, for they imposed upon us all.

Mir. Well, my dear Dulcinea, did your Don Quixote battle for you bravely? My father will answer for the force of my love.

Ori. Pray, Sir, don't insult the misfortunes of your own creating.

Dug. My prudence will be counted cowardice, if I stand tamely now.——[*Comes up between* Mirabel *and his Sister.*] Well, Sir!

Mir. Well, Sir! Do you take me for one of your tenants, Sir, that you put on your landlord's face at me?

Dug. On what presumption, Sir, dare you assume thus?   [*Draws.*

Old Mir. What's that to you, Sir.   [*Draws.*

Pet. Help! help! the lady faints.
[Oriana *falls into her Maid's arms.*

Mir. Vapours! vapours! she'll come to herself.——
' If it be an angry fit, a dram of Assa Fœtida——If jea-
' lousy, harts-horn in water——If the mother, burnt
' feathers——If grief, Ratifia——If it be straight stays,
' or corns, there's nothing like a dram of plain brandy.'

Ori. Hold off, give me air——O, my brother, would you preserve my life, endanger not your own; would you defend my reputation, leave it to itself; 'tis a dear vindication that's purchas'd by the sword; for though our champion proves victorious, yet our honour is wounded.

Old Mir. Ay, and your lover may be wounded, that's

                              another

another thing. But I think you are pretty brisk again, my child.

Ori. Ay, Sir, my indisposition was only a pretence to divert the quarrel; the capricious taste of your sex, excuses this artifice in ours.

' For often when our chief perfections fail,
' Our chief defects with foolish men prevail.'   [*Exit.*

Pet. Come, Mr. Dugard, take courage, there is a way still left to fetch him again.

Old Mir. Sir, I'll have no plot that has any relation to Spain.

Dug. I scorn all artifice whatsoever; my sword shall do her justice.

Pet. Pretty justice, truly ! Suppose you run him thro' the body ; you run her thro' the heart at the same time.

Old Mir. And me thro' the head—rot you sword——Sir, we'll have plots. Come, Petit, let's hear.

Pet. What if she pretended to go into a nunnery, and so bring him about to declare himself ?

Dug. That, I must confess, has a face.

Old Mir. A face ! A face like an angel, Sir. Ad's my life, Sir, 'tis the most beautiful plot in Christendom. We'll about it immediately.   [*Exeunt.*

' SCENE, The Street.

' Duretete and Mirabel.

' *Dur.* [*In a passion.*] And tho' I can't dance, nor
' sing, nor talk like you, yet I can fight, you know I
' can, Sir.

' *Mir.* I know thou can'st, man.

' *Dur.* 'Sdeath, Sir and I will: let me see the proud-
' est man alive make a jest of me ?

' *Mir.* But I'll engage to make you amends.—

' *Dur.* Danced to death ! Baited like a bear ! Ridicu-
' led ! Threatened to be kicked ! Confusion ! Sir, you
' set me on, and I will have satisfaction; all mankind
' will point at me.

' *Mir.* [*Aside.*] I must give this thunderbolt some pas-
' sage, or 'twill break upon my own head—Look'e, Du-
' retete, what do these gentlemen laugh at ?

Enter

' *Enter two Gentlemen.*

' *Dur.* At me to be sure——Sir, what made you laugh
' at me ?

' *1ſt Gen.* Your'e miſtaken, Sir, if we were merry,
' we had a private reaſon.

' *2d Gen.* Sir, we don't know you.

' *Dur.* Sir, I'll make you know me ; mark and ob-
' ſerve me, I won't be named ; it ſhan't be mentioned,
' not even whiſpered in your prayers at church. 'Sdeath,
' Sir, d'ye ſmile ?

' *1ſt Gen.* Not I, upon my word.

' *Dur.* Why then, look grave as an owl in a barn, or
' a Friar with his crown a ſhaving.

' *Mir.* [*Aſide to the Gent.*] Don't be bullied out of
' your humour, gentlemen ; the fellow's mad, laugh at
' him, and I'll ſtand by you.

' *1ſt Gen.* 'Egad and ſo we will.

' *Both.* Ha, ha, ha.

' *Dur.* Very pretty. [*Draws.*] She threatened to
' kick me. Ay, then you dogs, I'll murder ye.

' [*Fights, and beats them off* ; Mir. *Runs over to his ſide.*

' *Mir.* Ha, ha, ha ! bravely done, Duretete, there
' you had him, noble Captain. Hey, they run, they
' run, *victoria ! victoria !*—Ha, ha, ha—how happy am
' I in an excellent friend ! Tell me of your Virtuoſo's
' and men of ſenſe, a parcel of ſour-faced ſplenetic
' rogues —a man of my thin conſtitution ſhould never
' want a fool in his company : I don't affect your fine
' things that improve the underſtanding, but hearty
' laughing to fatten my carcaſe : and in my conſcience,
' a man of ſenſe is as melancholy without a coxcomb,
' as a lion without a jackall ; he hunts for our diverſion,
' ſtarts game for our ſpleen, and perfectly feeds us with
' pleaſure.

' I hate the man who makes acquaintance nice,
' And ſtill diſcreetly plagues me with advice ;
' Who moves by caution, and mature delays,
' And muſt give reaſons for whate'er he ſays.
' The man, indeed, whoſe converſe is ſo full,
' Makes me attentive, but it makes me dull :
' Give me the careleſs rogue, who never thinks,
' That plays the fool as freely as he drinks.

' Not

‘ Not a buffoon, who is buffoon by trade,
‘ But one that nature, not his wants have made.
‘ Who ſtill is merry, but does ne’er deſign it ;
‘ And ſtill is ridicul’d, but ne’er can find it.
‘ Who when he’s moſt in earneſt, is the beſt ;
‘ And his moſt grave expreſſion is a jeſt.   [*Exeunt.*

END of the THIRD ACT.

ACT IV.

SCENE, *Old* Mirabel’s *Houſe.*

Enter Old Mirabel *and* Dugard.

DUGARD.

THE lady abbeſs is my relation, and privy to the
plot : ‘ your ſon has been there, but had no ad-
‘ mittance beyond the privilege of the grate, and there
‘ my ſiſter refus’d to ſee him. He went off more net-
‘ tled at his repulſe, than I thought his gaiety could ad-
‘ mit.’

Old Mir. Ay, ay, this nunnery will bring him about,
I warrant ye.

Enter Duretete.

Dur. Here, where are ye all ?—O, Mr. Mirabel ! you
have done fine things for your poſterity—And you, Mr.
Dugard, may come to anſwer this—I come to demand my
friend at your hands ; reſtore him, Sir, or—[*To Old* Mir.

Old Mir. Reſtore him ! what d’ye think I have got
him in my trunk, or my pocket ?

Dur. Sir, he’s mad, and you’re the cauſe on’t.

Old Mir. That may be ; for I was as mad as he when
I begot him.

Dug. Mad, Sir ! what d’ye mean ?

Dur. What do you mean, Sir, by ſhutting up your
ſiſter yonder to talk like a parrot thro’ a cage ? Or a de-
coy-duck, to draw others into the ſnare ? Your ſon, Sir,
becauſe ſhe has deſerted him, he has forſaken the world ;
and in three words, has——

Old Mir. Hanged himſelf !

Dur. The very ſame, turned friar.

Old Mir. You lie, Sir, ’tis ten times worſe. Bob turned

ed friar!—Why should the fellow shave his foolish crown when the same razor may cut his throat?

Dur. If you have any command, or you any interest over him, lose not a minute: he has thrown himself into the next monastery, and has ordered me to pay off his servants, and discharge his equipage.

Old Mir. Let me alone to ferret him out; I'll sacrifice the abbot, if he receives him; I'll try whether the spiritual or the natural father has the most right to the child.——But, dear Captain, what has he done with his estate?

Dur. Settled it upon the church, Sir.

Old Mir. The church! Nay, then the devil won't get him out of their clutches——Ten thousand livres a year upon the church! 'Tis downright sacrilege—Come, gentlemen, all hands to work; for half that sum, one of these monasteries shall protect you a traitor from the law, a rebellious wife from her husband, and a disobedient son from his own father.   [*Exit:*

Dug. But will ye persuade me that he's gone to a monastery?

Dur. Is your sister gone to the *filles repenties?* I tell you, Sir, she's not fit for the society of repenting maids.

Dug. Why so, Sir?

Dur. Because she's neither one nor t'other; she's too old to be a maid, and too young to repent.

[*Exit,* Dug. *after him.*

SCENE, *the Inside of a monastery;* Oriana *in a Nun's Habit;* Bisarre.

Ori. I hope, Bisarre, there is no harm in jesting with this religious habit.

Bis. To me, the greatest jest in the habit, is taking it in earnest: I don't understand this imprisoning people with the keys of Paradise, nor the merit of that virtue which comes by constraint.—' Besides, we may own to one ano-
' other, that we are in the worst company when among
' ourselves; for our private thoughts run us into those
' desires, which our pride resists from the attack of the
' world; and, you may remember, the first woman met
' the devil when she retired from her man.

' *Ori.* But I'm reconciled, methinks, to the mortifica-
' tion

' tion of a nunnery; becaufe, I fancy, the habit be-
' comes me.

' *Bif.* A well-contrived mortification, truly, that makes
' a woman look ten times handfomer than fhe did before!
' —Ay, my dear, were there any religion in becoming
' drefs, our fex's devotion were rightly placed; for our
' toilettes would do the work of the altar; we fhould all
' be canonized.

' *Ori.* But don't you think there is a great deal of me-
' rit in dedicating a beautiful face and perfon to the fer-
' vice of religion?

' *Bif.* Not half fo much as devoting them to a pretty
' fellow : if our feminality had no bufinefs in this world,
' why was it fent hither? Let us dedicate our beautiful
' minds to the fervice of heaven : and for our handfome
' perfons, they become a box at the play, as well as a
' pew in the church.

' *Ori.* But the viciffitude of fortune, the inconftancy
' of man, with other difappointments of life, require
' fome place of religion, for a refuge from their perfe-
' cution.

' *Bif.* Ha, ha, ha, and do you think there is any devo-
' tion in a fellow's going to church, when he takes it only
' for a fanctuary? Don't you know that religion confifts
' in charity with all mankind; and that you fhould never
' think of being friends with heaven, 'till you have quar-
' relled with all the world.' Come, come, mind your
bufinefs, Mirabel loves you, 'tis now plain, and hold him
to't; give frefh orders that he fhan't fee you: we get
more by hiding our faces fometimes, than by expofing
them, a very mafk, you fee, whets defire; but a pair
of keen eyes through an iron grate, fire double upon them,
with view and difguife. But I muft be gone upon my
affairs, I have brought my captain about again.

Ori. But why will you trouble yourfelf with that coxcomb?

Bif. Becaufe he is a coxcomb; had I not better have a
lover like him, that I can make an afs of, that a lover
like yours, to make a fool of me. [*Knocking below.*] A
meffage from Mirabel, I'll lay my life. [*She runs to the
door.*] Come hither, run, thou charming nun, come hither.

Ori. What's the news? [*Runs to her.*
　　　　　　　　　　　　　　　　　　　　　　Bif.

Bif. Don't you fee who's below?

Ori. I fee no body but a friar.

Bif. Ah! Thou poor blind Cupid! ' O' my con-
' fcience,' thefe hearts of ours fpoil our heads ' inftant-
' ly! the fellows no fooner turn knaves, than we turn
' fools.' A friar! Don't you fee a villainous genteel
mien under that cloak of hypocrify, the loofe carelefs
air of a tall rake helly fellow?

Ori. As I live, Mirabel turned friar! I hope, in heaven, he's not in earneft.

Bif. In earneft: ha, ha, ha, are you in earneft? ' Now's
' your time; this difguife has he certainly taken for a
' paffport, to get in and try your refolutions; ftick to
' your habit, to be fure; treat him with difdain, rather
' than anger; for pride becomes us more than paffion!'
Remember what I fay, if you would yield to advantage,
and hold out the attack: to draw him on, keep him off
to be fure.

　　The cunning gamefters never gain too faft,

　　But lofe at firft, to win the more at laft.　　[*Exit.*

' *Ori.* His coming puts me into fome ambiguity. I
' don't know how; I don't fear him, but I miftruft my-
' felf. Would he were not come; yet I would not have
' him gone neither; I'm afraid to talk with him, but I
' love to fee him though.

' What a ftrange power has this fantaftic fire,

' That makes us dread even what we moft defire!'

　　Enter Mirabel *in a Friar's Habit.*

Mir. Save you, fifter—Your brother, young lady,
having a regard for your foul's health, has fent me to
prepare you for the facred habit by confeffion.

Ori. That's falfe, the cloven foot already. [*Afide.*] My
brother's care I own; and to you, facred Sir, I confefs,
that the great crying fin which I have long indulged, and
now prepare to expiate, was love. My morning thoughts,
my evening prayers, my daily mufings, nightly cares,
was love! ' My prefent peace, my future blifs, the joy
' of earth, and hopes of heaven! I all contemned for
' love!'

Mir. She's downright ftark mad in earneft; death and
confufion, I have loft her! [*Afide.*] You confefs your

　　2　　　　　　　　　　　　fault,

fault, Madam, in such moving terms, that I could almost
be in love with the sin.

Ori. Take care, Sir; crimes, like virtues, are their
own rewards; my chief delight became my only grief;
he in whose breast I thought my heart secure, turned
robber, and despoiled the treasure that he kept.

Mir. Perhaps that treasure he esteems so much, that
like the miser, though afraid to use it, he reserves it safe.

Ori. No, holy father: who can be miser in another's
wealth, that's prodigal of his own? His heart was open,
shar'd to all he knew, and what, alas! must then become
of mine? But the same eyes that drew this passion in,
shall send it out in tears, to which now hear my vow.

Mir. [*Discovering himself.*] No, my fair angel, but let
me repent; here on my knees behold the criminal, that
vows repentance his.	Ha! No concern upon her!

‘ *Ori.* This turn is odd, and the time has been, that
‘ such a sudden change would have surprised me into some
‘ confusion.

‘ *Mir.* Restore that happy time, for I am now returned
‘ to myself, for I want but pardon to deserve your favour,
‘ and here I'll fix till you relent and give it.

‘ *Ori.* Groveling, sordid man; why would you act a
‘ thing to make you kneel, monarch in your pleasures to
‘ be slave to your faults? Are all the conquests of your
‘ wand'ring sway, your wit, your humour, fortune, all
‘ reduced to the base cringing of a bended knee? Servile
‘ and poor! Pray heav'n this change be real.	[*Aside.*

‘ *Mir.* I come not here to justify my fault but my sub-
‘ mission, for though there be a meanness in this humble
‘ posture, 'tis nobler still to bend when justice calls, than
‘ to resist conviction.

‘ *Ori.* No more——thy oft repeated violated words re-
‘ proach my weak belief, 'tis the severest calumny to hear
‘ thee speak; that humble posture which once could raise,
‘ now mortifies my pride; how can'st thou hope for par-
‘ don, from one that you affront by asking it?

‘ *Mir.* [*Rises.*] In my own cause I'll plead no more;
‘ but give me leave to intercede for you against the hard
‘ injunctions of that habit, which for my fault you wear.

‘ *Ori.* Surprising insolence! My greatest foe pretends
‘ to give me counsel; but I am too warm upon to cool a

‘ sub-

‘ subject. My resolutions, Sir, are fixed! but as our
‘ hearts were united with the ceremony of our eyes, so
‘ I shall spare some tears to the separation. [*Weeps.*] That's
‘ all; farewel.

‘ *Mir.* And must I lose her? No. [*Runs and catches
‘ her.*] Since all my prayers are vain, I'll use the nobler
‘ argument of man, and force you to the justice you re-
‘ fuse; you're mine by pre-contract: and where's the
‘ vow so sacred to disannul another? I'll urge my love,
‘ your oath, and plead my cause against all monastic
‘ shifts upon the earth.

‘ *Ori.* Unhand me, ravisher! Would you prophane
‘ these holy walls with violence? Revenge for all my
‘ past disgrace now offers, thy life should answer this,
‘ would I provoke the law: urge me no farther, but be
‘ gone.

‘ *Mir.* Inexorable woman! let me kneel again.

[Kneels.’

Enter Old Mirabel.

Old Mir. Where, where's this counterfeit nun?

Ori. Madness! Confusion! I'm ruined!

Mir. What do I hear? [*Puts on his hood.*] What did
you say, Sir?

Old Mir. I say, she's a counterfeit, and you may be
another for ought I know, Sir; I have lost my child by
these tricks, Sir.

Mir. What tricks, Sir?

Old Mir. By a pretended trick, Sir. A contrivance
to bring my son to reason, and it has made him stark
mad; I have lost him and a thousand pounds a year.

Mir. [*Discovering himself.*] My dear father, I'm your
most humble servant.

Old Mir. My dear boy. [*Runs and kisses him.*] Welcome
ex inferis, my dear boy, 'tis all a trick, she's no more a
nun than I am.

Mir. No!

Old Mir. The devil a bit.

Mir. Then kiss me again, my dear dad, for the most
happy news—And now most venerable holy sister,

[Kneels.

Your mercy and your pardon I implore,
For the offence of asking it before.

E ‘ Look'e,

' Look'e, my dear counterfeiting nun, take my advice,
' be a nun in good earneſt; women make the beſt nuns
' always when they can't do otherwiſe. Ah, my dear
' father! there is a merit in your ſon's behaviour that you
' little think: the free deportment of ſuch fellows as I,
' makes more ladies religious, than all the pulpits in
' France.'

Ori. Oh, Sir, how unhappily have you deſtroyed what
was ſo near perfection! He is the counterfeit that has deceived you.

Old Mir. Ha! Look'e, Sir, I recant, ſhe is a nun.

Mir. Sir, your humble ſervant, then I'm a friar this
moment.

Old Mir. Was ever an old fool ſo bantered by a brace
o'young ones; hang you borh, you're both counterfeits,
and my plot's ſpoiled, that's all.

Ori. Shame and confuſion, love, anger, and diſappoint-
ment, will work my brain to madneſs.

[Takes off her habit. Exit.

Mir. Ay, ay, throw by the rags, they have ſerved a
turn for us both, and they ſhall e'en go off together.

[Takes off his habit.

' Thus the ſick wretch, when tortur'd by his pain,
' And finding all eſſays for life are vain;
' When the phyſician can no more deſign,
' Then call the other doctor, the divine.
' What vows to Heaven, would Heaven reſtore his
　　　　health!
' Vows all to Heaven, his thoughts, his actions, wealth!
' But if reſtor'd to vigour as before,
' His health refuſes what his ſickneſs ſwore.
' The body is no ſooner rais'd and well,
' But the weak ſoul relapſes into ill;
' To all its former ſwing of life is led,
' And leaves its vows and promiſes in bed.'

[Exit, throwing away the habit.

SCENE *changes to Old* Mirabel's *Houſe.* Duretete *with a
Letter.*

Dur. [*Reads.*] " My rudeneſs was only a proof of your
humour, which I have found ſo agreeable, that I own
myſelf

myself penitent, and willing to make any reparation upon your first appearance to   BISARRE."

Mirabel swears she loves me, and this confirms it; then farewel gallantry, and welcome revenge; 'tis my turn now to be upon the sublime, I'll take her off, I warrant her.

Enter Bisarre.

Well, mistress, do you love me?

Bis. I hope, Sir, you will pardon the modesty of——

Dur. Of what? Of a dancing devil!——Do you love me, I say?

Bis. Perhaps I——

Dur. What?

Bis. Perhaps I do not.

Dur. Ha! abused again! Death, woman, I'll——

Bis. Hold, hold, Sir, I do, I do!

Dur. Confirm it then by your obedience, stand there; and ogle me now, as if your heart, blood and soul were like to fly out at your eyes——First, the direct surprise [*She looks full upon him.*] Right; next the *deux yeux par oblique.* [*She gives him the side glance.*] Right; now depart, and languish. [*She turns from him and looks over her shoulder.*] Very well; now sigh. [*She sighs.*] Now drop your fan on purpose. [*She drops her fan.*] Now take it up again. Come now, confess your faults; are not you a proud——say after me.

Bis. Proud.

Dur. Impertinent.

Bis. Impertinent.

Dur. Ridiculous.

Bis. Ridiculous.

Dur. Flirt.

Bis. Puppy.

Dur. Zoons! Woman, don't provoke me, we are alone, and you don't know but the devil may tempt me to do you a mischief; ask my pardon immediately.

Bis. I do, Sir, I only mistook the word.

Dur. Cry then. Have you got e'er a handkerchief?

Bis. Yes, Sir.

Bis. Cry then, handsomely; cry like a queen in a tragedy. [*She pretending to cry, bursts out a laughing, and enter two ladies laughing.*

                                                 Bis.

Bif. Ha, ha, ha.

Ladies both. Ha, ha, ha.

Dur. Hell broke loose upon me, and all the furies fluttered about my ears ! Betrayed again ?

Bif. That you are, upon my word, my dear Captain ; ha, ha, ha.

Dur. The lord deliver me !

' *1ſt Lady.* What ! Is this the mighty man with the
' bull-face that comes to frighten ladies ? I long to ſee
' him angry ; come begin.'

Dur. Ah, Madam, I'm the beſt natured fellow in the world.

' *2d Lady.* A man ! We're miſtaken, a man has man-
' ners ; the aukward creature is ſome tinker's trull in a
' periwig.'

Bif. Come, ladies, let's examine him.

[They lay hold on him.

Dur. Examine ! the devil you will !

Bif. I'll lay my life, ſome great dairy maid in man's clothes.

Dur. They will do't ;—look'e, dear Chriſtian women, pray hear me.

Bif. Will you ever attempt a lady's honour again ?

Dur. If you pleaſe to let me get away with my honour, I'll do any thing in the world.

Bif. Will you perſuade your friend to marry mine ?

Dur. Oh, yes, to be ſure.

Bif. And will you do the ſame by me ?

Dur. Burn me, if I do, if the coaſt be clear. [*Runs out.*

Bif. Ha, ha, ha, the viſit, ladies, was critical for our diverſions, we'll go make an end of our tea.　　　[*Exeunt.*

Enter Mirabel and Old Mirabel.

Mir. Your patience, Sir, I tell you I won't marry ; and though you ſend all the biſhops in France to perſuade me, I ſhall never believe their doctrine againſt their prac‑ tice.

' *Old Mir.* But will you diſobey your father Sir ?

' *Mir.* Would my father have his youthful ſon lie laz-
' ing here, bound to a wife, chained like a monkey to
' make ſport to a woman, ſubject to her whims, humours,
' longings, vapours, and caprices, to have her one day
' pleaſed, to-morrow peeviſh ; the next day mad, the

' fourth

‘ fourth rebellious; and nothing but this fucceffion of·
‘ impertinence for ages together. Be merciful, Sir, to·
‘ your own flefh and blood.
  ‘ *Old Mir.* But, Sir, did not I bear all this, why fhould
‘ not you ?
   ‘ *Mir.* Then you think that marriage, like treafon,
‘ fhould attaint the whole body ; pray confider, Sir, is it
‘ reafonable becaufe you throw yourfelf down from one·
‘ ftory, that I muft caft myfelf headlong from the garret
‘ window ?’ You would compel me to that ftate, which
I have heard you curfe yourfelf, when my mother and.
you have battled it for a whole week together.

Old Mir. Never but once, you rogue, and that was
when fhe longed for fix Flanders mares : ay, Sir, then
fhe was breeding of you, which fhewed what an expenfive dog I fhould have of you.

Enter Petit.

Well, Petit, how does fhe now ?

Pet. Mad, Sir, *con pompos*—Ay, Mr. Mirabel, you’ll
believe that I fpeak truth now, when I confefs that I have
told you hitherto nothing but lies ; our jefting is come to
a fad earneft, fhe’s downright diftracted.

Enter Bifarre.

Bif. Where is this mighty victor !——The great ex-·
ploit is done ; ‘ go triumph in the glory of your con-
‘ queft, inhuman, barbarous man !’ Oh, Sir, [*To the old
gentleman.*] your wretched ward has found a tender guar-
·dian of you, where her young innocence expected pro-·
tection, here has fhe found her ruin.

Old Mir. Ay, the fault is mine, for I believe that
rogue won’t marry, for fearing of begetting fuch another.
difobedient fon as his father did. I have done all I can,
Madam, and now can do no more than run mad for company.   [*Cries.*

Enter Dugard, *with his fword drawn.*

Dug. Away ! Revenge, revenge,
Old Mir. Patience, patience, Sir. [*Old* Mirabel *holds.
him.*] Bob, draw.   · [*Afide.*
Dug. Patience ! The coward’s virtue, and the brave
man’s failing, when thus provoked——Villain !
Mir. Your fifter’s frenzy fhall excufe your madnefs ;
and to fhew my concern for what fhe fuffers, I’ll bear the

E 3   villain

villain from her brother.—Put up your anger with your sword; I have a heart like yours, that swells at an affront received, but melts at an injury given; and if the lovely Oriana's grief be such a moving scene, 'twill find a part within this breast, perhaps as tender as a brother's.

Dug. To prove that soft compassion for her grief, endeavour to remove it.—There, there, behold an object that's infective; I cannot view her, but I am as mad as she: [*Enter* Oriana, *held by two maids, who put her in a chair.*] A sister that my dying parents left, with their last words and blessing to my care. Sister, dearest sister.

                              [*Goes to her.*

Old Mir. Ay, poor child, poor child, d'ye know me?

Ori. You! you are *Amadis de Gaul*, Sir;—Oh! Oh, my heart! Were you never in love, fair lady? And do you never dream of flowers and gardens?—I dream of walking fires, and tall gigantic fights. Take heed, it comes now—What's that? Pray stand away: I have seen that face sure.——How light my head is!

Mir. What piercing charms has beauty, even in madness! ' these sudden starts of undigested words shoot ' through my soul, with more persuasive force than all ' the studied art of laboured eloquence.'—Come, Madam, try to repose a little.

Ori. I cannot; for I must be up to go to church, and I must dress me, put on my new gown, and be so fine, to meet my love. Hey ho!——Will not you tell me where my heart lies buried?

Mir. My very soul is touch'd—Your hand, my fair.

Ori. How soft and gentle you feel? I'll tell you your fortune, friend.

Mir. How she stares upon me!

Ori. You have a flattering face; but 'tis a fine one— I warrant you have five hundred mistresses—Ay, to be sure, a mistress for every guinea in his pocket——Will you pray for me? I shall die to-morrow——And will you ring my passing-bell?

Mir. ' Oh, woman, woman, of artifice created! whose ' nature, even distracted, has a cunning: in vain let man ' his sense, his learning boast, when woman's madness ' over-rules his reason.' Do you know me, injured creature?

                                      Ori.

Ori. No; but you shall be my intimate acquaintance in the grave.   [*Weeps.*

Mir. Oh, tears, I muſt believe you! Sure there is a kind of ſympathy in madneſs; for even I, obdurate as I am, do feel my ſoul ſo toſſed with ſtorms of paſſion, that I could cry for help as well as ſhe.   [*Wipes his eyes.*

Ori. What, have you loſt your lover? No, you mock me. I'll go home and pray.

Mir. Stay, my fair innocence, and hear me own my love ſo loud, that I may call your ſenſes to their place, reſtore them to their charming happy functions, and rein-ſtate myſelf into your favour.

Biſ. Let her alone, Sir; 'tis all too late; ſhe trembles; hold her, her fits grow ſtronger by her talking. Don't trouble her; ſhe don't know you, Sir.

Old Mir. Not know him! What then? ſhe loves to ſee him, for all that.

Enter Duretete.

Dur. Where are you all? What the devil! melancho-ly, and I here! Are ye ſad, and ſuch a ridiculous ſubject, ſuch a very good jeſt among you as I am?

Mir. Away with this impertinence! this is no place for *bagatelle:* I have murdered my honour, deſtroyed a lady, and my deſire of reparation is come at length too late. See there.

Dur. What ails her?

Mir. Alas, ſhe's mad!

Dur. Mad! doſt wonder at that? By this light, they're all ſo; they're cozening mad, they're brawling mad, they're proud mad; I juſt now came from a whole world of mad women, that had almoſt—What, is ſhe dead?

Mir. Dead! Heavens forbid!

Dur. Heavens further it! for till they be as cold as a key, there's no truſting them; you're never ſure that a woman's in earneſt, till ſhe is nailed in her coffin. Shall I talk to her? Are you mad, miſtreſs?

Biſ. What's that to you, Sir?

Dur. Oons, Madam, are you there?   [*Runs off.*

Mir. Away, thou wild buffoon! how poor and mean this humour now appears! His follies and my own I here diſclaim; this lady's frenzy has reſtor'd my ſenſes; and was ſhe perfect now, as once ſhe was, (before you all I

4

ſpeak

fpeak it) fhe fhould be mine; and as fhe is, my tears and prayers fhall wed her.

Dug. How happy had this declaration been fome hours ago!

Bif. Sir, fhe beckons to you, and waves us to go off. Come, come, let's leave them. [*Ex. all but* Mir. *and* Ori.

Ori. Oh, Sir!

Mir. Speak, my charming angel, if your dear fenfes have regained their order; fpeak, fair, and blefs me with the news.

Ori. Firft, let me blefs the cunning of my fex, that happy counterfeited frenzy, that has reftored to my poor labouring breaft the deareft, beft beloved of men.

Mir. Tune, all ye fpheres, your inftruments of joy, and carry round your fpacious orbs the happy found of Oriana's health! her foul, whofe harmony was next to yours, is now in tune again; the counterfeiting fair has played the fool.

> She was fo mad to counterfeit for me; }
> I was fo mad to pawn my liberty: }
> But now we both are well, and both are free. }

Ori. How, Sir, free!

Mir. As air, my dear bedlamite. What, marry a lunatic! Look ye, my dear, you have counterfeited madnefs fo very well this bout, that you'll be apt to play the fool all your life long. Here, gentlemen——

Ori. Monfter! you won't difgrace me?

Mir. O' my faith, but I will—here, come in, gentlemen—A miracle, a miracle! the woman's difpoffeffed! the devil's vanifhed!

Enter Old Mirabel *and* Dugard.

Old Mir. Blefs us! was fhe poffeffed?

Mir. With the worft of dæmons, Sir, a marriage-devil, a horrid devil. Mr. Dugard, don't be furprifed; I promifed my endeavours to cure your fifter; no mad-doctor in Chriftendom could have done it more effectually. Take her into your charge; and have a care fhe don't relapfe; if fhe fhould, employ me not again; for I am no more infallible than others of the faculty; I do cure fometimes.

Ori. Your remedy, moft barbarous man, will prove the
greateft

greatest poison to my health ; for tho' my former frenzy was but counterfeit, I shall now run into a real madness.

[*Exit*; Old Mir. *after.*

' *Dug.* This was a turn beyond my knowledge. I'm
' so confus'd, I know not how to resent it.   [*Exit.*'

Mir. What dangerous precipice have I escaped! Was not I just now upon the brink of destruction ?

' *Enter* Duretete.

' Oh, my friend, let me run into thy bosom ! no lark,
' escaped from the devouring pounces of a hawk, quakes
' with more dismal apprehension.

' *Dur.* The matter, man ?

' *Mir.* Marriage, hanging; I was just at the gallows-
' foot, the running noose about my neck, and the cart
' wheeling from me.   Oh, I shan't be myself this month
' again !

' *Dur.* Did not I tell you so ? They are all alike, saints
' or devils: their counterfeiting can't be reputed a deceit;
' for 'tis the nature of the sex, not their contrivance.

' *Mir.* Ay, ay; there's no living here with security;
' this house is so full of stratagem and design, that I must
' abroad again.

' *Dur.* With all my heart; I'll bear thee company,
' my lad.   I'll meet you at the play, and we'll set out
' for Italy to-morrow morning.

' *Mir.* A match ; I'll go pay my compliment of leave
' to my father presently.

' *Dur.* I'm afraid he'll stop you.

' *Mir.* What, pretend a command over me, after his
' settlement of a thousand pounds a year upon me ! No,
' no, he has passed away his authority with the convey-
' ance; the will of a living father is chiefly obeyed for
' the sake of the dying one.

' What makes the world attend and croud the great ?
' Hopes, interest and dependance make their state.
' Behold the antichamber fill'd with beaus ;
' A horse's levee crown'd with courtly crows.
' Tho' grumbling subjects make the crown their sport,
' Hopes of a place will bring the sparks to court.
' Dependance ev'n a father's sway secures;
' For tho' the son rebels, the heir is yours. [*Exeunt.*'

END OF THE FOURTH ACT.

ACT

ACT V.

SCENE, *the Street before the Play-house.*

Enter Mirabel *and* Duretete, *as coming from the Play.*

DURETETE.

HOW d'ye like this play?

Mir. I liked the company; the lady, the rich beauty, in the front box had my attention. Thefe impudent poets bring the ladies together to fupport them, and to kill every body elfe.

For deaths upon the ftage the ladies cry;
But ne'er mind us that in the audience die.
The poet's hero fhould not move their pain;
But they fhould weep for thofe their eyes have flain.

Dur. Hoity toity! did Phillis infpire you with all this?

Mir. Ten times more; the play-houfe is the element of poetry, becaufe the region of beauty; the ladies, methinks, have a more infpiring triumphant air in the boxes than any where elfe; they fit commanding on their thrones, with all their fubject flaves about them; their beft cloaths, beft looks, fhining jewels, fparkling eyes, the treafure of the world in a ring. ' Then there's fuch ' a hurry of pleafure to tranfport us; the buftle, noife, ' gallantry, equipage, garters, feathers, wigs, bows, fmiles, ' ogles, love, mufic, and applaufe.' I could wifh that my whole life long were the firft night of a new play.

Dug. The fellow has quite forgot this journey. Have you befpoke poft horfes?

Mir. Grant me but three days, dear Captain, one to difcover the lady, one to unfold myfelf, and one to make me happy, and then I'm yours to the world's end.

Dur. Haft thou the impudence to promife thyfelf a lady of her figure and quality in fo fhort a time?

Mir. Yes Sir; I have a confident addrefs, no difagreeable perfon, and five hundred louis d'ors in my pocket.

Dur. Five hundred louis d'ors! You an't mad?

Mir. I tell you, fhe's worth five thoufand; one of her black brilliant eyes is worth a diamond as big as her head. I compared her necklace with her looks, and the living jewels out-fparkled the dead ones by a million.

Dur.

Dur. But you have owned to me, that, abating Oriana's pretension's to marriage, you loved her paffionately : then how can you wander at this rate ?

Mir. I longed for partridge t'other day off the King's plate ; but, d'ye think, becaufe I could not have it, I muft eat nothing ?

Dur. Pr'ythee, Mirabel, be quiet ; you may remember what narrow efcapes you have had abroad, by following ftrangers ; you forget your leap out of the courtefan's window at Bologna, to fave your fine ring there.

Mir. My ring's a trifle ; there's nothing we poffefs comparable to what we defire. Be fhy of a lady, bare-faced, in the front-box, with a thoufand pounds in jewels about her neck !—For fhame ! no more——

Enter Oriana *in boy's cloaths, with a letter.*

Ori. Is your name Mirabel, Sir ?

Mir. Yes, Sir.

Ori. A letter from your uncle in Picardy.

[Gives the letter.

Mir. [*Reads.*] " The bearer is the fon of a proteftant gentleman who, flying for his religion, left me the charge of this youth."—A pretty boy.—" He's fond of fome handfome fervice that may afford him an opportunity of improvement. Your care of him will oblige

Your's."

Haft a mind to travel, child ?

Ori. 'Tis my defire, Sir ; I fhould be pleafed to ferve a traveller in any capacity.

Mir. A hopeful inclination. You fhall along with me into Italy as my page.

Dur. I don't think it fafe ; the rogue's too handfome. [*Noife without.*] The play is done, and fome of the ladies come this way.

Enter Lamorce, *with her train borne up by a page.*

Mir. Duretere, the very dear, identical fhe !

Dur. And what then ?

Mir. Why, 'tis fhe.

Du.. And what then, Sir ?

Mir. Then ! Why—Look ye, firrah, the firft piece of fervice I put you upon, is to follow that lady's coach, and bring me word where fhe lives. [*To* Oriana.

Ori.

Ori. I don't know the town, Sir, and am afraid of losing myself.

Mir. Pshaw!

Lam. Page, what's become of all my people?

Page. I can't tell, Madam; I can see no sign of your ladyship's coach.

Lam. That fellow is got into his old pranks, and fallen drunk somewhere—None of my footmen there?

Page. Not one, Madam.

Lam. These servants are the plague of our lives. What shall I do?

Mir. By all my hopes, Fortune pimps for me! Now, Duretete, for a piece of gallantry.

Dur. Why, you won't, sure?

Mir. Won't, brute!—Let not your servants' neglect, Madam, put your ladyship to any inconyenience; for you can't be disappointed of an equipage whilst mine waits below; and would you honour the matter so far, he would be proud to pay his attendance.

Dur. Ay, to be sure.   [*Aside.*

Lam. Sir, I won't presume to be troublesome; for my habitation is a great way off.

Dur. Very true, Madam; and he is a little engaged: besides, Madam, a hackney-coach will do as well, Madam.

Mir. Rude beast, be quiet. [*To* Duretete.]—The farther from home, Madam, the more occasion you have for a guard——Pray, Madam——

Lam. Lard, Sir!——

        [*He seems to press, she to decline it, in dumb show.*

Dur. Ah, the devil's in his impudence! Now he wheedles, she smiles; he flatters, she simpers; he swears, she believes; he's a rogue, and she's a w—— in a moment.

Mir. Without there! my coach!—Duretete, wish me joy.   [*Hands the lady out.*

Dur. Wish you a surgeon—Here, you little Picard; go follow your master, and he'll lead you——

Ori. Whither, Sir?

Dur. To the academy, child; 'tis the fashion with men of quality to teach their pages their exercises—Go.

Ori. Won't you go with him too, Sir? That woman may do him some harm; I don't like her.

Dur. Why, how now, Mr. Page? Do you start up to
                            give

give laws of a fudden ? Do you pretend to rife at court,
and difapprove the pleafure of your betters ? Look ye,
firrah, if ever you would rife by a great man, be fure to
be with him in his little actions; and, as a ftep to your
advancement, follow your mafter immediately, and make
it your hope that he goes to a bawdy-houfe.

Ori. Heavens forbid !   [*Exit.*

Dur. Now would I fooner take a cart in company of
the hangman, than a coach with that woman. What a
ftrange antipathy have I taken againft thefe creatures ! a
woman to me is averfion upon averfion ; a cheefe, a cat, a
breaft of mutton, the fqualling of children, the grinding
of knives, and the fnuff of a candle.   [*Exit.*

S C E N E, *a handfome Apartment.*

Enter Mirabel *and* Lamorce.

Lam. To convince me, Sir, that your fervice was
fomething more than good breeding, pleafe to lay out an
hour of your company upon my defire, as you have already upon my neceffity.

Mir. Your defire, Madam, has only prevented my requeft. My hours! make them yours, Madam ; eleven,
twelve, one, two, three, and all that belong to thofe happy minutes.

Lam. But I muft trouble you, Sir, to difmifs your retinue ; becaufe an equipage at my door, at this time of
night, will not be confiftent with my reputation.

Mir. By all means, Madam, all but one little boy——
Here, page, order my coach and fervants home, and do
you ftay ; 'tis a foolifh country boy, that knows nothing
but innocence.

Lam. Innocence, Sir ! I fhould be forry if you made
any finifter conftructions of my freedom.

Mir. Oh, Madam, I muft not pretend to remark upon
any body's freedom, having fo entirely forfeited my own.

Lam. Well, Sir, 'twere convenient towards our eafy
correfpondence, that we entered into a free confidence of
each other, by a mutual declaration of what we are, and
what we think of one another. Now, Sir, what are you ?

Mir. In three words, Madam,——I am a gentleman,
I have five hundred pounds in my pocket, and a clean
fhirt on.

F

Lam.

Lam. And your name is————

Mir. Muſtapha——Now, Madam, the inventory of your fortunes.

Lam. My name is Lamorce; my birth noble; I was married young, to a proud, rude, ſullen, impetuous fellow; the huſband ſpoiled the gentleman; crying ruined my face, till at laſt I took heart, leaped out of a window, got away to my friends, ſued my tyrant, and recovered my fortune. I lived from fifteen to twenty to pleaſe a huſband; from twenty to forty I'm reſolved to pleaſe myſelf, and from thence upwards I'll humour the world.

Mir. The charming wild notes of a bird broke out of its cage.

Lam. I marked you at the play, and ſomething I ſaw of a well-furniſhed, careleſs, agreeable *tour* about you. Methought your eyes made their mannerly demands with ſuch an arch modeſty, that I don't know how—but I'm elop'd. Ha, ha, ha! I'm elop'd.

Mir. Ha, ha, ha! I rejoice in your good fortune with all my heart.

Lam. Oh, now I think on't, Mr. Muſtapha, you have got the fineſt ring there; I could ſcarcely believe it right; pray, let me ſee it.

Mir. Hum!—Yes, Madam, 'tis, 'tis right—but, but, but, but, but it was given me by my mother; an old family ring, Madam, an old-faſhioned family ring.

Lam. Ay, Sir—If you can entertain yourſelf 'with a
' ſong' for a moment, I'll wait on you immediately.
' Come in there.'

' *Enter Singers.*

' Call what you pleaſe, Sir.'   [*Exit.*

Mir. ' The new ſong——" Pr'ythee, Phillis." [*Song.*'
Certainly the ſtars have been in a ſtrange intriguing humour when I was born. Ay, this night ſhould I have had a bride in my arms, and that I ſhould like well enough: but what ſhould I have to-morrow night? The ſame. And what next night? The ſame. And what next night? The very ſame—Soup for breakfaſt, ſoup for dinner, ſoup for ſupper, and ſoup for breakfaſt again—But here's variety.

' I love the fair who freely gives her heart,
' That's mine by ties of nature, not of art;

' Who

' Who boldly owns whate'er her thoughts indite,
' And is too modeſt for a hypocrite.'

[Lamorce *appears at the daor*; *as he runs towards her,* four
Bravoes *ſtep in before her.* He ſtarts back.
She comes, ſhe comes!—Hum, hum—Bitch—Murdered,
murdered to be ſure! The curſed ſtrumpet, to make me
ſend away my ſervants!—Nobody near me—Theſe cut-
throats always make ſure work. What ſhall I do? I
have but one way. Are theſe gentlemen your relations,
Madam?

Lam. Yes, Sir.

Mir. Gentlemen, your moſt humble ſervant. Sir,
your moſt faithful; yours, Sir, with all my heart; your
moſt obedient. Come, gentlemen, [*Salutes all round.*]
pleaſe to ſit— no ceremony—next the lady, pray, Sir.

Lam. Well, Sir, and how d'ye like my friends?
[*They all ſit.*

Mir. Oh, Madam, the moſt finiſhed gentlemen! I was
never more happy in good company in my life. I ſuppoſe, Sir, you have travelled?

1 *Bra.* Yes, Sir.

Mir. Which way, Sir, may I preſume?

1 *Bra.* In a weſtern barge, Sir.

Mir. Ha, ha, ha, very pretty! facetious pretty gentleman.

Lam. Ha, ha, ha! Sir, you have got the prettieſt ring
upon your finger there——

Mir. Ah, Madam, 'tis at your ſervice with all my
heart! [*Offering the ring.*

Lam. By no means, Sir; a family ring! [*Takes it.*

Mir. No matter, Madam. Seven hundred pounds, by
this light! [*Aſide.*

2 *Bra.* Pray, Sir, what's o'clock?

Mir. Hum!—Sir, I have left my watch at home.

2 *Bra.* I thought I ſaw the ſtring of it juſt now.

Mir. Ods my life, Sir, I beg your pardon, here it is;
but it don't go. [*Putting it up.*

Lam. Oh, dear Sir, an Engliſh watch! Tompion's, I
preſume.

Mir. D'ye like it, Madam?—No ceremony—'tis at
your ſervice with all my heart and ſoul——Tompion's!
Hang ye! [*Aſide.*

                                    1 *Bra.*

1 Bra. But, Sir, above all things, I admire the fashion and make of your sword-hilt.

Mir. I am mighty glad you like it, Sir.

1 Bra. Will you part with it, Sir?

Mir. Sir, I won't sell it.

1 Bra. Not sell it, Sir!

Mir. No, gentlemen; but I'll bestow it with all my heart.   [*Offering it.*

1 Bra Oh, Sir, we shall rob you!

Mir. That you do, I'll be sworn. [*Aside.*] I have another at home; pray, Sir—Gentlemen, you're too modest; have I any thing else that you can fancy? Sir, will you do me a favour? [*To the 1st Bravo.*] I am extremely in love with that wig which you wear; will you do me the favour to change with me?

1 Bra. Look ye, Sir, this is a family wig, and I would not part with it; but if you like it——

Mir. Sir, your most humble servant. [*They change wigs.*

1 Bra. Madam, your most humble slave.

[*Goes up foppishly to the lady, salutes her.*

2 Bra. The fellow's very liberal; shall we murder him?

[*Aside.*

1 Bra. What, let him escape to hang us all, and I to lose my wig! No, no; I want but a handsome pretence to quarrel with him; for you know we must act like gentlemen. [*Aside.*] Here, some wine. [*Wine here.*] Sir, your good health.   [*Pulls Mirabel by the nose.*

Mir. Oh, Sir, your most humble servant! A pleasant frolic enough, to drink a man's health, and pull him by the nose. Ha, ha, ha! the pleasantest pretty-humoured gentleman!

Lam. Help the gentleman to a glass.   [*Mir. drinks.*

1 Bra. How d'ye like the wine, Sir?

Mir. Very good o' the kind, Sir. But I tell ye what; I find we're all inclined to be frolicsome, and, 'egad, for my own part, I was never more disposed to be merry. Let's make a night on't, ha!—This wine is pretty; but I have such Burgundy at home—Look ye, gentlemen, let me send for half a dozen flasks of my Burgundy, I defy France to match it—'Twill make us all life, all air; pray, gentlemen——

2 Bra. Eh——Shall us have the Burgundy?

1 *Bra.* Yes, faith, we'll have all we can. Here, call up the gentleman's servant—What think you, Lamorce?

Lam. Yes, yes. Your servant is a foolish country boy, Sir, he understands nothing but innocence.

Mir. Ay, ay, Madam. Here, page!

Enter Oriana.

Take this key, and go to my butler, order him to send half a dozen flasks of the red Burgundy, marked a thousand: and be sure you make haste; I long to entertain my friends here, my very good friends.

Omnes. Ah, dear Sir!

1 *Bra.* Here, child, take a glass of wine—Your master and I have changed wigs, honey, in a frolic. Where had you this pretty boy, honest Mustapha?

Ori. Mustapha!

Mir. Out of Picardy. This is the first errand he has made for me, and if he does it right, I'll encourage him.

Ori. The red Burgundy, Sir?

Mir. The red, marked a thousand; and be sure you make haste.

Ori. I shall, Sir.   [*Exit.*

1 *Bra.* Sir, you were pleased to like my wig, have you any fancy for my coat? Look ye, Sir, it has served a great many honest gentlemen very faithfully.

Mir. Not so faithfully; for I'm afraid it has got a scurvy trick of leaving all its masters in necessity. The insolence of these dogs is beyond their cruelty.   [*Aside.*

Lam. You're melancholy, Sir.

Mir. Only concerned, Madam, that I should have no servant here but this little boy; he'll make some confounded blunder, I'll lay my life on't: I would not be disappointed of my wine for the universe.

Lam. He'll do well enough, Sir. But supper's ready; will you please to eat a bit, Sir?

Mir. Oh, Madam, I never had a better stomach in my life!

Lam. Come, then; we have nothing but a plate of soup.

Mir. [*Aside.*] Ah, the marriage-soup I could dispense with now!   [*Exit, handing the lady.*

2 *Bra.* That wig won't fall to your share.

1 *Bra.* No, no, we'll settle that after supper; in the mean time the gentleman shall wear it.

2 Bra. Shall we difpatch him?

3 Bra. To be fure.   I think he knows me.

1 Bra. Ay, ay, dead men tell no tales; I wonder at the impudence of the Englifh rogues, that will hazard the meeting a man at the bar, whom they have encountered upon the road.   I ha'n't the confidence to look a man in the face after I have done him an injury ; therefore we'll murder him.   [*Exeunt.*

SCENE *changes to* Old Mirabel's *Houfe.*

Enter Duretete.

Dur. My friend has forfaken me, I have abandoned my miftrefs, my time lies heavy upon my hands, and my money burns in my pocket.   But, now I think on't, my Myrmidons are upon duty to-night ; I'll fairly ftroll down to the guard, and nod away the night with my honeft Lieutenant, over a flafk of wine, a rakehelly ftory, and a pipe of tobacco.   [*Going off,* Bifarre *meets him.*

Bif. Who comes there ? Stand !

Dur. Hey-day ! now fhe's turn'd dragoon.

Bif. Look ye, Sir, I'm told you intend to travel again. I defign to wait on you as far as Italy.

Dur. Then I'll travel into Wales.

Bif. Wales ! What country's that ?

Dur. The land of mountains, child, where you're never out of the way, becaufe there's no fuch thing as a high-road.

Bif. Rather always in a high-road, becaufe you travel all upon hills.   But be it as it will, I'll jog along with you.

Dur. But we intend to fail to the Eaft-Indies.

Bif. Eaft or Weft, 'tis all one to me ; I'm tight and light, and the fitter for failing.

Dur. But fuppofe we take thro' Germany, and drink hard.

Bif. Suppofe I take thro' Germany, and drink harder than you.

Dur. Suppofe I go to a bawdy-houfe.

Bif. Suppofe I fhew you the way.

Dur. 'Sdeath, woman, will you go to the guard with me, and fmoak a pipe ?

Bif. Allons donc !

Dur. The devil's in the woman ! Suppofe I hang myfelf.

2

Bif.

Bif. There I'll leave you,

Dur. And a happy riddance; the gallows is welcome.

Bif. Hold, hold, Sir; [*Catches him by the arm, going.*] one word before we part.

Dur. Let me go, Madam, or I shall think that you are a man, and perhaps examine you. .

Bif. Stir if you dare; I have still spirits to attend me; and can raise such a muster of fairies as shall punish you to death. Come, Sir, stand there now and ogle me. [*He frowns upon her.*] Now a languishing sigh. [*He groans.*] Now run and take my fan—faster. [*He runs and takes it up.*] Now play with it handsomely

Dur. Ay, ay.   [*He tears it all in pieces.*

Bif. Hold, hold, dear humourous coxcomb! Captain, spare my fan, and I'll——Why, you rude, inhuman monster, don't you expect to pay for this?

Dur. Yes, Madam, there's twelve-pence; for that is the price on't.

Bif. Sir, it cost a guinea.

Dur. Well, Madam, you shall have the sticks again.
                    [*Throws them to her, and exit.*

Bif. Ha, ha, ha! ridiculous below my concern. I must follow him, however, to know if he can give me any news of Oriana.   [*Exit.*

SCENE changes to Lamorce's Lodgings.

Enter Mirabel.

Mir. Bloody hell-hounds! I over-heard you. Was not I, two hours ago, the happy, gay, rejoicing Mirabel? How did I plume my hopes in a fair coming prospect of a long scene of years? Life courted me with all the charms of vigour, youth, and fortune; and to be torn away from all my promised joys, is more than death--the manner too, by villains. Oh, my Oriana, this very moment might have bless'd me in thy arms! and my poor boy; the innocent boy!—Confusion!—But, hush, they come; I must dissemble still—No news of my wine, gentlemen?

Enter the four Bravoes.

1 *Bra.* No, Sir; I believe your country booby has lost himself, and we can wait no longer for it—True, Sir, you're a pleasant gentleman; but I suppose you understand our business.

Mir.

Mir. Sir, I may go near to gueſs at your employments ;
you, Sir, are a lawyer, I preſume ; you a phyſician, you
a ſcrivener, and you a ſtock-jobber——All cut-throats,
'egad.   [*Aſide.*

4 *Bra.* Sir, I am a broken officer ; I was caſhiered at the
head of the army for a coward ; ſo I took up the trade of
murder to retrieve the reputation of my courage.

3 *Bra.* I am a ſoldier too, and would ſerve my king ;
but I don't like the quarrel, and I have more honour than
to fight in a bad cauſe.

2 *Bra.* I was bred a gentleman, and have no eſtate ;
but I muſt have my whore and my bottle, through the
prejudice of education.

1 *Bra.* I am a ruffian too, by the prejudice of education ; I was bred a butcher. In ſhort, Sir, if your wine had
come, we might have trifled a little longer. Come, Sir,
which ſword will you fall by ? Mine, Sir ?   [*Draws.*

2 *Bra.* Or mine ?   [*Draws.*

3 *Bra.* Or mine ?   [*Draws.*

4 *Bra.* Or mine ?   [*Draws.*

Mir. I ſcorn to beg my life ; but to be butcher'd thus !
[*Knocking.*] Oh, there's the wine !——This moment for
my life or death.

Enter Oriana.

Loſt, for ever loſt !—Where's the wine, child ? [*Faintly.*

Ori. Coming up, Sir.   [*Stamps.*

Enter Duretete *with his ſword drawn, and ſix of the
grand Muſqueteers with their pieces preſented ; the Ruffians drop their ſwords. Oriana goes off.*

Mir. The wine, the wine, the wine ! Youth, pleaſure,
fortune, days and years are now my own again !—Ah,
my dear friends ! did not I tell you this wine would make
me merry ?—Dear Captain, theſe gentlemen are the beſt-
natured, facetious, witty creatures, that ever you knew.

Enter Lamorce.

Lam. Is the wine come, Sir?

Mir. Oh, yes, Madam, the wine is come—See there !
[*Pointing to the ſoldiers.*] Your Ladyſhip has got a very
fine ring upon your finger.

Lam. Sir, 'tis at your ſervice.

Mir. Oh, ho! is it ſo? Thou dear ſeven hundred pounds,
thou'rt welcome home again, with all my heart—Ad's my
life.

life, Madam, you have got the finest built watch there ! Tompion's, I presume.

Lam. Sir, you may wear it.

Mir. Oh, Madam, by no means, 'tis too much—Rob you of all !—[*Taking it from her.*] Good dear time, thou'rt a precious thing, I'm glad I have retrieved thee. [*Putting it up.*] What, my friends neglected all this while ! Gentlemen, you'll pardon my complaisance to the lady.—How now— is it civil to be so out of humour at my entertainment, and I so pleased with yours ? Captain, you are surprized at all this ! but we're in our frolics, you must know.——Some wine here.

Enter Servant with Wine.

Come, Captain, this worthy gentleman's health. (*Tweaks the first Bravo by the nose; he roars.*] But now, where ——where's my dear deliverer, my boy, my charming boy !

1st Bra. I hope some of our crew below-stairs have dispatched him.

Mir. Villain, what sayest thou ? Dispatched ! I'll have ye all tortured, racked, torn to pieces alive, if you have touched my boy.—Here, Page ! Page ! Page !

[*Runs out.*

Dur. Here, gentlemen, be sure you secure those fellows.

1st Bra. Yes, Sir, we know you and your guard will be very civil to us.

Dur. Now for you, Madam ;—— He, he, he.—I'm so pleased to think that I shall be revenged of one woman before I die—Well, Mistress Snap-Dragon, which of these honourable gentlemen is so happy to call you wife ?

1st Brav. Sir, she should have been mine to-night, because Sampre here had her last night. Sir, she's very true to us all four.

Dug. Take them to justice.

[*The Guards carry off the Bravoes.*
Enter Old Mirabel, Dugard, *and* Bisarre.

Old Mir. Robin, Robin, where's Bob ? Where's my boy ?—What, is this the lady ? a pretty whore, faith ?—Heark'e, child, because my son was so civil as to oblige you with a coach, I'll treat you with a cart, indeed I will.

Dug. Ay, Madam,—and you shall have a swinging
equi-

equipage, three or four thousand footmen at your heels at least.

Dur. No less becomes her quality.

Bif. Faugh! the monster!

Dur. Monster! ay, you're all a little monstrous, let me tell you.

Enter Mirabel.

Old Mir. Ah, my dear Bob, art thou safe, man?

Mir. No, no, Sir, I'm ruin'd, the saver of my life is lost.

Old Mir. No, he came and brought us the news.

Mir. But where is he?——

Enter Oriana.

Ha! [*Runs and embraces her.*] My dear preserver, what shall I do to recompense your trust?—' Father, friends, ' gentlemen, behold the youth that has relieved me from ' the most ignominious death, from the scandalous po- ' niards of these bloody Ruffians, where to have fallen ' would have defamed my memory with vile reproach— ' My life, estate, my all, is due to such a favour'—— Command me, child; before you all, before my late so kind indulgent stars, I swear to grant whate'er you ask.

Ori. To the same stars, indulgent now to me, I will appeal as to the justice of my claim; I shall demand but what was mine before——the just performance of your contract to Oriana.   [*Discovering herself.*

Om. Oriana!

Ori. In this disguise I resolved to follow you abroad, counterfeited that letter that got me into your service; and so, by this strange turn of fate, I became the instru- ment of your preservation; few common servants would have had such cunning; my love inspired me with the meaning of your message, because my concern for your safety made me suspect your company.

Dur. Mirabel, you're caught.

Mir. Caught! I scorn the thought of imposition, ' the ' tricks and artful cunning of the sex I have despised, and ' broke through all contrivance.' Caught! No, 'tis my voluntary act; this was no human stratagem, but by my providential stars designed, to shew the dangers wan- dering youth incurs by the pursuit of an unlawful love, to plunge me headlong in the snares of vice, and then

to

to free me by the hands of virtue. Here, on my knees, I humbly beg my fair preferver's pardon; my thanks are needlefs, for myfelf I owe. And now for ever do proteft me yours.

Old Mir. Tall, all, di, dall. [*Sings.*] Kifs me, daughter —No, you fhall kifs me firft, [*To* Lamorce.] for you're the caufe on't. Well, Bifarre, what fay you to the Captain ?

Bif. I like the beaft well enough, but don't underftand his paces fo well as to venture him in a ftrange road.

Old Mir. But marriage is fo beaten a path that you can't go wrong.

Bif. Ay, 'tis fo beaten that the way is fpoiled.

Dur. There is but one thing fhould make me thy hufband—I could marry thee to-day for the privilege of beating thee to-morrow.

Old Mir. Come, come, you may agree for all this. Mr. Dugard, are not you pleafed with this ?

Dug. So pleafed, that if I thought it might fecure your fon's affection to my fifter, I would double her fortune.

Mir. Fortune! has fhe not given me mine, my life, eftate, my all, and what is more, her virtuous felf?——
‘ Virtue, in this fo advantageous life, has her own fpark-
‘ ling charms, more tempting far than glittering gold or
‘ glory.’ Behold the foil [*Pointing to* Lamorce.] that fets this brightnefs off! [*To* Oriana] Here view the pride [*To* Oriana.] and fcandal of the fex. [*To* Lam.] ‘ There
‘ [*To* Lam.] the falfe meteor, whofe deluding light leads
‘ mankind to deftruction. Here [*To* Oriana.] the bright
‘ fhining ftar that guides to a fecurity of happinefs. A
‘ garden, and a fingle fhe, [*To* Oriana.] was our firft fa-
‘ ther's blifs ; the tempter, [*To* Lam.] and to wander, was
‘ his curfe.’

What liberty can be fo tempting there,   [*To* Lam.
As a foft, virtuous, am'rous bondage here ?   [*To* Ori.

END of the FIFTH ACT.

EPI-

EPILOGUE.

Written by Nathaniel Rowe, Esq.

FROM Fletcher's great original, to-day
  We took the hint of this our modern play:
Our author, from his lines, has strove to paint
A witty, wild, inconstant, free gallant:
With a gay soul, with sense, and will to rove,
With language, and with softness fram'd to move,
With little truth, but with a world of love.
Such forms on maids in morning slumbers wait,
When fancy first instructs their hearts to beat,
When first they wish, and sigh for what they know not yet.
Frown not, ye fair, to think your lovers may
Reach your cold hearts by some unguarded way;
Let Villeroy's misfortune make you wise,
There's danger still in darkness and surprise;
Though from his rampart he defy'd the foe,
Prince Eugene found an aqueduct below.
With easy freedom, and a gay address,
A pressing lover seldom wants success:
Whilst the respectful, like the Greek, sits down,
And wastes a ten years siege before one town.
For her own sake, let no forsaken maid,
Our wanderer, for want of love, upbraid;
Since 'tis a secret, none should e'er confess,
That they have lost the happy pow'r to please.
If you suspect the rogue inclin'd to break,
Break first, and swear you've turn'd him off a week;
As princes, when they resty statesmen doubt,
Before they can surrender, turn them out.
Whate'er you think, grave uses may be made,
And much even for inconstancy be said
Let the good man for marriage-rites design'd,
With studious care, and diligence of mind,
Turn over every page of womankind;
Mark every sense, and how the readings vary,
And, when he knows the worst on't,—let him marry.

Publish'd for Bells British Theatre July 1777

Mr BOOTH in the Character of LORD FROTH.

Now when I laugh, I always laugh alone.

THE
DOUBLE DEALER.

A COMEDY,

As written by CONGREVE.

DISTINGUISHING ALSO THE

VARIATIONS OF THE THEATRE,

AS PERFORMED AT THE

Theatre-Royal in Drury-Lane.

Regulated from the Prompt-Book.

By PERMISSION *of the* MANAGERS.

By Mr. HOPKINS, Prompter.

LONDON:

Printed for JOHN BELL, near *Exeter Exchange*, in the *Strand.*

MDCCLXXVII.

To the Right Honourable

CHARLES MONTAGUE,

ONE OF THE

LORDS OF THE TREASURY.

SIR,

I Heartily wish this play were as perfect as I intended
it, that it might be more worthy your acceptance;
and that my Dedication of it to you might be more becoming that honour and esteem which I, with every body who is so fortunate as to know you, have for you.
It had your countenance when yet unknown; and now it
is made public, it wants your protection.

I would not have any body imagine, that I think this
play without its faults, for I am conscious of several. I
confess I designed (whatever vanity or ambition occa-
sioned that design) to have written a true and regular comedy; but I found it an undertaking which put me in
mind of——*Sudet multum, frustraque laboret ausus idem.*
And now to make amends for the vanity of such a design, I do confess both the attempt, and the imperfect
performance. Yet I must take the boldness to say, I
have not miscarried in the whole; for the mechanical
part of it is regular. That I may say with a little vanity, as a builder may say, he has built a house according
to the model laid down before him; or a gardener that
he has set his flowers in a knot of such or such a figure.
I designed the moral first, and to that moral I invented
the fable, and do not know that I have borrowed one
hint of it any where. I made the plot as strong as I
could, because it was single; and I made it single, because I would avoid confusion, and was resolved to preserve the three unities of the Drama. Sir, this discourse is very impertinent to you, whose judgment much
better can discern the faults, than I can excuse them;
and whose good-nature, like that of a lover, will find

A 2

out

out thofe hidden beauties (if there are any fuch) which it would be great immodefty for me to difcover. I think I do not fpeak improperly when I call you a *Lover* of Poetry; for it is very well known fhe has been a very kind miftrefs to you; fhe has not denied you the laft favour, and fhe has been fruitful to you in a moft beautiful iffue—If I break off abruptly here, I hope every body will underftand that it is to avoid a commendation, which, as it is your due, would be moft eafy for me to pay, and too troublefome for you to receive.

I have, fince the acting of this play, hearkened after the objections which have been made to it; for I was confcious where a true critic might have put me upon my defence, I was prepared for the attack; and am pretty confident I could have vindicated fome parts, and excufed others; and where there were any plain mifcarriages, I would moft ingenuoufly have confeffed them. But I have not heard any thing faid fufficient to provoke an anfwer. That which looks moft like an objection, does not relate in particular to this play, but to all or moft that ever have been written; and that is foliloquy. Therefore I will anfwer it, not only for my own fake, but to fave others the trouble, to whom it may hereafter be objected.

I grant, that for a man to talk to himfelf, appears abfurd and unnatural; and indeed it is fo in moft cafes: but the circumftances which may attend the occafion make great alteration. It oftentimes happens to a man, to have defigns which require him to himfelf, and in their nature cannot admit of a confident. Such, for certain, is all villainy; and other lefs mifchievous intentions may be very improper to be communicated to a fecond perfon. In fuch a cafe, therefore, the audience muft obferve whether the perfon upon the ftage takes any notice of them at all, or no. For if he fuppofes any one to be by, when he talks to himfelf, it is monftrous and ridiculous to the laft degree; nay, not only in this cafe, but in any part of a play, if there is expreffed any knowledge of an audience, it is infufferable. But otherwife, when a man in foliloquy reafons with himfelf, and *pro*'s and *con*'s, and weighs all his defigns, we ought not to imagine that this man either talks to us, or to himfelf; he is only thinking, and thinking fuch matter as were

in-

inexcufable folly in him to fpeak. But becaufe we are concealed fpectators of the plot in agitation, and the poet finds it neceffary to let us know the whole myftery of this contrivance, he is willing to inform us of this perfon's thoughts; and to that end is forced to make ufe of the expedient of fpeech, no better way being yet invented for the communication of thought.

Another very wrong objection has been made by fome who have not taken leifure to diftinguifh the characters. The hero of the play, as they are pleafed to call him, (meaning Mellefont) is a gull, and made a fool, and cheated. Is every man a gull and a fool that is deceived? At that rate I am afraid the two claffes of men will be reduced to one, and the knaves themfelves be at a lofs to juftify their title; but if an open-hearted honeft man, who has an entire confidence in one whom he takes to be his friend, and whom he has obliged to be fo; and who (to confirm him in his opinion) in all appearance, and upon feveral trials, has been fo; if this man be deceived by the treachery of the other, muft he of neceffity commence fool immediately, only becaufe the other has proved a villain? Ay, but there was a caution given to Mellefont, in the firft act, by his friend Carelefs. Of what nature was that caution? only to give the audience fome light into the character of Mafkwell before his appearance, and not to convince Mellefont of his treachery; for that was more than Carelefs was then able to do: he never knew Mafkwell guilty of any villainy; he was only a fort of man which he did not like. As for his fufpecting his familarity with my Lady Touchwood, let them examine the anfwer that Mellefont makes him, and compare it with the conduct of Mafkwell's character through the play.

I would beg them again to look into the character of Mafkwell before they accufe Mellefont of weaknefs for being deceived by him. For upon fumming up the enquiry into this objection, it may be found they have miftaken cunning in one character for folly in another.

But there is one thing, at which I am more concerned than all the falfe criticifms that are made upon me; and that is, fome of the ladies are offended. I am heartily forry for it; for I declare I would rather difoblige all the critics in the world, than one of the fair-fex. They

are

are concerned that I have reprefented fome women vicious and affected : How can I help it ? It is the bufinefs of
a comic poet to paint the vices and follies of human-kind;
and there are but two fexes, male and female, *men* and
women, which have a title to humanity : and if I leave
one half of them out, the work will be imperfect. I
fhould be very glad of an opportunity to make my compliment to thofe ladies who are offended; but they can
no more expect it in a comedy, than to be tickled by a furgeon when he is letting them blood. They who are virtuous or difcreet fhould not be offended; for fuch characters as thefe diftinguifh *them*, and make their beauties
more fhining and obferved : and they who are of the
other kind, may neverthelefs pafs for fuch, by feeming
not to be difpleafed, or touched with the fatire of this
Comedy. Thus have they alfo wrongfully accufed me of
doing them a prejudice, when I have in reality done
them a fervice.

You will pardon me, Sir, for the freedom I take of
making anfwers to other people, in an epiftle which
ought wholly to be facred to you : but fince I intend the
play to be fo too, I hope I may take the more liberty of
juftifying it where it is in the right.

I muft now, Sir, declare to the world how kind you
have been to my endeavours; for in regard of what was
well meant, you have excufed what was ill performed.
I beg you would continue the fame method in your acceptance of this dedication. I know no other way of making a return to that humanity you fhewed, in protecting
an infant, but by enrolling it in your fervice, now that
it is of age, and come into the world. Therefore, be
pleafed to accept of this as an acknowledgment of the
favour you have fhewn me, and an earneft of the real fervice and gratitude of,

S I R,

Your moft obliged,

Humble Servant,

WILLIAM CONGREVE.

T

To my dear Friend Mr. CONGREVE, *on his* Comedy, *called, The* DOUBLE DEALER.

WELL then; the promis'd hour is come at laſt;
    The preſent age of wit obſcures the paſt:
Strong were our ſires, and as they fought they writ,
Conqu'ring with force of arms, and dint of wit;
'Theirs was the giant race, before the flood;
And thus, when Charles return'd, our empire ſtood.
Like Janus, he the ſtubborn ſoil manur'd,
With rules of huſbandry the rankneſs cur'd:
Tam'd us to manners, when the ſtage was rude,
And boiſt'rous Engliſh wit with art indu'd.
Our age was cultivated thus at length;
But what we gain'd in ſkill we loſt in ſtrength.
Our builders were, with want of genius, curſt;
The ſecond temple was not like the firſt:
'Till you the beſt Vitruvius come at length,
Our beauties equal, but excel our ſtrength.
Firm Doric pillars found your ſolid baſe;
The fair Corinthian crowns the higher ſpace;   }
Thus all below is ſtrength, and all above is grace.
In eaſy dialogue is Fletcher's praiſe:
He mov'd the mind, but had no pow'r to raiſe.
Great Johnſon did by ſtrength of judgment pleaſe:
Yet doubling Fletcher's force, he wants his eaſe.
In diff'rent talents both adorn'd their age;
One for the ſtudy, t'other for the ſtage.
But both to Congreve juſtly ſhall ſubmit,
One match'd in judgment, both o'er-match'd in wit.
In him all beauties of this age we ſee,
Etherege's courtſhip, Southerne's purity;   }
The ſatire, wit, and ſtrength of manly Wycherley.
All this in blooming youth you have achiev'd;
Nor are your foil'd cotemporaries griev'd;
So much the ſweetneſs of your manners move,
We cannot envy you, becauſe we love.
Fabius might joy with Scipio, when he ſaw
A beardleſs Conſul made againſt the law,
And join his ſuffrage to the votes of Rome;
Though he with Hannibal was overcome.

    4   Thus

Thus old Romano bow'd to Raphael's fame,
And scholar to the youth he taught, became.
   Oh, that your brows my laurel had sustain'd,
Well had I been depos'd, if you had reign'd!
The father had descended for the son;
For only you are lineal to the throne.
Thus when the State one Edward did depose,
A greater Edward in his room arose.
But now, not I, but poetry is curs'd,
For Tom the second reigns, like Tom the first.
But let them not mistake my patron's part,
Nor call his charity their own desert.
Yet this I prophesy ; thou shalt be seen
(Tho' with some short parenthesis between)
High on the throne of Wit ; and seated there,
Not mine (that's little) but thy laurel wear.
Thy first attempt an early promise made,
That early promise this has more than paid,
So bold, yet so judiciously you dare,
That your least praise, is to be regular.
Time, place, and action, may with pains be wrought,
But genius must be born, and never can be taught.
This is your portion ; this your native store ;
Heav'n. that but once was prodigal before,
To Shakespeare gave as much ; she could not give him
      more.
   Maintain your post ; that's all the fame you need ;
For 'tis impossible you should proceed.
Already I am worn with cares and age,
And just abandoning th' ungrateful stage ;
Unprofitably kept at Heaven's expence,
I live a rent-charge on his providence :
But you, whom ev'ry muse and grace adorn,
Whom I foresee to better fortune born,
Be kind to my remains ; and Oh, defend,
Against your judgment, your departed friend !
Let not th' insulting foe my fame pursue ;
But shade those laurels which descend to you :
And take for tribute what these lines express :
You merit more ; nor could my love do less.
                              JOHN DRYDEN.

                              P R O-

PROLOGUE.

MOORS have this way (as story tells) to know
Whether their brats are truly got, or no;
Into the sea the new-born babe is thrown,
There, as instinct directs, to swim or drown.
A barbarous device, to try if spouse
Has kept religiously her nuptial vows.

Such are the trials poets make of plays;
Only they trust to more inconstant seas;
So does our author, this his child commit
To the tempestuous mercy of the pit,
To know if it be truly born of Wit.

Critics, avaunt; for you are fish of prey,
And feed, like sharks, upon an infant play.
Be ev'ry monster of the deep away;
Let's have fair trial, and a clear sea.

Let Nature work, and do not damn too soon,
For life will struggle long, ere it sink down:
And will at least rise thrice before it drown.
Let us consider, had it been our fate,
Thus hardly to be prov'd legitimate!
I will not say we'd all in danger been,
Were each to suffer for his mother's sin:
But by my troth I cannot avoid thinking,
How nearly some good men might have 'scap'd sinking.
But, Heaven be prais'd, this custom is confin'd
Alone to th' offspring of the muses kind:
Our Christian cuckolds are more bent to pity;
I know not one Moor-husband in the city.
I'th' good man's arms the chopping bastard thrives,
For he thinks all his own that is his wives.

Whatever fate is for this play design'd,
The poet's sure he shall some comfort find:
For if his muse has play'd him false, the worst
That can befal him, is, to be divorced;
You husbands judge, if that be to be curs'd.

D R

DRAMATIS PERSONÆ.

MEN.

Covent-Garden.

Maskwell, a villain; pretended friend to *Mellefont*, gallant to Lady *Touch-wood*, and in love with *Cynthia* — Mr. Sheridan.
Lord *Touchwood*, uncle to *Mellefont* — Mr. Clarke.
Mellefont, promised to, and in love with *Cynthia* — Mr. Wroughton.
Careless, his friend — Mr. Lewis.
Lord *Froth*, a solemn coxcomb — Mr. Booth.
Brisk — Mr. Woodward.
Sir *Paul Plyant*, an uxorious, foolish, old Knight; brother to Lady *Touch-wood*, and father to *Cynthia* — Mr. Macklin.

WOMEN.

Lady *Touchwood*, in love with *Mellefont* — Mrs. Jackson.
Cynthia, daughter to Sir *Paul* by a for-mer wife, promised to *Mellefont* — Miss Dayes.
Lady *Froth*, a great coquet; preten-der to poetry, wit, and learning — Mrs. Mattocks.
Lady *Plyant*, insolent to her husband, and easy to any pretender — Miss Macklin.

Chaplain, Boy, Footmen, and *Attendants.*

The SCENE, *a Gallery in Lord* Touchwood's *House, with Chambers adjoining.*

THE

THE
DOUBLE DEALER,

⁎⁎⁎ *The lines diftinguifhed by inverted comas, ' thus,' are omitted in the reprefentation.*

ACT I.

SCENE, *A Gallery in Lord* Touchwood'*s Houfe, with Chambers adjoining.*

Enter Carelefs, *croffing the ftage, with his hat, gloves, and fword in his hands, as juft rifen from table;* Mellefont *following him.*

MELLEFONT.

NED, Ned, whither fo faft! What, turn'd ftincher! Why, you wo'not leave us?

Care. Where are the women? I'm weary of guzzling, and begin to think them the better company.

Mel. Then thy reafon ftaggers, and thou'rt almoft drunk.

Care. No, faith, but your fools grow noify; and if a man muft endure the noife of words without fenfe, I think the women have more mufical voices, and become nonfenfe better.

Mel. Why, they are at the end of the gallery, retired to their tea and fcandal, according to their ancient cuftom after dinner.————But I made a pretence to follow you, becaufe I had fomething to fay to you in private, and I am not like to have many opportunities this evening.

Care. And here's this coxcomb moft critically come to interrupt you.

Enter

Enter Brisk.

Brisk. Boys, boys, lads, where are you? What, do you give ground? Mortgage for a bottle, ha? Careless, this is your trick; you are always spoiling company by leaving it.

Care. And thou art always spoiling company by coming into it.

Brisk. Pooh, ha, ha, ha, I know you envy me. Spite, proud spite, by the gods! and burning envy.——I'll be judged by Mellefont here, who gives and takes raillery better, you or I. Pshaw, man, when I say you spoil company by leaving it, I mean you leave nobody for the company to laugh at. I think there I was with you, ha! Mellefont.

Mel. O' my word, Brisk, that was a home thrust—— you have silenced him.

Brisk. Oh, my dear Mellefont, let me perish if thou art not the soul of conversation, the very essence of wit, and spirit of wine——The deuce take me, if there were three good things said, or one understood, since thy amputation from the body of our society——He, I think that's pretty and metaphorical enough: 'Egad, I could not have said it out of thy company—Careless, ha!

Care. Hum, what is it?

Brisk. O, *mon cœur!* What is't! Nay, gad I'll punish you for want of apprehension:—the deuce take me if I tell you.

Mel. No, no, hang him, he has no taste—But, dear Brisk, excuse me, I have a little business.

Care. Pr'ythee, get thee gone: thou seest we are serious.

Mel. We'll come immediately if you'll but go in, and keep up good humour and sense in the company:: Pr'ythee do——they'll fall asleep else.

Brisk. 'Egad so they will——Well I will, I will; gad you shall command me from the zenith to the nadir.—— But the deuce take me if I say a good thing 'till you come.—But pr'ythee, dear rogue, make haste, pr'ythee make haste, I shall burst else.—And yonder your uncle, my Lord Touchwood, swears he'll disinherit you, and Sir Paul Plyant threatens to disclaim you for a son-in-law, and my Lord Froth won't dance at your wedding to-mor-

row;

crow; nor the deuce take me, I won't write your epithala-
mium——and see what a condition you're like to be
brought to.

Mel. Well, I'll speak but three words, and follow
you.

Brisk. Enough, enough. Careless, bring your apprehension along with you.   [*Exit.*

Care. Pert coxcomb.

Mel. Faith, 'tis a good-natured coxcomb, and has very entertaining follies——You must be more humane
to him; at this juncture it will do me service. I'll tell
you, I would have mirth continued this day at any rate;
tho' patience purchase folly, and attention be paid with
noise. There are times when sense may be unseasona-
ble, as well as truth. Pr'ythee do thou wear none to-
day; but allow Brisk to have wit, that thou mayst seem a
fool.

Care. Why, how now, why this extravagant propo-
sition?

Mel. O, I would have no room for serious design, for
I am jealous of a plot. I would have noise and impertinence keep my Lady Touchwood's head from working:
for Hell is not more busy than her brain, nor contains
more devils than that imaginations.

Care. I thought your fear of her had been over —— Is
not to-morrow appointed for your marriage with Cynthia, and her father Sir Paul Plyant come to settle the
writings this day, on purpose?

Mel. True; but you shall judge whether I have not
reason to be alarmed. None besides you and Maskwell
are acquainted with the secret of my aunt Touchwood's
violent passion for me. Since my first refusal of her addresses, she has endeavoured to do me all ill offices with
my uncle; yet has managed them with that subtilty,
that to him they have borne the face of kindness, while
her malice, like a dark lanthorn, only shone upon me,
where it was directed. Still it gave me less perplexity to
prevent the success of her displeasure, than to avoid the
importunities of her love; and of two evils, I thought
myself favoured in her aversion: but whether urged by
her despair, and the short prospect of time she saw, to
accomplish her designs; whether the hopes of revenge,
or of her love, terminated in the view of this my mar-

B

riage

riage with Cynthia, I know not; but this morning she surprized me in my bed ————

Care. Was there ever such a fury! 'Tis well Nature has not put it into her sex's power to ravish.——Well, bless us! proceed. What followed?

Mel. What at first amazed me; for I looked to have seen her in all the transports of a slighted and revengeful woman: but when I expected thunder from her voice, and lightning in her eyes, I saw her melted into tears, and hushed into a sigh. It was long before either of us spoke, passion had tied her tongue, and amazement mine. —In short, the consequence was thus: she omitted nothing that the most violent love could urge, or tender words express; which when she saw had no effect, but still I pleaded honour and nearness of blood to my uncle, then came the storm I feared at first; for starting from my bed-side like a fury, she flew to my sword, and with much ado I prevented her doing me or herself a mischief: having disarmed her, in a gust of passion she left me, and in a resolution, confirmed by a thousand curses, not to close her eyes, 'till they had seen my ruin.

Care. Exquisite woman! But what the devil does she think thou hast no more sense than to get an heir upon her body to disinherit thyself: for, as I take it, this settlement upon you, is with a proviso that your uncle have no children.

Mel. It is so. Well, the service you are to do me, will be a pleasure to yourself; I must get you to engage my Lady Plyant all this evening, that my pious aunt may not work her to her interest. And if you chance to secure her to yourself, you may incline her to mine. She is handsome, and knows it; is very silly, and thinks she has sense, and has an old fond husband.

Care. I confess a very fair foundation for a lover to build upon.

Mel. For my Lord Froth, he and his wife will be sufficiently taken up with admiring one another, and Brisk's galantry, as they call it. I'll observe my uncle myself; and Jack Maskwell has promised me to watch my aunt narrowly, and give me notice upon any suspicion. As for Sir Paul, my wife father-in-law that is to be, my dear Cynthia has such a share in his fatherly fondness, he

would

would scarce make her a moment uneasy, to have her, happy hereafter.

Care. So, you have manned your works; but I wish you may not have the weakest guard where the enemy is strongest.

Mel. Maskwell, you mean; pr'ythee why should you suspect him?

Care. Faith, I cannot help it; you know I never liked him; I am a little superstitious in physiognomy.

Mel. He has obligations of gratitude to bind him to me; his dependence upon my uncle is through my means.

Care. Upon your aunt, you mean.

Mel. My aunt!

Care. I am mistaken if there be not a familiarity between them you do not suspect, notwithstanding her passion for you.

Mel. Pooh, pooh, nothing in the world but his design to do me service; and he endeavours to be well in her esteem, that he may be able to effect it.

Care. Well, I shall be glad to be mistaken: but your aunt's aversion in her revenge cannot be any way so effectually shewn, as in bringing forth a child to disinherit you. She is handsome and cunning, and naturally wanton. Maskwell is flesh and blood at best, and opportunities between them are frequent. His affection to you, you have confessed, is grounded upon his interest, that you have transplanted; and should it take root in my lady, I do not see what you can expect from the fruit.

Mel. I confess the consequence is visible, were your suspicions just.—But see, the company is broke up, let us meet them.

Enter Lord Touchwood, *Lord* Froth, *Sir* Paul Plyant, *and* Brisk.

Ld. T. Out upon't, nephew——leave your father-in-law, and me, to maintain our ground against young people.

Mel. I beg your Lordship's pardom—we were just returning.————

Sir P. Were you, son? Gadsbud, much better as it is—Good, strange! I swear I'm almost tipsy——t'other bottle would have been too powerful for me—as sure as

can

can be it would.—We wanted your company, but Mr. Brisk—where is he? I swear and vow he's a most facerious person—and the best company.——And my Lord Froth, your Lordship is so merry a man, he, he, he.

Ld. F. O foy, Sir Paul, what do you mean? Merry! O barbarous! I'd as lieve you called me fool.

Sir P. Nay, I protest and vow now, 'tis true; when Mr. Brisk jokes, your Lordship's laugh does so become you, he, he, he.

Ld. F. Ridiculous! Sir Paul, you're strangely mistaken; I find Champagne is powerful. I assure you, Sir Paul. I laugh at nobody's jest but my own, or a lady's; I assure you, Sir Paul.

Brisk. How! how, my Lord! What, affront my wit! Let me perish, do I never say any thing worthy to be laughed at?

Ld. F. O foy, don't misapprehend me; I don't say so, for I often smile at your conceptions. But there is nothing more unbecoming a man of quality, than to laugh; 'tis such a vulgar expression of the passion! every body can laugh. Then especially to laugh at the jest of an inferior person, or when any body else of the same quality does not laugh with one. Ridiculous! to be pleased with what pleases the croud! Now, when I laugh, I always laugh alone.

Brisk. I suppose that's because you laugh at your own jests, 'egad, ha, ha, ha.

Ld. F. He, he, I swear tho', your raillery provokes me to a smile.

Brisk. Ay, my Lord, it's a sign I hit you in the teeth, if you shew 'em.

Ld. F. He, he, he, I swear that's so very pretty, I can't forbear.

' *Care.* I find a quibble bears more sway in your Lord-
' ship's face than a jest.'

Ld. T. Sir Paul, if you please we'll retire to the ladies, and drink a dish of tea to settle our heads.

Sir P. With all my heart.—Mr. Brisk, you'll come to us — or call me when you joke—I'll be ready to laugh incontinently.   [*Exeunt Ld.* Touch. *and Sir* Paul.

Mel. But does your Lordship never see comedies?

Ld. F. O yes, sometimes, but I never laugh.

Mel.

Mel. No?

Ld. F. Oh, no——never laugh indeed, Sir.

Care. No! Why, what d'ye go there for?

Ld. F. To diftinguifh myfelf from the commonalty, and mortify the poets;——the fellows grow fo conceited when any of their foolifh wit prevails upon the fide-boxes.——I fwear——he, he, he, I have often conftrained my inclinations to laugh——he, he, he, to avoid giving them encouragement

Mel. You are cruel to yourfelf, my Lord, as well as malicious to them.

Ld. F. I confefs I did myfelf fome violence at firft, but now I think I have conquered it.

Brisk. Let me perifh, my Lord, but there is fomething very particular in the humour; 'tis true, it makes againft wit, and I'm forry for fome friends of mine that write, but 'egad, I love to be malicious.——Nay, deuce take me, there's wit in't too——and wit muft be foiled by wit; cut a diamond with a diamond, no other way, 'egad.

Ld. F. Oh, I thought you would not be long before you found out the wit.

Care. Wit! In what? Where the Devil's the wit in not laughing when a man has a mind to't?

Brisk. O lord, why, can't you find it out?——Why, there 'tis, in the not laughing——Don't you apprehend me?—— My Lord, Carelefs is a very honeft fellow, but hark ye—you underftand me, fomewhat heavy, a little fhallow, or fo.—Why, I'll tell you now, fuppofe now you come up to me——Nay, pr'ythee Carelefs be inftructed. Suppofe, as I was faying, you come up to me holding your fides, and laughing, as if you would—— Well—I look grave, and afk the caufe of this immoderate mirth—— You laugh on ftill, and are not able to tell me——Still I look grave, not fo much as fmile.————

Care. Smile, no, what the Devil fhould you fmile at, when you fuppofe I can't tell you?

Brisk. Pfhaw, pfhaw, pr'ythee don't interrupt me.—— But I tell you, you fhall tell me—at laft—But it fhall be a great while firft.

Care. Well; but pr'ythee don't let it be a great while, becaufe I long to have it over.

B 3

Brifk.

Brisk. Well then, you tell me fome good jeft, or very witty thing, laughing all the while as if you were ready to die——and I hear it, and look thus.——Would not you be difappointed?

Care. No: for if it were a witty thing, I fhould not expect you to underftand it.

Ld. F. O foy, Mr. Carelefs, all the world allows Mr. Brifk to have wit; my wife fays he has a great deal. I hope you think her a judge.

Brisk. Pooh, my Lord, his voice goes for nothing.—— I can't tell how to make him apprehend.—Take it t'other way. Suppofe I fay a witty thing to you?

Care. Then I fhall be difappointed indeed.

Mel. Let him alone, Brifk, he is obftinately bent not to be inftructed.

Brisk. I'm forry for him, the deuce take me.

Mel. Shall we go to the ladies, my Lord?

Ld. F. With all my heart;——methinks we are a folitude without them.

Mel. Or, what fay you to another bottle of Champagne?

Ld. F. O, for the univerfe, not a drop more, I befeech you. Oh, intemperate! I have a flufhing in my face already.   [*Takes out a pocket glafs, and looks in it.*

Brisk. Let me fee, let me fee, my Lord, I broke my glafs that was in the lid of my fnuff-box. Hum! Deuce take me, I have encouraged a pimple here too.

[*Takes the glafs, and looks.*

Ld. F. Then you muft mortify him with a patch; my wife fhall fupply you. Come, gentlemen, *allons*, here is company coming.   [*Exeunt.*

Enter Lady Touchwood *and* Mafkwell.

L. T. I'll hear no more——Y'are falfe and ungrateful; come, I know you falfe.

Mask. I have been frail I confefs, Madam, for your Ladyfhip's fervice.

L. T. That I fhould truft a man whom I had known betray his friend!

Mask. What friend have I betrayed; Or to whom?

L. T. Your fond friend Mellefont, and to me—————— Can you deny it?

Mask. I do not.

L. T.

L. T. Have you not wronged my Lord, who has been a father to you in your wants, and given you being? Have you not wronged him in the higheſt manner, in his bed?

Mask. With your Ladyſhip's help, and for your ſervice, as I told you before. I cannot deny that neither. Any thing more, Madam?

L. T. More! audacious villain. Oh, what's more is moſt my ſhame——Have you not diſhonoured me?

Mask. No, that I deny; for I never told in all my life: ſo that accuſation's anſwered.——On to the next.

L. T. Death, do you dally with my paſſion? Inſolent devil! But have a care——provoke me not; for, by the eternal fire, you ſhall not eſcape my vengeance.—— Calm villain! how unconcerned he ſtands, confeſſing treachery and ingratitude! Is there a vice more black! ——Oh, I have excuſes, thouſands, for my faults; fire in my temper, paſſions in my ſoul, apt to every provocation; oppreſſed at once with love and with deſpair: but a ſedate, a thinking villain, whoſe black blood runs temperately bad, what excuſe can clear?

Mask. Will you be in temper, Madam? I would not talk not to be heard. I have been [*She walks about diſordered.*] a very great rogue for your ſake, and you reproach me with it; I am ready to be a rogue ſtill, to do you ſervice; and you are flinging conſcience and honour in my face, to rebate my inclinations. How am I to behave myſelf? You know I am your creature, my life and fortune in your power; to diſoblige you brings me certain ruin. Allow it, I would betray you, I would not be a traitor to myſelf: I do not pretend to honeſty, becauſe you know I am a raſcal: but I would convince you from the neceſſity of my being firm to you.

L. T. Neceſſity, impudence! Can no gratitude incline you, no obligations touch you? ' Have not my ' fortune and my perſon been ſubjected to your plea-' ſure?' Were you not in the nature of a ſervant, and have not I in effect made you lord of all, of me, and of my Lord? Where is that humble love, the languiſhing, that adoration, which once was paid me, and everlaſting-ly engaged?

Mask.

Mask. Fixed, rooted in my heart, whence nothing can remove them, yet you———

L. T. Yet, what yet?

Mask. Nay, misconceive me not, Madam, when I say I have had a generous and a faithful paffion, which you had never favoured but thro' revenge and policy.

L. T. Ha!

Mask. Look you, Madam, we are alone,——Pray contain yourfelf, and hear me. You know you loved your nephew when I firft fighed for you; I quickly found it; an argument that I loved: for with that art you veiled your paffion, 'twas imperceptible to all but jealous eyes. This difcovery made me bold, I confefs it; for by it I thought you in my power. Your nephew's fcorn of you added to my hopes; I watched the occafion, and took you, juft repulfed by him, warm at once with love and indignation; your difpofition, my argaments, and happy opportunity, accomplifhed my defign; I preft the yielding minute, and was bleft. How I have loved you fince, words have not fhewn, then how fhould words exprefs?

L. T. Well, mollifying devil!——And have I not met your love with forward fire?

Mask. Your zeal I grant was ardent, but mifplaced; there was revenge in view; that woman's idol had defiled the temple of the god, and love was made a mock-worfhip.——A fon and heir would have edged young Mellefont upon the brink of ruin, and left him none but you to catch at for prevention.

L. T. Again, provoke me! Do you wind me like a larum, only to roufe my ftilled foul for your diverfion? Confufion!

Mask. Nay, Madam, I am gone, if you relapfe——What needs this? I fay nothing but what you yourfelf, in open hours of love, have told me. Why fhould you deny it? Nay, how can you? Is not all this prefent heat owing to the fame fire? Do you not love him ftill? How have I this day offended you, but in not breaking off his match with Cynthia? which, ere to-morrow, fhall be done——had you but patience.

L. T. How, what faid you, Mafkwell,——Another caprice to unwind my temper?

Mask.

Mask. By Heav'n, no; I am your flave, the flave of all your pleafures; and will not reft 'till I have given you peace, would you fuffer me.

L. T. Oh, Mafkwell, in vain do I difguife me from thee, thou knoweft me, knoweft the very inmoft windings ' and receffes' of my foul.————' Oh, Mellefont! I ' burn :' married to-morrow! Defpair ftrikes me! Yet my foul knows I hate him too : let him but once be mine, ' and next immediate ruin feize him.'

Mask. Compofe yourfelf, you fhall poffefs and ruin him too—Will that pleafe you?

L. T. How, how? thou dear, thou precious villain, how?

Mask. You have already been tampering with my Lady Plyant.

L. T. I have; fhe is ready for any impreffion I think fit.

Mask. She muft be thoroughly perfuaded that Mellefont loves her.

L. T. She is fo credulous that way naturally, and likes him fo well, that fhe will believe it fafter than I can perfuade her. But I don't fee what you can propofe from fuch a trifling defign; for her firft converfing with Mellefont will convince her of the contrary.

Mask. I know it—I don't depend upon it.——But it will prepare fomething elfe; and gain us leifure to lay a ftronger plot.——If I gain a little time, I fhall not want contrivance.

One minute gives invention to deftroy,
What to rebuild, will a whole age employ.

[*Exeunt.*

END of the FIRST ACT.

A C T   II.

Enter Lady Froth *and* Cynthia.

CYNTHIA.

INDEED, Madam! Is it poffible your Ladyfhip could have been fo much in love?

L. F. I could not fleep; I did not fleep one wink for three weeks together.

Cyn.

Cyn. Prodigious! I wonder want of sleep, and so much love, and so much wit as your Ladyship has, did not turn your brain.

L. F. O my dear Cynthia, you must not rally your friend—but really, as you say, I wonder too—but then I had a way. For between you and I, I had whimsies and vapours, but I gave them vent.

Cyn. How, pray Madam?

L. F. O, I writ, writ abundantly——Do you never write?

Cyn. Write, what?

L. F Songs, elegies, satires, encomiums, panegyrics, lampoons, plays, or heroic poems.

Cyn. O lord, not I, Madam; I am content to be a courteous reader.

L. F. O inconsistent! in love, and not write! If my Lord and I had been both of your temper, we had never come together——O bless me! what a sad thing would that have been, if my Lord and I should never have met!

Cyn. Then neither my Lord nor you would ever have met with your match, on my conscience.

L. F. O' my conscience no more we should; thou say'st right—— for sure my Lord Froth is as fine a gentleman, and as much a man of quality! Ah! nothing at all of the common air——I think I may say he wants nothing but a blue ribband and a star, to make him shine the very phosphorus of our hemisphere. Do you understand those two hard words? If you don't, I'll explain them to you.

Cyn. Yes, yes, Madam, I am not so ignorant.—— At least I won't own it, to be troubled with your instructions   [*Aside.*

L. F. Nay, I beg your pardon; but being derived from the Greek, I thought you might have escaped the etymology.——But I am the more amazed, to find you a woman of letters, and not write! Bless me! how can Mellefont believe you love him?

Cyn. Why faith, Madam, he that won't take my word, shall never have it under my hand.

L. F. I vow Mellefont's a pretty gentleman, but methinks he wants a manner.

Cyn.

Cyn. A manner! What's that, Madam?

L. F. Some diftinguifhing quality, as for example, the *bel air* or *brillant* of Mr. Brifk; the folemnity, yet complaifance of my Lord, or fomething of his own that fhould look a little *je ne fçai quoi*; he is too much a mediocrity in my mind.

Cyn. He does not indeed affect either pertnefs or formality, for which I like him——Here he comes.

Enter Lord Froth, Mellefont, *and* Brifk.

Impertinent creature! I could almoft be angry with her now.   [*Afide.*

L. F. My Lord, I have been telling Cynthia how much I have been in love with you; I fwear I have; I'm not afhamed to own it now; Ah! it makes my heart leap, I vow I figh when I think on't :—My dear Lord! ha, ha, ha, do you remember, my Lord?

[*Squeezes him by the hand, looks kindly on him, fighs, and then laughs out.*

Ld. F. Pleafant creature! Perfectly well, Ah! that look! Ay, there it is; who could refift!——'Twas fo my heart was made a captive at firft, and ever fince it has been in love with happy flavery.

L. F. O that tongue, that dear deceitful tongue! that charming foftnefs in your mien and your expreffion, and then your bow! Good, my Lord, bow as you did when I gave you my picture; here, fuppofe this my picture— [*Gives him a pocket glafs.*] Pray mind, my Lord; ah! he bows charmingly. Nay, my Lord, you fhan't kifs it fo much; I fhall grow jealous, I vow now.

[*He bows profoundly low, then kiffes the glafs.*

Ld. F. I faw myfelf there, and kiffed it for your fake.

L. F. Ah! gallantry to the laft degree—Mr. Brifk, you are a judge; was ever any thing fo well bred as my Lord?

Brisk. Never any thing but your Ladyfhip, let me perifh.

L. F. O prettily turned again; let me die but you have a great deal of wit.——Mr. Mellefont, don't you think Mr. Brifk has a world of wit?

Mel. O yes, Madam.

Brisk. O dear, Madam——

L. F. An infinite deal!

Brisk.

Brisk. Oh Heavens, Madam————

L. F. More wit than any body,

Brisk. I am everlastingly your humble servant, deuce take me, Madam.

Ld. F. Don't you think us a happy couple?

Cyn. I vow, my Lord, I think you the happiest couple in the world; ' for you are not only happy in one ' another and when you are together, but happy in ' yourselves, and by yourselves.'

Ld. F. I hope Mellefont will make a good husband too.

Cyn. 'Tis my interest to believe he will, my Lord.

Ld. F. D'ye think he'll love you as well as I do my wife? I am afraid not.

Cyn. I believe he'll love me better.

Ld. F. Heav'ns! that can never be; but why do you think so?

Cyn. Because he has not so much reason to be fond of himself.

Ld. F. O your humble servant for that, dear Madam. Well, Mellefont, you'll be a happy creature.

Mel. Ay, my Lord, I shall have the same reason for my happiness that your Lordship has; I shall think myself happy.

Ld. F. Ah, that's all.

Brisk. [*To Lady* Froth.] Your Ladyship is in the right; but 'egad I'm wholly turned into satire. I confess I write but seldom, but when I do——keen Iambics, 'egad. But my Lord was telling me, your Ladyship has made an essay toward an heroic poem.

L. F. Did my Lord tell you? Yes, I vow, and the subject is my Lord's love to me. And what do you think I call it? I dare swear you won't guess——*The Sillabub,* ha, ha, ha.

Brisk. Because my Lord's title's Froth, 'egad; ha, ha, ha, ha, deuce take me, very *à propos,* and surprizing, ha, ha, ha.

L. F. He, ay, is not it?——And then I call my Lord Spumosa; and myself, what do ye think I call myself?

Brisk. Lactilla, may be——'Egad I cannot tell.

L. F. Biddy, that's all; just my own name.

Brisk.

Brisk. Biddy! 'Egad very pretty——Deuce take me, if your Ladyſhip has not the art of ſuprizing the moſt naturally in the world——I hope you'll make me happy in communicating the poem.

L. F. O, you muſt be my confident, I muſt aſk your advice.

Brisk. I'm your humble ſervant, let me periſh——I preſume your Ladyſhip has read Boſſu?

L. F. O yes, and Rapine, and Dacier upon Ariſtotle and Horace.——My Lord, you muſt not be jealous, I'm communicating all to Mr. Briſk.

Ld. F. No, no, I'll allow Mr. Briſk; have you nothing about you to ſhew him, my dear?

L. F. Yes, I believe I have.—— Mr. Briſk, come will you go into the next room, and there I'll ſhew you what I have.   · [*Exeunt L.* Froth *and* Briſk.

Ld. F. I'll walk a turn in the garden, and come to you.   [*Exit Ld.* Froth.

Mel. You are thoughtful, Cynthia.

Cyn. I am thinking, tho' marriage makes man and wife one fleſh, it leaves them ſtill two fools; and they become more conſpicuous by ſetting off one another.

Mel. That's only when two fools meet, and their follies are oppoſed.

Cyn. Nay, I have known two wits meet, and by the oppoſition of their wit, render themſelves as ridiculous as fools. 'Tis an odd game we are going to play at; what think you of drawing ſtakes, and giving over in time?

Mel. No, hang it, that's not endeavouring to win, becauſe it is poſſible we may loſe; ſince we have ſhuffled and cut, let's e'en turn up trump now.

Cyn. Then I find it is like cards, if either of us have a good hand it is an accident of fortune.

Mel. No, marriage is rather like a game at bowls: fortune indeed makes the match, and the two neareſt, and ſometimes the two fartheſt are together, but the game depends entirely upon judgment.

Cyn. Still it is a game, and conſequently one of us muſt be a loſer.

Mel. Not at all; only a friendly trial of ſkill, and the winnings to be laid out in an entertaiment.——' What's
' here, the muſic!——Oh, my Lord has promiſed the
                    C   ' com-

' company a new song, we'll get them to give it us by
' the way. [*Musicians crossing the stage.*] Pray let us have
' the favour of you, to practise the song before the com-
' pany hear it.

S O N G.

' Cynthia frowns whene'er I woo her,
' Yet she's vex'd if I give over;
' Much she fears I should undo her,
' But much more to lose her lover:
' Thus, in doubting, she refuses;
' And not winning, thus she loses.

' Pr'ythee, Cynthia, look behind you,
' Age and wrinkles will o'ertake you;
' Then too late desire will find you,
' When the power must forsake you:
' Think, O think o'th' sad condition,
' To be past, yet wish fruition.'

Mel. You shall have my thanks below.

[*To the music, they go out.*

   Enter Sir Paul Plyant *and Lady* Plyant.

Sir P. Gads bud! I am provoked into a fermentation,
as my Lady Froth says; was ever the like read of in
story?

L. P. Sir Paul, have patience; let me alone to rattle
him up.

Sir P. Pray your Ladyship give me leave to be angry
——I'll rattle him up, I warrant you, I'll firk him with
a *certiorari*.

L. P. You firk him! I'll firk him myself. Pray, Sir
Paul, hold you contented.

' *Cyn.* Bless me, what makes my father in such a pas-
' sion!————I never saw him thus before.'

Sir. P. Hold yourself contented, my Lady Plyant,—
I find passion coming upon me by inflation, and I cannot
submit as formerly, therefore give way.

L. P. How now! will you be pleased to retire, and—

Sir P. No marry will I not be pleased; I am pleased
to be angry, that's my pleasure at this time.

Mel. What can this mean!

3

L. P.

L. P. Gads my life, the man's diftracted; why how now, who are you? What am I? Slidikins, can't I govern you? What did I marry you for? Am I not to be abfolute and uncontroulable? Is it fit a woman of my fpirit and conduct fhould be contradicted in a matter of this concern!

Sir P. It concerns me, and only me:——Befides, I am not to be governed at all times. When I am in tranquility my Lady Plyant fhall command Sir Paul; but when I am provoked to fury, I cannot incorporate with patience and reafon,——as foon may tigers match with tigers, lambs with lambs, and every creature couple with its foe, as the poet fays.————

L. P. He's hot-headed ftill! 'tis in vain to talk to you; but remember I have a curtain-lecture for you, you difobedient, headftrong brute.

Sir P. No, 'tis becaufe I won't be headftrong, becaufe I won't be a brute, and have my head fortified, that I am thus exafperated.—But I will protect my honour, and yonder is the violator of my fame.

L. P. 'Tis my honour that is concerned, and the violation was intended to me.——Your honour! you have none but what is in my keeping, and I can difpofe of it when I pleafe—therefore don't provoke me.

Sir P. Hum, gads-bud fhe fays true——Well, my Lady, march on, I will fight under you then; I am convinced as far as paffion will permit.

[*Lady* Pl. *and Sir* Paul *come up to* Mellefont.

L. P Inhuman and treacherous————

Sir P. Thou ferpent, and firft tempter of womankind.————

Cyn. Blefs me, Sir! Madam, what mean you?

Sir P. Thy, Thy, come away Thy, touch him not; come hither, girl, go not near him, there is nothing but deceit about him; fnakes are in his peruke, and the crocodile of Nilus is in his belly, he will eat thee up alive.

L. P. Difhonourable, impudent creature!

Mel. For Heaven's fake, Madam, to whom do you direct this language?

L. P. Have I behaved myfelf with all the decorum and nicety, befitting the perfon of Sir Paul's wife? Have I preferved my honour as it were in a fnow-houfe for

thefe

thefe three years paft? Have I been white and unfullied even by Sir Paul himfelf?

Sir P. Nay, fhe has been an invincible wife, even to me, that's the truth on't.

L. P. Have I, I fay, preferved myfelf like a fair fheet of paper for you to make a blot upon?

Sir P. And fhe fhall make a fimile with any woman in England.

Mel. I am fo amazed, I know not what to fay.

Sir P. Do you think my daughter, this pretty creature; gads-bud fhe's a wife for a cherubin! Do you think her fit for nothing but to be a ftalking horfe, to ftand before you while you take aim at my wife? Gads-bud I was never angry before in my life, and I'll never be appeafed again.

Mel. Hell and damnation! this is my aunt; fuch malice can be engendered no where elfe. [*Afide.*

L. P. Sir Paul, take Cynthia from his fight; leave me to ftrike him with the remorfe of his intended crime.

Cyn. Pray Sir, ftay, hear him, I dare affirm he's innocent.

Sir P. Innocent! Why, hark'ee, come hither, Thy, hark'ee, I had it from his aunt, my fifter Touchwood—Gads-bud, he does not care a farthing for any thing of thee, but thy portion; why, he's in love with my wife; he would have tantalized thee, and made a cuckold of thy poor father,—and that would certainly have broke my heart—I am fure if ever I fhould have horns, they would kill me; they would never come kindly, I fhould die of them, like a child that was cutting his teeth——I fhould indeed, Thy—— therefore come away; but Providence has prevented all, therefore come away when I bid you.

Cyn. I muft obey. [*Exeunt Sir* Paul *and* Cynthia.

L. P. Oh, fuch a thing! the impiety of it ftartles me—to wrong fo good, fo fair a creature, and one that loves you tenderly—'Tis a barbarity of barbarities, and nothing could be guilty of it——

Mel. But the greateft villain imagination can form, I grant it; and next to the villainy of fuch a fact, is the villainy of afperfing me with the guilt. How? Which way was I to wrong her? For yet I underftand you not.

L. P.

L. P. Why, gads my life, coufin Mellefont, you cannot be fo peremptory as to deny it, when I tax you with it to your face; for, now Sir Paul is gone, you are *corum nobus.*

Mel. By Heaven I love her more than life, or——

L. P. Fiddle, faddle, don't tell of this and that, and every thing in the world, but give me mathemacular demonftration, anfwer me directly——But I have not patience——Oh! the impiety of it, as I was faying, and the unparalleled wickednefs! O merciful father! How could you think to reverfe nature fo, to make the daughter the means of procuring the mother?

Mel. The daughter to procure the mother!

L. P. Ay, for tho' I am not Cynthia's own mother, I am her father's wife, and that's near enough to make it inceft.

Mel. Inceft! O my precious aunt, and the devil in conjunction. [*Afide.*

L. P. O reflect upon the horror of that, and then the guilt of deceiving every body; marrying the daughter only to make a cuckold of the father; and then feducing me, debauching my purity, and perverting me from the road of virtue, in which I have trod thus long, and never made one trip, not one *faux pas*; O confider it, what would you have to anfwer for, if you fhould provoke me to frailty? Alas! humanity is feeble, Heaven knows! very feeble, and unable to fupport itfelf.

Mel. Where am I? Is it day? and am I awake? Madam——

L. P. And nobody knows how circumftances may happen together;——to my thinking, now I could refift the ftrongeft temptation——but yet I know, 'tis impoffible for me to know whether I could or not; there's no certainty in the things of this life.

Mel. Madam, pray give me leave to afk you one queftion.——

L. P. O lord, afk me the queftion! I'll fwear I'll refufe it; I fwear I'll deny it—therefore don't afk me; nay you fhan't afk me, I fwear I'll deny it. O Gemini, you have brought all the blood into my face; I warrant I am as red as a turky-cock; O fye, coufin Mellefont.

Mel. Nay, Madam, hear me; I mean——

C 3

L. P.

L. P. Hear you, no, no; I'll deny you firſt, and hear you afterwards. For one does not know how one's mind may change upon hearing.——Hearing is one of the ſenſes, and all the ſenſes are fallible; I won't truſt my honour, I aſſure you; my honour is infallible and uncomatible.

Mel. For Heaven's ſake, Madam.

L. P. O name it no more——Bleſs me, how can you talk of Heaven, and have ſo much wickedneſs in your heart? May be you don't think it a ſin,——they ſay ſome of you gentlemen don't think it a ſin——may be it is no ſin to them that don't think it ſo; indeed, if I did not think it a ſin——but ſtill my honour, if it were no ſin——but then to marry my daughter for the conveniency of frequent opportunities——I'll never conſent to that; as ſure as can be I'll break the match.

Mel. Death and amazement——Madam, upon my knees————

L. P. Nay, nay, riſe up; come, you ſhall ſee my good-nature. I know love is powerful, and nobody can help his paſſion: 'tis not your fault, nor I ſwear it is not mine.——How can I help it if I have charms? And how can you help it if you are made a captive? I ſwear it is pity it ſhould be a fault—— but my honour——well, but your honour too—but the ſin!—well, but the neceſſity —O lord, here's ſomebody coming, I dare not ſtay.—— Well, you muſt conſider of your crime, and ſtrive as much as can be againſt it—ſtrive, be ſure—but don't be melancholic, don't deſpair——but never think that I'll grant you any thing; O lord, no;—but be ſure you lay aſide all thoughts of the marriage; for tho' I know you don't love Cynthia, only as a blind for your paſſion to me, yet it will make me jealous—O lord, what did I ſay? Jealous! no, no, I can't be jealous, for I muſt not love you—therefore don't hope—but don't deſpair neither— O, they're coming, I muſt fly.   [*Exit.*

Mel. [*after a pauſe.*] So then——ſpite of my care and foreſight I am caught, caught in my ſecurity.—Yet this was but a ſhallow artifice, ' unworthy of my Machia-' ' velian aunt.' There muſt be more behind, this is but the firſt flaſh, the priming of her engine; deſtruction follows hard, if not moſt preſently prevented.

Enter Maſkwell.

Maſkwell, welcome, thy preſence is a view of land, appearing to my ſhipwrecked hopes; the witch has raiſed the ſtorm, and her miniſters have done their work; you ſee the veſſels are parted.

Maſk. I know it; I met Sir Paul towing away Cynthia. Come, trouble not your head, I'll join you together ere to-morrow morning, or drown between you in the attempt.

Mel. There's comfort in a hand ſtretched out to one that's ſinking, though never ſo far off.

Maſk. No ſinking, nor no danger——Come, cheer up; why you don't know that while I plead for you, your aunt has given me a retaining fee;——nay, I am your greateſt enemy, and ſhe does but journey-work under me.

Mel. Ha! how's this?

Maſk. What do ye think of my being employed in the execution of all her plots? Ha, ha, ha, by Heaven it is true; I have undertaken to break the match, I have undertaken to make your uncle diſinherit you, to get you turned out of doors, and to——ha, ha, ha, I can't tell you for laughing ——— Oh, ſhe has opened her heart to me——I am to turn you a grazing, and to—ha, ha, ha, marry Cynthia myſelf; there's a plot for you.

Mel. Ha! O ſee, I ſee my riſing ſun! light breaks thro' clouds upon me, and I ſhall live in day ——O my Maſkwell! how ſhall I thank or praiſe thee; thou haſt outwitted woman.—But tell me, how couldſt thou thus get into her confidence? Ha! how? But was it her contrivance to perſuade my Lady Plyant into this extravagant belief?

Maſk. It was, and to tell you the truth I encouraged it for your diverſion; tho' it make you a little uneaſy for the preſent, yet the reflexion of it muſt needs be entertaining—I warrant ſhe was very violent at firſt.

Mel. Ha, ha, ha, ay, a very fury; but I was moſt afraid of her violence at laſt—If you had not come as you did, I don't know what ſhe might have attempted.

Maſk. Ha, ha, ha, I know her temper.—Well, you muſt know then, that all my contrivances were but bubbles; 'till at laſt I pretended to have been long ſecretly

in

in love with Cynthia; that did my bufinefs; that convinced your aunt I might be trufted; fince it was as
much my intereft as hers to break the match: then, fhe
thought my jealoufy might qualify me to affift her in her
revenge. And, in fhort, in that belief told me the fecrets of her heart. At length, we made this agreement,
if I accomplifh her defigns (as I told you before) fhe has
engaged to put Cynthia with all her fortune into my
power.

Mel. She is moft gracious in her favour.——Well, and
dear Jack, how haft thou contrived?

Mask. I would not have you ftay to hear it now: for I
don't know but fhe may come this way; I am to meet
her anon; after that, I'll tell you the whole matter; be
here in this gallery an hour hence, by that time I imagine our confultation may be over.

Mel. I will; 'till then fuccefs attend thee. [*Exit.*

Mask. 'Till then fuccefs will attend me; for when I
meet you I meet the only obftacle to my fortune. Cynthia, let thy beauty gild my crimes; and whatfoever I
commit of treachery or deceit fhall be imputed to me as a
merit—Treachery, what treachery? Love cancels all the
bonds of friendfhip, and fets men right upon their firft
foundations. Duty to kings, piety to parents, gratitude to
benefactors, and fidelity to friends, are different and particular ties; but the name of rival cuts them all afunder,
and is a general acquittance—Rival is equal, and Love,
like Death, an univerfal leveller of mankind. Ha! but
is there not fuch a thing as honefty? Yes, and whofoever
has it about him, bears an enemy in his breaft: for your
honeft man, as I take it, is that nice, fcrupulous, confcientious perfon who will cheat nobody but himfelf; fuch
another coxcomb as your wife man, who is too hard for
all the world, and will be made a fool of by nobody but
himfelf. Ha, ha, ha; well, for wifdom and honefty,
give me cunning and hypocrify; Oh, 'tis fuch a pleafure
to angle for fair-faced fools!—Then that hungry gudgeon
Credulity will bite at any thing——Why, let me fee, I
have the fame face, the fame words and accents when I
fpeak what I do think, and when I fpeak what I do not
think——the very fame——and dear diffimulation is the
only art not to be known from nature.

Why will mankind be fools, and be deceiv'd?
And why are friends' and lovers' oaths believ'd?
When each who searches strictly his own mind,
May so much fraud and power of baseness find.

[Exit.

END of the SECOND ACT.

ACT III.

Enter Lord Touchwood, and Lady Touchwood.

LADY TOUCHWOOD.

MY Lord, can you blame my brother Plyant, if he refuse his daughter upon this provocation? The contract is void by this unheard of impiety.

Ld. T. I don't believe it true; he has better principles ——pho, 'tis nonsense. Come, come, I know my Lady Plyant has a large eye, and would centre every thing in her own circle; 'tis not the first time she has mistaken respect for love, and made Sir Paul jealous of the civility of an undesigning person, the better to bespeak his security in her unfeigned pleasures.

L. T. You censure hardly, my Lord; my sister's honour is very well known.

Ld. T. Yes, I believe I know some that have been familiarly acquainted with it. This is a little trick wrought by some pitiful contriver, envious of my nephew's merit.

L. T. Nay, my Lord, it may be so, and I hope it will be found so: but that will require some time; for, in such a case as this, demonstration is necessary.

Ld. T. There should have been demonstration of the contrary too before it had been believed——

L. T. So I suppose there was.

Ld. T. How? Where? When?

L. T. That I can't tell; nay, I don't say there was—I am willing to believe as favourably of my nephew as I can.

Ld. T. I don't know that.   [*Half aside.*

L. T. How? Don't you believe that, say you, my Lord?

Ld. T.

Ld. T. No, I don't fay fo—I confefs I am troubled to find you fo cold in his defence.

L. T. His defence ! Blefs me, would you have me defend an ill thing ?

Ld. T. You believe it then ?

L. T. I don't know ; I am very unwilling to fpeak my thoughts in any thing that may be to my coufin's difadvantage ; befides, I find, my Lord, you are prepared to receive an ill impreffion from any opinion of mine which is not confenting with your own : but fince I am like to be fufpected in the end, and 'tis a pain any longer to diffemble, I own it to you ; in fhort I do believe it, nay, and can believe any thing worfe, if it were laid to his charge————Don't afk me my reafons, my Lord, for they are not fit to be told you.

Ld. T. I am amazed ! Here muft be fomething more than ordinary in this. [*Afide.*] Not fit to be told me, Madam ? You can have no intereft wherein I am not concerned, and confequently the fame reafons ought to be convincing to me, which create your fatisfaction or difquiet.

L. T. But thofe which caufe my difquiet I am willing to have remote from your hearing. Good my Lord, don't prefs me.

Ld. T. Don't oblige me to prefs you.

L. T. Whatever it was, 'tis paft ; and that is better to be unknown which cannot be prevented ; therefore, let me beg you to reft fatisfied.————

Ld. T. When you have told me, I will ————

L. T. You won't.

Ld. T. By my life, my dear, I will.

L. T. What if you cannot.

Ld. T. How ? Then I muft know ; nay, I will. No more trifling—I charge you tell me—By all our mutual peace to come ; upon your duty————

L. T. Nay, my Lord, you need fay no more to make me lay my heart before you, but don't be thus tranfported ; compofe yourfelf ; it is not of concern to make you lofe one minute's temper ; 'tis not, indeed, my dear.—
' Nay, by this kifs you fhan't be angry.' O lord, I wifh I had not told you any thing——Indeed, my Lord, you have frighted me. Nay, look pleafed, I'll tell you.

Ld. T.

Ld. T. Well, well.

L. T. Nay, but will you be calm?——Indeed it is nothing but——

Ld. T. But what?

L. T. But will you promife me not to be angry?——Nay, you muft—not to be angry with Mellefont—I dare fwear he's forry—and were it to do again, would not——

Ld. T. Sorry, for what? 'Death, you rack me with delay.

L. T. Nay, no great matter, only——Well, I have your promife— pho, why nothing, only your nephew had a mind to amufe himfelf fometimes with a little gallantry towards me. Nay, I can't think he meant any thing ferioufly, but methought it looked oddly.

Ld. T. Confufion and Hell, what do I hear!

L. T. Or, may be, he thought he was not enough akin to me upon upon your account, and had a mind to create a nearer relation on his own; a lover, you know, my Lord—ha, ha, ha. Well, but that's all—' Now ' you have it;' well, remember your promife, my Lord, and don't take any notice of it to him.

Ld. T. No, no, no—Damnation!

L. T. Nay, I fwear you muft not—A little harmlefs mirth—only mifplaced, that's all.—But if it were more 'tis over now, and all is well. For my part, I have forgot it; and fo has he, I hope—for I have not heard any thing from him thefe two days.

Ld. T. Thefe two days! Is it fo frefh? Unnatural villain! 'Death, I'll have him ftripped and turned naked out of my doors this moment, and let him rot and perifh, inceftuous brute!

L. T. Oh, for Heaven's fake, my Lord, you'll ruin me if you take fuch public notice of it, it will be a towntalk: confider your own and my honour—Nay, I told you, you would not be fatisfied when you knew it.

Ld. T. Before I've done I will be fatisfied. Ungrateful monfter! How long?

L. T. Lord, I don't know:——I wifh my lips had grown together when I told you—Almoft a twelvemonth —Nay, I won't tell you any more 'till you are yourfelf. Pray, my Lord, don't let the company fee you in this diforder—Yet, I confefs, I cannot blame you; for I

think

hink I was never fo furprized in my life—Who would have thought my nephew could have, fo mifconftrued my kindnefs—But will you go into your clofet, and recover your temper. I'll make an excufe of fudden bufinefs to the company, and come to you. Pray, good dear my Lord, let me beg you do now : I'll come immediately, and tell you all —— Will you, my Lord ?

Ld. T. I will——I am mute with wonder.

L. T. Well, but go now, here is fomebody coming.

Ld. T. Well, I go—You won't ftay, for I would hear more of this.   [*Exit.*

L. T. I follow inftantly——So.

Enter Mafkwell.

Mask. This was a mafter-piece, and did not need my help—though I ftood ready for a cue to come in and confirm all, had there been occafion.

L. T. Have you feen Mellefont ?

Mask. I have ; and am to meet him here about this time.

L. T. How does he bear his difappointment ?

Mask. Secure in my affiftance, he feemed not much afflicted, but rather laughed at the fhallow artifice, which fo little time muft of neceffity difcover. Yet he is apprehenfive of fome farther defign of yours, and has engaged me to watch you. I believe he will hardly be able to prevent your plot, yet I would have you ufe caution and expedition.

L. T. Expedition indeed ; for all we do muft be performed in the remaining part of this evening, and before the company break up, left my Lord fhould cool, and have an opportunity to talk with him privately——My Lord muft not fee him again.

Mask. By no means ; therefore you muft aggravate my Lord's difpleafure to a degree that will admit of no conference with him.——What think you of mentioning me ?

L. T. How ?

Mask. To my Lord, as having been privy to Mellefont's defign upon you, but ftill ufing my utmoft endeavours to diffuade him: ' tho' my friendfhip and love to ' him has made me conceal it ; yet you may fay, I threa-

' tened

' tened the next time he attempted any thing of that
' kind, to difcover it to my Lord.'

L. T. To what end is this?

Mask. It will confirm my Lord's opinion of my honour and honefty, and create in him a new confidence
in me, which (fhould this defign mifcarry) will be neceffary to the forming another plot that I have in my
head——to cheat you as well as the reft.   [*Afide.*

L. T. I'll do it—I'll tell him you hindered him once
from forcing me.

Mask. Excellent! your Ladyfhip has a moft improving
fancy. You had beft go to my Lord, keep him as long
as you can in his clofet, and I doubt not but you will
mould him to what you pleafe; your guefts are fo engaged in their own follies and intrigues, they'll mifs neither of you.

L. T. When fhall we meet?—At eight this evening
in my chamber; there rejoice at our fuccefs, and toy
away an hour in mirth.   [*Exit.*

Mask. I will not fail.————I know what fhe means
by toying away an hour well enough. Pox, I have loft
all my appetite to her; yet fhe's a fine woman, and I
loved her once. ' But I don't know, fince I have been
' in a great meafure kept by her, the cafe is altered;'
what was my pleafure is become my duty: and I have as
little ftomach to her now as if I were her hufband.
Should fhe fmoke my defign upon Cynthia, I were in a
fine pickle. She has a damned penetrating head, and
knows how to interpret a coldnefs the right way; therefore I muft diffemble ardour and ecftafy, that's refolved:
How eafily and pleafantly is that diffembled before fruition! Pox on it, that a man can't drink without quench-
ing his thirft. Ha! yonder comes Mellefont thoughtful.
Let me think: meet her at eight—hum—ha! by Heaven I have it—if I can fpeak to my Lord before—' Was
' it my brain or Providence? no matter which'—I will
deceive them all, and yet fecure myfelf, 'twas a lucky
thought! Well, this double-dealing is a jewel. Here
he comes, now for me————

[*Mafkwell pretending not to fee him, walks by him, and
fpeaks as it were to himfelf.*

D   *Enter*

Enter Mellefont *musing.*

Mask. Mercy on us, what will the wickedness of this world come to?

Mel. How now, Jack? What, so full of contemplation that you run over!

Mask. I'm glad you are come, for I could not contain myself any longer, and was just going to give vent to a secret, which nobody but you ought to drink down.——— Your aunt is just gone from hence.

Mel. And having trusted thee with the secrets of her soul, thou art villainously bent to discover them all to me, ha?

Mask. I am afraid my frailty leans that way———But I don't know whether I can in honour discover them all.

Mel. All, all man. What, you may in honour betray her as far as she betrays herself. No tragical design upon my person, I hope.

Mask. No, but it is a comical design upon mine.

Mel. What dost thou mean?

Mask. Listen and be dumb———We have been bargaining about the rate of your ruin———

Mel. Like any two guardians to an orphan heiress——— Well.

Mask. And whereas pleasure is generally paid with mischief, what mischief I do is to be paid with pleasure.

Mel. So when you've swallowed the potion, you sweeten your mouth with a plumb.

Mask. You are merry, Sir, but I shall probe your constitution. In short, the price of your banishment is to be paid with the person of———

Mel. Of Cynthia, and her fortune—Why you forget you told me this before.

Mask. No, no———So far you are right; and I am, as an earnest of that bargain, to have full and free possession of the person of———your aunt.

Mel. Ha!———Pho, you trifle.

Mask. By this light, I am serious; all raillery apart— I knew 'twould stun you :———This evening at eight she will receive me in her bed-chamber.

Mel. Hell and the Devil, is she abandoned of all grace —Why the woman is possessed———

Mask. Well, will you go in my stead?

Mel. By Heaven into a hot furnace sooner.

Mask. No, you would not—it would not be so convenient, as I can order matters.

Mel. What do ye mean?

Mask. Mean? Not to disappoint the lady, I assure you ——Ha, ha, ha, how gravely he looks——Come, come, I won't perplex you. 'Tis the only thing that Providence could have contrived to make me capable of serving you, either to my inclination or your own necessity.

Mel. How, how, for Heaven's sake, dear Maskwell?

Mask. Why thus—I'll go according to appointment; you shall have notice at the critical minute to come and surprize your aunt and me together; counterfeit a rage against me, and I will make my escape through the private passage from her chamber, which I'll take care to leave open: 'twill be hard, if then you can't bring her to any conditions. For this discovery will disarm her of all defence, and leave her entirely at your mercy: nay, she must ever after be in awe of you.

Mel. Let me adore thee, my better genius! By Heaven I think it is not in the power of Fate to disappoint my hopes ——My hopes, my certainty!

Mask. Well, I'll meet you here within a quarter of eight, and give you notice.   *[Exit.*

Mel. Good fortune ever go along with thee.

Enter Careless.

Care. Mellefont, get out of the way, my Lady Plyant's coming, and I shall never succeed while thou art in sight——Tho' she begins to tack about; but I made love a great while to no purpose.

Mel. Why, what's the matter? She is convinced that I don't care for her.

Care. I cannot get an answer from her that does not begin with her honour, or her virtue, her religion, or some such cant. Then she has told me the whole story of Sir Paul's nine years courtship; how he has lain for whole nights together upon the stairs before her chamber-door; and that the first favour he received from her was a piece of an old scarlet petticoat for a stomacher; which, since the day of his marriage, he has, out of a piece of gallantry, converted into a night-cap, and wears it still with much solemnity on his anniversary wedding night.

D 2   *Mel.*

Mel. That I have seen, with the ceremony thereunto belonging—For on that night he creeps in at the bed's feet, like a gulled Baſſa that has married a relation of the Grand Signior, ' and that night he has his arms at li- ' berty. Did ſhe not tell you at what a diſtance ſhe keeps ' him ? He has confeſſed to me, that but at ſome ' certain times, that is, I ſuppoſe, when ſhe apprehends ' being with child, he never has the privilege of uſing ' the familiarity of a huſband with a wife. He was once ' given to ſcrambling with his hands, and ſprawling in ' his ſleep, and ever ſince ſhe has ſwaddled him up in ' blankets, and his hands and feet ſwathed down, and ſo ' put to bed ; and there he lies with a great beard, like a ' Ruſſian bear upon a drift of ſnow. You are very great ' with him,' I wonder he never told you his grievances; he will, I warrant you.

Care. Exceſſively fooliſh !——But that which gives me moſt hopes of her, is her telling me of the many temptations ſhe has reſiſted.

Mel. Nay, then you have her ; for a woman's brag- ging to a man that ſhe has overcome temptations, is an ar- gument that they were weakly offered, and a challenge to him to engage her more irreſiſtibly. 'Tis only an en- hancing the price of the commodity, by telling you how many cuſtomers have underbid her.

Care. Nay, I don't deſpair—But ſtill ſhe has a grud- ging to you——I talked to her t'other night at my Lord Froth's maſquerade, when I am ſatisfied ſhe knew me, and I had no reaſon to complain of my reception ; but I find women are not the ſame bare-faced and in maſks—— and a vizor diſguiſes their inclinations as much as their faces.

Mel. ' Tis a miſtake ; for women may moſt properly ' be ſaid to be unmaſked when they wear vizors ; for ' that ſecures them from bluſhing, and being out of ' countenance, and next to being in the dark, or alone, ' they are moſt truly themſelves in a vizor-maſk.' Here they come. I'll leave you. Ply her cloſe, and by and by clap a *billet-doux* into her hand : for a woman never thinks a man truly in love with her 'till he has been fool enough to think of her out of her ſight, and to loſe ſo much time as to write to her.   [*Exit.*

                                                        Enter

Enter Sir Paul *and Lady* Plyant.

Sir P. Shan't we difturb your meditation, Mr. Care-lefs? You would be in private?

Care. You bring that along with you, Sir Paul, that fhall be always welcome to my privacy.

Sir P. O, fweet Sir, you load your humble fervants, both me and my wife, with continual favours.

L. P. Sir Paul, what a phrafe was there! You will be making anfwers, and taking that upon you which ought to lie upon me: that you fhould have fo little breeding to think Mr. Carelefs did not apply himfelf to me. Pray, what have you to entertain any body's privacy? I fwear and declare in the face of the world I'm ready to blufh for your ignorance.

Sir P. I acquiefce, my Lady; but don't fnub fo loud.
                                        [*Afide to her.*

L. P. Mr. Carelefs, if a perfon that is wholly illite-rate might be fuppofed to be capable of being qualified to make a fuitable return to thofe obligations which you are pleafed to confer upon one that is wholly incapable of being qualified in all thofe circumftances, I am fure I fhould rather attempt it than any thing in the world, [*Courtefies.*] for I'm fure there's nothing in the world that I would rather. [*Courtefies.*] But I know Mr. Care-lefs is fo great a critic, and fo fine a gentleman, that it is impoffible for me———

Care. O Heavens! Madam, you confound me.

Sir P. Gads-bud, fhe's a fine perfon———

L. P. O lord! Sir, pardon me; we women have not thofe advantages: I know my own imperfections—but at the fame time you muft give me leave to declare in the face of the world that nobody is more fenfible of favours and things; for, with the referve of my honour, I af-fure you, Mr. Carelefs, I don't know any thing in the world I would refufe to a perfon fo meritorious———You'll pardon my want of expreffion.

Care. O, your Ladyfhip is abounding in all excellence, particularly that of phrafe.

L. P. You are fo obliging, Sir.

Care. Your Ladyfhip is fo charming.

Sir P. So, now, now; now, my Lady.

L. P. So well bred.

                                        Care.

Care. So furprizing.

L. P. So well dreft, fo *bonne mien*, fo eloquent, fo un-
affected, fo eafy, fo free, fo particular, fo agreeable——

Sir P. Ay, fo, fo, there.

Care. O lord, I befeech you, Madam, don't——

L. P. So gay, fo graceful, fo good teeth, fo fine
fhape, fo fine limbs, fo fine linen, and I don't doubt but
you have a very good fkin, Sir.

Care. For Heaven's fake, Madam——I am quite out
of countenance.

Sir P. And my Lady's quite out of breath; or elfe
you fhould hear—Gad's-bud, you may talk of my Lady
Froth.

Care. O fy, fy, not to be named of a day---My Lady
Froth is very well in her accomplifhments——but it is
when my Lady Plyant is not thought of——If that can
ever be.

L. P. O, you overcome me——That is fo exceffive.

Sir P. Nay, I fwear and vow that was pretty.

Care. O, Sir Paul, you are the happieft man alive.
Such a lady! that is the envy of her own fex, and the
admiration of ours.

Sir P. Your humble fervant; I am, I thank Heaven,
in a fine way of living, as I may fay, peacefully and
happily, and I think need not envy any of my neighbours, bleffed be Providence——Ay, truly, Mr. Carelefs, my Lady is a great bleffing, a fine, difcreet, well-
fpoken woman as you fhall fee——if it becomes me to fay
fo; and we live very comfortably together; fhe is a little
hafty fometimes, and fo am I; but mine's foon over,
and then I am fo forry—O, Mr. Carelefs, if it were not
for one thing——

Enter Boy with a letter.

L. P. How often have you been told of that, you
jackanapes?

Sir P. Gad fo, gads-bud——Tim, carry it to my
Lady, you fhould have carried it to my Lady firft.

Boy. 'Tis directed to your worfhip.

Sir P. Well, well, my Lady reads all letters firft——
Child, do fo no more; d'ye hear, Tim.

Boy. No, and pleafe you.   [*Exit.*

Sir P.

Sir P. A humour of my wife's; you know women have little fancies——But as I was telling you, Mr. Carelefs, if it were not for one thing, I fhould think myfelf the happieft man in the world; indeed that touches me near, very near.

Care. What can that be, Sir Paul?

Sir P. Why, I have, I thank Heaven, a very plentiful fortune, a good eftate in the country, fome houfes in town, and fome money, a pretty tolerable perfonal eftate; and it is a great grief to me, indeed it is, Mr. Carelefs, that I have not a fon to inherit this. 'Tis true, I have a daughter, and a fine dutiful child fhe is, though I fay it, bleffed be Providence I may fay; for indeed, Mr. Carelefs, I am mightily beholden to Providence---A poor unworthy finner---But if I had a fon, ah! that's my affliction, and my only affliction; indeed, I cannot refrain tears when it comes into my mind. [*Cries.*

Care. Why, methinks that might be eafily remedied; my Lady is a fine likely woman.

Sir P. Oh, a fine likely woman as you fhall fee in a fummer's day——Indeed fhe is, Mr. Carelefs, in all refpects.

Care. And I fhould not have taken you to have been fo old ——

Sir P. Alas! that's not it, Mr. Carelefs: ah! that's not it; no, no, you fhoot wide of the mark a mile; indeed you do; that's not it, Mr. Carelefs; no, no, that's not it.

Care. No, what can be the matter then?

Sir P. You'll fcarcely believe me when I fhall tell you ——my Lady is fo nice——It is very ftrange, but it is true: too true—fhe is fo very nice, that I don't believe fhe would touch a man for the world.——'. At leaft not ' above once a year; I am fure I have found it fo; and ' alas, what's once a year to an old man, who would do ' good in his generation!' Indeed, it is true, Mr. Carelefs, it breaks my heart—I am her hufband, as I may fay; though far unworthy of that honour, yet I am her hufband; but alas-a-day, I have no more familiarity with her perfon—' as to that matter'——than with my own mother——no indeed.

Care.

Care. Alas-a-day! this is a lamentable story; my Làdy muſt be told on't; ſhe muſt, i'faith, Sir Paul; 'tis an injury to the world.

Sir P. Ah! would to Heaven you would, Mr. Careleſs; you are mightily in her favour.

Care. I warrant you, what, we muſt have a ſon ſome way or other.

Sir P. Indeed, I ſhould be mightily bound to you, if you could bring it about, Mr. Careleſs.

L. P. Here, Sir Paul, it is from your ſteward, here's a return of 600l. you may take fifty of it for the next half-year.   [*Gives him the letter.*

Enter Lord Froth *and* Cynthia.

Sir P. How does my girl? Come hither to thy father, poor lamb, thou art melancholic.

Ld. F. Heaven, Sir Paul, you amaze me of all things in the world—You are never pleaſed but when we are all upon the broad grin; all laugh and no company; ah! then 'tis ſuch a ſight to ſee ſome teeth——Sure you are a great admirer of my Lady Whifler, Mr. Sneer, and Sir Laurence Loud, and that gang.

Sir P. I vow and ſwear ſhe is a very merry woman, but I think ſhe laughs a little too much.

Ld. F. Merry! O lord, what a character that is of a woman of quality——You have been at my Lady Whifler's upon her day, Madam?

Cyn. Yes, my Lord—I muſt humour this fool. [*Aſide.*

Ld. F. Well and how? hee! What is your ſenſe of the converſation?

Cyn. O, moſt ridiculous, a perpetual concert of laughing without any harmony; for ſure, my Lord, to laugh out of time, is as diſagreeable as to ſing out of time or out of tune.

Ld. F. Hee, hee, hee, right; and then my Lady Whifler is ſo ready—ſhe always comes in three bars too ſoon—And then, what do they laugh at? For you know laughing without a jeſt is as impertinent, hee! as——

Cyn. As dancing without a fiddle.

Ld. F. Juſt i'faith, that was at my tongue's end.

Cyn. But that cannot be properly ſaid of them, for I think they are all in good nature with the world, and only laugh at one another; and you muſt allow they

have

have all jeſts in their perſons, though they have none in their converſation.

Ld. F. True, as I am a perſon of honour————For Heaven's ſake let us ſacrifice them to mirth a little.

[*Enter Boy and whiſpers Sir* Paul.

Sir P. Gad ſo—Wife, Wife, my Lady Plyant, I have a word.

L. P. I am buſy, Sir Paul, I wonder at your imperinence————

Care. Sir Paul, harkee, I am reaſoning the matter you know: Madam, if your Ladyſhip pleaſe we'll diſcourſe of this in the next room. [*Ex. Lady* P. *and* Care.

Sir P. O ho, I wiſh you good ſucceſs, I wiſh you good ſucceſs. Boy, tell my Lady, when ſhe has done, I would ſpeak with her below. [*Exit Sir* Paul.

Enter Lady Froth *and* Briſk.

L. F. Then you think that epiſode between Suſan the dairy-maid, and our coachman, is not amiſs; you know I may ſuppoſe the dairy in town, as well as in the country.

Brisk. Incomparable, let me periſh—But then being an heroic poem, had you not better call him a Charioteer? Charioteer ſounds great: beſides your Ladyſhip's coachman having a red face, and you comparing him to the ſun————And you know the ſun is called Heaven's Charioteer.

L. F. Oh, infinitely better; I am extremely beholden to you for the hint; ſtay, we'll read over thoſe half a ſcore lines again. [*Pulls out a paper.*] Let me ſee here, you know what goes before————the compariſon, you know. [*Reads.*]

For as the ſun ſhines every day,
So of our coachman I may ſay.

Brisk. I am afraid that ſimile won't do in wet weather ————Becauſe you ſay the ſun ſhines every day.

L. F. No, for the ſun it won't, but it will do for the coachman, for you know there's moſt occaſion for a coach in wet weather.

Brisk. Right, right, that ſaves all.

L. F. Then I don't ſay the ſun ſhines all the day, but that he peeps now and then, yet he does ſhine all the day too, you know, though we don't ſee him.

Brisk.

Brisk. Right, but the vulgar will never comprehend that.

L.-F. Well, you shall hear—Let me see.

[*Reads.*] For as the sun shines every day,
    So of our coachman I may say ;
    He shews his drunken fiery face,
    Just as the sun does, more or less.

Brisk. That's right, all's well, all's well. More or less.

L. F. [*Reads.*]
    And when at night his labour's done,
    Then too, like Heaven's charioteer, the sun :

Ay, Charioteer does better.
    Into the dairy he descends,
    And there his whipping and his driving ends ;
    There he's secure from danger of a bilk,
    His fare is paid him, and he sets in milk.

For Susan, you know, is Thetis, and so ————

Brisk. Incomparable well and proper, 'egad—But I have one exception to make——Don't you think bilk. (I know it is good rhyme) but don't you think bilk and fare too like a hackney coachman ?

L. F. I swear and vow I am afraid so ————And yet our Jehu was a hackney coachman when my Lord took him.

Brisk. Was he? I am answered, if Jehu was a hack-ney coachman—You may put that in the marginal notes tho' to prevent criticism—Only mark it with a small aste-rism, and say—Jehu was formerly a hackney coachman.

L. F. I will; you'll oblige me extremely to write notes to the whole poem.

Brisk. With all my heart and soul, and proud of the vast honour, let me perish.

Ld. F. Hee, hee, hee, my dear, have you done?—— Won't you join with us ? we were laughing at my Lady Whifler and Mr. Sneer.

L. F. ——Ay, my dear——Were you ? Oh filthy Mr. Sneer ; he's a nauseous figure, a most fulsamic fop, foh————He spent two days together in going about Covent-Garden to suit the lining of his coach with his complexion.

            Ld F.

Ld. F. O filly! yet his aunt is as fond of him as if fhe had brought the ape into the world herfelf.

Brisk. Who, my Lady Toothlefs; O, fhe's a mortifying fpectacle; fhe's always chewing the cud like an old ewe.

Cyn. Fy, Mr. Brifk, eringo is for her cough.

L. F. I have feen her take them half-chewed out of her mouth to laugh, and then put them in again—Foh.

Ld. F. Foh.

L. F. Then fhe is always ready to laugh when Sneer offers to fpeak—and fits in expectation of his no jeft, with her gums bare, and her mouth open————

Brisk. Like an oyfter at low ebb, 'egad—Ha, ha, ha.

' *Cyn.* [*Afide.*] Well, I find there are no fools fo in-
' confiderable in themfelves, but they can render other
' people contemptible by expofing their infirmities.'

L. F. Then that t'other great ftrapping lady——I cannot hit of her name; the old fat fool that paints fo exorbitantly.

Brisk. I know whom you mean—But deuce take me, I cannot hit of her name neither——Paints, d'ye fay? Why, fhe lays it on with a trowel——Then fhe has a great beard that briftles through it, and makes her look as if fhe were plaiftered with lime and hair, let me perifh.

L. F. Oh, you made a fong upon her, Mr. Brifk.

Brisk. He! 'egad, fo I did——My Lord can fing it.

' *Cyn.* O good, my Lord, let us hear it.'

Brisk. 'Tis not a fong neither——It is a fort of an epigram, or rather an epigrammatic fonnet; I don't know what to call it, but it is fatire.—' Sing it, my
' Lord.'

Lord Froth *fings.*

Ancient Phillis has young graces,
'Tis a ftrange thing, but a true one;
   Shall I tell you how?
She herfelf makes her own faces,
And each morning wears a new one?
   Where's the wonder now?

Brisk. Short, but there is falt in it; my way of writing, 'egad.

4

Enter

Enter Footman.

L. F. How now?

Foot. Your Ladyfhip's chair is come.

L. F. Is nurfe and the child in it?

Foot. Yes, Madam.   [*Exit.*

L. F. O, the dear creature! let us go fee it.

Ld. F. I fwear, my dear, you'll fpoil that child with fending it to and again fo often; this is the feventh time the chair has gone for her to-day.

L. F. O-la, I fwear it's but the fixth——and I han't feen her thefe two hours——The poor dear creature—— I fwear, my Lord, you don't love poor little Sappho, ——Come, my dear Cynthia, Mr. Brifk, we'll go fee Sappho, though my Lord won't.

Cyn. I'll wait upon your Ladyfhip.

Brisk. Pray, Madam, how old is Lady Sappho?

L. F. Three quarters, but I fwear fhe has a world of wit, and can fing a tune already. My Lord, won't you go? Won't you? What, not to fee Saph? Pray, my Lord, come fee little Saph. I knew you could not ftay.

       [*Exeunt all but* Cynthia.

' *Cyn.* 'Tis not fo hard to counterfeit joy in the
' depth of affliction, as to diffemble mirth in the com-
' pany of fools——Why fhould I call them fools? The
' world thinks better of them; for thefe have quality
' and education, wit and fine converfation, are received
' and admired by the world——If not, they like and
' admire themfelves——And why is not that true wif-
' dom, for it is happinefs? And for ought I know, we
' have mifapplied the name all this while, and miftaken
' the thing: fince

' If happinefs in felf-content is plac'd,
' The wife are wretched, and fools only blefs'd.

          [*Exit.*

END of the THIRD ACT.

A C T   IV.

' *Enter* Mellefont *and* Cynthia.

' CYNTHIA.

' I Heard him loud as I came by the clofet-door, and
' my Lady with him; but fhe feemed to moderate

'*Mel.* Ay, Hell thank her, as gentle breezes moderate
'a fire; but I shall counter-work her spells, and ride
'the witch in her own bridle.

'*Cyn.* It is impossible; she'll cast beyond you still——
'I'll lay my life it will never be a match.

'*Mel.* What?

'*Cyn.* Between you and me.

'*Mel.* Why so?

'*Cyn.* My mind gives me it won't——because we are
'both willing; we each of us strive to reach the goal,
'and hinder one another in the race; I swear it never
'does well when parties are so agreed—For when people
'walk hand in hand, there's neither overtaking nor
'meeting: we hunt in couples where we both pursue
'the same game, but forget one another; and 'tis be-
'cause we are so near that we don't think of coming to-
'gether.

'*Mel.* Hum, 'egad I believe there's something in it—
'Marriage is the game that we hunt, and while we
'think that we only have it in view, I don't see but
'we have it in our power.

'*Cyn.* Within reach; for example, give me your
'hand; you have looked through the wrong end of the
'perspective all this while; for nothing has been be-
'tween us but our fears.

'*Mel.* I don't know why we should not steal out of
'the house this very moment, and marry one another,
'without consideration, or the fear of repentance. Pox
'o'fortune, portion, settlements, and jointures.

'*Cyn.* Ay, ay, what have we to do with them; you
'know we marry for love.

'*Mel.* Love, love, downright very villainous love.

'*Cyn.* And he that cannot live upon love deserves to
'die in a ditch.—— Here then, I give you my promise,
'in spite of duty, any temptation of wealth, your in-
'constancy, or my own inclination to change————

'*Mel.* To run most wilfully and unreasonably away
'with me this moment, and be married.

'*Cyn.* Hold—Never to marry any body else.

'*Mel.* That's but a kind of negative consent—Why,
'you won't baulk the frolic?

E

'*Cyn.*

' *Cyn.* If you had not been ſo aſſured of your own
' conduct I would not——— But 'tis but reaſonable that
' ſince I conſent to like a man without the vile conſide-
' ration of money, he ſhould give me a very evident de-
' monſtration of his wit : therefore, let me ſee you un-
' dermine my Lady Touchwood, as you boaſted, and
' force her to give her conſent, and then———

' *Mel.* I'll do it.

' *Cyn.* And I'll do it.

' *Mel.* This very next enſuing hour of eight o'clock,
' is the laſt minute of her reign, unleſs the Devil aſſiſt
' her in *propria perſona.*

' *Cyn.* Well, if the Devil ſhould aſſiſt her, and your
' plot miſcarry.———

' *Mel.* Ay, what am I to truſt to then ?

' *Cyn.* Why, if you give me very clear demonſtration
' that it was the Devil, I will allow for irreſiſtible odds.
' But if I find it to be only chance, or deſtiny, or un-
' lucky ſtars, or any thing but the very Devil, I am in-
' exorable: only ſtill I'll keep my word, and live a maid
' for your ſake.

' *Mel.* And you won't die one for your own, ſo ſtill
' there's hope.

' *Cyn.* Here is my mother-in-law, and your friend
' Careleſs, I would not have them ſee us together yet.

' *[Exeunt.']*

Enter Careleſs *and Lady* Plyant.*

L. P. I ſwear, Mr. Careleſs, you are very alluring—
and ſay ſo many fine things, and nothing is ſo moving to
me as a fine thing. Well, I muſt do you this juſtice,
and declare in the face of the world, never any body
gained ſo far upon me as yourſelf; with bluſhes I muſt
own it, you have ſhaken, as I may ſay, the very foundation of my honour—Well, ſure if I eſcape your importunities, I ſhall value myſelf as long as I live, I ſwear.

Care. And deſpiſe me. 				*[Sighing.*

L. P. The laſt of any man in the world, by my purity ; now you make me ſwear—O, gratitude forbid that
I ſhould ever be wanting in a reſpectful acknowledgment
of an entire reſignation of all my beſt wiſhes for the per-

---

* The fourth act, in repreſentation, begins here.

ſon

fon and parts of fo accomplifhed a perfon, whofe merit challenges much more, I am fure, than my illiterate praifes can defcription.————

Care. [*In a whining tone.*] Ah, Heavens, Madam, you ruin me with kindnefs ; your charming tongue purfues the victory of your eyes, while at your feet your poor adorer dies.

L. P. Ah ! very fine.

Care. [*Still whining.*] Ah, why are you fo fair, fo bewitching fair ? O, let me grow to the ground here, and feaft upon that hand ; O, let me prefs it to my heart, my trembling heart, the nimble movement fhall inftruct your pulfe, and teach it to alarm defire.—Zoons I am almoft at the end of my cant, if fhe does not yield quickly.
[*Afide.*

L. P. O that's fo paffionate and fine, I cannot hear it— I am not fafe if I ftay, and muft leave you.

Care. And muft you leave me ! Rather let me languifh out a wretched life, and breathe my foul beneath your feet————I muft fay the fame thing over again, and cannot help it.   [*Afide.*

L. P. I fwear I am ready to languifh too————O my honour ! Whither is it going ? I proteft you have given me the palpitation of the heart.

Care. Can you be fo cruel ?

L. P. O rife, I befeech you, fay no more 'till you rife—Why did you kneel fo long ? I fwear I was fo tranfported I did not fee it————Well, to fhew you how far you have gained upon me, I affure you, if Sir Paul fhould die, of all mankind there's none I'd fooner make my fecond choice.

Care. O Heaven ! I cannot out-live this night without your favour————I feel my fpirits faint, a general dampnefs over-fpreads my face, a cold deadly dew already vents through all my pores, and will to-morrow wafh me for ever from your fight, and drown me in my tomb.

L. P. O, you have conquered, fweet, melting, moving Sir, you have conquered—What heart of marble can refrain to-weep, and yield to fuch fad fayings.—
[*Cries.*

Care. I thank Heaven, they are the faddeft that I ever faid—Oh ! ' I fhall never contain laughter.'   [*Afide.*
E 2   *L. P.*

L. P. Oh, I yield myself all up to your uncontroulable embraces——Say, thou dear dying man, when, where, and how?——' Ah, there's Sir Paul.'

Care. 'Slife, yonder's Sir Paul, but if he were not come, I am so transported I cannot speak——This note will inform you.   *[Gives her a note. Exit.*

Enter Sir Paul *and* Cynthia.

Sir P. Thou art my tender lambkin, and shalt do what thou wilt—But endeavour to forget this Mellefont.

Cyn. I would obey you to my power, Sir; but if I have not him, I have sworn never to marry.

Sir P. Never to marry! Heavens forbid! Must I neither have sons nor grandsons? Must the family of the Plyants be utterly extinct for want of issue male. Oh, impiety! But did you swear, did that sweet creature swear! ha? How durst you swear without my consent, ah? Gads-bud, who am I?

Cyn. Pray don't be angry, Sir; when I swore I had your consent, and therefore I swore.

Sir P. Why then the revoking my consent does annul, or make of none effect your oath; so you may unswear it again——The law will allow it.

Cyn. Ay, but my conscience never will.

Sir P. Gads-bud, no matter for that; conscience and law never go together; you must not expect that.

L. P. Ay, but Sir Paul, I conceive if she has sworn, d'ye mark me, if she has once sworn, it is most unchristian, inhuman, and obscene that she should break it.—— I'll make up the match again, because Mr. Carelefs said it would oblige him.   *[Afide.*

Sir P. Does your Ladyship conceive so?——Why, I was of that opinion once too——Nay, if your Ladyship conceives so, I am of that opinion again; but I can neither find my Lord nor my Lady, to know what they intend.

L. P. I am satisfied that my cousin Mellefont has been much wronged.

Cyn. [*Afide.*] I am amazed to find her of our side, for I am sure she loved him.

L. P. I know my Lady Touchwood has no kindness for him; and besides, I have been informed by Mr. Carelefs, that Mellefont had never any thing more than

a pro-a profound refpect—That he has owned himfelf to be my admirer, 'tis true, but he was never fo prefumptuous to entertain any difhonourable notions of things; fo that if this be made plain—I don't fee how my daughter can in confcience, or honour, or any thing in the world——

Sir P. Indeed if this be made plain, as my Lady your mother fays, child——

L. P. Plain! I was informed of it by Mr. Carelefs—And I affure you Mr. Carelefs is a perfon—that has a moft extraordinary refpect and honour for you, Sir Paul.

Cyn. [*Afide.*] And for your Ladyfhip too, I believe, or elfe you had not changed fides fo foon; now I begin to find it.

Sir P. I am much obliged to Mr. Carelefs, really, he is a perfon that I have a great value for, not only for that, but becaufe he has a great veneration for your Ladyfhip.

L. P. O la, no indeed, Sir Paul, it is upon your account.

Sir P. No, I proteft and vow I have no title to his efteem, but in having the honour to appertain in fome meafure to your Ladyfhip, that's all.

L. P. O la, now, I fwear and declare, it fhan't be fo, you are too modeft, Sir Paul.

Sir P. It becomes me, when there is any comparifon made between ——

L. P. O fy, fy, Sir Paul, you'll put me out of countenance——Your very obedient and affectionate wife, that's all——And highly honoured in that title.

Sir P. Gads-bud I am tranfported! Give me leave to kifs your Ladyfhip's hand.

' *Cyn.* That my poor father fhould be fo very filly!'
                                                    [*Afide.*

L. P. My lip, indeed, Sir Paul, I fwear you fhall.
                    [*He kiffes her, and bows very low.*

Sir P. I humbly thank your Ladyfhip—I don't know whether I fly on ground, or walk in air——Gads-bud, fhe was never thus before——Well, I muft own myfelf beholden to Mr. Carelefs—As fure as can be this is all his doing—fomething that he has faid; well, 'tis a rare thing to have an ingenious friend. Well, your Lady-fhip is of opinion that the match may go forward.

E 3

L. P.

L. P. By all means—Mr. Careless has satisfied me of the matter.

Sir P. Well, why then, lamb, you may keep your oath, but have a care of making rash vows; come hither to me, and kiss papa.

L. P. I swear and declare, I am in such a twitter to read Mr. Careless's letter, that I cannot forbear any longer—But though I may read all letters first by prerogative, yet I'll be sure to be unsuspected this time.—— Sir Paul.

Sir P. Did your Ladyship call?

L. P. Nay, not to interrupt you, my dear——Only lend me your letter, which you had from your steward to-day: I would look upon the account again; and may be increase the allowance.

Sir P. There it is, Madam. Do you want a pen and ink?   [*Bows and gives the letter.*

L. P. No, no, nothing else, I thank you, Sir Paul— So now I can read my own letter under the cover of his.   [*Aside.*

Sir P. He? and wilt thou bring a grandson at nine months end---He? A brave chopping boy.—I'll settle a thousand pounds a year upon the rogue as soon as ever he looks me in the face, I will Gads-bud. I am overjoyed to think I have any of my family that will bring children into the world. For I would fain have some resemblance of myself in my posterity, he, Thy! 'Cannot you contrive that affair, girl? Do; Gads-bud think on thy old father;' heh! Make the young rogue as like as you can.

Cyn. I am glad to see you so merry, Sir.

Sir P. Merry! Gads-bud I am serious! I'll give thee 500 l. for every inch of him that resembles me; ah, this eye, this left eye! A thousand pounds for this left eye. This has done execution in its time, girl; why, thou hast my leer, hussy, just thy father's leer.—Let it be transmitted to the young rogue by the help of imagination---- Why 'tis the mark of our family, Thy; our house is distinguished by a languishing eye, as the house of Austria is by a thick lip ——Ah! when I was of your age, hussy, I would have held fifty to one I could have drawn my own picture——Gads-bud, but I could have done——

                                        not

not fo much as you neither,——but————nay, don't blufh——————

Cyn. I don't blufh, Sir, for I vow I don't underftand.

Sir P. Pfhaw, pfhaw, you fib, you baggage, you do underftand, and you fhall underftand : Come, don't be fo nice ; Gads-bud don't learn after your mother-in-law, my Lady here——Marry Heaven forbid that you fhould follow her example, that would fpoil all indeed. Blefs us, if you fhould take a vagary, and make a rafh refolution on your wedding-night to die a maid, as fhe did, all were ruined, all my hopes loft————My heart would break, and my eftate would be left to the wide world, he ! I hope you are a better Chriftian than to think of living a nun, he ? Anfwer me.

Cyn. I am all obedience, Sir, to your commands.

L. P. [*Having read the letter.*] O dear Mr. Carelefs, I fwear he writes charmingly, and he looks charmingly, and he has charmed me as much as I have charmed him ; and fo I'll tell him in the wardrobe when 'tis dark. O Crimine ! I hope Sir Paul has not feen both letters———— [*Puts the wrong letter haftily up, and gives him her own.*] Sir Paul, here's your letter, to-morrow morning I'll fettle accounts to your advantage.

Enter Brifk.

Brisk. Sir Paul, Gad's-bud you are an uncivil perfon, let me tell you, and all that ; and I did not think it had been in you.

Sir P. O la, what's the matter now ? I hope you are not angry, Mr. Brifk ?

Brisk. Deuce take me, I believe you intend to marry your daughter yourfelf ; you are always brooding over her like an old hen, as if fhe were not well hatched, 'egad, he ?

Sir P. Good ftrange ! Mr. Brifk is fuch a merry facetious perfon, he, he, he. No, no, I have done with her, I have done with her now.

Brisk. The fiddles have ftayed this hour in the hall, and my Lord Froth wants a partner ; we can never begin without her.

Sir P. Go, go, child, go, get you gone and dance, and be merry ; I will come and look at you by and by.————{ Where is my fon Mellefont ?

L. P.

L. P. I'll send him to them, I know where he is——

Brisk. Sir Paul, will you send Careless into the hall if you meet him.

Sir P. I will, I will, I'll go and look for him on purpose.   [*Ex. all but* Brisk.

Brisk. So now they are all gone, and I have an opportunity to practise——Ah! my dear Lady Froth! She's a most engaging creature, if she were not so fond of that damned coxcombly Lord of hers; and yet I am forced to allow him wit too, to keep in with him——No matter, she's a woman of parts, and 'egad parts will carry her. She said, she would follow me into the gallery——Now to make my approaches—Hem, hem! Ah, Ma- [*Bows.*] dam!——Pox on't, why should I disparage my parts by thinking what to say; None but dull rogues *think:* witty men, like rich fellows, are always ready for all expences, while your blockheads, like poor needy scoundrels, are forced to examine their stock, and forecast the charges of the day.   Here she comes; I'll seem not to see her, and try to win her with a new airy invention of my own, hem!

Enter Lady Froth.

[Brisk *sings, walking about.*] I'm sick with love, ha, ha, ha, pr'ythee come cure me.

I'm sick with, &c.

O ye powers! O my Lady Froth, my Lady Froth! My Lady Froth! Heigho! Break heart; Gods I thank you.
[*Stands musing with his arms across.*

L. F. O Heavens, Mr. Brisk! What's the matter?

Brisk. My Lady Froth! Your Ladyship's most humble servant——The matter, Madam? Nothing, Madam, nothing at all 'egad.   I was fallen into the most agreeable amusement in the whole province of contemplation: That is all——(I'll seem to conceal my passion, and that will look like respect.)
[*Aside.*

L. F. Bless me, why did you call out upon me so loud?——

Brisk. O lord, I Madam! I beseech your Ladyship.——When?

L. F. Just now as I came in; bless me, why don't you know it?

Brisk.

Brisk. Not I, let me perifh——But did I? Strange! I confefs your Ladyfhip was in my thoughts; and I was in a fort of dream that did in a manner reprefent a very pleafing object to my imagination, but——but did I indeed?——To fee how love and murder will out. But did I really name my Lady Froth?

L. F. Three times aloud, as I love letters——But did you talk of love? O Parnaffus! Who would have thought Mr. Brifk could have been in love, ha, ha, ha. O Heavens! I thought you could have no miftrefs but the nine mufes.

Brifk. No more I have, 'egad, for I adore them all in your Ladyfhip——Let me perifh, I don't know whether to be fplenetic or airy upon it; the deuce take me if I can tell whether I am glad or forry that your Ladyfhip has made the difcovery.

L. F. O, be merry by all means——Prince Volfcius in love! Ha, ha, ha.

Brisk. O, barbarous, to turn me into ridicule! Yet, ha, ha, ha. The deuce take me, I cannot help laughing myfelf, ha, ha, ha; yet by Heavens I have a violent paffion for your Ladyfhip ferioufly.

L. F. Serioufly! Ha, ha, ha.

Brisk. Serioufly, ha, ha, ha. Gad I have for all I laugh.

L. F. Ha, ha, ha! What d'ye think I laugh at? Ha, ha, ha.

Brisk. Me 'egad, ha ha.

L. F. No, the deuce take me if I don't laugh at myfelf; for hang me if I have not a violent paffion for Mr. Brifk, ha, ha, ha.

Brisk. Serioufly?

L. F. Serioufly, ha, ha, ha.

Brisk. That's well enough, let me perifh, ha, ha, ha. O miraculous, what a happy difcovery! Ay, my dear charming Lady Froth!

L. F. Oh, my adored Mr. Brifk!   [*Embrace.*
        Enter Lord Froth.

Ld. F. The company are all ready——How now!

Brisk. Zoons, Madam, there's my Lord. [*Softly to her.*]

L. F. Take no notice——but obferve me——Now caft off, and meet me at the lower end of the room, and
                            then

then join hands again; I could teach my Lord this dance purely, but I vow, Mr. Brisk, I can't tell how to come so near any other man. Oh, here's my Lord, now you shall see me do it with him.

              [*They pretend to practise part of a country dance.*

    Ld. F. ——Oh, I see there's no harm yet——But I don't like this familiarity.   [*Afide.*

    L. F. —Shall you and I do our clofe dance, to fhew Mr. Brisk ?

    Ld. F. No, my dear, do it with him.

    L. F. I'll do it with him, my Lord, when you are out of the way.

    Brisk. That's good 'egad, that's good; deuce take me I can hardly hold laughing in his face.   [*Afide.*

    Ld. F. Any other time, my dear, or we'll dance it below.

    L. F. With all my heart.

    Brisk. Come, my Lord, I'll wait on you—My charming witty angel !   [*To her.*

    L. F. We fhall have whifpering time enough, you know, fince we are partners.   [*Exeunt.*

         Enter Lady Plyant *and* Carelefs.

    L. P. O Mr. Carelefs, Mr. Carelefs, I'm ruined, I'm undone.

    Care. What's the matter, Madam ?

    L. P. O the unluckieft accident, I'm afraid I fhan't live to tell it you.

    Care. Heaven forbid ! What is it ?

    L. P. I'm in fuch a fright; the ftrangeft quandary and premunire ! I'm all over in an univerfal agitation, I dare fwear every circumftance of me trembles.——O your letter, your letter ! By an unfortunate miftake, I have given Sir Paul your letter inftead of his own.

    Care. That was unlucky.

    L. P. O yonder he comes reading of it, for Heaven's fake ftep in here and advife me quickly, before he fees.

                 [*Exeunt.*

       Enter Sir Paul *with the letter.*

    Sir P. —O Providence, what a confpiracy have I difcovered——But let me fee to make an end on't————— [*Reads.*] Hum——*After fupper in the wardrobe by the gallery. If Sir* Paul *fhould furprize us, I have a commiffion from*

from him to treat with you about the very matter of fact——
Matter of fact! Very pretty; it seems, then, I am con-
ducing to my own cuckoldom; why this is a very trai-
terous position of taking up arms by my authority against
my person! Well, let me see—'*Till then I languish in expectation of my adored charmer.*

Dying Ned Careless.

Gads-bud, would that were matter of fact too.   Die and
be damned for a Judas Maccabeus and Iscariot both.   O
friendship, what art thou but a name!   Henceforward
let no man make a friend that would not be a cuckold:
for whomsoever he receives into his bosom, will find the
way to his bed, and there return his caresses with interest
to his wife. ' Have I for this been pinioned night after
' night for three years past? Have I been swathed in
' blankets 'till I have been even deprived of motion?'
Have I approached the marriage-bed with reverence, as
to a sacred shrine, ' and denied myself the enjoyment of
' lawful domestic pleasures to preserve its purity,' and
must I now find it polluted by foreign iniquity? O my
Lady Plyant, you were chaste as ice, but you are melted
now, and false as water.——But Providence has been
constant to me in discovering this conspiracy; still I am
beholden to Providence; if it were not for Providence,
sure, poor Sir Paul, thy heart would break.

Enter Lady Plyant.

L. P. So, Sir, I see you have read the letter—Well,
now, Sir Paul, what do you think of your friend Careless? Has he been treacherous, or did you give his insolence a licence to make trial of your wife's suspected virtue? D'ye see here? [*Snatches the letter as in anger.*]
Look, read it! Gad's my life, if I thought it were so, I
would this moment renounce all communication with
you.   Ungrateful monster! He? Is it so? Ay, I see it,
a plot upon my honour; your guilty cheeks confess it:
Oh, where shall wronged virtue fly for reparation! I'll
be divorced this instant.

Sir P. Gads-bud, what shall I say? This is the strangest surprize! Why I don't know any thing at all, nor I
don't know whether there be any thing at all in the world,
or no.

I

L. P.

L. P. I thought I should try you, false man. I that never dissembled in my life; yet to make trial of you, pretended to like that monster of iniquity, Careless, and found out that contrivance to let you see this letter; which now I find was of your own inditing———— I do, Heathen, I do; see my face no more; ' I'll be divorced ' presently.'

Sir P. O strange, what will become of me!———I am so amazed, and so overjoyed, so afraid, and so sorry.——— But did you give me this letter on purpose, he? Did you?

L. P. Did I? Do you doubt me, Turk, Saracen? I have a cousin that's a proctor in the Commons, I'll go to him instantly————

Sir P. Hold, stay, I beseech your Ladyship———I am so overjoyed, stay, I'll confess all.

L. P. What will you confess, Jew?

Sir P. Why now as I hope to be saved, I had no hand in this letter—Nay, hear me, I beseech your Ladyship: The Devil take me now if he did not go beyond my com- mission———If I desired him to do any more than speak a good word only just for me; Gads-bud, only for poor Sir Paul, I am an Anabaptist, or a Jew, or what you please to call me.

L. P. Why, is not here matter of fact?

Sir P. Ay, but by your own virtue and continency that matter of fact is all his own doing.—I confess I had a great desire to have some honours conferred upon me, which lie all in your Ladyship's breast, and he being a well-spoken man, I desired him to intercede for me.———

L. P. Did you so, Presumption! ' Oh! he comes, ' the Tarquin comes; I cannot bear his sight.'   [*Exit.*

Enter Careless.

Care. Sir Paul, I am glad I have met with you; 'egad I have said all I could, but cannot prevail———Then my friendship to you has carried me a little further in this matter————

Sir P. Indeed———Well, Sir—I'll dissemble with him a little.   [*Aside.*

Care. Why, faith, I have in my time known honest gentlemen abused by a pretended coyness in their wives, and I had a mind to try my Lady's virtue—And when I

could

could not prevail for you, 'egad I pretended to be in love myfelf—but all in vain, fhe would not hear a word upon that fubject; then I writ a letter to her; I don't know what effects that will have, but I'll be fure to tell you when I do; though, by this light, I believe her virtue is impregnable.

Sir P. O Providence! Providence! What difcoveries are here made! Why, this is better and more miraculous than the reft.

Care. What do you mean?

Sir P. I cannot tell you, I am fo overjoyed; come along with me to my Lady, I cannot contain myfelf; come my dear friend.

Care. So, fo, fo, this difficulty's over.   [*Afide.*
[*Exit.*

Enter Mellefont *and* Mafkwell *from different doors.*

Mel. Mafkwell, I have been looking for you——It is within a quarter of eight.

Mask. My Lady is juft gone into my Lord's clofet, you had beft fteal into her chamber before fhe comes, and lie concealed there, otherwife fhe may lock the door when we are together, and you not eafily get in to fur-prize us.

Mel. He? You fay true.

Mask. You had beft make hafte, for after fhe has made fome apology to the company for her own and my Lord's abfence all this while, fhe'll retire to her chamber inftantly.

Mel. I go this moment: Now, Fortune, I defy thee.
[*Exit.*

Mask. I confefs you may be allowed to be fecure in your own opinion; the appearance is very fair, but I have an after-game to play that fhall turn the tables, and here comes the man that I muft manage.

Enter Lord Touchwood.

Ld. T. Mafkwell, you are the man I wifhed to meet.

Mask. I am happy to be in the way of your Lordfhip's commands.

Ld. T. I have always found you prudent and careful in any thing that has concerned me or my family.

Mask. I were a villain elfe—I am bound by duty and
F   grati-

gratitude, and my own inclination, to be ever your Lordſhip's ſervant.

Ld. T. Enough——You are my friend; I know it: Yet there has been a thing in your knowledge which has concerned me nearly, that you have concealed from me.

Mask. My Lord!

Ld. T. Nay, I excuſe your friendſhip to my unnatural nephew thus far——But I know you have been privy to his impious deſigns upon my wife. This evening ſhe has told me all: her good-nature concealed it as long as was poſſible; but he perſeveres ſo in villainy, that ſhe has told me even you were weary of diſſuading him, tho' you have once actually hindered him from forcing her.

Mask. I am ſorry, my Lord, I cannot make you an anſwer; this is an occaſion in which I would not willingly be ſilent.

Ld. T. I know you would excuſe him—And I know as well that you cannot.

Mask. Indeed I was in hopes it had been but a youthful heat that might have ſoon boiled over; but——

Ld. T. Say on.

Mask. I have nothing more to ſay, my Lord——but to expreſs my concern; for I think his frenzy increaſes daily.

Ld. T. How! give me but proof of it, ocular proof, that I may juſtify my dealing with him to the world, and ſhare my fortunes.

Mask. O my Lord! conſider that is hard: beſides, time may work upon him: then, for me to do it! I have profeſſed an everlaſting friendſhip to him.

Ld. T. He is your friend, and what am I?

Mask. I am anſwered.

Ld. T. Fear not his diſpleaſure; I will put you out of his and Fortune's power; and for that thou art ſcrupulouſly honeſt, I will ſecure thy fidelity to him, and give my honour never to own any diſcovery that you ſhall make me. Can you give me a demonſtrative proof? Speak.

Mask. I wiſh I could not——To be plain, my Lord, I intended this evening to have tried all arguments to diſſuade him from a deſign, which I ſuſpect; and if I had not fucceeded, to have informed your Lordſhip of what I knew.

Ld. T. I thank you.   What is the villain's purpofe?

Mask. He has owned nothing to me of late, and what I mean now is only a bare fufpicion of my own.   If your Lordſhip will meet me a quarter of an hour hence there, in that lobby by my Lady's bed-chamber, I ſhall be able to tell you more.

Ld T. I will.

Mask. My duty to your Lordſhip makes me do a fevere piece of juſtice.

Ld. T. I will be fecret, and reward your honeſty beyond your hopes.   [*Exeunt.*

SCENE *opening, ſhews Lady* Touchwood's *chamber.*

Mellefont *folus.*

Mel. Pray Heaven my aunt keep touch with her affignation.——Oh, that her Lord were but fweating behind this hanging, with the expeċtation of what I ſhall fee —— Hiſt, ſhe comes——Little does ſhe think what a mine is juſt ready to fpring under her feet.   But to my poſt.

[*Goes behind the hangings.*

Enter Lady Touchwood.

L. T. 'Tis eight o'clock: methinks I ſhould have found him here—Who does not prevent the hour of love, outſtays the time ; for to be duly punċtual is too flow.—— I was accufing you of negleċt.

Enter Maſkwell.

Mellefont *abfconding.*

Mask. I confefs you do reproach me when I fee you here before me ; but 'tis fit I ſhould be ſtill behind-hand, ſtill to be more and more indebted to your goodnefs.

L. T. You can excufe a fault too well, not to have been to blame————A ready anfwer ſhews you were prepared.

Mask. Guilt is ever at a lofs, and confufion waits upon it ; when innocence and bold truth are always ready for expreſſion————

L. T. Not in love ; words are the weak fupport of cold indifference ; love has no language to be heard.

Mask. Excefs of joy has made me ſtupid ! Thus may my lips be ever clofed. [*Kiſſes her.*] And thus—Oh, who

                    would

would not lofe his fpeech upon condition to have joys above it! -

L. T. Hold, let me lock the door firft.

[*Goes to the door.*

Mask. [*Afide.*] That I believed; 'twas well I left the private paffage open.

L. T. So, that's fafe.

Mask. And fo may all your pleafures be, and fecret as this kifs ———

Mel. And may all treachery be thus difcovered.

[*Leaps out.*

L. T. Ah!

[*Shrieks.*

Mel. Villain!

[*Offers to draw.*

Mask. Nay then, there's but one way.   [*Runs out.*

Mel. Say you fo, were you provided for an efcape? Hold, Madam, you have no more holes to your burrow, I ftand between you and this fally-port.

L. T. Thunder ftrike thee dead for this deceit, immediate lightning blaft thee, me, and the whole world ——— Oh! I could rack myfelf, play the vulture to my own heart, and gnaw it piece-meal, for not boding to me this misfortune.

Mel. Be patient———

' *L. T.* Be damned.'

Mel. Confider I have you on the hook; you will but flounder yourfelf a weary, and be neverthelefs my prifoner.

L. T. I'll hold my breath and die, but I'll be free.

Mel. O Madam, have a care of dying unprepared, I doubt that you have fome unrepented fins that may hang heavy, and retard your flight.

L. T. Oh! what fhall I do? fay? Whither fhall I turn? Has Hell no remedy?

Mel. None.   Hell has ferved you even as Heaven has done, left you to yourfelf.—You are in a kind of Erafmus Paradife; yet if you pleafe, you may make it a purgatory; and with a little penance and my abfolution, all this may turn to a good account.

L. T. [*Afide.*] Hold in my paffion, and fall, fall a little, thou fwelling heart; let me have fome intermiffion of this rage, and one minute's coolnefs to diffemble.

[*She weeps.*

Mel.

Mel. You have been to blame——I like thofe tears, and hope they are of the pureft kind—Penitential tears.

L. T. O, the fcene was fhifted quick before me—I had not time to think——I was furprized to fee a monfter in the glafs, and now I find 'tis myfelf: Can you have mercy to forgive the faults I have imagined, but never put in practice——O confider, confider how fatal you have been to me, ‘ you have already killed the quiet of this ‘ life.’ The love of you was the firft wandering fire that e'er mifled my fteps, and while I had only that in view, I was betrayed into unthought-of ways of ruin.

Mel. May I believe this true ?

L. T. O be not cruelly incredulous——How can you doubt thefe ftreaming eyes ? Keep the fevereft eye over all my future conduct, and if I once relapfe, let me not hope forgivenefs, 'twill ever be in your power to ruin me —My Lord fhall fign to your defires ; I will myfelf create your happinefs, and Cynthia fhall be this night your bride—Do but conceal my failings, and forgive.

Mel. Upon fuch terms, I will be ever yours in every honeft way.

Mafkwell *foftly introduces Lord* Touchwood, *and retires.*

Mask. I have kept my word, he is here, but I muft not be feen.

Ld. T. Hell and amazement ! She is in tears.

L. T. [*Kneeling.*] Eternal bleffings thank you—Ha ! My Lord liftening ! O, Fortune has o'erpaid me all, all ! all's my own !   [*Afide.*

Mel. Nay, I befeech you rife.

L. T. [*Aloud.*] Never, never ! I'll grow to the ground, be buried quick beneath it, ere I'll be confenting to fo damned a fin as inceft ! unnatural inceft !

Mel. Ha !

L. T. O cruel man, will you not let me go—I'll forgive all that's paft—O Heaven, you will not ravifh me !.

Mel. Damnation !

Ld. T. Monfter ! Dog ! your life fhall anfwer this—

[*Draws and runs at* Mel. *is held by Lady* Touchwood.

L. T. O Heavens, my Lord ! Hold, hold, for Heaven's fake.

Mel. Confufion, my uncle ! O, the damned forcerefs.

L. T. Moderate your rage, good my Lord! He's mad, alas, he's mad—Indeed he is my Lord, and knows not what he does——See how wild he looks.

Mel. By Heaven, 'twere fenfelefs not to be mad, and fee fuch witchcraft.

L. T. My Lord, you hear him, he talks idly.

Ld. T. Hence from my fight, thou living infamy to my name: when next I fee that face, I'll write villain in it with my fword's point.

Mel. Now, by my foul, I will not go 'till I have made known my wrongs——Nay, 'till I have made known yours, which (if poffible) are greater—though fhe has all the hoft of Hell her fervants.

L. T. Alas, he raves! ' Talks very poetry.' For Heaven's fake away my Lord, he'll either tempt you to extravagance, or commit fome himfelf.

Mel. Death and furies, will you not hear me—Why, by Heaven fhe laughs, grins, points to your back; fhe forks out cuckoldom with her fingers, and you are running horn-mad after your fortune.

　　　　[As fhe is going fhe turns back and fmiles at him.

Ld. T. I fear he's mad indeed—Let's fend Mafkwell to him.

Mel. Send him to her.

' *L. T.* Come, come, good my Lord, my heart achs ' fo, I fhall faint if I ftay.'　　　*[Exeunt Ld. and L. T.*

Mel. Oh, I could curfe my ftars, fate, and chance; all caufes and accidents of fortune in this life! But to what purpofe? ' Yet, 'fdeath, for a man to have the fruit of ' all his induftry grow full and ripe, ready to drop into ' his mouth, and juft when he holds out his hand to ga-' ther it, to have a fudden whirlwind come, tear up tree ' and all, and bear away the very root and foundation of ' his hopes; What temper can contain?' They talk of fending Mafkwell to me; I never had more need of him ——But what can he do? Imagination cannot form a fairer and more plaufible defign than this of his which has mifcarried——O my precious aunt! I fhall never thrive without I deal with the devil, or another woman.

' Women, like flames, have a deftroying pow'r,

' Ne'er to be quench'd 'till they themfelves devour.'

　　　　　　　　　　　　　　　　　[Exit.

END of the FOURTH ACT.

A C T

A C T   V.

Enter Lady Touchwood *and* Maſkwell.

LADY TOUCHWOOD.

WAS it not lucky?

Mask. Lucky! Fortune is your own, and 'tis her intereſt ſo to be; by Heaven I believe you can controul her power, and ſhe fears it; though chance brought my Lord, 'twas your own art that turned it to advantage.

L. T. 'Tis true, it might have been my ruin——But yonder's my Lord, I believe he is coming to find you, I'll not be ſeen.   [*Exit.*

Mask. So; I durſt not own my introducing my Lord, though it ſucceeded well for her, for ſhe would have ſuſpected a deſign which I ſhould have been puzzled to excuſe. My Lord is thoughtful—I'll be ſo too; yet he ſhall know my thoughts; or think he does——

Enter Lord Touchwood.

What have I done?

Ld. T. Talking to himſelf!

Mask. 'Twas honeſt—and ſhall I be rewarded for it? No, 'twas honeſt, therefore I ſhall not:—Nay, rather therefore I ought not; for it rewards itſelf.

Ld. T. Unequalled virtue!   [*Aſide.*

Mask. But ſhould it be known! then I have loſt a friend! He was an ill man, and I have gained; for half myſelf I lent him, and that I have recalled; ſo I have ſerved myſelf, and what is yet better, I have ſerved a worthy Lord, to whom I owe myſelf.

Ld. T. Excellent man!   [*Aſide.*

Mask. Yet I am wretched—O, there is a ſecret burns within this breaſt, which, ſhould it once blaze forth, would ruin all, conſume my honeſt character, and brand me with the name of villain.

Ld. T. Ha!

Mask. Why do I love! Yet Heaven and my waking conſcience are my witneſſes, I never gave one working thought a vent, which might diſcover that I loved, nor ever muſt; no, let it prey upon my heart; for I would rather die than ſeem once, barely ſeem, once diſhoneſt:—

O, ſhould

O, fhould it once be known I love fair Cynthia, all this that I have done would look like rival's malice, falfe friendfhip to my Lord, and bafe felf-intereft. Let me perifh firft, and from this hour avoid all fight and fpeech, and, if I can, all thought of that pernicious beauty. Ha! but what is my diftraction doing? I am wildly talking to myfelf, and fome ill chance might have directed malicious ears this way.   [*Seems to ftart, feeing my Lord.*

Ld. T. Start not——let guilty and difhoneft fouls ftart at the revelation of their thoughts, but be thou fixed, as is thy virtue.

Mask. I am confounded, and beg your Lordfhip's pardon for thofe free difcourfes which I have had with myfelf.

Ld. T. Come, I beg your pardon that I over-heard you, and yet it fhall not need—Honeft Mafkwell! Thy and my good genius led me hither—Mine, in that I have difcovered fo much manly virtue; thine, in that thou fhalt have due reward of all thy worth. Give me thy hand——my nephew is the alone remaining branch of all our ancient family; him I thus blow away, and conftitute thee in his room to be my heir——

Mask. Now Heaven forbid————

Ld. T. No more——I have refolved——The writings are ready drawn, and wanted nothing but to be figned, and have his name inferted—Yours will fill the blank as well——I will have no reply——Let me command this time, for 'tis the laft in which I will affume authority— hereafter you fhall rule where I have power.

Mask. I humbly would petition————

Ld. T. Is it for yourfelf? [Mafk. *paufes.*] I'll hear of nought for any body elfe.

Mask. Then witnefs Heaven for me, this wealth and honour was not of my feeking, nor would I build my fortune on another's ruin: I had but one defire——

Ld T. Thou fhalt enjoy it.——If all I am worth in wealth or intereft can purchafe Cynthia, fhe is thine.—— I am fure Sir Paul's confent will follow fortune; I will quickly fhew him which way that is going.

Mask. You opprefs me with bounty; my gratitude is weak, and fhrinks beneath the weight, and cannot rife to thank you——What, enjoy my love! Forgive the
tranf-

tranſports of a bleſſing ſo unexpected, ſo unhoped for, ſo unthought of !

Ld. T. I will confirm it, and rejoice with thee.

[*Exit.*

Mask. This is proſperous indeed !—Why, let him find me out a villain, ſettled in poſſeſſion of a fair eſtate, and full fruition of my love, I'll bear the railings of a loſing gameſter—But ſhould he find me out before !—'tis dangerous to delay—Let me think———Should my Lord proceed to treat openly of my marriage with Cynthia, all muſt be diſcovered, and Mellefont can be no longer blinded.—It muſt not be ; nay, ſhould my Lady know it———Ay, then were fine work indeed ! Her fury would ſpare nothing, though ſhe involved herſelf in ruin. No, it muſt be by ſtratagem——— I muſt deceive Mellefont once more, and get my Lord to conſent to my private management. He comes opportunely———Now will I, in my old way, diſcover the whole and real truth of the matter to him, that he may not ſuſpect one word on't.

    No maſk like open truth to cover lies,
    As to go naked is the beſt diſguiſe.
       Enter Mellefont.

Mel. O, Maſkwell, what hopes ? I am confounded in a maze of thoughts, each leading into another, and all ending in perplexity. My uncle will not ſee nor hear me.

Mask. No matter, Sir, don't trouble your head, all is in my power.

Mel. How, for Heaven's ſake ?

Mask. Little do you think that your aunt has kept her word——How the devil ſhe wrought my Lord into this dotage I know not ; but he is gone to Sir Paul about my marriage with Cynthia, and has appointed me his heir.

Mel. The devil he has ! What's to be done?

Mask. I have it, it muſt be by ſtratagem ; for it is in vain to make application to him. I think I have that in my head which cannot fail. Where is Cynthia?

Mel. In the garden.

Mask. Let us go and conſult her :—My life for yours, I cheat my Lord.

[*Exeunt.*
Enter

Enter Lord and Lady Touchwood.

L. T. Maſkwell your heir, and marry Cynthia!

Ld. T. I cannot do too much for ſo much merit.

L. T. But this is a thing of too great moment to be ſo ſuddenly reſolved. Why Cynthia? Why muſt he be married? Is there not reward enough in raiſing his low fortune, but he muſt mix his blood with mine, and wed my niece? How know you that my brother will conſent, or ſhe? Nay, he himſelf perhaps may have affections otherwhere.

Ld. T. No, I am convinced he loves her.

L. T. Maſkwell love Cynthia, impoſſible!

Ld. T. I tell you, he confeſſed it to me.

L. T. Confuſion! How is this!   [*Aſide.*

Ld. T. His humility long ſtifled his paſſion; and his love of Mellefont would have made him ſtill conceal it: but by encouragement I wrung the ſecret from him, and know he is no way to be rewarded but in her. I will defer my farther proceedings in it 'till you have conſidered it: but remember how we are both indebted to him.

    [*Exit.*

L. T. Both indebted to him! Yes, we are both indebted to him, if you knew all, ‘ villain!’ Oh, I am wild with this ſurprize of treachery: it is impoſſible, it cannot be——He love Cynthia! ‘ What, have I been ‘ bawd to his deſigns!’ his property only, ‘ a baiting- ‘ place! Now I ſee what made him falſe to Mellefont--- ‘ Shame and diſtraction! I cannot bear it, Oh! What ‘ woman can bear to be a property? To be kindled to a ‘ flame, only to light him to another’s arms: Oh! that ‘ I were fire indeed, that I might burn the vile traitor.’ What ſhall I do? How ſhall I think? I cannot think—— All my deſigns are loſt, my love unſated, my revenge unfiniſhed, and freſh cauſe of fury from unthought-of plagues.

Enter Sir Paul.

Sir P. Madam, ſiſter, my Lady ſiſter, did you ſee my Lady, my wife?

L. T. Oh! Torture!

Sir P. Gads-bud, I cannot find her high nor low; Where can ſhe be, think you?

L. T. Where ſhe is ſerving you as all your ſex ought

to

to be ferved; making you a beaft. Don't you know that
you are a fool, brother?

Sir P. A fool; he, he, he, you are merry—No, no,
not I, I know no fuch matter.

L. T. Why then you don't know half your happinefs.

Sir P. That's a jeft with all my heart, faith and troth
—But hark ye, my Lord told me fomething of a revolution of things; I don't know what to make on't——
Gads-bud I muft confult my wife——He talks of difin-
heriting his nephew, and I don't know what——Look
you, fifter, I muft know what my girl has to truft to;
or not a fyllable of a wedding, Gads-bud——to fhew you
that I am not a fool.

L. T. Hear me; confent to the breaking off this marriage, and the promoting any other, without confulting
me, and I will renounce all blood, all relation and concern with you for ever——Nay, I'll be your enemy, and
purfue you to deftruction; I'll tear your eyes out, and
tread you under my feet.——

Sir P. Why, what's the matter now? Good Lord,
what's all this for? Pooh, here's a joke indeed——Why,
where's my wife?

L. T. With Carelefs, in the clofe arbour; he may
want you by this time, as much as you want her.

Sir P. Oh, if fhe be with Mr. Carelefs, 'tis well
enough.

L. T. Fool, fot, infenfible ox! But remember what I
faid to you, or you had better eat your own horns, by
this light you had.

Sir P. You are a paffionate woman, Gads-bud——
But to fay truth, all our family are choleric; I am the
only peaceable perfon amongft them.   [*Exeunt.*

Enter Mellefont, Mafkwell, *and* Cynthia.

Mel. I know no other way but this he has propofed;
if you have love enough to run the venture.

Cyn. I don't know whether I have love enough——
but I find I have obftinacy enough to purfue whatever I
have once refolved; and a true female courage to oppofe
any thing that refifts my will, though it were reafon itfelf.

Mask. That's right——Well, I'll fecure the writings,
and run the hazard along with you.

Cyn.

Cyn. But how can the coach and fix horfes be got ready without fufpicion?

Mask. Leave it to my care; that fhall be fo far from being fufpected, that it fhall be got ready by my Lord's own order.

Mel. How?

Mask. Why, I intend to tell my Lord the whole matter of our contrivance, that's my way.

Mel. I do not underftand you.

Mask. Why, I'll tell my Lord I laid this plot with you on purpofe to betray you; and that which put me upon it, was the finding it impoffible to gain the lady any other way, but in the hopes of her marrying you.

Mel. So.————

Mask. So, why fo, while you are bufied in making yourfelf ready, I'll wheedle her into the coach; and inftead of you, borrow my Lord's chaplain, and fo run away with her myfelf.

Mel. O, I conceive you, you'll tell him fo.

Mask. Tell him fo! Ay, why, you don't think I mean to do fo.

Mel. No, no; ha, ha, I dare fwear thou wilt not.

Mask. Therefore, for our farther fecurity I would have you difguifed like a parfon, that if my Lord fhould have curiofity to peep, he may not difcover you in the coach, but think the cheat is carried on as he would have it.

Mel. Excellent Mafkwell! thou wert certainly meant for a ftatefman or a Jefuit———— but thou art too honeft for one, and too pious for the other.

Mask. Well, get yourfelves ready, and meet me in half an hour yonder in my Lady's dreffing-room; go by the back-ftairs, and fo we may flip down without being obferved————I'll fend the chaplain to you with his robes; I have made him my own—and ordered him to meet us to-morrow morning at St. Albans; there we will fum up this account to all our fatisfactions.

Mel. Should I begin to thank or praife thee, I fhould wafte the little time we have. [*Exit.*

Mask. Madam, you will be ready.

Cyn. I will be punctual to the minute. [*Going.*
                                          Mask.

Mask. Stay, I have a doubt—Upon second thoughts, we had better meet in the chaplain's chamber here, the corner chamber at this end of the gallery; there is a back way into it, so that you need not come through this door——and a pair of private stairs leading down to the stables——It will be more convenient.

Cyn. I am guided by you—but Mellefont will mistake.

Mask. No, no, I'll after him immediately, and tell him.

Cyn. I will not fail. [*Exit.*

Mask. Why, *qui vult decipi decipiatur.*—'Tis no fault of mine, I have told them in plain terms how easy it is for me to cheat them; and if they will not hear the serpent's hiss, they must be stung into experience and future caution.——Now to prepare my Lord to consent to this.————But first I must instruct my little Levite; there is no plot, public or private, that can expect to prosper without one of them has a finger in it; he promised me to be within at this hour—Mr. Saygrace, Mr. Saygrace. [*Goes to the chamber door, and knocks.*

[Mr. Saygrace *looking out.*] Sweet Sir, I will but pen the last line of an acrostick, and be with you in the twinkling of an ejaculation, in the pronouncing of an *Amen,* or before you can————

Mask. Nay, good Mr. Saygrace, do not prolong the time by describing to me the shortness of your stay; rather, if you please, defer the finishing of your wit, and let us talk about our business; it shall be tithes in your way.

Enter Saygrace.

Sayg. You shall prevail; I would break off in the middle of a sermon to do you a pleasure.

Mask. You could not do me a greater——except——— the business in hand————Have you provided a habit for Mellefont?

Sayg. I have; they are ready in my chamber, together with a clean starched band and cuffs.

Mask. Good: let them be carried to him——Have you stitched the gown-sleeve, that he may be puzzled, and waste time in putting it on?

Sayg. I have; the gown will not be indued without perplexity.

G

Mask.

Mask. Meet me in half an hour, here in your own chamber. When Cynthia comes, let there be no light; and do not speak, that she may not distinguish you from Mellefont. I'll urge haste to excuse your silence.

Sayg. You have no more commands?

Mask. None, your text is short.

Sayg. But pithy, and I will handle it with discretion.

Mask. It will be the first you have so served. [*Exeunt.*
     Enter Lord Touchwood and Maskwell.

Ld. T. Sure I was born to be controuled by those I should command: my very slaves will shortly give me rules how I shall govern them.

Mask. I am concerned to see your Lordship discomposed———

Ld. T. Have you seen my wife lately, or disobliged her?

Mask. No, my Lord.——What can this mean?
                                  [*Aside.*

Ld. T. Then Mellefont has urged somebody to incense her——Something she has heard of you, which carries her beyond the bounds of patience.

Mask. This I feared. [*Aside.*] Did not your Lordship tell her of the honours you designed me?

Ld. T. Yes.

Mask. 'Tis that; you know my Lady has a high spirit, she thinks I am unworthy.

Ld. T. Unworthy! 'Tis an ignorant pride in her to think so———Honesty to me is true nobility. However, 'tis my will it shall be so, and that should be convincing to her as much as reason———By Heaven, I'll not be wife-ridden! Were it possible, it should be done this night.

Mask. By Heaven he meets my wishes! [*Aside.*] Few things are impossible to willing minds.

Ld. T. Instruct me how this may be done, you shall see I want no inclination.

Mask. I had laid a small design for to-morrow (as love will be inventing) which I thought to communicate to your Lordship——But it may be as well done to-night.

Ld. T. Here is company——Come this way, and tell me.   [*Exeunt.*
                                     Enter

Enter Careless *and* Cynthia.

Care. Is not that he, now gone out with my Lord?

Cyn. Yes.

Care. By Heaven there's treachery——The confusion that I saw your father in, my Lady Touchwood's passion, with what imperfectly I overheard between my Lord and her, confirm me in my fears. Where's Mellefont?

Cyn. Here he comes.

Enter Mellefont.

——Did Maskwell tell you any thing of the chaplain's chamber?

Mel. No; my dear, will you get ready?—The things are all in my chamber; I want nothing but the habit.

Care. You are betrayed, and Maskwell is the villain I always thought him.

Cyn. When you were gone, he said his mind was changed, and bid me meet him in the chaplain's room, pretending immediately to follow you, and give you notice.

Care. There's Saygrace tripping by with a bundle under his arm—He cannot be ignorant that Maskwell means to use his chamber; let's follow and examine him.

Mel. 'Tis loss of time——I cannot think him false.

[*Exeunt* Mel. *and* Care.

Enter Lord Touchwood.

Cyn. My Lord musing!

Ld. T. He has a quick invention, if this were suddenly designed——Yet he says he had prepared my chaplain already.

Cyn. How is this! Now I fear, indeed.

Ld. T. Cynthia here! Alone, fair cousin, and melancholy?

Cyn. Your Lordship was thoughtful.

Ld. T. My thoughts were on serious business, not worth your hearing.

Cyn. Mine were on treachery concerning you, and may be worth your hearing.

Ld. T. Treachery concerning me! Pray, be plain—— Hark! What noise!

Mask. [*Within.*] Will you not hear me?

Lady T. [*Within.*] No, monster! Traitor! No.

Cyn. My Lady and Maſkwell! This may be lucky---
My Lord, let me intreat you to ſtand behind this ſcreen,
and liſten ; perhaps this chance may give you proof of
what you never could have believed from my ſuſpicions.
Enter Lady Touchwood, *with a dagger, and* Maſkwell :
   Cynthia *and Lord* Touchwood *abſcond, liſtening.*
   L. T. You want but leiſure to invent freſh falſhood,
and ſooth me to a fond belief of all your fictions ; but I
will ſtab the lie that's forming in your heart, and ſave a
ſin in pity to your ſoul.
   Mask. Strike then----ſince you will have it ſo.
   L. T. Ha ! a ſteady villain to the laſt !
   Mask. Come, why do you dally with me thus ?
   ' *L. T.* Thy ſtubborn temper ſhocks me, and you
' know it would----This is cunning all, and not cou-
' rage ; no, I know thee well----But thou ſhalt miſs
' thy aim.'
   Mask. Ha, ha, ha.
   L. T. Ha ! Do you mock my rage ? Then this ſhall
puniſh your fond, raſh contempt ! Again ſmile !
                                        [*Goes to ſtrike.*
And ſuch a ſmile as ſpeaks in ambiguity !
Ten thouſand meanings lurk in each corner of that various face.
O ! that they were written in thy heart,
That I, with this, might lay thee open to my ſight !
But then 'twill be too late to know----
Thou haſt, thou haſt found the only way to turn my
rage ; too well thou knoweſt my jealous ſoul could never
bear uncertainty.   Speak then, and tell me----Yet are
you ſilent ? Oh, I am wildered in all paſſions ! But thus
my anger melts. [*Weeps.*] Here, take this poniard, for
my very ſpirits faint, and I want ſtrength to hold it,
thou haſt diſarmed my ſoul.   [*Gives the dagger.*
   Ld. T. Amazement ſhakes me—Where will this end ?
   Mask. So 'tis well----let your wild fury have a vent,
and when you have temper, tell me.
   L. T. Now, now, now I am calm, and can hear you.
   Mask. [*Aſide.*] Thanks, my invention : and now I have
it for you.----Firſt tell me, what urged you to this violence ? For your paſſion broke out in ſuch imperfect
terms, that yet I am to learn the cauſe.
                                        L. T.

L. T. My Lord himself furprized me with the news, you were to marry Cynthia—That you had owned your love to him, and his indulgence would affift you to attain your ends.

Cyn. How, my Lord!

Ld. T. Pray forbear all refentments for a while, and let us hear the reft.

Mask. I grant you in appearance all is true; I feemed confenting to my Lord; nay, tranfported with the blef-fing——But could you think that I, who had been happy in your loved embraces, could e'er be fond of inferior flavery?

Cyn. Nay, good my Lord, forbear refentment, let us hear it out.

Ld. T. Yes, I will contain, though I could burft.

Mask. I that had wantoned in the rich circle of your world of love, could be confined within the puny province of a girl? No——Yet tho' I dote on each laft favour more than all the reft, though I would give a limb for every look you cheaply throw away on any other ob-ject of your love; yet fo far I prize your pleafures o'er my own, that all this feeming plot that I have laid, has been to gratify your tafte, and cheat the world, to prove a faithful rogue to you.

L. T. If this were true——But how can it be?

Mask. I have fo contrived, that Mellefont will prefent-ly, in the chaplain's habit, wait for Cynthia in your dreffing-room: but I have put the change upon her, that fhe may be otherwhere employed—Do you procure her night-gown, and with your hoods tied over your face, meet him in her ftead; you may go privately by the back-ftairs, and, unperceived, there you may propofe to reinftate him in his uncle's favour, if he will comply with your defires; his cafe is defperate, and I believe he'll yield to any conditions——If not, here, take this; you may employ it better than in the heart of one who is nothing when not yours.   [*Gives the dagger.*

L. T. Thou canft deceive every body——Nay, thou haft deceived me; but 'tis as I would wifh——Trufty villain! I could worfhip thee. ————

Mask. No more——it wants but a few minutes of the time; and Mellefont's love will carry him there before

L. T. I go, I fly, incomparable Maſkwell!-   [*Exit.*

Mask. So, this was a pinch indeed; my invention was, upon the rack, and made diſcovery of her laſt plot; I hope Cynthia and my chaplain will be ready. I'll prepare for the expedition.   [*Exit.*

Cynthia *and Lord* Touchwood *come forward.*

Cyn. Now, my Lord!

Ld. T. Aſtoniſhment binds up my rage! Villainy upon villainy! Heavens, what a long track of dark deceit has this diſcovered! I am confounded when I look back, and want a clue to guide me through the various mazes of unheard-of treachery. My wife! Damnation! My Hell!

Cyn. My Lord, have patience, and be ſenſible how great our happineſs is, that this diſcovery was not made too late.

Ld. T. I thank you, yet it may be ſtill too late, if we don't preſently prevent the execution of their plots :——. Ha! I'll do it. Where is Mellefont, my poor injured nephew? How ſhall I make him ample ſatisfaction?

Cyn. I dare anſwer for him.

Ld. T. I do him freſh wrong to queſtion his forgiveneſs, for I know him to be all goodneſs——Yet my wife! Damn her——She'll think to meet him in that dreſſing-room—Was't not ſo? And Maſkwell will expect you in the chaplain's chamber——For once I'll add my plot too——let us haſte to find out, and inform my nephew; and do you, quickly, as you can, bring all the company into this gallery.—I'll expoſe the ſtrumpet and the villain.   [*Exeunt.*

Enter Lord Froth *and Sir* Paul.

Ld. F. By Heavens, I have ſlept an age—Sir Paul, what o'clock is it? Paſt eight, on my conſcience, my Lady's is the moſt inviting couch, and a ſlumber there is the prettieſt amuſement! But where is all the company?

Sir P. The company, Gad's-bud, I don't know; my Lord; but here's the ſtrangeſt revolution, all turned topſy-turvy, as I hope for Providence.

Ld. F. O Heavens! What's the matter? Where is my wife?

Sir P. All turned topſy-turvy, as ſure as a gun.

Ld. F. How do you mean? My wife!

Sir. P.

Sir P. The ftrangeft pofture of affairs !

Ld. F. What, my wife ?

Sir P. No, no, I mean the family. Your Lady's affairs may be in a very good pofture ; I faw her go into,
the garden with Mr. Brifk.

Ld. F. How ? Where, when, what to do ?

Sir P. I fuppofe they have been laying their heads
together.

Ld. F. How ?

Sir P. Nay, only about poetry, I fuppofe, my Lord ;
making couplets.

Ld. F. Couplets.

Sir P. O, here they come.

Enter Lady Froth *and* Brifk.

Brisk. My Lord, your humble fervant ; Sir Paul,
yours ————The fineft night !

L. F. My dear, Mr. Brifk and I have been ftar-ga-
zing I don't know how long.

Sir P. Does it not tire your Ladyfhip ? Are not you
weary with looking up ?

L. F. Oh, no ! I love it violently————My dear,
you are melancholy.

Ld. F. No, my dear, I am but juft awake.

L. F. Snuff fome of my fpirit of hartfhorn.

Ld. F. I have fome of my own, thank you, my dear.

L. F. Well, I fwear, Mr. Brifk, you underftood
aftronomy like an old Egyptian.

Brisk. Not comparably to your Ladyfhip ; you are
the very Cynthia of the fkies, and queen of ftars.

L. F. That's becaufe I have no light ; but what's by
reflexion from you, who are the fun.

Brisk. Madam, you have eclipfed me quite, let me
perifh————I cannot anfwer that.

L. F. No matter————Harkee, fhall you and I make
an almanack together ?

Brisk. With all my foul, ————Your Ladyfhip has
made me the man in it already, I am fo full of the
wounds which you have given.

L. F. O, finely taken ! I fwear now you are even with
me ; O Parnaffus, you have an infinite deal of wit.

Sir P. So he has, Gads-bud, and fo has your Ladyfhip.

Enter

Enter Lady Plyant, Carelefs, *and* Cynthia.

L. P. You tell me moft furprizing things ; blefs me, who would ever truft a man ? O; my heart achs for fear they fhould be all deceitful alike.

Care. You need not fear, Madam, you have charms to fix inconftancy itfelf.

L. P. O dear, you make me blufh.

Ld. F. Come, my dear, fhall we take leave of my Lord and Lady ?

Cyn. They'll wait upon your Lordfhip prefently.

L. F. Mr. Brifk, my coach fhall fet you down.

All. What's the matter ?

[*A great fhriek from the corner of the ftage.*
Enter Lady Touchwood, *and runs out affrighted, my Lord after her, like a parfon.*

L. T. O, I'm betrayed——Save me, help me !

Ld. T. Now what evafion, ftrumpet ?

L. T. Stand off, let me go.

Ld. T. Go, and thy own infamy purfue thee----You ftare as you were all amazed——I do not wonder at it, ——But too foon you'll know mine, and that woman's fhame.

Enter Mellefont, *difguifed in a parfon's habit, and pul-ling in* Mafkwell.

Mel. Nay, by Heaven you fhall be feen——Carelefs, your hand—Do you hold down your head ? Yes, I am your chaplain ; look in the face of your injured friend, thou wonder of all falfhood.

Ld. T. Are you filent, monfter ?

Mel. Good Heavens ! How I believed and loved this man !—Take him hence, for he is a difeafe to my fight.

Ld. T. Secure that manifold villain.

[*Servants feize him.*

Care. Miracle of ingratitude !

Brisk. This is all very furprizing, let me perifh.

L. F. You know I told you Saturn looked a little more angry than ufual.

Ld. T. We'll think of punifhment at leifure, but let me haften to do juftice, in rewarding virtue and wronged innocence.——Nephew, I hope I have your pardon, and Cynthia's.

Mel. We are your Lordfhip's creatures.

Ld. T.

Ld. T. And be each other's comfort :----Let me join
your hands————Unwearied nights, and wishing days
attend you both ; mutual love, lasting health, and cir-
cling joys, tread round each happy year of your long
lives.

> Let secret villainy from hence be warn'd ;
> Howe'er in private mischiefs are conceiv'd,
> Torture and shame attend their open birth :
> Like vipers in the womb, base treachery lies
> Still gnawing that whence first it did arise ;
> No sooner born, but the vile parent dies.

[*Exeunt.*

END of the FIFTH ACT.

E P I-

EPILOGUE.

COULD poets but foresee how plays would take,
Then they could tell what epilogues to make ;
Whether to thank or blame their audience most :
But that late knowledge does much hazard cost,
'Till dice are thrown, there's nothing won, nor lost.
So 'till the thief has stol'n, he cannot know
Whether he shall escape the law, or no.
But poets run much greater hazards far,
Than they who stand their trials at the bar ;
The law provides a curb for its own fury,
And suffers judges to direct the jury.
But in this court, what diff'rence does appear !
For every one's both judge and jury here ;
Nay, and what's worse, an executioner.
All have a right and title to some part,
Each choosing that in which he has most art.
The dreadful men of learning all confound,
Unless the fable's good, and moral sound.
The vizor-masks that are in pit and gallery,
Approve or damn the repartee and raillery.
The lady critics, who are better read,
Inquire if characters are nicely bred ;
If the soft things are penn'd and spoke with grace :
They judge of action too, and time, and place ;
In which we do not doubt but they're discerning,
For that's a kind of assignation learning.
Beaus judge of dress ; the witlings judge of songs ;
The cuckoldom, of ancient right, to Cits belongs.
Thus poor poets the favour are deny'd,
Even to make exceptions, when they're try'd.
'Tis hard that they must every one admit :
Methinks I see some faces in the pit,
Which must of consequence be foes to wit.
You who can judge, to sentence may proceed ;
But tho' he cannot write, let him be freed,
At least, from their contempt who cannot read.

MISS POPE in the Character of ROSETTA.

THE
FOUNDLING.
A COMEDY,

As written by Mr. MOORE.

DISTINGUISHING ALSO THE

VARIATIONS OF THE THEATRE,

AS PERFORMED AT THE

Theatre-Royal in Drury-Lane.

Regulated from the Prompt-Book,

By PERMISSION of the MANAGERS,

By Mr. HOPKINS, Prompter.

LONDON:

Printed for JOHN BELL, near Exeter-Exchange, in the Strand.

MDCCLXXVII.

TO HER GRACE THE

DUCHESS

OF

BEDFORD.

MADAM,

THE permission your Grace honours me with, of presenting the Foundling to your protection, is the highest gratification of my pride, and my best security for the indulgence of the town. It is in writing as in life; an introduction to the world by a great name is a sanction, even where merit is wanting, and can adorn it where it is. And though my pretensions are inconsiderable, my fears are lessened, while I can boast the Duchess of Bedford for my patroness.

I have no intention to alarm your Grace with the common flattery of dedications. The mind that deserves praise, is above receiving it. Your own consciousness, though in your humblest hours, will afford truer satisfaction than the best written panegyric. But while your Grace forbids me praise, I am at liberty to indulge my wishes for your happiness and honour. In those, I may be allowed to name the Duke of Bedford with his Duchess, and to rejoice, with every Englishman, that the highest dignities are the reward of the highest merit.

If I descend to say a little of myself, I shall hope for your Grace's pardon. This is my first attempt in dramatic poetry. Whether I deserve the favour the town

A 2　　　　has

has shewn me, is submitted to your Grace's candour, and the judgment of my readers. The disapprobation which the character of Faddle met with the first night, made it necessary for me to shorten it in almost every scene, where it was not immediately connected with the fable. But though success has attended the alteration, I have ventured to publish it in its original dress; submitting it still to your Grace and the public, from whom I have no appeal to my own partiality. But I am detaining your Grace too long, and shall only add, that I am,

Madam,

Your Grace's

Most obliged, and

Most obedient servant,

E D W. M O O R E.

PROLOGUE.

Written by Mr. BROOKE.

UNPRACTIS'D in the drama's artful page,
   And new to all the dangers of the stage,
Where judgment sits to save or damn his play,
Our poet trembles for his first essay.
He, like all authors, a conforming race!
Writes to the taste and genius of the place;
Intent to fix, and emulous to please
The happy sense of these politer days,
He forms a model of a virtuous sort,
And gives you more of moral than of sport;
He rather aims to draw the melting sigh,
Or steal the pitying tear from beauty's eye;
To touch the strings that humanise our kind,
Man's sweetest strain, the music of the mind.
Ladies, he bids me tell you, that from you
His first, his fav'rite character, he drew;
A young, a lovely, unexperienc'd maid,
In honest truth and innocence array'd;
Of fortune destitute, with wrongs oppress'd,
By fraud attempted, and by love distress'd;
Yet, guarded still, and every suff'ring past,
Her virtue meets the sure reward at last.
From such examples shall the sex be taught,
How virtue fixes whom their eyes have caught;
How honour beautifies the fairest face,
Improves the mien, and dignifies the grace.
And hence the libertine, who builds a name
On the base ruins of a woman's fame,
Shall own, the best of human blessings lie
In the chaste honours of the nuptial tie;
There lives the homefelt sweet, the near delight,
There peace reposes, and there joys unite;
And female virtue was by Heav'n design'd
To charm, to polish, and to bless mankind.

DRA-

DRAMATIS PERSONÆ.

MEN.

		Drury-Lane.
Sir Roger Belmont,	—— ——	Mr. Yates.
Sir Charles Raymond,	—— ——	Mr. Bannister.
Young Belmont,	—— ——	Mr. Reddish.
Colonel Raymond,	—— ——	Mr. Packer.
Villiard,	—— ——	Mr. Bransby.
Faddle,	—— ——	Mr. Dodd.

WOMEN.

Rosetta,	—— ——	Miss Pope.
Fidelia,	—— ——	Miss Younge.

SCENE, Sir Roger Belmont's house in *LONDON.*

THE

THE
FOUNDLING.

⁂ The lines marked with inverted commas, 'thus,' are omitted in the representation.

ACT I.

SCENE, *an Apartment in* Sir Roger Belmont's *House.*

Enter Young Belmont *and* Col. Raymond.

BELMONT.

MY dear Colonel, you are as unlettered in love as I am in war. What, a woman, a fine woman, a coquette, and my sister!——and to be won by whining! Mercy on us! that a well-built fellow, with common sense, should take pains to unman himself, to tempt a warm girl of two-and-twenty to come to bed to him!—— I say, again, and again, Colonel, my sister's a woman.

Col. And the very individual woman that I want, Charles.

Bel. And of all women in the world, the least fit for thee. An April day is less changeable than her humour. She laughs behind her fan at what she should not understand; calls humility meanness, and blushing the want of education. In all affairs with a man, she goes by contraries; if you tell her a merry story, she sighs; if a serious one, she laughs; for yes, she says no, and for no, yes; and is mistress of such obedient features, that her looks are always ready to confirm what her tongue utters.

Col. Fine painting, upon my word, and no flattery!

Bel. This is the lady. Now for the lover. A fellow made up of credulity and suspicion; believing where he should doubt, and doubting where he should believe; jealous without cause, and satisfied without proof. A great
boy,

boy, that has loſt his way, and blubbering through every road, but the right, to find his home again ; ha, ha, ha !

Col. Mighty florid, indeed, Sir !

Bel. Come, come, Colonel ; Love, that can exalt the brute to a man, has ſet you upon all-fours. Women are indeed delicious creatures ; but not what you think them. The firſt wiſh of every mother's daughter is power, the ſecond miſchief : the way to her heart is by indifference, or abuſe ; for whoever owns her beauty, will feel her tyranny : but if he calls her ugly, or a fool, ſhe'll ſet her cap at him, and take pains for his good opinion.

Col. And ſo, ſubmiſſion and flattery are out of your ſyſtem ?

Bel. For ſubmiſſion and flattery, I ſubſtitute impudence and contradiction ; theſe two, well managed, my dear, will do more with beauty in an hour, than fine ſpeeches in a year. Your fine woman expects adoration, and receives it as common incenſe, which every fool offers ; while the rude fellow, who tells her truth, claims all her attention. Difficulty endears conqueſt. To him only ſhe appears what ſhe ſhould be to all ; and while ſhe labours with her natural charms to ſecure him, ſhe's loſt herſelf.

Col. Why, faith, Charles, there may be ſome muſic in theſe wild notes ; but I am ſo far gone in the old ballad, that I can ſing no other words to any tune.

Bel. Ha, ha ! Thou poor mournful nightingale in a cage, ſing on then ; and I'll whiſtle an upper part with thee, to give a little life to the meaſure.

Col. That will be kind ; for Heaven knows, I have need of aſſiſtance !—Pr'ythee, tell me, doſt think Roſetta wants underſtanding ?

Bel. N——o, faith, I think not.

Col. Good-humour ?

Bel. Hum——She's generally pleaſed.

Col. What then can reconcile her behaviour to me, and her fondneſs for ſuch a reptile as Faddle ? A fellow made up of knavery and noiſe, with ſcandal for wit, and impudence for raillery ; and ſo needy, that the very devil might buy him for a ſingle guinea. I ſay, Charles, what can tempt her even to an acquaintance with this fellow ?

Bel. Why, the very underſtanding and good-humour

you

you fpeak of. A woman's underftanding is defign, and her good-humour mifchief. Her advances to one fool are made only to teize another.

Col. Sir, your moft humble fervant.

Bel. And her good-humour is kept alive by the fuccefs of her plots.

Col. But why fo conftant to her fool?

Bel. Becaufe her fool's the fitteft for her purpofe——He has more tricks than her monkey, more prate than her parrot, more fervility than her lap-dog, more lies than her woman, and more wit than her—Colonel. And faith, all thefe things confidered, I can't blame my fifter for her conftancy.

Col. Thou art a wild fellow, and in earneft about nothing but thy own pleafures—and fo we'll change the fubject. What fays Fidelia?

Bel. Why, there, now!—That a man can't inftruct another, but he muft be told, by way of thanks, how much he ftands in need of affiftance himfelf!

Col. Any new difficulties?

Bel. Mountains, Colonel, a few mountains in my way. But if I want faith to remove them, I hope I fhall have ftrength to climb them, and that will do my bufinefs.

Col. She's a woman, Charles.

Bel. By her outfide one would guefs fo; but look a little farther, and, except the ftubbornnefs of her temper, fhe has nothing feminine about her. She has wit without pertnefs, beauty without confcioufnefs, pride without infolence, and defire without wantonnefs. In fhort, fhe has every thing ——

Col. That you would wifh to ruin in her. Why, what a devil are you, Charles, to fpeak fo feelingly of virtues, which you only admire to deftroy!

Bel. A very pretty comforter, truly!

Col. Come, come, Charles, if fhe is as well born as you pretend, what hinders you from cherifhing thefe qualities in a wife, which you would ruin in a miftrefs? Marry her, marry her.

Bel. And hang myfelf in her garters the next morning, to give her virtues the reward of widowhood. Faith, I muft read Pamela twice over firft. But fuppofe her not

born

born as I pretend, but the outcaft of a beggar, and obliged to chance for a little education.

Col. Why, then her mind is dignified by her obfcurity; and you will have the merit of raifing her to a rank which fhe was meant to adorn. And where's the mighty matter in all this? You want no addition to your fortune, and have only to facrifice a little unneceffary pride to neceffary happinefs.

Bel. Very heroical, upon my word! And fo, my dear Colonel, one way or other, I muft be married, it feems.

Col. If Fidelia can be honeft, my life on't, you are of my mind within this fortnight. But, pr'ythee, fince I am not to believe your former account of her, who is this delicious girl, that muft and will get the better of your pride?

Bel. A fifter of the Graces, without mortal father or mother; fhe dropped from the clouds in her cradle, was lulled by the winds, chriftened by the rains, foftered by a hag, fold for a whore, fentenced to a rape, and refcued by a rogue—to be ravifhed by her own confent. There's myftery and hieroglyphic for you! and every fyllable, my dear, a truth, beyond apocrypha.

Col. And what am I to underftand by all this?

Bel. Faith, juft as much as your underftanding can carry. A man in love is not to be trufted with a fecret.

Col. And, pray, moft difcreet Sir, is Rofetta acquainted with her real hiftory?

Bel. Not a circumftance. She has been amufed, like you, and ftill believes her to be the fifter of a dead friend of mine at college, bequeathed to my guardianfhip. But the devil, I find, owes me a grudge, for former virtues; for this fifter of mine, who doats upon Fidelia, and believes every thing I have told her of her family and fortune, has very fairly turned the tables upon me. She talks of equality of birth, forfooth; of virtue, prudence, and good fenfe; and bids me blefs my ftars for throwing in my way the only woman in the world that has good qualities enough to redeem my bad ones, and make me, what fhe fays every man ought to be—a good hufband.

Col. Was ever poor innocent fellow in fuch diftrefs!— But what fays the old gentleman, your father?

Bel.

Bel. Why, faith, the certainty of a little money would set him at work the same way——But I'll have one trial of skill with them yet.——As I brought her in by one lie, I'll take her out by another——I'll swear she's a whore——that I may get an opportunity to make her one.

Col. Most religiously resolved, upon my word!

Bel. Between you and me, Colonel, has not your old gentleman, Sir Charles, a liquorish look out for Fide-delia himself?

Col. No, upon my honour. I believe his affiduities there, are more to prevent the designs of another, than to forward any of his own.

Bel. As who should say, because I have no teeth for a crust, I'll muzzle the young dog that has. A pox of every thing that's old, but a woman!—for 'tis but varying her vocation a little, and you may make her as useful at fif-ty-five, as fifteen. But what say you to a little chat with the girls this morning? I believe we shall find them in the next room.

Col. Not immediately———I have an appointment at White's.

Bel. For half an hour, I am your man there too.— D'ye return so soon?

Col. Sooner, if you will.

Bel. With all my heart. *Alons!* [*Exeunt.*

SCENE, Another Apartment.

Enter Rosetta and Fidelia meeting.

Ros. O, my dear! I was just coming to see if you were dressed. You look as if you had pleasant dreams last night.

Fid. Whatever my dreams were, they can't disturb the morning's happiness, of meeting my dear Rosetta so gay and charming.

Ros. My sweet creature!———But what were your dreams?

Fid. O, nothing—A confusion of gay castles, built by Hope, and thrown down by Disappointment.

Ros. O barbarous! Well, for my part, I never built a castle in my sleep, that would not last till doomf-day. Give me a dream, and I am mistress of the crea-

tion. I can do what I will with every man in it—And
power, power, my dear, sleeping or waking, is a charming thing !

Fid. Now, in my opinion, a woman has no business
with power——— Power admits no equal, and dismisses
friendship for flattery. Besides, it keeps the men at a
distance, and that is not always what we wish.

Ros. But then, my dear, they'll come when we call
them, and do what we bid them, and go when we send
them——There's something pretty in that, sure—And
for flattery—take my word for't, 'tis the highest proof
of a man's esteem—'Tis only allowing one what one has
not, because the fellow admires what one has—And she,
that can keep that, need not be afraid of believing she
has more.

Fid. Ay, if she can keep that. But the danger is,
in giving up the substance for the shadow. Come,
come, my dear, we are weak by nature; and 'tis but
knowing that we are so, to be always upon our guard.
Fear may make a woman strong, but confidence un-
does her.

Ros. Ha ! ha ! How different circumstances direct different opinions ! You are in love with a rake of a fellow, who makes you afraid of yourself——And I hold
in chains a mighty Colonel, who's afraid of me. And
so, my dear, we both go upon right principles. Your
weakness keeps you upon your guard, and my power
leaves me without danger.

Fid. And yet you must forgive me, if I tell you, that
you love this Colonel.

Ros. Who told you so, my dear creature ?

Fid. I know it by the pains you take to vex him. Besides, I have seen you look as if you did.

Ros. Look, child ! Why don't I look like other people ?

Fid. Ay, like other people in love. Oh, my dear,
I have seen just such looks in the glass, when my heart
has beat at my very lips.

Ros. Thou art the most provoking creature—

Fid. You must pardon me, Rosetta——I have a heart
but little inclined to gaiety ; and am rather wondering,
that when happiness is in a woman's power, she should

neglect

neglect it for trifles—or how it should ever enter her thoughts, that the rigour of a mistress can endear the submission of a wife.

Rof. As certain, my dear, as the repentance of a sinner out-weighs in opinion the life of a saint. But, to come to serious confession, I have, besides a woman's inclination to mischief, another reason for keeping off a little——I am afraid of being thought mercenary.

Fid. Hey day!—why, are you not his equal every way?

Rof. That's not it—I have told you, that before his father's return from exile—You know his unhappy attachments to a succesless party—This Colonel (brough up in our family, and favoured by Sir Roger and my brother) laid violent siege to me for a whole year. Now, tho' I own I never disliked him, in all that time, either thro' pride, folly, or a little mischief, I never gave him the least hint, by which he could guess at my inclinations.

Fid. Right woman, upon my word!

Rof. 'Tis now about three months, since the king in his goodness recalled Sir Charles; and, by restoring the estate, made the Colonel heir to a fortune, more than equal to my expectations. And now, to confess all, the airs that Folly gave me before, Reason bids me continue ——for to surrender my heart at once to this new-made commander, would look as if the poor Colonel had wanted a bribe for the governor. Besides, he has affronted my pride, in daring to imagine I could descend so low, as to be fond of that creature, Faddle. A fellow, formed only to make one laugh—a cordial for the spleen, to be bought by every body; and just as necessary in a family as a monkey. For which insolence, I must and will be revenged.

Fid. Well, I confess, this looks a little like reason. But are you sure, all this while, the Colonel, in despair, won't raise the siege, and draw off his forces to another place?

Rof. Pshah! I have a better opinion of the men, child. Do but ply them with ill usage, and they are the gentlest creatures in the world. ' Like other beasts of ' prey, you must tame them by hunger—but if once ' you feed them high, they are apt to run wild, and for- ' get their keepers.'

B

Fid.

Fid. And are all men so, Rosetta?

Rof. By the gravity of that question, I'll be whipped now, if you don't expect me to say something civil of my brother---Take care of him, Fidelia, 'for hunger 'can't tame him, nor fulness make him wilder.'——To leave you to his guardianship, was setting the fox to keep the chicken.

Fid. Wild as he is, my heart can never beat to another ---And then I have obligations, that would amaze you.

Rofet. Obligations!—Let me die, if I would not marry my Colonel's papa, and put it out of his power to oblige, or disoblige me.

Fid. Still you banter me with Sir Charles—Upon my life, he has no more designs upon me than you have—I know no reason for his friendship, but his general humanity, or perhaps the particularity of my circumstances.

Rofet. Why, as you say, youth and beauty are particular circumstances to move humanity—Ha, ha, ha!—Oh, my dear, time's a great tell-tale, and will discover all—What a sweet mamma shall I have, when I marry the Colonel!

Enter Young Belmont, *and the* Colonel.

Bel. When you marry the Colonel, sister!—A match, a match, child!—Here he is, just in the nick; and, faith, as men go, very excellent stuff for a husband.

Col. Those were lucky words, Madam.

Rofet. Perhaps not so lucky, if you knew all, Sir.— Now, or never, for a little lying, Fidelia, if you love me.
[Apart to Fid.

Fid. I'll warrant you, my dear—You must know, Sir, [*To* Bel.] that your sister has taken it into her head, that the Colonel's father is my lover.

Rofet. What is she going to say now?   [*Afide.*

Fid. And as she looks upon herself to be as good as married to the Colonel.

Rofet. Who I!—I!—

Fid. She has been settling some family affairs with her new mamma here: and upon my word, she's a sweet contriver.

Rof. And you think I won't be even with you for this, Fidelia?

Bel. Sister!

Col.

Col. And was it fo, Madam ?—And may I hope ?

Rof. Was it fo, Madam ?—And may I hope ? [*Mocking him.*] No, Sir, it was not fo, and you may not hope. —Do you call this wit, Fidelia ?

Fid. My dear creature, you muft allow me to laugh a little—Ha, ha, ha !

Rof. 'Tis mighty well, Madam---Oh, for a little devil at my elbow now, to help out invention. [*Afide.*

Bel. Ha, ha, ha !---Won't it come, fifter?

Rof. As foon as your manners, brother. You and your grave friend there, have been genteelly employed indeed, in liftening at the door of a lady's chamber : and then, becaufe you heard nothing for your purpofe, to turn my own words to a meaning, I fhould hate myfelf for dreaming of.

Bel. Why, indeed, child, we might have perplexed you a little, if Fidelia had not fo artfully brought you off.

Rof. Greatly obliged to her, really.

[*Walking in diforder.*

Col. I never knew till now, Rofetta, that I could find a pleafure in your uneafinefs.

Rof. And you think, Sir, that I fhall eafily forgive this infolence ? But you may be miftaken, Sir.

Bel. Poor thing, how it pants ! Come, it fhall have a hufband ! We muft about it immediately, Colonel, for fhe's all over in a flame.

Rof. You grow impertinent, brother. Is there no relief ? [*Afide.*

Bel. Shall I lift up the fafh for a little air, child ?

Enter Servant.

Rof. So, John !---Have you delivered the card, I gave you ?

Serv. Yes, Madam ; and Mr. Faddle defires his compliments to your Ladyfhip, and Madam Fidelia.

Rof. Mr. Faddle, John !——Where did you fee him ?

Serv. He met me in the ftreet, Madam, and made me ftep into a coffee-houfe with him, 'till he wrote this, Madam. [*Delivers a letter, and Exit.*

Rof. Oh, the kind creature !---Here's a letter from Mr. Faddle, Fidelia !---Fortune, I thank thee for this little refpite. [*Afide, and reading the letter.*

Col. Does fhe fuffer the fool to write to her too ?

B 2

Fid.

Fid. What, pining, Colonel, in the midſt of victory?

Col. To receive his letters, Madam!---I ſhall run mad.

Bel. So!---Away prop, and down ſcaffold ---All's over, I ſee.

Roſ. Oh, Fidelia!---You ſhall hear it---You ſhall all hear it---And there's ſomething in't about the Colonel too.

Col. About me, Madam.   [*Peeviſhly.*

Roſ. Nay, Colonel, I am not at all angry now.   Methinks th's letter has made me quite another creature.— To be ſure, Mr. Faddle has the moſt gallant way of writing! But his own words will ſpeak beſt for him. [*Reads.*

   " Dear creature,

   " Since I ſaw you yeſterday, time has hung upon me like a winter in the country; and unleſs you appear at rehearſal of the new opera this morning, my ſun will be in total eclipſe for two hours. Lady Fanny made us laugh laſt night, at What's my Thought like, by comparing your Colonel to a great box o' the ear---Becauſe it was very rude, ſhe ſaid, and what nobody cared for---I have a thouſand things to ſay, but the clamour of a coffee-houſe is an interruption to the ſentiments of love and veneration, with which I am,

           " Madam, moſt unſpeakably yours,

               " WM. FADDLE."

——Is it not very polite, Colonel?

Col. Extremely, Madam!---Only a little out as to the box o' the ear : for you ſhall ſee him take it, Madam, as careleſsly as a pinch of ſnuff.

Roſ. Fie, Colonel! You would not quarrel before a lady, I hope. Fidelia, you muſt oblige me with your company to rehearſal---I'll go put on my capuchin, and ſtep into the coach, this moment.

Fid. I am no friend to public places; but I'll attend you, Madam.

Roſ. You'll come, Colonel?

Col. To be ſure, Madam.

Bel. Siſter!---Oh, you're a good creature!

           [*Exit* Roſetta, *laughing affectedly.*

Fid. Shall we have your company, Sir?   [*To* Bel.

Bel. We could find a way to employ time better, child ——But I am your ſhadow, and muſt move with you
                         every

every where. [*Exit* Fidelia.]——Ha, ha, ha !——How
like a beaten general doſt thou look now !——while the
enemy is upon the march, to proclaim *Te Deum* for a
complete victory.

Col. I am but a man, Charles, and find myſelf no
match for the devil and a woman.

Bel. Courage, boy !—and the fleſh and the devil may
be ſubdued—Ha, ha, ha !—Such a colonel !   [*Exit.*

‘ *Col.* Why this it is to be in love !——Well !——Let
‘ me but ſlip my leading-ſtrings !—and if ever I am a
‘ woman’s baby again !——

‘ To cheat our wiſhes nature meant the ſex,

‘ And form’d them, leſs to pleaſe us, than perplex.

‘ [Exit.’

END of the FIRST ACT.

ACT II.

SCENE *continues.*

Enter Sir Roger Belmont, *and Sir* Charles Raymond.

SIR ROGER.

A Voracious young dog !—Muſt I feed ortolans to
pamper his gluttony !

Sir Char. Be under no apprehenſions, Sir Roger ; Mr.
Belmont’s exceſſes are mitigated by the levity of youth,
and a too early indulgence. In his moments of thinking, I know him generous and noble—And for Fidelia !
——I think I can be anſwerable for her conduct, both in
regard to what ſhe owes herſelf, and you.

Sir Ro. Why, look you, Sir Charles, the girl’s a ſweet
girl, and a good girl—and beauty’s a fine thing, and virtue’s a fine thing——But as for marriage !——Why—a
man may buy fine things too dear.—A little money, Sir
Charles, would ſet off her beauty, and find her virtue employment—But the young rogue does not ſay a word of
that, of late.

Sir Cha. Nor of marriage, I am ſure——His love of
liberty will prevent your fears one way ; and, I hope,
Fidelia’s honour, another.

B 3

Sir

Sir Ro. Muſt not have her ruined though!

Sir Char. Fear it not, Sir Roger——And when next you ſee your ſon, be a little particular in your enquiries about her family and circumſtances—If ſhe is what her behaviour beſpeaks her, and he pretends, a lady of birth and fortune—why, ſecrets are unneceſſary : if he declines an explanation, look upon the whole as a contrivance to cover purpoſes, which we muſt guard againſt.

Sir Ro. What you don't think the rogue has had her, hah, Sir Charles ?

Sir Char. No, upon my honour——I hold her innocence to be without ſtain——But to deal freely with my friend, I look upon her ſtory, as ſtrange and improbable. —An orphan, of beauty, family, and fortune ; committed by a dying brother to the ſole care of a licentious young fellow !—You muſt pardon me, Sir Roger.

Sir Ro. Pray go on, Sir.

Sir Char. Brought in at midnight too!——And then a young creature, ſo educated, and ſo irreſiſtibly amiable, to be, in all appearance, without alliance, friend, or acquaintance in the wide world !——a link, torn off from the general chain !——I ſay, Sir Roger, this is ſtrange.

Sir Ro. By my troth, and ſo it is !

Sir Char. I know not why I am ſo intereſted in this lady's concerns ; but yeſterday, I indulged my curioſity with her, perhaps, beyond the bounds of good-manners —I gave a looſe to my ſuſpicion, and added oaths of ſecrecy to my enquiries. But her anſwers only ſerved to multiply my doubts ; and ſtill as I perſiſted, I ſaw her cheeks covered with bluſhes, and her eyes ſwimming in tears——But my life upon't, they were the bluſhes and the tears of innocence !

Sir Ro. We muſt and will be ſatisfied, Sir Charles.

Sir Char. For who knows, while we are delaying, but ſome unhappy mother, perhaps, of rank too, may be wringing her hands in bitterneſs of miſery for this loſt daughter.—Girls, who have kept their virtue, Sir Roger, have done mad things for a man they love.

Sir Ro. And ſo indeed they have——I remember when I was a young fellow myſelf——But is not that my Charles coming through the hall yonder ?

Sir Char. Ay, Sir Roger. Attack him now—But let.

L

your.

your enquiries have more the shew of accidental chat than
design; for too much earnestness may beget suspicion——
And so, Sir, I leave you to your discretion.   [*Exit.*

Sir Ro. You shall see me again before dinner——A pox
of these young, rakehelly rogues!—a girl's worth twenty
of them—if one could but manage her.

    Enter Young Belmont, *repeating;*

Bel. No warning of th' approaching flame,
    Swiftly like sudden death, it came;
    Like mariners, by lightning kill'd,
    I burnt the moment————
My dear Sir, I have not seen you to-day before!

Sir Ro. What, studying poetry, boy, to help out the
year's allowance?

Bel. Faith, Sir, times are hard—and unless you come
down with a fresh hundred now and then, I may go near
to disgrace your family——and turn poet.

Sir Ro. And so want friends all thy life after! But now
we talk of money, Charles, what art thou doing with
Fidelia's money?—I am thinking, that a round sum
thrown into the stocks now, might turn to pretty tolerable account.

Bel. The stocks, Sir?

Sir Ro. Ay, boy. My broker will be here after dinner, and he shall have a little chat with thee, about laying out a few of her thousands.

Bel. I hope, he'll tell us where we shall get these
thousands.   [*Aside.*

Sir Ro. Thou dost not answer me, Charles—Art dumb,
boy?

Bel. Why, to be sure, Sir, as to that——Fidelia——
I can't say, but that she may——However, that is, you
know, Sir——If as to possibility——Will your broker
be here after dinner, Sir?

Sir Ro. Take a little time, Charles; for at present,
thou dost not make thyself so clearly understood.

Bel. Quite right, to be sure, Sir—Nothing could, beyond all doubt, be more judicious, or more advantageous,
—Her interest, Sir—why as to that—a pretty fortune—
but—did you know her brother, Sir?

Sir Ro. Who I, child?——No.

Bel. Faith, nor I neither. [*Aside.*]—Not know, Jack,
                    Sir?

Sir ?——The rogue would have made you laugh.——Did I never read you any of his epigrams ?—But then he had such an itch for play !—Why he would set you a whole fortune at a caft !—And such a mimic too !—but no œconomy in the world—— Why, it coft him a cool fix thoufand, to ftand for member once—— Oh, I could tell you such ftories of that election, Sir——

Sir Ro. Pr'ythee, what borough did he ftand for ?

Bel. Lord, Sir !——He was flung all to nothing—— My Lord What-d'ye-call-um's fon carried it fifteen to one, at half the expence——In fhort, Sir, by his extravagance, affairs are fo perplexed, fo very intricate, that upon my word, Sir, I declare it, I don't know what to think of them——A pox of thefe queftions !   [*Afide.*

Sir Ro. But fhe has friends and relations, Charles :—I fancy, if I knew who they were, fomething might be done.

Bel. Yes, yes, Sir, fhe has friends and relations——I fee, Sir, you know nothing of her affairs—Such a ftring of them !——The only wife thing her brother ever did, was making me her guardian, to take her out of the reach of thofe wretches——I fhall never forget his laft words ——Whatever you do, my dear Charles, fays he, taking me by the hand, keep that girl from her relations. Why, I would not for a thoufand pounds, Sir, that any of them fhould know where fhe is.

Sir Ro. Why, we have been a little cautious, Charles ——But where does the eftate lie ?

Bel. Lord, Sir !——an eftate and no eftate——I wonder a man of your knowledge would afk the queftion.— An earthquake may fwallow it for any thing I care.

Sir Ro. But where does it lie, Charles ?——In what county, I fay ?

Bel. And then there's the fix thoufand pounds, that her father left her——

Sir Ro. What, that gone too, Charles ?

Bel. Juft as good, I believe——Every fhilling on't in a lawyer's hands.

Sir Ro. But fhe is not afraid to fee him too, Charles ? ——Where does he live ?

Bel. Live, Sir !——Do you think fuch a fellow ought to live ?—Why he has trumpt up a contract of marriage

with

with this girl, Sir, under the penalty of her whole fortune
—There's a piece of work for you!

Sir Ro. But has he no name, Charles?———What is
he called, I say?

Bel. You can't call him by any name, that's too bad for
him—But if I don't draw his gown over his ears—why
say, I am a bad guardian, Sir—that's all.

Sir Ro. If this should be apocryphal now?

Bel. Sir?

Sir Ro. A fetch! a fib, Charles!———to conceal some
honeſt man's daughter, that you have ſtolen, child!

Bel. And brought into a ſober family, to have the entire poſſeſſion of, without lett, or moleſtation?———Why,
what a deal of money have you laviſhed away, Sir, upon
the education of a fool?

Sir Ro. There is but that one circumſtance to bring
thee off———For to be ſure, her affairs might have been as
well ſettled in private lodgings—And beſides, Charles, a
world of troubleſome queſtions, and lying anſwers, might
have been ſaved. But take care, boy;—for I may be in
the ſecret before thou art aware on't———A great rogue,
Charles!   [*Exit.*

Bel. So! The mine's ſprung, I ſee———and Fidelia has
betrayed me. And yet, upon cooler thoughts, ſhe durſt
not break her word with me; for though ſhe's a woman, the devil has no part in her———Now will I be
hanged, if my loving ſiſter is not at the bottom of all this
———But if I don't out-plot her!———Let me ſee!———
Ay———Faddle ſhall be called in———for the fool loves
miſchief like an old maid; and will out-lie an attorney.

Enter Roſetta.

Roſet. What, muſing, brother!———Now would I fain
know, which of all the virtues has been the ſubjeƈt of
your contemplations?

Bel. Patience, patience, child———for he that has con-
neƈtion with a woman, let her be wife, miſtreſs, or ſiſter,
muſt have patience.

Roſet. The moſt uſeful virtue in the world, brother!
—and Fidelia ſhall be your tutoreſs———I'll hold ſix to
four, that ſhe leads you into the practice on't with more
dexterity, than the beſt philoſopher in England———She
ſhall

shall teach it, and yet keep the heart without hope, brother.

Bel. Why that's a contrary method to yours, fifter;— for you give hope, where you mean to try patience moft ——and I take it, that you are the abler miftrefs in the art. Why every coxcomb in town has been your fcholar, child.

Rofet. Not to learn patience—there's your miftake now; for it has been my conftant practice, to put my fcholars out of all patience. What are you thinking of, brother?

Bel. Why, I was thinking, child, that 'twould be a queftion to puzzle a conjurer, what a coquette was made for?

Rofet. Am I one, brother?

Bel. Oh, fie, fifter!

Rofet. Lord! I, that am no conjurer, can tell you that ——A coquette!——Oh!—Why, a coquette is a fort of beautiful defert in wax-work, that tempts the fool to an entertainment, merely to baulk his appetite.——And will any one tell me, that nature had no hand in the making a coquette, when fhe anfwers fuch wife and neceffary purpofes?—Now, pray, Sir, tell me what a rake was made for?

Bel. Am I one, fifter?

Rofet. Oh, fie, brother!

Bel. Nay, child, if a coquette be fo ufeful in the fyftem of morals, a rake muft be the moft horrid thing in nature——He was born for her deftruction, child——fhe lofes her being at the very fight of him——and drops plump into his arms, like a charmed bird into the mouth of a rattle-fnake.

Rofet. Blefs us all!——What a mercy it is, that we are brother and fifter!

Bel. Be thankful for't night and morning upon your knees, huffy——for I fhould certainly have been the ruin of you——But come, Rofetta——'tis allowed then that we are rake and coquette—And now, do you know, that the effential difference between us lies only in two words——petticoat and breeches.

Rofet. Ay, make that out, and you'll do fomething.

Bel. Pleafure, child, is the bufinefs of both——and
the

the same principles, that make me a rake, would make you——no better than you should be——were it not for that tax upon the petticoat, called Scandal. Your wishes are restrained by fear; mine, authorised by custom: and while you are forced to sit down with the starved comfort of making men fools, I am upon the wing to make girls——women, child.

Roset. Now, as I hope to be married, I would not be a rake for the whole world—unless I were a man; and then I do verily believe, I should turn out just such another.

Bel. That's my dear sister! Give me your hand, child. ——Why now thou art the honestest girl in St James's parish——and I'll trust thee for the future with all my secrets——I am going to Fidelia, child.

Roset. What a pity 'tis, brother, that she is not such a coquette as I am?

Bel. Not so neither, my sweet sister; for, faith, the conquest would be too easy to keep a man constant.

Roset. Civil creature!

Bel. But here comes the Colonel——Now to our several vocations———You to fooling, and I to business—— At dinner we'll meet, and compare notes, child.

Roset. For a pot of coffee, I succeed best.

Bel. Faith, I'm afraid so.   [*Exit.*

Enter the Colonel.

Col. To meet you alone, Madam, is a happiness—

Roset. Pray, Colonel, are you a rake? Methinks I would fain have you a rake.

Col. Why so, Madam?——'Tis a character I never was fond of.

Roset. Because I am tired of being a coquette—and my brother says, that a rake can transform one, in the flirt of a fan.

Col. I would be any thing, Madam, to be better in your opinion.

Roset. If you were a rake now, what would you say to me?

Col. Nothing, Madam——I would———
[*Snatches her hand, and kisses it.*

Roset. Bless me !—— is the man mad!——I only asked what you would say to me?

Col.

Col. I would fay, Madam, that you are my life, my foul, my angel!——That all my hopes of happinefs are built upon your kindnefs!

Rofet. Very well!——keep it up!

Col. That your fmiles are brighter than virtue, and your chains fweeter than liberty!

Rofet. Upon my word!

Col. Oh, Rofetta!——How can you trifle fo with a heart that loves you?

Rofet. Very well!——Pathetic too!

' *Col.* Nay, nay, this is carrying the jeft too far—If ' you knew the fituation of my mind, you would not tor-
' ture me thus.

' *Rofet.* Situation of the mind!——Very geographi-
' cal!——Go on!

' *Col.* Pfhah!——This is not in your nature.

' *Rofet.* Sufpicion!——pretty enough!

' *Col.* You know I have not deferved this.

' *Rofet.* Anger too!'——Go on!,

Col. No, Madam,——Faddle can divert you this way at an eafier price.

Rofet. And jealoufy!——All the viciffitudes of love!——Incomparable!

Col. You will force me to tell you, Madam, that I can bear to be your jeft no longer.

Rofet. Or thus————

Am I the jeft of her I love!
Forbid it all the gods above!

——It may be rendered either way——But I am for the rhyme——I love poetry vaftly—Don't you love poetry, Colonel?

Col. This is beyond all patience, Madam.

[*Very angrily.*

Rofet. Blefs me!—Why, you have not been in earneft, Colonel?——Lord, Lord, how a filly woman may be miftaken!

Col. Shall I afk you one ferious queftion, Madam?

Rofet. Why, I find myfelf fomewhat whimfical this morning—and I don't care if I do take a little ftuff——but don't let it be bitter.

Col. Am I to be your fool always, Madam, or, like

other

other fools, to be made a hufband of, when my time's out ?

Rofet. Lord, you men-creatures do afk the ftrangeft queftions !—Why how can I poffibly fay now, what I. fhall do ten years hence ?

Col. I am anfwered, Madam.   [*Walking in diforder.*

Enter Servant.

Serv. Mr. Faddle, Madam.   [*Exit.*

Enter Faddle.

Fad. Oh, my dear, foft toad !——And the Colonel, by all that's fcarlet !—Now pox catch me, if nature ever formed fo complete a couple——fince the firft pair in Paradife.

Rofet. 'Tis well you are come, Faddle—Give me fomething to laugh at, or I fhall die with the fpleen.

Col. Ay, Sir, make the lady laugh this moment, or I fhall break your bones, rafcal.

Fad. Lord, Colonel !—What !—What !—hah !—

Col. Make her laugh this inftant, I fay, or I'll make you cry—Not make her laugh, when fhe bids you !——Why, firrah !——I have made her laugh this half hour, without bidding.

Rofet. Ha, ha, ha !

Fad. Why there, there, there, Colonel !—She does, fhe does, fhe does !——

Enter young Belmont, *and* Fidelia.

Bel. Why, how now, Faddle !——What has been the matter, pr'ythee ?

Col. A rafcal !——Not make a lady laugh

Fad. What, Charles, and my little Fiddy, too !—Stand by me a little——for this robuft Colonel has relaxed my very finews, and quite tremulated my whole fyftem.—— . I could not have collected myfelf, without your prefence.

Fid. And was he angry with you, Faddle ?

Fad. To a degree, my dear——But I have forgot it— I bear no malice to any one in the world, child.

Rofet. Do you know, Faddle, that I have a quarrel with you too ?

Fad. You, child !—Heh ! heh !—What, I am inconftant, I fuppofe—and have been the ruin of a few families this winter, hah, child ?—Murder will out, though it's done in the centre——But come, *vivace !* Let the

ftorm

storm loofe———and you fhall fee me weather it, like the ofier in the fable———It may bend, but not break me.

Rofet. Nay, it fhall come in a breeze———I'll whifper it.   [*Whifpers* Faddle.

Bel. Colonel!

Col. Now I could cut my throat, for being vexed at this puppy : and yet the devil, jealoufy, will have it fo.
                    [*Apart to* Belmont.

Fad. Oh, what a creature have you named, child !—— Heh, heh, heh !———May grace renounce me, and darknefs feal my eye-lids, if I would not as foon make love to a millener's doll.

Bel. Pr'ythee, what miftrefs has fhe found out for thee, Faddle ?

Fad. By all that's odious, Charles, Mifs Gargle, the 'pothecary's daughter : the toad is fond of me, that's pofitive : but fuch a mefs of water-gruel !—Ugh !—— To all purpofes of joy, fhe's an armful of dry fhavings ! And then fhe's fo jealous of one ! Lord, fays fhe, Mr. Faddle, you are eternally at Sir Roger's ; one can't fet eyes upon you in a whole day---Heh, heh ! And then the tears do fo trickle down thofe white-wafh cheeks of hers, that if fhe could but warm me to the leaft fit of the heart-burn, I believe I fhould be tempted to take her, by way of chalk and water.---Heh, heh, heh !

Bel. ⎫
Rof. ⎬ Ha, ha, ha !
Fid. ⎭

Rof. Ifn't he a pleafant creature, Colonel ?

Col. Certainly, Madam, of infinite wit, with abundance of modefty.

Fad. Pugh !—Pox of modefty, Colonel ! But do you know, you flim toad you, [*To* Rofet.] what a battle I had laft night, in a certain company, about you, and that ugly gipfy there ?

Fid. Meaning me, Sir ?

Fad. Pert, and pretty !—You muft know, there was Jack Taffety, Billy Cruel, Lord Harry Gymp, and I, at Jack's lodgings, all in tip-top fpirits, over a pint of Burgundy—A pox of all drinking though ! I fhall never get it out of my head.—Well, we were toafting a round of beauties, you muft know ; the girl of your heart, Faddle,
                              fays

says my Lord. Rosetta Belmont, my Lord, says I—and, faith, down you went, you delicate devil you, in almost half a glass.——Rot your toast, says my Lord, I was fond of her last winter.——She's a wit, says Jack; and a scold, by all that's noisy, says Billy.——Isn't she a little freckled, says my Lord? Damnationly padded, says Jack; and painted like a Dutch doll, by Jupiter, says Billy. She's very unsusceptible, says my Lord. No more warmth than a snow-ball, says Jack.—A mere cold-bath to a lover, curse catch me, says Billy.---Heh, heh, heh! Says I, that's because you want heart to warm her, my dears: to me now, she's all over combustibles; I can electrify her by a look: touch but her lip, and snap she goes off in a flash of fire.

Ros. Oh, the wretch! what a picture has he drawn of me! ˌ   [*To* Fidelia.

Fid. You must be curious, my dear.

Bel. Ha, ha! But you forget Fidelia, Faddle.

Fad. Oh!——And there's the new face, says Billy---Fidelia, I think they call her.——If she was an appurtenance of mine, says my Lord, I'd hang her upon a peg in my wardrobe, amongst my cast clothes.—With those demure looks of hers, says Jack, I'd send her to my aunt in Worcestershire, to set her face by, when she went to church. Or what think you, says Billy, of keeping her in a show-glass, by way of---Gentlemen and Ladies, walk in, and see the curiosity of curiosities——the perfect Pamela in high life! Observe, gentlemen, the blushing of her cheeks, the turning up of her eyes, and her tongue, that says nothing but fie! fie!——Ha, ha, ha!——Incomparable! said all three——Pugh, pox, says I, not so bad as that neither: the little toad has not seen much of the town indeed: but she'll do in time; and a glass of Preniac may serve one's turn, you know, when Champaign is not to be had.   [*Bowing to* Rosetta.

All. Ha, ha, ha!

' *Bel.* Why, thou didst give it them, faith, bully.

' *Fid.* I think, Rosetta, we were mighty lucky in an
' advocate.

' *Ros.* Prodigious!

' *Fad.* Poor toads!---Oh!---I had forgot: you left
' the rehearsal of the new opera this morning in the most
                ' un-

‘ unlucky time ! The very moment you were gone, souse
‘ came into the pit, my friend the alderman and his fat
‘ wife, tricked out in sun-shine : you must know, I drank
‘ chocolate with them in the morning, and heard all the
‘ ceremony of their proceedings---Sir Barnaby, says my
‘ Lady, I shall wear my pink and silver, and my best
‘ jewels; and, d’ye hear ? Do you get Betty to tack on
‘ your Dresdens, and let Pompey comb out the white tie,
‘ and bring down the blue coat lined with buff, and the
‘ brown silk breeches, and the gold-headed cane : I think
‘ as you always wear your coat buttoned, that green
‘ waistcoat may do; but ’tis so besmeared, that I vow it’s
‘ a filthy sight with your night-gown open : and as you
‘ go in the coach with me, you may get your white
‘ stockings aired——But you are determined never to
‘ oblige me with a pair of roll-ups upon these occasions,
‘ notwithstanding all I have said. We are to mix with
‘ quality this morning, Mr. Faddle, and it may be proper
‘ to let them know as how, there are people in the city,
‘ who live of the Westminster side of Wapping. Your
‘ Ladyship’s perfectly in the right, Madam, says I——
‘ [*Stifling a laugh.*] and for fear of a horse-laugh in her
‘ face, slap-dash, I made a leg, and brushed off like light-
‘ ning.

‘ *All.* Ha, ha, ha !’

Enter Servant, *and whispers* Rosetta.

Rof. Come, gentlemen, dinner waits——We shall have
all your companies, I hope.

Bel. You know, you dine with me at the King’s-Arms,
Faddle.   [*Apart to* Faddle.

Fad. Do I ? I am sorry, my dear creature, that a particular appointment robs me of the honour. [*To* Rosetta.

Rof. Pshah ! you are always engaged, I think. Come,
Fidelia.   [*Exeunt* Rosetta *and* Fidelia.

Col. Why then, thank heaven, there’s some respite !
                                                          [*Exit.*

Bel. Hark you, Faddle ; I hope you are not in the least
ignorant, that upon particular occasions, you can be a
very great rascal ?

Fad. Who I, Charles ?—Pugh !—Pox !—Is this the
dinner I am to have ?

Bel. Courage, boy ! And because I think so well of
                                                          thee,

thee, there : [*Gives him a purse.*] 'twill buy thee a new laced coat, and a feather.

Fad. Why ay, this is fomething, Charles. But what am I to do, hah? I won't fight, upon my foul, I won't fight.

Bel. Thou canft lie a little.

Fad. A great deal, Charles, or I have fpent my time among women of quality to little purpofe.

Bel. I'll tell thee then. This fweet girl, this angel, this ftubborn Fidelia, fticks fo at my heart, that I muft either get the better of her, or run mad.

Fad. And fo thou wouldft have me aiding and abetting, hah, Charles? Muft not be tucked up for a rape neither.

Bel. Peace, fool! About three months ago, by a very extraordinary adventure, this lady dropped into my arms. It happened that our hearts took fire at firft fight ——But as the devil would have it, in the hurry of my firft thoughts, not knowing where to place her, I was tempted, for fecurity, to bring her to this haunted houfe here, where, between the jealoufy of Sir Charles, the gravity of the Colonel, the curiofity of a fifter, and the awkward care of a father, fhe muft become a veftal, or I—a hufband.

Fad. And fo, by way of a little fimple fornication, you want to remove her to private lodgings, hah, Charles?

Bel. But how, how, how—thou dear rafcal?

Fad. Let me fee——Hum——And fo, you are not her guardian, Charles?

Bel. Nor fhe the woman fhe pretends, boy——I tell thee, fhe was mine by fortune——I tilted for her at midnight——But the devil tempted me, I fay, to bring her hither——The family was in bed, which gave me time for contrivance——I prevailed upon her to call me guardian——that by pretending authority over her, I might remove her at pleafure——But here too I was deceived——My fifter's fondnefs for her has rendered every plot of mine to part them impracticable ——And without thy wicked affiftance, we muft both die in our virginity.

C 3 *Fad.*

Fad. Hum! That would be a pity, Charles————
But let me fee——Ay——I have it.——Within thefe
three hours, we'll contrive to fet the houfe in fuch a
flame, that the devil himfelf may take her——if he ftand
at the ftreet-door————To dinner, to dinner, boy! 'Tis
here, here, here, Charles!

Bel. If thou doft————

Fad. And if I don't——why no more purfes, Charles.
———— I tell thee, 'tis here, here, boy! To dinner, to
dinner!   [*Exeunt.*

END of the SECOND ACT.

A C T   III.

SCENE *continues.*

Enter Rofetta *and* Fidelia.

FIDELIA.

'TIS all your own doing, my dear. You firft teize
him into madnefs, and then wonder to hear his
chains rattle.

Rof. And yet how one of my heavenly fmiles fobered
him again!

Fid. If I were a man, you fhould ufe me fo but once,
Rofetta.

Rof. Pfhah!——If you were a man, you would do, as
men do, child——Ha, ha, ha!——They are creatures
of robuft conftitutions, and will bear a great deal————
Befides, for my part, I can't fee what a reafonable fellow ought to expect before marriage, but ill ufage.——
You can't imagine, my dear, how it fweetens kindnefs
afterwards——' 'Tis bringing a poor ftarved creature to
' a warm fire, after a whole night's wandering through
' froft and fnow.

' *Fid.* But, to carry on the image, my dear——won't
' he be apt to curfe the tongue that mifguided him; and
' take up with the firft fire he meets with, rather than
' perifh in the cold?————I could fing you a fong,
' Rofetta, that one would fwear was made o' purpofe
' for you.

                                            ' *Rof.*

I

‘ *Rof.* O, pray let me hear it.

‘ SONG, Fidelia.

‘ I.

‘ For a ſhape, and a bloom, and an air, and a mien,
‘ Myrtilla was brighteſt of all the gay green ;
‘ But artfully wild, and affectedly coy,
‘ Thoſe her beauties invited, her pride would deſtroy.

II.

‘ By the flocks, as ſhe ſtray’d with the nymphs of the
      vale,
‘ Not a ſhepherd but woo’d her to hear his ſoft tale ;
‘ Tho’ fatal the paſſion, ſhe laugh’d at the ſwain,
‘ And return’d with neglect, what ſhe heard with diſdain.

III.

‘ But beauty has wings, and too haſtily flies,
‘ And love, unrewarded, ſoon ſickens and dies.
‘ The nymph cur’d, by time, of her folly and pride,
‘ Now ſighs in her turn for the bliſs ſhe den‚’d.

IV.

‘ No longer ſhe frolicks it wide o’er the plain,
‘ To kill with her coyneſs the languiſhing ſwain ;
‘ So humbled her pride is, ſo ſoften’d her mind,
‘ That, tho’ courted by none, ſhe to all would be kind.

  ‘ *Rof.* Pſhah !———there’s a ſong indeed !———You
‘ ſhould ſing of men’s perjuries, my dear———of kind
‘ nymphs, and cloy’d ſhepherds’———For, take my word
for’t, there’s no charm like cruelty, to keep the men
conſtant ; nor no deformity like kindneſs, to make them
loath you.
               Enter Servant.
Serv. A letter for your Ladyſhip, Madam.   *[Exit.*
Rof. For me ? I don’t remember the hand.
          [Opens and reads the letter to herſelf.
                  ‘ *Fid.*

Fid. ' I have little inclination to be chearful, tho' I
' sing songs, and prattle thro' the whole day—Belmont !
' Belmont ! [*Aside.*] ' You seem strangely concerned,
Madam——I hope no ill news ?

Rof. The worst in the world, Fidelia, if it be true.

Fid. Pray Heaven it be false then !—But must it be a
secret ?—I hope, my dear Rosetta knows, that whatever
affects her quiet, can't leave mine undisturbed.

Rof. Who's there ?

Enter Servant.

How did you receive this letter ?

Ser. From a porter, Madam.

Rof. Is he without ?

Ser. No, Madam ; he said it required no answer.

Rof. Had you any knowledge of him ?

Ser. Not that I remember, Madam.

Rof. Should you know him again ?

Ser. Certainly, Madam.

Rof. Where did my brother say he dined to-day ?

Ser. At the King's-Arms, Madam.

Rof. And Mr. Faddle with him ?

Ser. They went out together, Madam.

Rof. Run this moment, and say I desire to speak with
both of them immediately, upon an extraordinary affair.

Ser. Yes, Madam.   [*Exit.*

Fid. What can this mean, Rosetta ?———Am I unfit
to be trusted ?

Rof. Tell me, Fidelia—But no matter—Why should I
disturb you ?—I have been too grave.

Fid. Still more and more perplexing !———But my enquiries are at an end———I shall learn to be less troublesome, as you are less kind, Rosetta.

Rof. Pr'ythee don't talk so, Fidelia———I can never be
less kind.

Fid. Indeed, I won't deserve you should.

Rof. I know it, Fidelia.———But tell me then.—Is there
a circumstance in your life, that would call a blush to
your cheeks, if 't'were laid as open to the world's knowledge, as to your own ?

Fid. If from the letter you ask me that strange question, Madam, surely I should see it.

Rof.

Rof. I think not, Fidelia—For, upon fecond thoughts, 'tis a trifle, not worth your notice.

Fid. Why were you fo much alarmed then ?

Rof. I confefs, it ftartled me at firft—But 'tis a lying letter, and fhould not trouble you.

Fid. Then it relates to me, Madam ?

Rof. No matter, Fidelia.

Fid. I have loft my friend then—I begged at firft, to be a fharer in Rofetta's griefs—but now I find they are all my own, and fhe denies my right to them.

Rof. This is too much, Fidelia——And now to keep you longer in fufpenfe would be cruelty——But the writer of this fcroll has a mind darker than night. You fhall join with me in wondering, that there is fuch a mon-fter in the world. [*Reads.*

To *Mifs* Rofetta Belmont.

Madam,

As I write without a name, I am alike indifferent to your thanks or refentment.——Fidelia is not what fhe feems——She has deceived you, and may your brother, to his ruin.—Women of the town know how to wear the face of innocence, when it ferves the purpofes of guilt. ——Faddle, if he pleafes, can inform you farther—— But be affured, I have my intelligence from more fuffi-cient authority.

P. S. There needs no farther addrefs in this matter, than a plain queftion to Fidelia—Is fhe the fifter of Mr. Belmont's friend ?

Fid. Then I am loft ! [*Afide.*

Rof. What, in tears, Fidelia ?—Nay, I meant to raife your contempt only—Pr'ythee, look up, and let us laugh at the malice of this namelefs libeller.

Fid. No, Rofetta——The mind muft be wrapt in its own innocence, that can ftand againft the ftorms of ma-lice—I fear, I have not that mind.

Rof. What mind, Fidelia ?

Fid. And yet that letter is a falfe one.

Rof. Upon my life, it is——For you are innocence itfelf.

Fid.

Fid. Oh, Rosetta!——No sister of Mr. Belmont's friend kneels to you for pardon——but a poor wretched out-cast of fortune, that with an artful tale has imposed upon your nature, and won you to a friendship for a helpless stranger, that never knew herself.

Rof. Rise, Fidelia—But take care!—For if you have deceived me, honesty is nothing but a name.

Fid. Think not too hardly of me neither——For tho' I am not what I seem, I would not be what that letter calls me, to be mistress of the world.

Rof. I have no words, Fidelia——Speak on——But methinks you should not weep so.

Fid. Nay, now, Rosetta, you compel me—For this gentleness is too much for me—I have deceived you, and you are kind——If you would dry up my tears, call forth your resentment——Anger might turn me into stone—but compassion melts me.

Rof. I have no anger, Fidelia —— Pray go on.

Fid. When my tears will let me——I have played a foolish game, Rosetta—and yet my utmost fault has been consenting to deceive you.—What I am, I know not—— That I am not what I seem, I know.—But why I have seemed otherwise than I am, again I know not.—'Tis a riddle, that your brother only can explain.——He knows the story of my life, and will in honour reveal it. Would he were here!

Rof. Would he were, Fidelia!—for I am upon the rack—Pr'ythee, go on, and inform me farther.

Fid. There's my grief, Rosetta—For I am bound by such promises to silence, that to clear my innocence, would be to wound it——All I have left to say is, that my condition of life only has been assumed, my virtue never.

Enter Servant.

Rof. Well, Sir!

Ser. Mr. Belmont, Madam, was just gone; but Mr. Faddle will wait upon your Ladyship immediately.

Rof. Did they say where my brother went?

Ser. They did not know——Mr. Faddle is here, Madam.   [*Exit.*
Enter

Enter Faddle, *humming a tune.*

Fad. In obedience to your extraordinary commands, Madam——But you should h ve been alone, child.

Rof. No trifling, Sir——Do you know this hand-writing?   [*Gives him the letter.*

Fad. Hum!——Not I, as I hope to be faved——Nor you neither, I believe. [*Afide.*]——Is it for my perufal, Madam?

Fid. And your anfwering too, Sir.

Fad. Mighty well, Madam. [*Reads.*] Hum!—Fidelia—Women—of the town—Innocence—Guilt——Faddle inform you farther!——Why, what a-pox am I brought in for?——Intelligence—Queſtion—Fidelia ?——Siſter of Mr. Belmont's friend.
                [*Stares and whiſtles.*

Rof. Well, Sir!   [*Takes the letter.*

Fad. Oh!—I am to guefs at the writer—Can't, upon my foul——Upon my foul, I can't, child——'Tis a woman, I believe tho', by the damned blabbing that's in't.

Fid. The letter fays, Sir, that you can inform this lady farther concerning me.—Now, Sir, whatever you happen to know, or to have heard of me, deliver it freely, and without difguife.—I entreat it, as an act of friendfhip, that will for ever oblige me.

Fad. Let me fee——No——It can't be her neither—She is a woman of too much honour—and yet, I don't remember to have opened my lips about it, to any foul but her.

Fid. You know me then, Sir?

Rof. Speak out, Sir.

Fad. Methinks, if thefe letter-writers were a little more communicative of their own names, and lefs fo of their neighbours; there would be more honeſty in them, —Why am I introduced here!—Truly, forfooth, becaufe a certain perfon in the world is overburthened with the fecrets of her own flips, and for a little vent, chufes to blab thofe of another—Faddle inform you farther! Faddle will be damned as foon.

Rof. Hark you, Sir—If you intend to enter thefe doors again, tell me all you know, for I will have it. You have owned your telling it elfewhere, Sir.

                                        Fid.

Fid. What is it you told, Sir?

Fad. What I shan't tell here, Madam. Her angry ladyship must excuse me, faith.

Ros. 'Tis very well, Sir!

Fid. Indeed, Rosetta, he knows nothing.

Fad. Nothing in the world, Madam, as I hope to be saved. Mine is all hear-say. And, curse upon them! the whole town may be in a lie, for any thing I know. So they said of Lady Bridget, that she went off with her footman; but 'twas all slander, for 'twas a horse grenadier, that she bought a commission for last week.

Ros. What has Lady Bridget, or the town, to do with Fidelia, Sir?

Fad. So I said, Madam—the very words. Says I, a woman of the town? Does a slip or two with particulars make a lady a woman of the town? Or if it did, says I, many a one has taken up, and lived honestly afterwards. A woman of the town indeed!

Fid. Hold your licentious tongue, Sir! Upon my life, Rosetta, 'tis all malice. 'Tis his own contrivance. I dare him to produce another villain, that's base enough to say this of me.

Fad. Right, Madam! Stick to that, and 'egad, I'll be of your side.   [*Aloud in her ear.*

Fid. Insolence! [*Strikes him.*] Oh, I am hurt beyond all bearing!

Ros. And I, lost in perplexity. If thou art linked with any wretch base enough to contrive this paper, or art thyself the contriver, may poverty and a bad heart, be thy companions: but if thou art privy to any thing, that concerns the honour of this family, give it breath, and I'll insure thee both protection and reward.

Fid. I dare him to discovery.

Fad. Ladies, I have had the honour of a blow conferred on me by one of you, and am favoured with the offer of protection and reward from the other; now to convince both, that, in spite of indignities, or obligations, I can keep a secret, if ever I open my lips upon this matter, may plague, famine, and the horned devil consume and seize me. And so, ladies, I take my leave.

                              [*Exit singing.*
                                   Ros.

Rof. What can this fellow mean, Fidelia? Has he not abufed you?

Fid. Is it a doubt then? Would I had leave to fpeak!

Rof. And why not, Fidelia? Promifes unjuftly extortsd, have no right to obfervance. You have deceived me, by your own acknowledgment, and methinks, at fuch a time, matters of punctilio fhould give place to reafon and neceffity.

Fid. I dare not, Rofetta. 'Twould be a crime to your brother, and I owe him more than all the world.

Rof. And what are thofe obligations, Fidelia?

Fid. Not for me to mention. Indeed, I dare not, Rofetta.

Rof. 'Tis well, Madam! And when you are inclined to admit me to your confidence, I fhall perhaps know better how to conduct myfelf.　　[*Going.*

Enter Young Belmont, *meeting her.*

Oh, are you come, brother! Your friend's fifter, your ward there, has wanted you, Sir.

Bel. What is it, Fidelia?

Fid. I have no breath to fpeak it. Your fifter, Sir, can better inform you.

Rof. Read that, Sir.

[*Gives him the letter, which he reads to himfelf.*

Fid. Now, Rofetta, all fhall be fet right. Your brother will do me juftice, and account for his own conduct.

Rof. I expect fo, Fidelia.

Bel. Impertinent! [*Gives back the letter.*] I met Faddle as I came in, and I fuppofe in pure love of mifchief, he has made my believing fifter here, a convert to the villainy of that letter. But I'll make the rafcal unfay every thing he has faid, or his bones fhall ake for't.

[*Going.*

Fid. Stay, Sir, I entreat you. That I am a counterfeit, in part, I have already confeffed——

Bel. You have done wrong then.

Fid. But am I a creature of the town, Sir? Your fifter muft learn that from you. You have been once my deliverer—be fo now. Tell her, I am poor and miferable, but not difhoneft. That I have only confented to

D　　deceive

deceive her, not defired it. Tell her, I deferve her pity, not her anger. 'Tis my only requeft. Can you deny it me?

Bel. You have faid too much, Fidelia. And for your own fake, I fhall forbear to mention what I know of your ftory. How far your own honour is bound, you are the beft judge. But a breach of the moft folemn promifes, let me tell you, Madam, will be a wretched vindication of the innocence you contend for.

Fid. And is this all, Sir?

Bel. For my own part, I muft have better authority than Faddle, or a namelefs writer, to believe any thing to your difhonour. And for you, fifter, I muft not have this lady ill-treated. While I am fatisfied of her inno-cence, your fufpicions are impertinent. Nor will I con-fent to her removal, Madam, mark that, whatever you, in your great wifdom, may have privately determined.
[*Exit.*

Rof. You are a villain, brother.

Fid. Now I have loft you, Rofetta!

Rof. When you incline to be a friend to yourfelf, Fi-delia, you may find one in me. But while explanations are avoided, I muft be allowed to act from my own opinion, and agreeable to the character I am to fupport.
[*Exit.*

Fid. Then I am wretched! But that's no novelty. I have wandered from my cradle, the very child of mif-fortune. To retire and weep, muft now be my only in-dulgence.
[*Exit.*

Enter Belmont.

Bel. Why, what a rogue am I! Here have I thrown a whole family, and that my own too, into perplexities, that innocence can't oppofe, nor cunning guard againft. And all for what? Why, a woman—Take away that excufe, and the devil himfelf would be a faint to me; for all the reft is finning without temptation. In my com-merce with the world, I am guarded againft the mer-cenary vices.—I think, I have honour above lying, courage above cruelty, pride above meannefs, and ho-nefly above deceit; and yet, throw but coy beauty in my way, and all the vices, by turns, take poffeffion of
me.

me. Fortune, Fortune, give me succefs this once——
and I'll build churches !

Enter Faddle.

Fad. What, Charles—Is the coaft clear, and the finifhing ftroke given to my embaffy, hah ?

Bel. Thou haft been a moft excellent rafcal, and faith,
matters feem to be in a promifing condition. For I have
flung that in Rofetta's way, which if fhe keeps her wo-
manhood, will do the bufinefs.

Fad. Pr'ythee, what's that, Charles ?

Bel. Why, I have bid her not to think of parting with
Fidelia.

Fad. Nay, then, tip fhe goes headlong out at window. But haft thou no bowels, Charles ? for, methinks, I begin to feel fome twitches of compunction
about me.

Bel. I underftand you, Sir ; but I have no more
purfes.

Fad. Why, look you, Charles, we muft find a way to
lull this confcience of mine—here will be the devil to do
elfe. That's a very pretty ring, Charles.

Bel. Is it fo, Sir ? Hark you, Mr. Dog, if you de-
mur one moment to fetching and carrying in this bufinefs, as I bid you, you fhall find my hand a little heavy
upon you.

Fad. Pugh, pox, Charles ! can't a body fpeak ? People may be in good-humour, when they want people to
do things for people, methinks.

Bel. Troop this moment, with your rafcally confcience to the King's Arms, and wait there till I come,
Sir.

Fad. Why fo I will, Charles——A pox of the fwag-
gering fon of a—Not fo big neither, if one had but a little courage. *[Afide and going.*

Bel. Hark you, Faddle—Now I think on't, there is
a way yet for thee to make another purfe out of this
bufinefs.

Fad. Why, one would not be a rogue for nothing,
methinks.

Bel. I faw Sir Charles going into Fidelia's chamber—
thou mayeft fteal upon them unobferved—they'll have
their plots too, I fuppofe.

D 2

Fad.

Fad. And where am I to come and tell thee, hah ?

Bel. At the King's Arms, boy.

Fad. But you'll remember the purse, Charles.

Bel. Softly, rascal ! [*Exit* Fad.] Why there it is again now ! I am a fellow of principle ! and so I will be, some time or other. But these appetites are the devil, and at present I am under their direction.   [*Exit.*

SCENE, *Another Apartment.*

Sir Charles *and* Fidelia *discovered sitting.*

Sir Cha. He durst not say, directly, you were that creature the letter called you !

Fid. Not in terms, Sir ; but his concealments struck deeper than the sharpest accusations.

Sir Cha. And could Mr. Belmont be silent to all this ?

Fid. He said he had his reasons, Sir, and it was my part to submit. I had no heart to disoblige him.

Sir Cha. You are too nice, Madam. Rosetta loves you, and should be trusted.

Fid. Alas, Sir ! if it concerned me only, I should have no concealment.

Sir Cha. It concerns you most, Madam. I must deal plainly with you. You have deceived your friend ; and, tho' I believe it not, a severer reproach rests upon you. And shall an idle promise, an extorted one too, and that from a man who solicits your undoing, forbid your vindication ? You must think better of it.

Fid. 'Tis not an extorted promise, Sir, that seals my lips—but I love him—and tho' he pursues me to my ruin, I will obey him in this, whatever happens. He may desert me, but never shall have reason to upbraid me.

Sir Cha. 'Tis your own cause, Madam, and you must act in it as you think proper. Yet still, if I might advise———

Fid. Leave it to time, Sir Charles. And if you believe me innocent, your friendly thoughts of me, and my own conscience, shall keep me chearful.

Enter Faddle, *listening.*

Fad. O, pox, is it so ! Now for a secret worth twenty pieces !

Sir

Sir Cha. Has it ever appeared to you, Madam, that Faddle was a confidant of Mr. Belmont's?

Fid. Never, Sir. On the contrary, a wretch most heartily defpifed by him.

Fad. If fhe fhould be a little miftaken now.   [*Afide.*

Sir Cha. Can you guefs at any other means of his coming to a knowledge of you?

Fid. None that I know of, Sir.

Fad. Faith, I believe her.   [*Afide.*

Sir Cha. One queftion more, Madam, and I have done. Did Mr. Belmont ever folicit your removing from this houfe?

Fid. Never directly, Sir. He has often, when we have been alone, quarrelled with himfelf for bringing me into it.

Sir Cha. I thank you, Madam. And if my enquiries have been at any time too importunate, allow them to the warmth of an honeft friendfhip: for I have a heart that feels for your diftreffes, and beats to relieve them.

Fid. I have no words, Sir Charles; let my tears thank you.

Sir Cha. Be compofed, my child. And if Rofetta's fufpicions grow violent, I have apartments ready to receive you, with fuch welcome, as virtue fhould find with one who loves it.

Fid. Still, Sir Charles, my tears are all that I can thank you with——for this goodnefs is too much for me.

Fad. And fo fhe's a bit for the old gentleman at laft! Rare news for Charles! or with a little addition I fhall make it fo. But I muft decamp, to avoid danger.
                              [*Afide, and exit.*

Sir Cha. Dry up your tears, Fidelia. For, if my conjectures are well grounded, before night, perhaps, fomething may be done to ferve you. And fo I leave you to your beft thoughts.   [*Exit.*

Fid. Then I have one friend left. How long I am to hold him, Heaven knows. 'Tis a fickle world, and nothing in it is lafting, but misfortune——yet I'll have patience;

D 3

That

That fweet relief, the healing hand of Heav'n
Alone to fuff'ring innocence has giv'n ;
Come, friend of virtue, balm of every care,
Dwell in my bofom, and forbid defpair.　　　[*Exit.*

END of the THIRD ACT.

ACT IV.

SCENE, *An Apartment.*

Enter Colonel *and* Rofetta.

ROSETTA.

I Tell you, I will not be talked to.

Col. 'Tis my unhappinefs, Madam, to raife no paf-fion in you, but anger.

Rof. You are miftaken, Colonel. I am not angry, tho' I anfwer fo. My gaiety has been difturbed to-day ; and gravity always fits upon me like ill-humour. Fidelia has engroffed me, and you are talking of yourfelf. What would you have me fay ?

Col. That your neglect of me has been diffembled, and that I have leave to love you, and to hope for you.

Rof. This is very ftrange now! Why 'tis not in your power to avoid loving me, whether you have leave to hope or not. And as to my diffembling, I know nothing of that—all I know is, that I'm a woman, and women, I fuppofe, diffemble fometimes—I don't pretend to be a bit better than a woman.

Col. Be a kind one, and you're an angel.

Rof. Why there now! when if I wanted to be an angel, the very kindnefs that made me one, would leave me in a month or two, a mere forfaken woman. No, no, Colonel! ignorance is the mother of love, as well as devotion. We are angels before you know us to be wo-men, and lefs than women, when you know us to be no angels. If you would be pleafed with the tricks of a juggler, never enquire how they are done.

Col. Right, Madam, where the entertainment confifts only in the deceit.

Rof.

Rof. And philofophers will tell you, that the only happinefs of life is to be well deceived.

Col. 'Tis the philofophy of fools, Madam. Is the
pleafure that arifes from virtue a cheat? Or is there no
happinefs in conferring obligations, where the receiver
wifhes to be obliged, and labours to return? 'Tis the
happinefs of divinity, to diftribute good, and be paid
with gratitude.

Rof. But to give all at once, would be to lofe the
power of obliging.

Col. And to deny all, would be to lofe the pleafure of
obliging.

Rof. But where the gift is trifling, you know——

Col. That trifle, if lent to another's management,
might make both rich.

Rof. This is playing at crofs-purpofes. But if I were
inclined to liften, what have you to fay in favour of matrimony?

Col. ' To fools, Madam, 'tis the jewel of Æfop's
' cock; but to the wife, a diamond of price, in a fkilful
' hand, to enrich life.' 'Tis happinefs, or mifery, as
minds are differently difpofed. The neceflary requifites
are love, good fenfe, and good breeding. The firft to
unite, the fecond to advife, and the third to comply. If
you add to thefe, neatnefs and a competency, beauty will
always pleafe, and family cares become agreeable amufe-
ments.

' *Rof.* And yet I have known a very miferable cou-
' ple, with all thefe requifites.

' *Col.* Never, if you'll believe me, Rofetta--They have
' worn them in public, and may have diffembled with
' fuccefs. But marriage-intimacies deftroy diffimulation
' —And if their private hours have known no enjoy-
' ment, there muft have been wanting, either the affec-
' tion that fhould unite, the underftanding that fhould
' advife, or the complacency that fhould oblige.'

Rof. Do you know, now, that you never pleafed me fo
much in all your life?

Col. If fo, Rofetta, one queftion, and then to apply.

Rof. How if I fhould not anfwer your queftion?

Col. 'Tis a fair one, upon my word. Don't you think,

that

that you and I could muster up these requisites between us?

Rof. Let me consider a little——Who must have love, pray?

Col. Both of us.

Rof. No, I have no mind to have any thing to do with love. Do you take that, and give me understanding, to advise. ' So then you chuse again, and have all the good-
' breeding, for compliance; then I neatness; and last of
' all, competency shall be divided between us.'

Col. A match, Madam, upon your own terms. ' But
' if ever you should take it into your head to dispute love
' with me, what other requisite are you willing to give up
' for it?

' *Rof.* Why, neatness, I think; 'tis of little use to a
' married woman, you know.

' *Col.* A trifle, Madam.' But when are we to come together?

Rof. As soon as we can give proof that these ingredients are between us—In a few years, perhaps.

Col. If our virtues should starve in that time?

Rof. Psha!—You know nothing of the matter. Sense will improve every day, and love and good-breeding live an age, if we don't marry them. But we'll have done with these matters; for I can keep the ball up no longer. You did not say Fidelia upbraided me?

Col. The very reverse. 'Twas her only affliction, she said, that you had reason to think hardly of her.

Rof. Poor girl! If you would make love to me with success, Colonel, clear up these perplexities. Suppose I was to dismiss my pride a little, and make her a visit with you?

Col. 'Twould be a kind one.

Rof. Lead on then; for, in spite of my resentments, I have no heart to keep from her.　　　　　*[Exeunt.*

SCENE, *another Apartment.*

Enter Young Belmont *and* Faddle.

Bel. If this should be invention, Faddle?

Fad. I tell thee, I was behind the screen, and heard every syllable on't. Why, I'll say it to his face, pr'ythee.

　　　　　　　　　　　　　　　　　　　　Bel.

Bel. What, that he propofed to take her into keeping, and that fhe confented?

Fad. Not in thofe words, man—No, no, Sir Charles is a gentleman of politer elocution. Pray, child, fays he, did Young Belmont ever propofe your removing from this houfe? No, Sir, fays fhe, but he has curfed himfelf to damnation for bringing me into it. [*Mimicking* Sir Charles *and* Fidelia.] Well, child, fays he, the thing may be done to-night; apartments are ready for you. And then, in a lower voice, he faid fomething about virtue, that I could not very well hear; but I faw it fet the girl a cry-ing. And prefently, in anfwer to a whifper of his, I heard her fay, in a very pretty manner, that fhe thought it was too much for her. But what his propofals were, the devil a fyllable could I hear.

Bel. Ha, ha!—Yonder he is, Faddle, and coming this way. We muft not be feen together.

Fad. For a little fport, Charles, fuppofe I fling myfelf in his way, and make intereft to be commode to him, ha.!

Bel. And get thy nofe twifted for thy pains?

Fad. Why, I can run, if I can't fight, pr'ythee.

Bel. Faith, I never doubted thee that way. I'll to my room, then, and wait for thee.

Fad. But leave the door open, Charles.

Bel. Ha, ha, ha!—You'll not be tedious, Sir. [*Exit.*

Enter Sir Charles.

Fad. If the old gentleman fhould be in his airs tho'—Servant, fervant, Sir Charles.

Sir Cha. Oh, Sir, you are the man I was looking for!

Fad. If I can be of any fervice, Sir Charles—What, and fo—ha!——Faith, you're a fly one——But you old poachers have fuch a way with you?——Why here has Charles been racking his brains for ways and means, any time thefe three months; and juft in the nick, foufe comes me down the old kite——and, alack-a-day, poor chick!—the bufinefs is done.

Sir Cha. Make yourfelf a little intelligible, Sir.

Fad. And fo, I don't fpeak plain, ha?—Oh, the little rogue!—There's more beauty in the veins of her neck, than in a landfcape of Claude; and more mufic in the fmack of her lips, than in all Handel!

Sir Cha. Let me underftand you, Sir.

Fad. Methinks 'twas very laconic, tho'——If Rofet-

ta's

ta's fufpicions grow violent, I have apartments ready to receive you. [*Mimicking* Sir Charles.] But a word in your ear, old gentleman——Thofe apartments won't do.

Sir Cha. Oh, Sir, I begin to be a little in the fecret!

Fad. Mighty quick of apprehenfion, faith!——And the little innocent!——Still, Sir Charles, my tears are all that I can thank you with; for this goodnefs is too much for me. [*Mimicking* Fidelia.] Upon my foul, you have a great deal of goodnefs, Sir Charles; a great deal of goodnefs, upon my foul.

Sir Cha. Why, now I underftand you, Sir. And as thefe matters may require time, for the fake of privacy, we'll fhut this door.   [*Shuts the door.*

Fad. Any other time, Sir Charles. But I am really fo hurried at prefent, that—Oh, Lord!   [*Afide.*

Sir Cha. Why, what does the wretch tremble at?—— Broken bones are to be fet again; and thou mayeft yet die in thy bed. [*Takes hold of him.*] You have been a liftener, Sir.

Fad. Lord, Sir!—Indeed, Sir!—Not I, Sir!

Sir Cha. No denial, Sir.   [*Shakes him.*

Fad. Oh, Sir, I'll confefs! I did liften, Sir——I did, indeed, Sir.

Sir Cha. Does your memory furnifh you with any other villainy of yours, that may fave me the trouble of an explanation?

Fad. I'll think, Sir——What the devil fhall I fay now?
[*Afide.*

Sir Cha. Take care; for every lie thou telleft me, fhall be fcored ten fold upon thy flefh. Anfwer me—How came Mr. Belmont's fifter by that anonymous letter?

Fad. Letter, Sir!

Sir Cha. Whence came it, I fay?

Fad. Is there no remiffion, Sir?

Sir Cha. None that thou canft deferve: for honefty is not in thy nature.

Fad. If I confefs?

Sir Cha. Do fo, then; and truft me.

Fad. Yes, and fo be beat to mummy by Charles——— If you won't tell him, Sir———

Sir Cha. I'll think on't.

Fad. Why, then, Sir——But he'll certainly be the
death

death of me——It was by his contrivance I wrote the letter, and sent it from the King's-Arms.

Sir Cha. Very well, Sir.   And did you know to what purpose it was sent?

Fad. Yes, Sir; it was to alarm the family against Fidelia, that Charles might get her into private lodgings—That was all, as I hope to be sav'd, Sir.

Sir Cha. Was it, Sir? And upon what principles were you an accomplice in this villainy?

Fad. I was out of money, Sir, and not over-valiant; and Charles promised and threatened—'Twas either a small purse, or a great cudgel—And so, I took one, to avoid t'other, Sir.

Sir Cha. And what dost thou deserve for this?

Fad. Pray, Sir, consider my honest confession, and think me paid already, if you please, Sir.

Sir Cha. For that thou art safe. If thou wouldst continue so, avoid me. Begone, I say!

Fad. Yes, Sir——and well off, too, faith.

[Aside, and going.

Sir Cha. Yet stay——If thou art open to any sense of shame, hear me.

Fad. I will, Sir.

Sir Cha. Thy life is a disgrace to humanity. A foolish prodigality makes thee needy; need makes thee vicious, and both make thee contemptible. Thy wit is prostituted to slander and buffoonery; and thy judgment, if thou hast any, to meanness and villainy. Thy betters that laugh with thee, laugh at thee: and who are they? The fools of quality at court, and those who ape them in the city. The varieties of thy life are pitiful rewards, and painful abuses; for the same trick that gets thee a guinea to-day, shall get thee beaten out of doors to-morrow. Those who caress thee, are enemies to themselves; and when they know it, will be so to thee: in thy distresses they'll desert thee, and leave thee, at last, to sink in thy poverty, unregarded and unpitied. If thou canst be wise, think of me, and be honest.   [Exit.

Fad. I'll endeavour it, Sir——A most excellent discourse, faith,; and mighty well there was not a larger congregation.—— So, so!—I must be witty, with a vengeance!——What the devil shall I say to Charles, now?

—And

3

—And here he comes, like poverty and the plague, to deſtroy me at once——Let me ſee——Ay—as truth has ſaved me with one, I'll try what a little lying will do with t'other.

Enter Young Belmont.

Ha, ha, ha! Oh, the rareſt ſport, Charles!

Bel. What ſport, pr'ythee?

Fad. I ſhall burſt!——Ha, ha, ha!——The old gentleman has let me into all his ſecrets.

Bel. And like a faithful confident, you are going to reveal them.

Fad. Not a breath, Charles—Only that I am in commiſſion, my dear, that's all.

Bel. So I ſuppoſe, indeed.

Fad. Nay, Charles, if I tell thee a lie, cut my throat. The ſhort of the matter is, the old poacher, finding me in the ſecret, thought it the wiſeſt way to make a confident of me; and this very moment, my dear, I am upon the wing to provide lodgings for the occaſion.

Bel. If this ſhould be apocryphal, as my father ſays——

Fad. Goſpel every ſyllable, as I hope to be ſaved—— Why, what, in the devil's name, have I to do, to be inventing lies for thee?——But here comes the old gentleman again, faith—Oh, the devil! [*Aſide.*] —Pr'ythee, ſtroke him down a little, Charles, if 'tis only to ſee how awkward he takes it—I muſt about the lodgings, ha, ha, ha!——But if ever I ſet foot in this houſe again, may a horſe-pond be my portion.   [*Aſide, and exit.*

Enter Sir Charles, *with a letter in his hand, ſpeaking to a Servant.*

Sir Cha. Bid him wait a little, and I'll attend him. [*Exit Servant.*] What can this mean?—Let me read it again. [*Reads.*] " If the intereſt of Sir Charles Raymond's family be dear to him, he will follow the bearer with the ſame haſte that he would ſhun ruin."——That he would ſhun ruin! This is ſtrange! But, be it as it will, I have another concern, that muſt take place firſt.

Bel. Sir Charles, your ſervant. Any news, Sir?

Sir Cha. Not much, Sir; only, that a young gentleman, of honour and condition, had introduced a virtuous lady to his family; and when a worthleſs fellow defamed her innocence, and robbed her of her quiet, he, who

might

might have dried her tears, and vindicated her virtue, forfook her in her injuries, to debauch his mind with the affaffin of her reputation.

Bel. If your tale ends there, Sir, you have learned but half on't ; for my advices add, that a certain elderly gentleman, of title and fortune, pitying the forlorn circumftances of the lady, has offered her terms of friendfhip and accommodation : and this night fhe bids farewel to maidenhood, and a female bedfellow in private apartments.

Sir Cha. You treat me lightly, Mr. Belmont.

Bel. You ufe me roughly, Sir Charles.

Sir Cha. How, Sir ?

Bel. In the perfon of Fidelia.

Sir Cha. Make it appear, and you fhall find me a very boy in my fubmiffions.

Bel. 'Twould be time loft ; and I can employ it to advantage. But remember, Sir, that this houfe is another's, not yours ; that Fidelia is under my direction, not yours ; and that my will muft determine her removal, not yours.

Sir Cha. Is fhe your flave, Sir, to bear the burden of your infults without complaining, or the right of chufing another mafter ?

Bel. And who fhall be that mafter ? You, Sir ? The poor bird, that would efcape the kite, is like to find warm protection from the fox.

Sir Cha. Pr'ythee, think me a man, and treat me as fuch.

Bel. As the man I have found you, Sir Charles. Your grave deportment, and honefty of heart, are covers only for wantonnefs and defign. You preach up temperance and fobriety to youth, to monopolize, in age, the vices you are unfit for.

Sir Cha. Hark you, young man—you muft curb this impetuous fpirit of yours, or I fhall be tempted to teach you manners, in a method difagreeable to you.

Bel. Learn them firft yourfelf, Sir. You fay Fidelia is infulted by me ; how is it made out ? Why, truly, I would poffefs her without marriage !—I would fo. Marriage is the thing I would avoid : 'tis the trick of priefts, to make men miferable, and women infolent. I have dealt plainly, and told her fo. Have you faid as much ?

E   No ;

No; you wear the face of honesty, to quiet her fears; that when your blood boils, and security has stolen away her guard, you may rush at midnight upon her beauties, and do the ravage you are sworn to protect her from.

Sir Cha. Hold, Sir. You have driven me beyond the limits of my patience; and I must tell you, young man, that the obligations I owe your father, demand no returns that manhood must blush to make. Therefore, hold, I say; for I have a sword to do me justice, tho' it should leave my dearest friend childless.

Bel. I fear it not.

Sir Cha. Better tempt it not; for your fears may come too late. You have dealt openly with Fidelia, you say: deal so for once with me, and tell me, whence came that vile scroll to Rosetta this afternoon?

Bel. It seems, then, I wrote it. You dare not think so.

Sir Cha. I dare speak, as well as think, where honour directs me.

Bel. You are my accuser, then?

Sir Cha. When I become so, I shall take care, Mr. Belmont, that the proof waits upon the accusation.

Bel. I disdain the thought.

Sir Cha. Better have disdained the deed.

Bel. I do both—and him that suspects me.

Sir Cha. Away! You fear him that suspects you; and have disdained neither the thought nor the deed.

Bel. How, Sir? [*Drawing.*

Sir Cha. Put up your sword, young man, and use it in a better cause: this is a vile one. And now you shall be as still thro' shame, as you have been loud thro' pride. You should have known, that cowards are unfit for secrets.

Bel. And if I had, Sir?

Sir Cha. Why, then, Sir, you had not employed such a wretch as Faddle, to write that letter to Rosetta.

Bel. The villain has betrayed me! But I'll be sure on't. [*Aside.*] He durst not say I did.

Sir Cha. You should rather have built your innocence upon the probability of his unsaying it; for the same fear that made him confess to me, may make him deny every syllable to you.

Bel. What has he confessed, Sir?

Sir Cha. That, to-day, at dinner, you prompted the
letter

letter that he wrote.   That your defign was, by vilifying
Fidelia, to get her difmiffed, and the difmiffion to prepare
her ruin in private lodgings.   Was this your open behaviour, Sir?

Bel. Go on with your upbraidings, Sir.   Speak to me
as you will, and think of me as you will.   I have deferved
fhame, and am taught patience.

Sir Cha. Was this well done ? Did her innocence, and
her undiffembled love deferve this treatment ?

Bel. Proceed, Sir.

Sir Cha. No, Sir, I have done.   If you have fenfe of
your paft conduct, you want not humanity to heal the
wounds it has given.   Something muft be done, and
fpeedily.

Bel. What reparation can I make her ?

Sir Cha. Dry up her tears, by an immediate acknowledgment of her wrongs.

Bel. I would do more.

Sir Cha. Bid her farewel, then, and confent to her removal.

Bel. I cannot, Sir.

Sir Cha. Her peace demands it : but we'll talk of that
hereafter.   If you have honour, go and do her juftice,
and undeceive your abufed fifter.   Who waits there ?——
Indeed, you have been to blame, Mr. Belmont.

Enter Servant.

Show me to the bearer of this letter.

[*Exit with the Servant.*

Bel. Why, what a thing am I !——But 'tis the trick
of Vice to pay her votaries with fhame ; and I am rewarded amply.   To be a fool's fool too ! to link myfelf
in villainy with a wretch below the notice of a man ! and
to be outwitted by him !—So, fo !——I may have abufed
Sir Charles too——Let me think a little——I'll to Fidelia inftantly, and tell her what a rogue I have been.   But
will that be reparation ?—I know but of one way ; and
there my pride ftops me—— And then I lofe her—Worfe
and worfe !——I'll think no more on't ; but away to her
chamber, and bid her think for me.

[*Exit.*

END of the FOURTH ACT.

E 2   ACT

A C T   V.

S C E N E *continues.*

Enter Sir Roger *and Servant.* Sir Roger *with a letter in his hand.*

SIR ROGER.

VERY fine doings, indeed! But I'll teach the dog to play his tricks upon his father. A man had better let a lion loose in his family, than a town-rake. Where is Sir Charles, I say?

Serv. This moment come in, Sir.

Sir Ro. And why did not you say so, blockhead? Tell him I must speak with him this moment.

Serv. The servant says, he waits for an answer to that letter, Sir.

Sir Ro. Do as I bid you, rascal, and let him wait. Fly, I say.   [*Exit Servant.*
The riotous young dog! to bring his harlots home with him! But I'll out with the baggage.

Enter Sir Charles.

Oh, Sir Charles, 'tis every word as we said this morning! The boy has stolen her, and I am to be ruined by a law-suit.

Sir Cha. A law-suit! With whom, Sir?

Sir Ro. Read, read, read!   [*Gives the letter.*

Sir Cha. [*Reads.*] " I am guardian to that Fidelia, whom your son has stolen from me, and you unjustly detain. If you deny her to me, the law shall right me. I wait your answer by the bearer, to assert my claim, in the person of   George Villiard."

Why, then my doubts are at an end. But I must conceal my transports, and wear a face of coolness, while my heart overflows with passion.   [*Aside.*

Sir Ro. What, not a word, Sir Charles?—There's a piece of work for you!—And so I am to be ruined.

Sir Cha. Do you know this Villiard, Sir Roger?

Sir Ro. Whether I do or not, Sir, the slut shall go to him this moment.

Sir Cha. Hold a little. This gentleman must be heard, Sir, and, if his claim be good, the lady restored.

Sir Ro. Why, e'en let her go as it is, Sir Charles.

Sir

Sir Cha. That would be too hafty.   Go in with me,
Sir, and we'll confider how to write to him.

Sir Ro. Well, well, well——I wifh fhe was gone, tho'.
[*Exeunt.*

SCENE, *another apartment.*

Enter Young Belmont *and* Fidelia.

Bel. Afk me not why I did it, but forgive me.

Fid. No, Sir, 'tis impoffible.   I have a mind, Mr.
Belmont, above the wretchednefs of my fortunes ; and,
helplefs as I am, I can feel in this breaft a fenfe of injuries, and fpirit to refent them.

Bel. Nay, but hear me, Fidelia.

Fid. Was it not enough. to defert me in my diftreffes,
to deny me the poor requeft I made you, but muft you
own yourfelf the contriver of that letter ? Tis infup-
portable !   If I confented to affume a rank that belonged
not to me, my heart went not with the deceit. You
would have it fo, and I complied.   'Twas fhame enough,
that I had deceived your fifter ; it needed not, that I
fhould bring a proftitute to her friendfhip.   This was too
much, too much, Mr. Belmont.

Bel. Yet hear me, I fay.

Fid. And then, to leave me to the malice of that
wretch ; to have my fuppofed infamy the tavern jeft of
his licentious companions !——I never flattered myfelf,
Mr. Belmont, with your love ; but knew not, till now,
that I have been the objeft of your hatred.

Bel. My hatred !——But I have deferved your hardeft
thoughts of me.   And yet, believe me, Fidelia, when I
ufed you worft, I loved you moft.

Fid. Call it by another name ; for love delights in afts
of kindnefs.   Were yours fuch, Sir ?——And yet, muft I
forget all—for I owe you more than injuries can cancel,
or gratitude repay.

Bel. Generous creature ! This is to be amiable indeed !
But muft we part, Fidelia ?

Fid. I have refolved it, Sir, and you muft yield to it.

Bel. Never, my fweet obftinate.

Fid. That I have loved you, 'tis my pride to acknowledge ; but that muft be forgot.   And the hard tafk remains, to drive the paffion from my breaft, while I cherifh

                    the

memory of your humane offices. This day, then, fhall be the laft of our meeting. Painful tho' it may be, yet your own, mine, and the family's peace requires it. Heaven, in my diftreffes, has not left me deftitute of a friend; or if it had, I can find one in my innocence, to make even poverty fupportable.

Bel. You have touch'd me, Fidelia; and my heart yields to your virtues. Here, then, let my follies have an end; and thus let me receive you as the everlafting partner of my heart and fortune. [*Offers to embrace her.*

Fid. No, Sir. The conduct that has hitherto fecured my own honour, fhall protect yours. I have been the innocent difturber of your family; but never will confent to load it with difgrace.

Bel. Nor can it be difgraced. I mean to honour it, Fidelia. You muft comply.

Fid. And repay generofity with ruin! No, Mr. Belmont; I can forego happinefs, but never can confent to make another miferable.

Bel. When I repent, Fidelia!—But fee where my fifter comes, to be an advocate for my wifhes.

Enter Rofetta.

Rof. Oh, Sir, you are found! You have done nobly, indeed! But your thefts are difcovered, Sir. This lady's guardian has a word or two for you.

Bel. Her guardian!—Upon my life, Fidelia, Villiard! He comes as I could wifh him.

Rof. Say fo when you have anfwered him, brother. Am I to lofe you at laft then, Fidelia? And yet my hopes flatter me, that this too, as well as the letter, is a deceit. May I think fo, Fidelia?

Fid. As truly as of your own goodnefs, Rofetta. Your brother will tell you all. Oh, he has made me miferable by his generofity!

Bel. This pretended guardian, fifter, is a villain, and Fidelia the moft abufed of women. Bounteous he has been indeed; but to his vices, not his virtues, fhe ftands indebted for the beft of educations. The ftory will amaze you. At twelve years old——

Rof. He's here, brother, and with him my papa, Sir Charles, and the Colonel. Now, Fidelia.

Enter Sir Roger, Sir Charles, *the* Colonel, *and* Villiard.

Sir Cha. If that be the lady, Mr. Villiard, and your

claim

I

claim as you pretend, Sir Roger has told you, she shall be restored, Sir.

Sir Ro. Yes, Sir, and your claim as you pretend.

Vil. 'Tis well, Madam, I have found you. [*Going to* Fidelia] This, gentlemen, is the lady ; and this the robber who stole her from me: [*Pointing to* Belmont.] By violence, and at midnight he stole her.

Bel. Stole her, Sir !

Vil. By violence, and at midnight, I say.

Bel. You shall be heard, Sir.

Vil. Ay, Sir, and satisfied. I stand here, gentlemen, to demand my ward.

Sir Cha. Give us proofs, Sir, and you shall have justice.

Vil. Demand them there, Sir. [*Pointing to* Bel. *and* Fid.] I have told you, I am robbed: if you deny me justice, the law shall force it.

Sir Cha. A little patience, Sir. [*To* Villiard.] Do you know this gentleman, Fidelia ?

Fid. Too well, Sir.

Sir Cha. By what means, Sir, did you become her guardian ? [*To* Vil.

Vil. By the will of her who bore her, Sir.

Sir Cha. How will you reply to this, Fidelia ?

Fid. With truth and honesty, Sir.

Bel. Let him proceed, Madam.

Vil. Ay, Sir, to your part of the story ; tho' both are practised in a damn'd falshood to confront me.

Bel. Falshood !—But I am cool, Sir. Proceed.

Vil. My doors were broke open at midnight by this gentleman, [*Pointing to* Bel.] myself wounded, and Fidelia ravished from me. He ran off with her in his arms. Nor, till this morning, in a coach which brought her hither, have my eyes ever beheld her.

Sir Ro. A very fine businefs, truly, young man !
[*To* Belmont.

Fid. He has abused you, Sir. Mr. Belmont is noble—

Bel. No matter, Fidelia. Well, Sir, you have been robbed, you say ? [*To* Villiard.

Vil. And will have justice, Sir.

Bel. Take it from this hand then, [*Drawing.*

Sir Cha. Hold, Sir. This is adding insult to injuries. Fidelia must be restored, Sir.

Sir

Sir Ro. Ay, Sir, Fidelia muſt be reſtored.

Fid. But not to him. Hear but my ſtory, and, if I deceive you, let your friendſhip forſake me. He bought me, gentlemen, for the worſt of purpoſes; he bought me of the worſt of women. A thouſand times has he con-feſſed it, and as often pleaded his right of purchaſe to un-do me. Whole years have I endured his brutal ſolicita-tions; till, tired with entreaties, he had recourſe to vio-lence. The ſcene was laid, and I had been ruined be-yond redreſs, had not my cries brought the generous Mr. Belmont to my relief. He was accidentally paſſing by, and alarmed, at midnight, with a woman's ſhrieks, he forced open the door, and ſaved me from deſtruction.

Sir Cha. How will you anſwer this, Sir? [*To* Vil.

Vil. 'Tis falſe, Sir. That woman was her nurſe: theſe hands delivered her to her care.

Fid. Alas, gentlemen, ſhe found me a helpleſs infant at her door! So ſhe has always told me; and at twelve years old, betrayed me to that monſter. Search out the woman, if ſhe be alive, and let me be confronted.

Sir Ro. If this be true, Sir Charles, I ſhall bleſs myſelf as long as I live, for getting my boy. [*Weeps.*

Vil. 'Tis falſe, I ſay; a damn'd contrivance to eſcape me. I ſtand here, Sir, to demand my ward. [*To* Sir Ro.] Deny her to me at your peril.

Bel. He ſhall have my life as ſoon.

Vil. Hark you, Sir. [*To* Sir Ro.] There are things, called laws, to do right to the injured. My appeal ſhall be to them.

Sir Cha. That woman muſt be produced, Sir. [*To* Vil.

Vil. And ſhall, Sir, in a court of juſtice. Our next meeting ſhall be there. Till then, Madam, you are ſe-cure. [*To* Fidelia.

Bel. Take care that you are ſo, Sir, when we have oc-caſion to call upon you. You ſhall have juſtice.

Vil. And will, Sir, in defiance of you. [*Exit.*

Sir Cha. Fear not, Fidelia; we believe, and will pro-tect you.

Ros. My ſweet girl!——But whence came the letter this afternoon?

Bel. 'Twas I that wrote it.

Ros.

Rof. Oh, monftrous!—And could you be that wretch, brother?

Bel. And will atone for it, by the only recompence that's left me.

Sir Ro. And what recompence will you make her, ha, rogue?

Bel. I have injured her, Sir, and muft do her juftice. If you would retrieve my honour, or promote my hap-pinefs, give me your confent, Sir, to make her your daughter.

Rof. Why, that's my brother! Now I am fure fhe's innocent. And fo you will, papa.

Sir Ro. But, pofitively, I will not, child. Marry her, indeed! What, without a fhilling! and be ruined by Vil-liard into the bargain! If your ftory be true, Fidelia, you fhall be provided for. But no marrying, d'ye hear, child?

Fid. You need not doubt me, Sir.

Sir Ro. Why, that's well faid, Fidelia.

Rof. And deferves reward, Sir. Pray, Sir Charles, let us have your thoughts upon this matter.

Sir Cha. Your brother's propofal, Madam, and Fide-lia's denial, are as generous, as your father's determina-tion is juft.

Bel. I expected as much, Sir.

Sir Cha. My opinion was afked, Sir.

Bel. And you have given it. I thank you, Sir.

Sir Cha. Think of Villiard, Mr. Belmont; his claim may be renewed, Sir.

Bel. Fidelia has deceived you then. You think other-wife, Sir Charles.

Col. My life upon her innocence!—And where the fortune, on one fide, is more than fufficient, how light is all addition to it, compared to the poffeffion of her one loves!—Let me, Sir, be happy in Rofetta, [*To* Sir Ro.] and give her fortune to Fidelia, to make her an object worthy of your fon.

Rof. There's a Colonel for you!——What fays my fweet Fidelia?

Fid. I intended to be filent, Madam; but 'tis now my duty to fpeak. You have been my deliverer, Sir, from the worft of evils; [*To* Bel.] and now would nobly aug-

ment

ment the firſt obligation, by a generoſity, too mighty for acknowledgment. If I had the wealth of worlds, it would be too little to beſtow. But poor and friend-leſs as I am, my heart may break, but never ſhall con-ſent to make my benefactor a penitent to his virtues.

Sir Cha. 'Tis nobly ſaid, Fidelia. And now, Mr. Bel-mont, our diſputes will ſoon be at an end. You have this day, Sir, reproached me often; it remains now that you ſhould know me as I am.

Bel. If I have erred, Sir——

Sir Cha. Interrupt me not, but hear me. I have watched your follies with concern; and 'tis with equal pleaſure, I congratulate your return to honour. If I have oppoſed your generous inclinations, it was only to give them ſtrength. I am now a ſuppliant to your fa-ther, for the happineſs you deſire.

Bel. This is noble, Sir Charles!

Sir Cha. And to make Fidelia worthy of his ſon, a fortune ſhall be added, equal to his warmeſt expecta-tions.

Sir Ro. Why ay, Sir Charles, · let that be made out, and I ſhall have no objections.

Fid. What mean you, Sir? [*To Sir* Cha.

Sir Cha. A minute more, and my ſweet girl ſhall be in-ſtructed. You have often told me, Sir, [*To* Bel.] that I had an intereſt in this lovely creature. I have an inte-reſt! an intereſt, that you ſhall allow me! My heart doats upon her! Oh, I can hold no longer!———My daughter! my daughter!

[*Running to* Fidelia *and embracing her.*

Fid. Your daughter, Sir!

Sir Cha. Oh, my ſweet child!—Sir Roger, Mr. Bel-mont, my ſon!———Theſe tears!—theſe tears!—Fidelia is my daughter!

Col. Is't poſſible?

Sir Cha. Let not exceſs of wonder over-power you, Fidelia, for I have a tale to tell, that will exceed belief.

Fid. Oh, Sir!

Sir Cha. Upbraid me not, that I have kept it a mo-ment from your knowledge——'twas a hard trial! and while my tongue was taught diſſimulation, my heart bled for a child's diſtreſſes.

Bel.

Bel. Torture us not, Sir, but explain this wonder!

Sir Cha. My tears muſt have their way fiꞏſt——O, my child! my child! [*Turning to Sir. Roger and the reſt.*]—Know then, that wicked woman, ſo often mentioned, was my Fidelia's governante. When my miſtaken zeal drove me into baniſhment, I left her, an infant, to her care—To ſecure ſome jewels of value, I had lodged with her, ſhe became the woman you have heard——My child was taught to believe ſhe was a foundling——her name of Harriet changed to Fidelia——and to leſſen my ſolicitude for the theft, a letter was diſpatched to me in France, that my infant daughter had no longer a being. Thus was the father robbed of his child, and the brother taught to believe he had no ſiſter!

Fid. Am I that Siſter, and that daughter?——Oh, Heavens! [*Kneels.*

Bel. [*Running to her, and raiſing her.*] Be compoſed, my life! A moment's attention more, and your tranſports ſhall have a looſe. Proceed, Sir!

Sir Cha. Where ſhe withdrew herſelf, I could never learn. At twelve years old, ſhe ſold her, as you have heard, and never, till yeſterday, made enquiry about her. 'Twas then, that a ſudden fit of ſickneſs brought her to repentance. She ſent for Villiard, who told her minutely what happened. The knowledge of her deliverance gave her ſome conſolation. But more was to be done yet. She had information of my pardon and return, and ignorant of my child's deliverer, or the place of her conveyance, ſhe at laſt determined to unburthen herſelf to me. A letter was brought to me this afternoon, conjuring me to follow the bearer with the ſame haſte that I would ſhun ruin. I did follow him, and received from this wretched woman the ſtory I have told you.

Fid. Oh, my heart!—My father! [*Kneels.*] Have I at laſt found you! And were all my ſorrows paſt, meant only to endear the preſent tranſport—'Tis too much for me!

Sir Cha. Riſe, my child! To find thee thus virtuous, in the midſt of temptations, and thus lovely, in the midſt of poverty and diſtreſs——after an abſence of eighteen melancholy years, when imaginary death had torn thee from my hopes——to find thee thus unexpected, and

thus

thus amiable, is happiness that the uninterrupted enjoy-
-ment of the fairest life never equalled!

Fid. What must be mine then! Have I a brother too!
.[*Turning to the* Col.] Oh, my kind fortune!

Col. My sister!   [*Embracing her.*

Fid. Still there is a dearer claim than all, and now I
can acknowledge it.   My deliverer!———

Bel. And husband, Fidelia! Let me receive you, as
the richest gift of Fortune!   [*Catching her in his arms.*

Rof. My generous girl! The pride of your alliance
is my utmost boast, as it is my brother's happiness.

Sir Ro. I have a right in her too, for now you are my
daughter, Fidelia.   [*Kisses her.*

Fid. I had forgot, Sir—If you will receive me as such,
you shall find my gratitude in my obedience.

Sir Cha. Take her, Mr. Belmont, and protect the virtue you have tried.   [*Joining their hands.*

Bel. The study of my life, Sir, shall be to deserve her.

Fid. Oh, Rosetta! yet it still remains with you, to
make this day's happiness compleat——I have a brother
that loves you.

Rof. I would be Fidelia's sister every way! So take
me, while I am warm, Colonel!   [*Giving him her hand.*

Col. And when we repent, Rosetta, let the next minute end us.

Rof. With all my heart!

Fid. Now, Rosetta, we are doubly sisters!

Sir Cha. And may your lives and your affections know
an end together.

Bel. [*Taking* Fidelia *by the hand.*] And now, Fidelia,
what you have made me, take me, a convert to honour!
I have at last learnt, that custom can be no authority for
vice; and however the mistaken world may judge, he
who solicits pleasure, at the expence of innocence, is the
vilest of betrayers.

Yet savage man, the wildest beast of prey,
Assumes the face of kindness to betray;
His giant strength against the weak employs,
And woman, whom he should protect, destroys.

                                               [*Exeunt.*

END of the FIFTH ACT.

EPI-

EPILOGUE.

Written by Mr. GARRICK.

Spoken by Mrs. CIBBER.

I Know you all expect, from seeing me,
An epilogue, of strictest purity;
Some formal lecture, spoke with prudish face,
To shew our present joking, giggling race,
True joy consists in——gravity and grace!
But why am I, for ever made the tool,
Of every squeamish, moralizing fool?
Condemn'd to sorrow all my life, must I
Ne'er make you laugh, because I make you cry?
Madam (say they) your face denotes your heart,
'Tis yours to melt us in the mournful part.
So from the looks, our hearts they prudish deem!
Alas, poor souls!——we are not what we seem!
Tho' prudence oft our inclination smothers,
We grave ones love a joke—as well as others.
From such dull stuff, what profit can you reap?
You cry—'Tis very fine—[Yawns.]—and fall asleep.
Happy that bard!——blest with uncommon art,
Whose wit can chear, and not corrupt the heart!
Happy that play'r, whose skill can chase the spleen,
And leave no worse inhabitant within.
'Mongst friends, our author is a modest man,
But wicked wits will cavil at his plan.
Damn it (says one) this stuff will never pass,
The girl wants nature, and the rake's an ass.
Had I, like Belmont, heard a damsel's cries,
I would have pink'd her keeper, seiz'd the prize,
Whipt to a coach, not valu'd tears a farthing,
But drove away like smoke——to Covent-Garden;
There to some house convenient would have carry'd her,
And then—dear soul!—the devil should have marry'd her.
But this our author thought too hard upon her;
Besides, his spark, forsooth, must have some honour:
The fool's a fabulist!——and deals in fiction;
Or he had giv'n him vice——without restriction.

G

Of fable, all his characters, partake,
Sir Charles is virtuous——and for Virtue's sake;
Nor vain, nor blust'ring is the soldier writ,
His rake has conscience, modesty, and wit.
The ladies too !——how oddly they appear !
His prude is chaste, and his coquet sincere :
In short, so strange a group ne'er trod the stage,
At once to please, and satirize the age !
For you, ye fair, his muse has chiefly sung,
'Tis you have touch'd his heart, and tun'd his tongue ;
The sex's champion, let the sex defend,
A soothing poet is a charming friend :
Your favours, here bestow'd, will meet reward,
So as you love dear flatt'ry——save your bard.

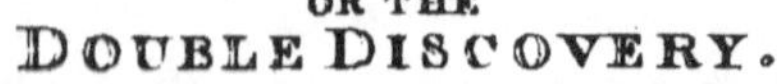

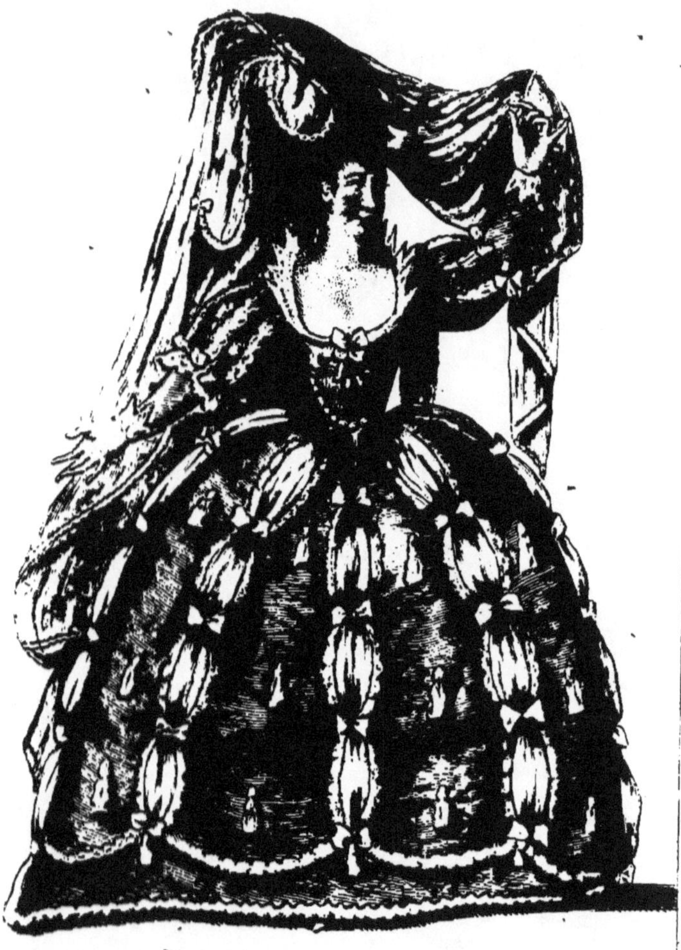

Mrs. MATTOCKS in the Character of ELVIRA.
:— but however I will not stand with you for a Sample

THE
SPANISH FRYAR:
OR, THE
DOUBLE DISCOVERY.

A COMEDY,

As written by Mr. DRYDEN.

DISTINGUISHING ALSO THE

VARIATIONS OF THE THEATRE,

AS PERFORMED AT THE

Theatre-Royal in Covent-Garden.

Regulated from the Prompt-Book,

By PERMISSION of the MANAGERS,

By Mr. WILD, Prompter.

Ut melius possis fallere, sume togam.—MART.

———————————*Alterna revisens
Lusit, et in solido rursus fortuna locavit.*—VIRGIL.

LONDON:

Printed for JOHN BELL, near *Exeter-Exchange*, in the *Strand.*

MDCCLXXVII.

J O H N,

Lord *HAUGHTON.*

MY LORD,

WHEN I firſt deſign'd this play, I found, or thought I found, ſomewhat ſo moving in the ſerious part of it, and ſo pleaſant in the comic, as might deſerve a more than ordinary care in both: accordingly I uſed the beſt of my endeavour, in the management of two plots, ſo very different from each other, that it was not perhaps the talent of every writer, to have made them of a piece. Neither have I attempted other plays of the ſame nature, in my opinion, with the ſame judgment; though with like ſucceſs. And though many poets may ſuſpect themſelves for the fondneſs and partiality of parents to their youngeſt children, yet I hope I may ſtand exempted from this rule, becauſe I know myſelf too well, to be ever ſatisfied with my own conceptions, which have ſeldom reached to thoſe ideas that I had within me: and conſequently, I preſume I may have liberty to judge when I write more or leſs pardonably, as an ordinary markſman may know certainly when he ſhoots leſs wide at what he aims. Beſides, the care and pains I have beſtowed on this beyond my other tragi-comedies, may reaſonably make the world conclude, that either I can do nothing tolerably, or that this poem is not much amiſs. Few good pictures have been finiſhed at one ſitting;

A 2

neither

neither can a true juft play, which is to bear the teft of ages, be produced at a heat, or by the force of fancy, without the maturity of judgment. For my own part, I have both fo juft a diffidence of myfelf, and fo great a reverence for my audience, that I dare venture nothing without a ftrict examination; and am as much afhamed to put a loofe indigefted play upon the public, as I fhould be to offer brafs money in a payment: for though it fhould be taken, (as it is too often on the ftage,) yet it will be found in the fecond telling: and a judicious reader will difcover in his clofet that trafhy ftuff, whofe glittering deceived him in the action. I have often heard the ftationer fighing in his fhop, and wifhing for thofe hands to take off his melancholy bargain which clapped its performance on the ftage. In a play-houfe every thing contributes to impofe upon the judgment; the lights, the fcenes, the habits, and, above all, the grace of action, which is commonly the beft where there is the moft need of it, furprize the audience, and caft a mift upon their underftandings; not unlike the cunning of a juggler, who is always ftaring us in the face, and over-whelming us with gibberifh, only that he may gain the opportunity of making the cleaner conveyance of his trick. But thefe falfe beauties of the ftage, are no more lafting than a rainbow, when the actor ceafes to fhine upon them, when he gilds them no longer with his reflection, they vanifh in a twinkling. I have fometimes wondered, in the reading, what was become of thofe glaring colours which amazed me in Buffy Damboys upon the theatre: but when I had taken up what I fuppofed a fallen ftar, I found I had been cozened with a jelly: nothing but a cold dull mafs, which glittered no longer than it was fhooting: a dwarfifh thought, dreffed up in gigantic words, repetition in abundance, loofenefs of expreffion, and grofs hyperboles; the fenfe of one line expanded prodigioufly into ten; and to fum up all, uncorrect Englifh, and a hideous mingle of falfe poetry and true nonfenfe; or, at beft, a fcantling of wit which lay gafping for life, and groaning beneath a heap of rubbifh. A famous modern poet ufed to facrifice every year a Statius to Virgil's manes: and I have indignation enough to burn a Damboys annually to the memory of

Johnfon.

Johnson.   But now, my Lord, I am senfible, perhaps too
late, that I have gone too far: for I remember some
verfes of my own, Maximin and Almanzor, which cry
vengeance upon me for their extravagance, and which I
wish heartily in the fame fire with Statius and Chapman:
all can fay for thofe paffages, which are, I hope, not many,
is, that I know they were bad enough to pleafe, even when
I writ them: but I repent of them amongft my fins; and
if any of their fellows intrude by chance into my prefent
writings, I draw a ftroke over all thofe Dalilahs of the
theatre; and am refolved I will fettle myfelf no reputation by the applaufe of fools.   'Tis not that I am mortified to all ambition, but I fcorn as much to take it from
half-witted judges, as I fhould to raife an eftate by cheating of bubbles.   Neither do I difcommend the lofty ftile
in tragedy, which is naturally pompous and magnificent:
but nothing is truly fublime that is not juft and proper.
If the ancients had judged by the fame meafures which
a common reader takes, they had concluded Statius to
have written higher than Virgil; for,

Quæ fuperimpofito moles geminata coloffo,

carries a more thundering kind of found than,

Tityre, tu patulæ recubans fub tegmine fagi.

Yet Virgil had all the majefty of a lawful prince; and
Statius only the bluftering of a tyrant.   But when men
affect a virtue which they cannot reach, they fall into a
vice, which bears the neareft refemblance to it.   Thus
an injudicious poet who aims at loftinefs, runs eafily into
the fwelling puffy ftile, becaufe it looks like greatnefs.   I
remember, when I was a boy, I thought inimitable Spen-
cer a mean poet in comparifon of Sylvefter's Dubartius;
and was rapt into an ecftafy when I read thefe lines:

Now, when the winter's keener breath began
To chryftallize the Baltic ocean;
To glaze the lakes, to bridle up the floods,
And periwig with fnow the bald-pate woods.

I am

I am much deceived if this be not abominable fuftian, that is, thoughts and words ill forted, and without the leaft relation to each other; yet I dare not anfwer for an audience, that they would not clap it on the ftage: fo little value there is to be given to the common cry, that nothing but madnefs can pleafe madmen, and a poet muft be of a piece with the fpectators, to gain a reputation with them. But, as in a room contrived for ftate, the height of the roof fhould bear a proportion to the area; fo, in the heightenings of poetry, the ftrength and vehemence of figures fhould be fuited to the occafion, the fubject, and the perfons. All beyond this is monftrous; 'tis out of nature, 'tis an excrefcence, and not a living part of poetry. I had not faid thus much, if fome young gallants, who pretend to criticifm, had not told me that this tragi-comedy wanted the dignity of ftyle: but as a man who is charged with a crime of which he thinks himfelf innocent, is apt to be eager in his own defence, fo perhaps I have vindicated my play with more partiality than I ought, or than fuch a trifle can deferve. Yet, whatever beauties it may want, 'tis free at leaft from the groffnefs of thofe faults I mentioned: what credit it has gained upon the ftage, I value no farther than in reference to my profit, and the fatisfaction I had in feeing it reprefented with all the juftnefs and gracefulnefs of action. But as it is my intereft to pleafe my audience, fo it is my ambition to be read; that I am fure is the more lafting and the nobler defign: for the propriety of thoughts and words, which are the hidden beauties of a play, are but confufedly judged in the vehemence of action: all things are there beheld, as in a hafty motion, where the objects only glide before the eye and difappear. The moft difcerning critic can judge no more of thefe filent graces in the action, than he who rides poft through an unknown country can diftinguifh the fituation of places, and the nature of the foil. The purity of phrafe, the clearnefs of conception and expreffion, the boldnefs maintained to majefty, the fignificancy and found of words, not ftrained into bombaft, but juftly elevated; in fhort, thofe very words and thoughts which cannot be changed but for the worfe, muft of neceffity efcape our tranfient view upon the theatre; and yet, without all thefe, a play

may

may take. For if either the story move us, or the actor help the lameness of it with his performance, or now and then a glittering beam of wit or passion strike through the obscurity of the poem, any of those are sufficient to effect a present liking, but not to fix a lasting admiration; for nothing but truth can long continue; and time is the surest judge of truth. I am not vain enough to think I have left no faults in this, which that touchstone will not discover; neither indeed is it possible to avoid them in a play of this nature. There are evidently two actions in it: but it will be clear to any judicious man, that with half the pains, I could have raised a play from either of them: for this time I satisfied my own humour, which was to tack two plays together; and to break a rule for the pleasure of variety. The truth is, the audience are grown weary of continued melancholy scenes: And I dare venture to prophesy, that few tragedies, except those in verse, shall succeed in this age, if they are not enlightened with a course of mirth. For the feast is too dull and solemn without the fiddles. But how difficult a task this is, will soon be tried: for a several genius is required to either way; and without both of them, a man, in my opinion, is but half a poet for the stage. Neither is it so trivial an undertaking, to make a tragedy end happily; for 'tis more difficult to save than it is to kill. The dagger and the cup of poison are always in a readiness; but to bring the action to the last extremity, and then by probable means to recover all, will require the art and judgment of a writer; and cost him many a pang in the performance.

And now, my Lord, I must confess that what I have written, looks more like a preface than a dedication; and truly it was thus far my design, that I might entertain you with somewhat in my own art, which might be more worthy of a noble mind, than the stale exploded trick of fulsome panegyricks. 'Tis difficult to write justly on any thing, but almost impossible in praise. I shall therefore wave so nice a subject; and only tell you, that in recommending a Protestant play to a Protestant patron, as I do myself an honour, so I do your noble family a right, who have been always eminent in the support and favour of our religion and liberties. And if the promises of

your

your youth, your education at home, and your experience abroad, deceive me not, the principles you have embraced are such as will no way degenerate from your anceftors, but refresh their memory in the minds of all true Englishmen, and renew their luftre in your person; which, my Lord, is not more the wish, than is it the conftant expectation of your Lordship's

Moft obedient, faithful fervant,

JOHN DRYDEN.

PROLOGUE.

NOW luck for us, and a kind hearty pit ;
  For he who pleases, never fails of wit :
Honour is yours ;
And you, like kings at city-treats bestow it ;
The writer kneels, and is bid rise a poet :
But you are fickle sovereigns, to our sorrow,
You dubb to-day, and hang a man to-morrow ;
You cry the same sense up, and down again,
Just like brass-money once a year in Spain :
Take you i'th' mood, whate'er base metal come,
You coin as fast as groats at Birmingham :
Though 'tis no more like sense in ancient plays,
Than Rome's religion's like St. Peter's days.
In short, so swift your judgments turn and wind,
You cast our fleetest wits a mile behind.
'Twere well your judgments but in plays did range,
But ev'n your follies and debauches change
With such a whirl, the poets of your age
Are tir'd, and cannot score them on the stage,
Unless each vice in short-hand they endite,
Ev'n as notcht 'prentices whole sermons write.
The heavy Hollanders no vices know,
But what they us'd a hundred years ago ;
Like honest plants, where they were stuck, they grow.
They cheat, but still from cheating sires they come ;
They drink, but they were chrift'ned first in mum.
Their patrimonial sloth the Spaniards keep,
And Philip first taught Philip how to sleep.
The French and we still change, but here's the curse,
They change for better, and we change for worse ;
They take up our old trade of conquering,
And we are taking theirs, to dance and sing :
Our fathers did, for change, to France repair,
And they, for change, will try our English air ;
As children, when they throw one toy away,
Strait a more foolish gewgaw comes in play :
So we, grown penitent, on serious thinking,
Leave whoring, and devoutly fall to drinking.

Scow'ring

Scow'ring the watch grows out-of-fashion wit :
Now we set up for tilting in the pit,
Where 'tis agreed by bullies, chicken-hearted,
To fright the ladies first, and then be parted.
A fair attempt has twice or thrice been made,
To hire night-murd'rers, and make death a trade.
When murder's out, what vice can we advance ?
Unless the new-found pois'ning trick of France :
And when their art of rats-bane we have got,
By way of thanks, we'll send them o'er our plot.

DRAMATIS PERSONÆ.

MEN.

	Drury-Lane.	Covent-Garden.
Torrismond, ——————	Mr. Holland.	Mr. Smith.
Bertran, ———— ——	Mr. Lee.	Mr. Clarke.
Alphonso, ——	Mr. Packer.	
Lorenzo, his son, —	Mr. Palmer.	Mr. Lewis.
Raymond, ————	Mr. Bransby.	Mr. Hull.
Pedro, ————	Mr. Wright.	Mr. Thompson.
Gomez, ————	Mr. Yates.	Mr. Shuter.
Dominick, the Spanish Fryar, ————	Mr. Love.	Mr. Dunstall.

WOMEN.

	Drury-Lane.	Covent-Garden.
Leonora, Queen of Arragon, ————	Mrs. Yates.	Mrs. Hartley.
Teresa, woman to Leonora, ————	Mrs. Bennet.	Mrs. Pouffin.
Elvira, wife of Gomez,	Mrs. Cibber.	Mrs. Mattocks.

THE

THE
SPANISH FRYAR.

⁎ *The lines distinguished by inverted commas, 'thus,' are omitted in the representation.*

ACT I.

Alphonso and Pedro *meet, with Soldiers on each side, Drums, &c.*

ALPHONSO.

STAND! give the word.
  Ped, The queen of Arragon.
  Alph. Pedro;—how goes the night?
  Ped. She wears apace.
  Alph. Then welcome, day-light; we shall have warm
The Moor will gage   [work on't:
His utmost forces on this next assault,
To win a queen and kingdom.
  Ped. Pox o' this lion-way of wooing, though:
Is the queen stirring yet?
  Alph. She has not been a-bed, but in her chapel
All night devoutly watch'd, and brib'd the saints
With vows for her deliverance.
  Ped. Oh, Alphonso,
I fear they come too late: her father's crimes
Sit heavy on her, and weigh down her prayers.
A crown usurp'd, a lawful king depos'd,
In bondage held, debarr'd the common light;
His children murder'd, and his friends destroy'd;
What can we less expect than what we feel?
And what we fear will follow.
  Alph. Heav'n avert it.

Ped.

Ped. Then heav'n muſt not be heav'n. Judge the event
By what has paſs'd.   Th' uſurper 'joy'd not long
His ill-got crown ! 'Tis true, he dy'd in peace :
(Unriddle that, ye Pow'rs ;) but left his daughter,
Our preſent queen, engag'd upon his death-bed,
To marry with young Bertran, whoſe curs'd father
Had help'd to make him great.
Hence, you well know, this fatal war aroſe ;
Becauſe the Moor Abdallah, with whoſe troops
Th' uſurper gain'd the kingdom, was refus'd,
And, as an infidel, his love deſpis'd.
Alph. Well, we are ſoldiers, Pedro, and, like lawyers,
Plead for our pay.
Ped. A good cauſe would do well though ;
It gives my ſword an edge.   You ſee this Bertran
Has now three times been beaten by the Moors :
What hope we have is in young Torriſmond,
Your brother's ſon.
Alph. He's a ſuccefsful warrior, -
' And has the ſoldiers hearts.   Upon the ſkirts
' Of Arragon our ſquander'd troops he rallies :'
Our watchmen from the tow'rs with longing eyes
Expect his ſwift arrival.
Ped. It muſt be ſwift, or it will come too late.
Alph. No more :——Duke Bertran.
Enter Bertran *attended.*
Bert. Relieve the centries that have watch'd all night.
[*To* Ped.] Now, Colonel, have you diſpos'd your men,
That you ſtand idle here?
Ped. Mine are drawn off,
To take a ſhort repoſe.
Bert. Short let it be,
For, from the Mooriſh camp, this hour and more,
There has been heard a diſtant humming noiſe,
Like bees diſturb'd, and arming in their hives.
What courage in our ſoldiers? Speak ! what hope ?
Ped. As much as when phyſicians ſhake their heads,
And bid their dying patient think of heaven.
' Our walls are thinly mann'd : our beſt men ſlain :
' The reſt, an heartleſs number, ſpent with watching,
' And harraſs'd out with duty.'
Bert. Good-night all then.

Ped.

Ped. Nay, for my part, 'tis but a single life
I have to lose : I'll plant my colours down
In the mid-breach, and by them fix my foot ;
Say a short soldier's pray'r, to spare the trouble
Of my few friends above ; and then expect
The next fair bullet.

  ' *Alph.* Never was known a night of such distraction ;
' Noise so confus'd and dreadful ; justling crowds,
' That run, and know not whither ; torches gliding,
' Like meteors, by each other in the streets.

  ' *Ped.* I met a reverend, fat, old, gouty fryar ;
' With a paunch swoll'n so high, his double chin
' Might rest upon't : a true son of the church ;
' Fresh colour'd, and well thriven on his trade,
' Came puffing with his greasy bald-pate choir,
' And fumbling o'er his beads, in such an agony,
' He told them false for fear : about his neck
' There hung a wench, the label of his function,
' Whom he shook off, i'faith, methought, unkindly.
' It seems the holy stallion durst not score
' Another sin before he left the world.'

Enter a Captain.

  Capt. To arms, my Lord, to arms !
From the Moors' camp the noise grows louder still :
' Rattling of armour, trumpets, drums and atabals ; '
' And sometimes peals of shouts that rend the heav'ns,
' Like victory : the groans again, and howlings,
' Like those of vanquish'd men ; but every echo
' Goes fainter off ; and dies in distant sounds.'

  Bert. Some false attack : expect on th' other side :
One to the gunners on St. Jago's tow'r ; bid them, for
Level their cannon lower : on my soul,   [shame,
They're all corrupted with the gold of Barbary
To carry over, and not hurt the Moor.

Enter a second Captain.

  2d Capt. My Lord, here's fresh intelligence arriv'd ;
Our army, led by valiant Torrismond,
Is now in hot engagement with the Moors ;
'Tis said, within their trenches.

  Bert. I think all fortune is reserv'd for him.
He might have sent us word though ;

B

And

And then we could have favour'd his attempt
With fallies from the town——
    Alph. It could not be:
We were fo clofe block'd up, that none could peep
Upon the walls and live; but yet 'tis time——
    Bert. No, 'tis too late; I will not hazard it:
On pain of death, let no man dare to fally.
    Ped. [*Afide.*] Oh, envy, envy, how it works within
How now! what means this fhow?   [him!
    Alph. 'Tis a proceffion:
The queen is going to the great cathedral,
To pray for our fuccefs againft the Moors.
    Ped. Very good: fhe ufurps the throne; keeps the
old king in prifon; and, at the fame time, is praying
for a bleffing: Oh, religion and roguery, how they go
together!   [*Shout and a flourifh of trumpets.*

'*A proceffion of priefts and chorifters in white, with tapers,*
 '*followed by the queen and ladies, goes over the ftage:*
 '*the chorifters finging.*

 '*Look down, ye blefs'd above, look down,*
   '*Behold our weeping matrons tears,*
   '*Behold our tender virgins fears,*
 '*And with fuccefs our armies crown.*

 '*Look down, ye blefs'd above, look down:*
   '*Oh, fave us, fave us, and our ftate reftore;*
   '*For pity, pity, pity, we implore;*
 '*For pity, pity, pity, we implore.*
             '[*The proceffion goes off, and fhout within.*'

        Enter Lorenzo, *who kneels to* Alphonzo.
    Bert. [*To* Alph.] A joyful cry; and fee your fon, Lo-
renzo: good news, kind Heav'n!
    Alph. [*To* Lor.] Oh, welcome, welcome! Is the Gene-
        ral fafe?
How near our army? When fhall we be fuccour'd?
Or, are we fuccour'd? Are the Moors remov'd?
Anfwer thefe queftions firft, and then a thoufand more;
Anfwer them all together.
    Lor. Yes, when I have a thoufand tongues, I will.
The General's well; his army too is fafe
As victory can make them: the Moors' king
Is fafe enough, I warrant him, for one.   At

At dawn of day our General cleft his pate,
Spite of his woollen night-cap: a flight wound;
Perhaps he may recover.

Alph. Thou reviv'ft me.

Ped. By my computation now, the victory was gained
before the proceffion was made for it; and yet it will go
hard but the priefts will make a miracle of it.

Lor. Yes, faith we came, like bold intruding guefts,
And took them unprepar'd to give us welcome.
Their fcouts we kill'd, then found their body fleeping;
And as they lay confus'd, we ftumbled o'er them,
And took what joint came next, arms, heads, or legs,
Somewhat undecently. But when men want light,
They make but bungling work.

Bert. I'll to the Queen,
And bear the news.

Ped. That's young Lorenzo's duty.

Bert. I'll fpare his trouble————
This Torrifmond begins to grow too faft;
He muft be mine, or ruin'd.   [*Afide.*

Lor. Pedro, a word. [*Whifper.*]   [*Exit* Bertran.

Alph. ' How fwift he fhot away! I find it ftung him,
' In fpite of his diffembling.'
To Lor.] How many of the enemy are flain?

Lor. Troth, Sir, we were in hafte, and could not ftay
To fcore the men we kill'd. But there they lie;
Beft fend our women out to take the tale;
There's circumcifion in abundance for them.
                              [*Turns to* Pedro *again.*

Alph. How far did you purfue them?

Lor. Some few miles.
To Ped.] Good ftore of harlots, fay you, and dog-cheap?
Pedro, they muft be had, and fpeedily.
I've kept a tedious faft.   [*Whifper again.*

Alph. When will he make his entry? He deferves
Such triumphs as were giv'n by ancient Rome.
Ha, boy, what fay'ft thou?

Lor. As you fay, Sir, that Rome was very ancient——
[*To* Ped.] I leave the choice to you; fair, black, tall, low;
Let her but have a nofe. And you may tell her
I'm rich in jewels, rings, and bobbing pearls
Pluck'd from Moors' ears.

B 2   Alph.

Alph. Lorenzo.

Lor. Somewhat bufy
About affairs relating to the public————
A feafouable girl, juft in the nick now.   [*To* Ped.
                                                                      [*Trumpets within.*

   Ped. I hear the General's trumpet.   Stand and mark
How he will be receiv'd : I fear, but coldly ;
There hung a cloud, methought, on Bertran's brow.

   Lor. Then look to fee a ftorm on Torrifmond's.
Looks fright not men : the General has feen Moors
With as bad faces, no difpraife to Bertran's.

   Ped. 'Twas rumour'd in the camp he loves the Queen.

   Lor. He drinks her health devoutly.

   Alph. That may breed bad blood 'twixt him and Bertran.

   Ped. Yes, in private.
But Bertran has heen taught the arts of courts,
To gild a face with fmiles, and leer a man to ruin.
Oh, here they come————
Enter Torrifmond *and Officers one fide*, Bertran, *attended,*
      on the other ; ' *they embrace,* Bertran *bowing low.*
' Juft as I prophefy'd.
   '. *Lor.* Death and hell, he laughs at him ! in's face too.
   ' *Ped.* Oh, you miftake him ! 'twas an humble grin,
' The fawning joy of courtiers and of dogs.'

   Lor. [*Afide.*] Here are nothing but lies to be expected ; I'll e'en go lofe myfelf in fome blind alley, and
try if any courteous damfel will think me worth the
finding.   [*Exit* Lor.

   ' *Alph.* Now he begins to open.'

   Bert. Your country refcu'd, and your Queen reliev'd !
A glorious conqueft, noble Torrifmond !
The people rend the fkies with loud applaufe,
And Heav'n can hear no other name but yours.
The thronging crouds prefs on you as you pafs,
And with their eager joy make triumph flow.

   Tor. My Lord, I have no tafte
Of popular applaufe ; the noify praife
Of giddy crouds, as changeable as winds,
Still vehement, and ftill without a caufe ;
Servants to chance, and blowing in the tide
Of fwol'n fuccefs ; but veering with its ebb,
It leaves the channel dry.

                                                                    Bert.

Bert. So young a ftoic !

Tor. You wrong me, if you think I'll fell one drop
Within thefe veins for pageants : but let honour
Call for my blood, and fluice it into ftreams ;
Turn fortune loofe again to my purfuit,
And let me hunt her through embattled foes,
In dufty plains, amidft the cannons roar,
There will I be the firft.

Bert. I'll try him farther————   [*Afide.*
Suppofe th' affembled ftates of Arragon
Decree a ftatue to you, thus infcrib'd,
To Torrifmond, who freed his native land.

' *Alph.* [*To* Ped.] Mark how he founds and fathoms
' The fhallows of his foul !   [him, to find

' *Bert.* The juft applaufe
' Of godlike fenates, is the ftamp of virtue,
' Which makes it pafs unqueftion'd through the world.
' Thefe honours you deferve ; nor fhall my fuffrage
' Be laft to fix them on you. If refus'd,
' You brand us all with black ingratitude ;
' For times to come fhall fay, Our Spain, like Rome,
' Neglects her champions after noble acts,
' And lets their laurels wither on their heads.'

Tor. A ftatue for a battle blindly fought,
Where darknefs and furprife made conqueft cheap !
Where Virtue borrow'd but the arms of Chance,
And ftruck a random blow ! 'Twas Fortune's work,
And Fortune take the praife.

Bert. Yet happinefs
Is the firft fame. Virtue, without fuccefs,
Is a fair picture fhewn by an ill light.
But lucky men are favourites of Heaven :
And whom fhould kings efteem above Heaven's darlings ?
The praifes of a young and beauteous queen
Shall crown your glorious acts.

Ped. [*To* Alph.] There fprung the mine.

Tor. The Queen ! that were a happinefs too great !
Nam'd you the Queen, my Lord ?

Bert. Yes. You have feen her, and you muft confefs,
A praife, a fmile, a look from her is worth
The fhouts of thoufand amphitheatres.
She, fhe fhall praife you ; for I can oblige her :

                    To-morrow

To-morrow will deliver all her charms
Into my arms, and make her mine for ever.
Why stand you mute ?
   Tor. Alas, I cannot speak !   [employ'd ?
   Bert. Not speak, my Lord ! How were your thoughts
   Tor. Nor can I think ; for I am lost in thought.
   Bert. Thought of the Queen, perhaps ?
   Tor. Why, if it were,
Heav'n may be thought on, though too high to climb.
   Bert. Oh, now I find where your ambition drives !
You ought not to think of her.
   Tor. So I say too,
I ought not : madmen ought not to be mad ;
But who can help his frenzy ?
   Bert. Fond young man !
The wings of your ambition must be clipp'd.
Your shame-fac'd virtue shunn'd the people's praise,
And senate's honours : but 'tis well we know
What price you hold yourself at. You have fought
With some success, and that has seal'd your pardon.
   Tor. Pardon from thee ! Oh, give me patience, Heaven !
Thrice vanquish'd Bertran, if thou dar'st, look out
Upon yon slaughter'd host, that field of blood ;
There seal my pardon, where thy fame was lost.
   Ped. He's ruin'd, past redemption !
   Alph. [*To* Tor.] Learn respect
To the first prince o' the blood.
   Bert. Oh, let him rave !
I'll not contend with madmen.
   Tor. I have done.
I know 'twere madness to declare this truth ;
And yet 'twere baseness to deny my love.
'Tis true, my hopes are vanishing as clouds,
Lighter than children's bubbles blown by winds.
My merit's but the rash result of chance ;
My birth unequal ; all the stars against me ;
Pow'r, promise, choice, the living and the dead ;
Mankind my foes, and only love my friend ;
But such a love, kept at such awful distance,
As, what it loudly dares to tell, a rival
Shall fear to whisper there. Queens may be lov'd,
And so may gods ; else why are altars rais'd ?
     3   Why

Why shines the sun, but that he may be view'd?
But, Oh, when he's *too* bright, if then we gaze,
'Tis but to weep, and clofe our eyes in darknefs!   [*Exit.*
‘ *Bert.* 'Tis well; the goddefs shall be told, she shall,
‘ Of her new worshipper.   [*Exit.*’
   Ped. So, here's fine work!
‘ He fupply'd his only foe with arms
‘ For his deftruction.   Old Penelope's talc
‘ Inverted: h' has unravell'd all by day,
‘ That; he has done by night.’   What, planet-ftruck!
   Alph. I wish I were, to be paft fenfe of this!
   Ped. Would I had but a leafe of life fo long,
As till my flesh and blood rebell'd this way,
Againft our fovereign lady! Mad for a queen,
With a globe in one hand, and a fceptre in t'other!
A very pretty moppet!
   Alph. Then to declare his madnefs to his rival,
His father abfent on an embaffy,
Himfelf a ftranger almoft, wholly friendlefs!
A torrent, rolling down a precipice,
Is eafier to be ftopp'd, than is his ruin.
   Ped. 'Tis fruitlefs to complain : hafte to the court;
Improve your intereft there, for pardon from the queen.
   Alph. Weak remedies;
But all muft be attempted.   [*Exit.*
           Enter Lorenzo.
   Lor. Well, I am the moft unlucky rogue! I have been
ranging over half the town, but have fprung no game.
Our women are worfe infidels than the Moors : I told
them I was one of their knights-errant, that delivered
them from ravishment; and I think in my confcience
that's their quarrel to me.
   Ped. Is this a time for fooling? Your coufin is run ho-
nonourably mad in love with her Majefty : he is fplit
upon a rock; and you, who are in chace of harlots, are
finking in the main ocean. I think the devil's in the family.   [*Exit.*
   Lor. My coufin ruined, fays he!—Hum!—Not that
I wish my coufin's ruin; that were unchriftian : but if
the General's ruined, I am heir; there's comfort for a
Chriftian. Money I have, I thank the honeft Moors for't;
                                                    ‘ but

but I want a miftrefs.   I am willing to be lewd; but the tempter is wanting on his part.

Enter Elvira *veiled.*

Elv. Stranger! cavalier! Will you not hear me, you Moor-killer, you *matador?*

Lor. Meaning me, Madam?

Elv. Face about, man; you a foldier, and afraid of the enemy!

Lor. I muft confefs, I did not expect to have been charged firft. I fee fouls will not be loft for want of diligence in this devil's reign. [*Afide.*]—Now, Madam Cynthia behind a cloud, your will and pleafure with me?

Elv. You have the appearance of a cavalier; and if you are as deferving as you feem, perhaps you may not repent of your adventure. If a lady like you well enough to hold difcourfe with you at firft fight, you are gentleman enough, I hope, to help her out with an apology, and to lay the blame on ftars, or deftiny, or what you pleafe, to excufe the frailty of a woman.

Lor. Oh, I love an eafy woman! there's fuch a-do to crack a thick-fhell'd miftrefs; we break our teeth, and find no kernel. 'Tis generous in you to take pity on a ftranger, and not to fuffer him to fall into ill hands at his firft arrival.

Elv. You have a better opinion of me than I deferve. You have not feen me yet; and therefore I am confident you are heart-whole.

Lor. Not abfolutely flain, I muft confefs; but I am drawing on apace. You have a dangerous tongue in your head, I can tell you that; and if your eyes prove of as killing metal, there's but one way with me. Let me fee you, for the fafe-guard of my honour: 'tis but decent the cannon fhould be drawn down upon me before I yield.

Elv. What a terrible fimilitude have you made, Colonel, to fhew that you are inclining to the wars! I could anfwer you with another in my profeffion. Suppofe you were in want of money; would you not be glad to take a fum upon content in a fealed bag, without peeping?——— But, however, I will not ftand with you for a fample.

[*Lifts up her veil.*

Lor. What eyes were there! how keen their glances!

you

you do well to keep them veiled : they are too sharp to be
trusted out of the scabbard.

Elv. Perhaps, now, you may accuse my forwardnefs :
but this day of jubilee is the only time of freedom I have
had; and there is nothing fo extravagant as a prisoner,
when he gets loofe a little, and is immediately to return
to his fetters.

Lor. To confefs freely to you, Madam, I was never in
love with lefs than your whole fex before : but now I
have feen you, I am in the direct road of languifhing and
fighing ; and, if love goes on as it begins, for ought I
know, by to-morrow morning you may hear of me in
rhyme and fonnet. I tell you truly, I do not like thefe
fymptoms in myfelf. Perhaps I may go fhufflingly at
firft ; for I was never before walked in trammels : yet I
fhall drudge and moil at conftancy, till I have worn off
the hitching in my pace.

Elv. Oh, Sir, there are arts to reclaim the wildeft men,
as there are to make fpaniels fetch and carry ! chide them
often, and feed them feldom. Now I know your temper,
you may thank yourfelf if you are kept to hard meat—
you are in for years, if you make love to me.

Lor. I hate a formal obligation, with an *anno domini* at
the end on't : there may be an evil meaning in the word
years, called matrimony.

Elv. I can eafily rid you of that fear : I wifh I could
rid myfelf as eafily of the bondage.

Lor. Then you are married ?

Elv. If a covetous, and a jealous, and an old man be
a hufband.

Lor. Three as good qualities for my purpofe as I could
wifh. Now, Love be praifed !

 Enter Elvira's *Duenna, and whifpers to her.*

Elv. [*Afide.*] If I get not home before my hufband, I
fhall be ruin'd——[*To him.*] I dare not ftay to tell you
where—Farewel—Could I once more——   [*Exit.*

Lor. This is unconfcionable dealing : to be made a
flave, and not know whofe livery I wear——Who have
we yonder ?

  Enter Gomez.

By that fhambling in his walk, it fhould be my rich old
       banker,

banker, Gomez, whom I knew at Barcelona. As I live 'tis he! [*To* Gom.] What, old Mammon here?

Gom. How! young Belzebub?

Lor. What devil has set his claws in thy haunches, and brought thee hither to Saragossa? Sure he meant a farther journey with thee.

Gom. I always remove before the enemy: when the Moors are ready to besiege one town, I shift my quarters to the next; I keep as far from the infidels as I can.

Lor. That's but a hair's breadth at farthest.

Gom. Well, you have got a famous victory; all true subjects are overjoyed at it: there are bonfires decreed; an the times had not been so hard, my billet should have burnt too.

Lor. I dare say for thee, thou hast such a respect for a single billet, that thou would'st almost have thrown on thyself to save it; thou art for saving every thing but thy soul.

Gom. Well, well, you'll not believe me generous till I carry you to the tavern, and crack half a pint with you at my own charge.

Lor. No; I'll keep thee from hanging thyself for such an extravagance; and instead of it, thou shalt do me a mere verbal courtesy: I have just now seen a most incomparable young lady.

Gom. Whereabouts did you see this most incomparable young lady?———My mind misgives me plaguily.

[*Aside.*

Lor. Here, man, just before this corner house: pray Heaven it prove no bawdy-house.

Gom. [*Aside.*] Pray Heaven he does not make it one.

Lor. What dost thou mutter to thyself? Hast thou any thing to say against the honesty of that house?

Gom. Not I, Colonel, the walls are very honest stone, and the timber very honest wood, for ought I know; but for the woman I cannot say, till I know her better. Describe her person, and if she live in this quarter I may give you tidings of her.

Lor. She's of a middle stature, dark-colour'd hair, the most bewitching leer with her eyes, the most roguish cast; her cheeks are dimpled when she smiles, and her smiles would tempt an hermit.

Gom.

Gom. [*Aside.*] I am dead, I am buried, I am damned.——Go on——Colonel——have you no other marks of her?

Lor. Thou haſt all her marks, but that ſhe has an huſband, a jealous, covetous, old huncks : ſpeak; canſt thou tell me news of her?

Gom. Yes, this news, Colonel, that you have ſeen your laſt of her.

Lor. If thou helpeſt me not to the knowledge of her, thou art a circumciſed Jew.

Gom. Circumciſe me no more than I circumciſe you, Colonel Hernando.　Once more, you have ſeen your laſt of her.

Lor. [*Aſide.*] I am glad he knows me only by that name of Hernando, by which I went at Barcelona; now he can tell no tales of me to my father. [*To him.*] Come, thou wert ever good-natured, when thou could'ſt get by it.　Look here, rogue, 'tis of the right damning colour : thou art not proof againſt gold, ſure!　Do not I know thee for a covetous————

Gom. Jealous old huncks; thoſe were the marks of your miſtreſs's huſband, as I remember, Colonel.

Lor. O the devil! what a rogue in underſtanding was I, not to find him out ſooner!　　　　　　[*Aſide.*

Gom. Do, do, look ſillily, good Colonel; 'tis a decent melancholy after an abſolute defeat.

Lor. Faith, not for that, dear Gomez :——but——

Gom. But—no pumping, my dear Colonel.

Lor. Hang pumping; I was—thinking a little upon a point of gratitude : we two have been long acquaintance; I know thy merits, and can make ſome intereſt; go to; thou wert born to authority; I'll make thee Alcaide, mayor of Saragoſſa.

Gom. Satisfy yourſelf; you ſhall not make me what you think, Colonel.

Lor. Faith but I will; thou haſt the face of a magiſtrate already.

Gom. And you would provide me with a magiſtrate's head to my magiſtrate's face; I thank you, Colonel.

Lor. Come, thou art ſo ſuſpicious upon an idle ſtory—that woman I ſaw, I mean that little crooked, ugly woman, for t'other was a lie—is no more thy wife——as

I'll

I'll go home with thee, and satisfy thee immediately, my dear friend.

Gom. I shall not put you to that trouble; no, not so much as a single visit; not so much as an embassy by a civil old woman, nor a serenade of twincledum twincledum under my windows: nay, I will advise you, out of tenderness to your person, that you walk not near yon corner-house by night; for to my certain knowledge, there are blunderbusses planted in every loop-hole, that go off constantly of their own accord at the squeaking of a fiddle and the thrummming of a guittar.

Lor. Art thou so obstinate? Then I denounce open war against thee: I'll demolish thy citadel by force; or, at least, I'll bring my whole regiment upon thee: my thousand red locusts, that shall devour thee in free quarter.——Farewel, wrought night-cap.   [*Exit.*

Gom. Farewel, Buff! free quarter for a regiment of red-coat locusts! I hope to see them all in the Red Sea first!——But Oh, this Jezabel of mine! I'll get a physician that shall prescribe her an ounce of camphire every morning for her breakfast, to abate incontinency. She shall never peep abroad, no, not to church for confession! and for never going, she shall be condemned for a heretic. She shall have stripes by Troy-weight, and sustenance by drachms and scruples: nay, I'll have a fasting almanack printed on purpose for her use, in which

No carnival nor Christmas shall appear,
But Lents and Ember-weeks shall fill the year.
                                        [*Exit.*

END of the FIRST ACT.

ACT II.

' SCENE, *The Queen's Antichamber.*

' Alphonso *and* Pedro.

' ALPHONSO.

' WHEN saw you my Lorenzo?
          ' *Ped.* I had a glimpse of him; but he shot
          by me
                                        ' Like

‘ Like a young hound upon a burning scent :
‘ He's gone a harlot hunting.
   ‘ *Alph.* His foreign breeding might have taught him
       better.
   ‘ *Ped.* 'Tis that has taught him this.
‘ What learn our youth abroad, but to refine
‘ The homely vices of their native land ?
‘ Give me an honeſt home-ſpun country clown
‘ Of our own growth ; his dulneſs is but plain,
‘ But theirs embroidered ; they are ſent out fools, ’
‘ And come back fops.
   ‘ *Alph.* You know what reaſons urg'd me ;
‘ But now I have accompliſhed my deſigns,
‘ I ſhould be glad he knew them.   His wild riots
‘ Diſturb my ſoul ; but they would ſit more cloſe,
‘ Did not the threaten'd downfall of our houſe,
‘ In Torriſmond, o'erwhelm my private ills.
‘ *Enter* Bertran *attended, and whiſpering with a Courtier*
       ‘ *aſide.*
   ‘ *Bert.* I would not have her think he dar'd to love
‘ If he preſumes to own it, ſhe's ſo proud,   [her ;
‘ He tempts his certain ruin.
   ‘ *Alph.* [*To* Ped.] Mark how diſdainfully he throws
       his eyes on us.
‘ Our old impriſon'd king wore no ſuch looks.
   ‘ *Ped.* O, would the General ſhake off his dotage to
      th'uſurping Queen,
‘ And re-inthrone good venerable Sancho ;
‘ I'll underdake, ſhould Bertran ſound his trumpets,
‘ And Torriſmond but whiſtle through his fingers,
‘ He draws his army off.
   ‘ *Alph.* I told him ſo ;
‘ But had an anſwer louder than a ſtorm.
   ‘ *Ped.* Now plague and pox on his ſmock-loyalty ;
‘ I hate to ſee a brave, bold fellow ſotted,
‘ Made ſour and ſenſeleſs, turn'd to whey, by love ;
‘ A driveling hero, fit for a romance.
‘ O, here he comes : what will their greeting be ?’
Enter Torriſmond *attended.* Bertran *and he meet and juſtle.*
  Bert. Make way, my lords, and let the pageant paſs.
  Tor. I make my way where-e'er I ſee my foe :
C

But

But you, my Lord, are good at a retreat.
I have no Moors behind me.
    Bert. Death and hell!
Dare to ſpeak thus when you come out again.
    Tor. Dare to provoke me thus, inſulting man.
                    Enter Tereſa.
    Ter. My Lords, you are too loud ſo near the Queen;
You, Torriſmond, have much offended her.
'Tis her command you inſtantly appear,
To anſwer your demeanour to the prince.
    [*Exit* Tereſa ; Bertran *with his company following her.*
    Tor. O, Pedro! O, Alphonſo! pity me!
A grove of pikes,
Whoſe poliſh'd ſteel from far ſeverely ſhines,
Are not ſo dreadful as this beauteous queen.
    Alph. Call up your courage timely to your aid,
And, like a lion preſs'd upon the toils,
Leap on your hunters.   Speak your actions boldly.
There is a time when modeſt virtue is
Allow'd to praiſe itſelf.
    Ped. Heart, you were hot enough, too hot, but now ;
Your fury then boil'd upward to a foam :
But ſince this meſſage came, you ſink and ſettle,
As if cold water had been pour'd upon you.
    Tor. Alas, thou know'ſt not what it is to love !
When we behold an angel, not to fear,
Is to be impudent: no, I'm reſolv'd,
Like a led victim, to my death I'll go,
And, dying, bleſs the hand that gave the blow.
                                [*Exeunt.*

The SCENE *draws, and ſhews the Queen ſitting in ſtate :*
    Bertran *ſtanding next her ; then* Tereſa, *&c. She riſes,*
    and comes to the front.

    Qu. [*To* Ber.] I blame not you, my Lord ; my fa-
            ther's will,
Your own deſerts, and all my people's voice,
Have plac'd you in the view of ſov'reign power.
But I would learn the cauſe, why Torriſmond,
Within my palace walls, within my hearing,
Almoſt within my ſight, affronts a prince
Who ſhortly ſhall command him.
                                Bert.

Ber. He thinks you owe him more than you can pay,
And looks as he were lord of human kind.
Enter Torrifmond, Alphonfo, *and* Pedro. Torrifmond
*bows low, then looks earneftly on the Queen, and keeps at
diftance.*
Ter. Madam, the General.——
Qu. Let me view him well.
My father fent him early to the frontiers.
I have not often feen him ; if I did,
He pafs'd unmark'd by my unheeding eyes.
But where's the fiercenefs, the difdainful pride,
The haughty port, the fiery arrogance ?
By all thefe marks, this is not fure the man.
Bert. Yet this is he who fill'd your court with tumult,
Whofe fierce demeanour, and whofe infolence,
The patience of a god could not fupport.
Qu. Name his offence, my Lord, and he fhall have
Immediate punifhment.
Bert. 'Tis of fo high a nature, fhould I fpeak it,
That my prefumption then would equal his.
Qu. Some one among you fpeak.
Ped. [*Afide.*] Now my tongue itches.
Qu. All dumb! On your allegiance, Torrifmond,
By all your hopes, I do command you, fpeak.
Tor. [*Kneeling.*] O feek not to convince me of a crime
Which I can ne'er repent, nor can you pardon ;
Or, if you needs will know it, think, Oh think,
That he who thus commanded dares to fpeak,
Unlefs commanded, would have dy'd in filence.
But you adjur'd me, Madam, by my hopes !
Hopes I have none, for I am all defpair ;
Friends I have none, for friendfhip follows favour ;
Defert I have none, for what I did was duty :
Oh, that it were ! that it were duty all !
Qu. Why do you paufe ? Proceed.
Tor. As one condemn'd to leap a precipice,
Who fees before his eyes the depth below,
Stops fhort, and looks about for fome kind fhrub
To break his dreadful fall—fo I—
But whither am I going ? If to death,
He looks fo lovely fweet in beauty's pomp,
He draws me to his dart.—I dare no more.

C 2

Bert.

Bert. He's mad beyond the cure of Hellebore.
Whips, darknefs, dungeons for this infolence.

Tor. Mad as I am, yet I know when to bear.

Qu. You're both too bold. You, Torrifmond, withdraw;
I'll teach you all what's owing to your queen.
For you, my Lord ——
The prieft to-morrow was to join our hands;
I'll try if I can live a day without you.
So both of you depart, and live in peace.

Alph. Who knows which way fhe points?
Doubling and turning like an hunted hare.
Find out the meaning of her mind who can.

Ped. Who ever found a woman's? Backward and forward. The whole fex in every word. In my confcience,
when fhe was getting, her mother was thinking of a
riddle.   [*Exeunt all but the Queen and* Terefa.

Qu. Hafte, my Terefa, hafte, and call him back.

Ter. Whom, Madam?

Qu. Him.

Ter. Prince Bertran?

Qu. Torrifmond;
There is no other he.

'-*Ter.* [*Afide.*] A rifing fun,
• Or I am much deceiv'd.'   [*Exit* Terefa.

Qu. A change fo fwift what heart did ever feel!
It rufh'd upon me like a mighty ftream,
And bore me in a moment far from fhore.
I've lov'd away myfelf; in one fhort hour
Already am I gone an age of paffion.
Was it his youth, his valour, or fuccefs?
Thefe might perhaps be found in other men.
'Twas that refpect, that awful homage paid me;
That fearful love which trembled in his eyes,
And with a filent earthquake fhook his foul.
But, when he fpoke, what tender words he faid!
So foftly, that, like flakes of feather'd fnow,
They melted as they fell.——
              Enter Terefa *with* Torrifmond.

Ter. He waits your pleafure.

Qu. 'Tis well; retire—Oh, Heav'ns, that I muft fpeak
So diftant from my heart——   [*Afide.*
                                                  [*To*

[*To* Tor.] How now ! What boldnefs brings you back
  Tor. I heard 'twas your command.   [again ?
  Qu. A fond miftake,
To credit fo unlikely a command.
And you return full of the fame prefumption,
T' affront me with your love ?
  Tor. If 'tis prefumption, for a wretch condemn'd,
To throw himfelf beneath his judge's feet :
A boldnefs more than this I never knew ;
Or, if I did, 'twas only to your foes.
  Qu. You would infinuate your paft fervices, ·
And thofe, I grant, were great ; but you confefs
A fault committed fince, that cancels all.
  Tor. And who could dare to difavow his crime,
When that for which he is accus'd and feiz'd,
He bears about him ftill ! My eyes confefs it ;
My every action fpeaks my heart aloud :
But, Oh, the madnefs of my high attempt
Speaks louder yet ! and all together cry,
I love and I defpair.
  Qu. Have you not heard,
My father, with his dying voice, bequeath'
My crown and me to Bertran ? And dare you,
A private man, prefume to love a queen ?
  Tor. That, that's the wound ! I fee you fet fo high,
As no defert or fervices can reach :
Good heav'ns, why gave you me a monarch's foul,
And crufted it with bafe Plebeian clay ?
Why gave you me defires of fuch extent,
And fuch a fpan to grafp them ? Sure my lot
By fome o'er-hafty angel was mifplac'd
In Fate's eternal volume !——But I rave,
And, like a giddy bird in dead of night,
Fly round the fire that fcorches me to death.
  Qu. Yes, Torrifmond, you've not fo ill deferv'd,
But I may give you counfel for your cure.
  Tor. I cannot, nay, I wifh not to be cur'd.
  Qu. [*Afide.*] Nor I, Heav'n knows !
  Tor. There is a pleafure fure
In being mad, which none but madmen know !
Let me indulge it ; let me gaze for ever !
C 3

And,

And, fince you are too great to be belov'd,
Be greater, greater yet, and be ador'd.

Qu. Thefe are the words which I muft only hear
From Bertran's mouth; they fhould difpleafe from you;
I fay they fhould; but women are fo vain
To like the love, though they defpife the lover.
Yet, that I may not fend you from my fight
In abfolute defpair——I pity you.

Tor. Am I then pity'd! I have liv'd enough!
Death, take me in this moment of my joy:
But when my foul is plung'd in long oblivion,
Spare this one thought, let me remember pity;
And fo deceiv'd, think all my life was blefs'd.

Qu. What if I add a little to my alms?
If that would help, I could caft in a tear
To your misfortunes.

Tor. A tear! you have o'erbid all my paft fufferings,
And all my future too!

Qu. Were I no queen——
Or you of royal blood——

Tor. What have I loft by my fore-fathers' fault!
Why was not I the twentieth by defcent
From a long reftive race of droning kings?
Love, what a poor omnipotence haft thou,
When gold and titles buy thee?

Qu. [*Sighs.*] Oh, my torture!

Tor. Might I prefume, but, Oh, I dare not hope
That figh was added to your alms for me!

Qu. I give you leave to guefs, and not forbid you
To make the beft conftruction for your love.
Be fecret and difcreet; thefe fairy favours
Are loft when not conceal'd;—provoke not Bertran—
Retire; I muft no more but this—Hope, Torrifmond.
                                       [*Exit.*

Tor. She bids me hope; Oh, Heav'ns, fhe pities me!
And pity ftill foreruns approaching love,
As lightning does the thunder! Tune your harps,
Ye angels, to that found; and thou, my heart,
Make room to entertain thy flowing joy.
Hence all my griefs and every anxious care;
One word, and one kind glance, can cure defpair. [*Exit.*

SCENE,

SCENE, *a Chamber. A table and wine set out.*

Enter Lorenzo.

Lor. This may hit, 'tis more than barely possible; for fryars have free admittance into every house. This Jacobin, whom I have sent to, is her confessor; and who can suspect a man of such reverence for a pimp? I'll try for once; I'll bribe him high; for commonly none love money better than they who have made a vow of poverty.

Enter Servant.

Serv. There's a huge, fat, religious gentleman coming up, Sir; he says he's but a fryar, but he's big enough to be a pope; his gills are as rosy as a turkey cock's; his great belly walks in state before him like an harbinger; and his gouty legs come limping after it: never was such a tun of devotion seen.

Lor. Bring him in, and vanish.   [*Exit.*

Enter Father Dominick.

Lor. Welcome, father.

Dom. Peace be here: I thought I had been sent for to a dying man, to have fitted him for another world.

Lor. No, faith, father, I was never for taking such long journies. Repose yourself, I beseech you, Sir, if those spindle legs of yours will carry you to the next chair.

Dom. I am old, I am infirm, I must confess, with fasting.

Lor. 'Tis a sign by your wan complexion, and your thin jowls, father. Come, to our better acquaintance: here's a sovereign remedy for old age and sorrow.

[*Drinks.*

Dom. The looks of it are indeed alluring: I'll do you reason.   [*Drinks.*

Lor. Is it to your palate, father?

Dom. Second thoughts, they say, are best: I'll consider of it once again. [*Drinks.*] It has a most delicious flavour with it. Gad, forgive me, I have forgotten to drink your health, son, I am not used to be so unmannerly.   [*Drinks again.*

Lor. No, I'll be sworn, by what I see of you, you are not. To the bottom, I warrant him, a true church-man.

Now,

Now, father, to our bufinefs, 'tis agreeable to your calling; I intend to do an act of charity.

Dom. And I love to hear of charity; 'tis a comfortable fubject.

Lor. Being in the late battle, in great hazard of my life, I recommended my perfon to good St. Dominick.

Dom. You could not have pitched upon a better: he's a fure card: I never knew him fail his votaries.

Lor. Troth I e'en made bold to ftrike up a bargain with him, that if I 'fcaped with life and plunder, I would prefent fome brother of his order with part of the booty taken from the infidels, to be employed in charitable ufes.

Dom. There you hit him; St. Dominick loves charity exceedingly; that argument never fails with him.

Lor. The fpoils were mighty; and I fcorn to wrong him of a farthing. To make fhort my ftory; I enquired among the Jacobins for an almoner, and the General has pointed out your reverence as the worthieft man: here are fifty pieces in this purfe.

Dom. How! fifty pieces? 'tis too much, too much in confcience.

Lor. Here, take them, father.

Dom. No, in troth, I dare not: do not tempt me to break my vow of poverty.

Lor. If you are modeft, I muft force you; for I am ftrongeft,

Dom. Nay, if you compel me, there's no contending; but will you fet your ftrength againft a decrepit, poor, old man? [*Takes the purfe.*] As I faid, 'tis too great a bounty? But St. Dominick fhall owe you another 'fcape; I'll put him in mind of you.

Lor. If you pleafe, father, we will not trouble him 'till the next battle. But you may do me a greater kindnefs, by conveying my prayers to a female faint.

Dom. A female faint! good now, good now, how your devotions jump with mine! I always loved the female faints.

Lor. I mean a female, mortal, married-woman faint. Look upon the fuperfcription of this note; you know Don Gomez's wife.　　　　　[*Gives him a letter.*
　　　　　　　　　　　　　　　　　　　　　　Dom.

Dom. Who, Donna Elvira? I think I have some reason; I am her ghostly father.

Lor. I have some business of importance with her,
which I have communicated in this paper; but her husband is so horribly given to be jealous.

Dom. Ho, jealous! he's the very quintessence of jealousy: he keeps no male creature in his house; and from
abroad he lets no man come near her.

Lor. Excepting you, father.

Dom. Me, I grant you: I am her director and her
guide in spiritual affairs. But he has his humours with
me too; for t'other day, he called me false apostle.

Lor. Did he so? that reflects upon you all; on my
word, father, that touches your copyhold. If you would
do a meritorious action, you might revenge the church's
quarrel. My letter, father.

Dom. Well, so far as a letter, I will take upon me;
for what can I refuse to a man so charitably given?

Lor. If you bring an answer back, that purse in your
hand has a twin-brother, as like him as ever he can
look; there are fifty pieces lie dormant in it, for more
charities.

Dom. That must not be: not a farthing more, upon
my priesthood. But what may be the purport and meaning of this letter; that, I confess, a little troubles me.

Lor. No harm, I warrant you.

Dom. Well, you are a charitable man; and I'll take
your word: my comfort is, I know not the contents;
and so far I am blameless. But an answer you shall
have; though not for the sake of your fifty pieces more:
I have sworn not to take them, they shall not be altogether fifty: your mistress—forgive me that I should
call her your mistress, I meant Elvira, lives but at next
door: I'll visit her immediately: but not a word more of
the nine and forty pieces.

Lor. Nay, I'll wait on you down stairs. Fifty pounds
for the postage of a letter! to send by the church is certainly the dearest road in Christendom.   [*Exeunt.*

SCENE, a Chamber.

Enter Gomez *and* Elvira.

Gom. Henceforth I banish flesh and wine: I'll have
none stirring within these walls these twelve months.

Elv.

Elv. I care not; the sooner I am starved, the sooner I am rid of wedlock. I shall learn the knack to fast a days: you have used me to fasting nights already.

Gom. How the gipsey answers me! Oh, 'tis a most notorious hilding.

Elv. [*Crying.*] But was ever poor innocent creature so hardly dealt with, for a little harmless chat?

Gom. 'Oh, the impudence of this wicked sex!' Lascivious dialogues are innocent chat with you!

Elv. Was it such a crime to enquire how the battle passed?

Gom. But that was not the business, gentlewoman; you were not asking news of a battle passed; you were engaging for a skirmish that was to come.

Elv. An honest woman would be glad to hear, that her honour was safe, and her enemies were slain.

Gom. [*In her tone.*] And to ask, if he were wounded in your defence; and, in case he were, to offer yourself to be his surgeon; then you did not describe your husband to him, for a covetous, jealous, rich, old hunks.

Elv. No, I need not: he describes himself sufficiently: but, in what dream did I do this?

Gom. You walked in your sleep, with your eyes broad open, at noon-day; and dreamed you were talking to the foresaid purpose with one Colonel Hernando——

Elv. Who, dear husband, who?

Gom. What the devil have I said? You would have farther information, would you.

Elv. No, but my dear, little old man, tell me now; that I may avoid him for your sake.

Gom. Get you up into your chamber, cockatrice; and there immure yourself: be confined, I say, during our royal pleasure: but, first, down on your marrowbones, upon your allegiance, and make an acknowledgement of your offences; for I will have ample satisfaction.

[*Pulls her down.*

Elv. I have done you no injury, and therefore I'll make you no submission: but I'll complain to my ghostly father.

Gom. Ay; there's your remedy: when you receive condign punishment, you run with open mouth to your confessor; that parcel of holy guts and garbage: he must

chuckle

chuckle you and moan you: but I'll rid my hands of his
ghostly authority one day,

Enter Dominick.

and make him know he's the son of a——[*Sees him.*] So;
——no sooner conjure, but the devil's in the circle.

Dom. Son of what, Don Gomez.

Gom. Why, a son of a church; I hope there's no
harm in that, father?

Dom. I will lay up your words for you till time shall
serve; and to-morrow I enjoin you to fast, for penance.

Gom. [*Aside.*] There's no harm in that; she shall fast
too; fasting saves money.

Dom. [*To* Elvira.] What was the reason that I found
you upon your knees, in that unseemly posture?

Gom. [*Aside.*] Oh, horrible! to find a woman upon
her knees, he says, is an unseemly posture; there's a
priest for you!

Elv. [*To* Dom.] I wish, father, you would give me an
opportunity of entertaining you in private: I have somewhat upon my spirits that presses me exceedingly.

Dom. [*Aside.*] This goes well: Gomez, stand you at
a distance,—farther yet,—stand out of ear-shot—I have
somewhat to say to your wife in private.

Gom. [*Aside.*] Was ever man thus priest-ridden?
Would the steeple of his church were in his belly: I am
sure there's room for it.

Elv. I am ashamed to acknowledge my infirmities;
but you have been always an indulgent father; and
therefore I will venture to—and yet I dare not.

Dom. Nay, if you are bashful; if you keep your
wound from the knowledge of your surgeon.

Elv. You know my husband is a man in years; but
he's my husband, and therefore I shall be silent; but
his humours are more intolerable than his age: he's
grown so froward, so covetous, and so jealous, that he
has turned my heart quite from him; and, if I durst confess it, has forced me to cast my affections on another
man.

Dom. Good!——hold, hold; I meant abominable.
——Pray, Heaven, this be my Colonel.   [*Aside.*

Elv. I have seen this man, father; and have encouraged his addresses: he's a young gentleman, a soldier,

of

of a moſt winning carriage; and what his courtſhip may produce at laſt, I know not; but I am afraid of my own frailty.

Dom. [*Aſide.*] 'Tis he for certain: ſhe has ſaved the credit of my function, by ſpeaking firſt; now I muſt take gravity upon me.

Gom. [*Aſide.*] This whiſpering bodes me no good for certain; but he has me ſo plaguily under the laſh, that I dare not interrupt him.

Dom. Daughter, daughter, do you remember your matrimonial vow?

Elv. Yes, to my ſorrow, father, I do remember it; a miſerable woman it has made me: but you know, father, a marriage vow is but a thing of courſe, which all women take, when they would get a huſband.

Dom. A vow is a very ſolemn thing; and it is good to keep it:—but, notwithſtanding, it may be broken, upon ſome occaſions. Have you ſtriven with all your might againſt this frailty?

Elv. Yes, I have ſtriven: but I found it was againſt the ſtream. Love, you know, father, is a great vow-maker; but he's a greater vow breaker.

Dom. 'Tis your duty to ſtrive always: but, notwith-ſtanding, when we have done our utmoſt, it extenuates the ſin.

Gom. I can hold no longer——Now, gentlewoman, you are confeſſing your enormities; I know it, by that hypocrital, down-caſt look: enjoin her to ſit bare upon a bed of nettles, father; you can do no leſs in conſcience.

Dom. Hold your peace; are you growing malapert? Will you force me to make uſe of my authority? Your wife's a well-diſpoſed and a virtuous lady; I ſay it, *in verbo ſarcedotis.*

Elv. I know not what to do, father; I find myſelf in a moſt deſperate condition; and ſo is the Colonel for love of me.

Dom. The Colonel, ſay you! I wiſh it be not the ſame young gentleman I know; 'tis a gallant young man, I muſt confeſs, worthy of any lady's love in Chriſtendom; in a lawful way, I mean: of ſuch a charming behaviour, ſo bewitching to a woman's eye; and furthermore, ſo charitably given; by all good tokens, this muft be my Colonel Hernando.

Elv. Ay, and my Colonel too, father: I am over-joyed; and are you then acquainted with him?

Dom. Acquainted with him! Why, he haunts me up and down; and, I am afraid, it is for love of you; for he preffed a letter upon me, within this hour, to deliver to you: I confefs, I received it, left he fhould fend it by fome other; but with full refolution never to put it into your hands.

Elv. Oh, dear father, let me have it, or I fhall die.

Gom. Whifpering ftill! A pox of your clofe commit-tee! I'll liften, I'm refolved.   [*Steals nearer.*

Dom. Nay, if you are obftinately bent to fee it, ufe your difcretion, but for my part, I wafh my hands on't. What makes you liftening there? Get farther off, I preach not to thee, thou wicked eves-dropper.

Elv. I'll kneel down, father, as if I were taking ab-folution, if you'll but pleafe to ftand before me.

Dom. At you peril be it then. I have told you the ill confequences; *& liberavi animam meam.*—Your reputa-tion is in danger, to fay nothing of your foul. Not-withftanding, when the fpiritual means have been ap-plied, and fail; in that cafe, the carnal may be ufed.—You are a 'tender child, you are; and muft not be put into defpair: your heart is as foft and melting as your hand.   [*He ftrokes her face; takes her by the hand; and gives the letter.*

Gom. Hold, hold, father, you go beyond your com-miffion; palming is always held foul play amongft game-fters.

Dom. Thus good intentions are mifconftrued by wick-ed men; you will never be warned 'till you are excom-municated.

Gom. [*Afide.*] Ah, devil on him; there's his hold! if there were no more in excommunication than the church's cenfure, a wife man would lick his confcience whole with a wet finger; but, if I am excommunicated, I am out-lawed; and then there's no calling in my money.

Elv. [*Rifing.*] I have read the note, father, and will fend him an anfwer immediately; for I know his lodg-ing by his letter.

D

Dom.

Dom. I underſtand it not, for my part; but I wiſh your intentions be honeſt. Remember, that adultery, though it be a ſilent ſin, yet it is a crying ſin alſo. Nevertheleſs, if you believe abſolutely he will die, unleſs you pity him, to ſave a man's life is a point of charity; and actions of charity do alleviate, as I may ſay, and take off from the mortality of the ſin. Farewel, daughter—Gomez, cheriſh your virtuous wife; and thereupon I give you my benediction.   [*Going.*

Gom. Stay; I'll conduct you to the door, that I may be ſure you ſteal nothing by the way. Fryars wear not their long ſleeves for nothing.—Oh, it is a Judas Iſcariot.
                                    [*Exit after the Fryar.*

Elv. This fryar is a comfortable man! He will underſtand nothing of the buſineſs, and yet does it all.

Pray, wives, and virgins, at your time of need,
For a true guide, of my good father's breed.   [*Exit.*

END of the SECOND ACT.

A C T   III.

SCENE, *the Street.*

Enter Lorenzo *in a Fryar's habit, following* Dominick.

LORENZO.

FATHER Dominick, father Dominick! Why in ſuch haſte, man?

Dom. It ſhould ſeem a brother of our order.

Lor. No, faith, I am only your brother in iniquity; my holineſs, like yours, is mere outſide.

Dom. What! my noble Colonel in metamorphoſis! On what occaſion are you transformed?

Lor. Love; almighty love; that which turned Jupiter into a town-bull, has transformed me into a fryar: I have had a letter from Elvira, in anſwer to that I ſent by you.

Dom. You ſee I have delivered my meſſage faithfully; I am a fryar of honour where I am engaged.

Lor. Oh, I underſtand your hint; the other fifty pieces are ready to be condemned to charity.

                                                    Dom.

Dom. But this habit, fon, this habit!

Lor. 'Tis a habit, that in all ages has been friendly to fornication : you have begun the defign in this cloath-ing, and I'll try to accomplifh it. The hufband is ab-fent ; that evil counfellor is removed ; and the fovereign is gracioufly difpofed to hear my grievances.

Dom. Go to ; go to ; I find good counfel is but thrown away upon you : fare you well, fare you well, fon ! ah——

Lor. How ! will you turn recreant at the laft caft ? You muft along to countenance my undertaking : we are at the door, man.

Dom. Well, I have thought on't, and I will not go.

Lor. You may ftay, father ; but no fifty pounds with-out it ; that was only promifed in the bond : but the con-dition of this obligation is fuch, that if the above-named father, father Dominick, do not well and faith-fully perform——

Dom. Now I better think on't, I will bear you compa-ny ; for the reverence of my prefence may be a curb to your exorbitances.

Lor. Lead up your myrmidon, and enter.   [*Exeunt.*
Enter Elvira *in her Chamber.*

Elv. He'll come, that's certain ; young appetites are fharp, and feldom need twice bidding to fuch a banquet. Well, if I prove frail, as I hope I fhall not, till I have compaffed my defign, never woman had fuch a hufband to provoke her, fuch a lover to allure her, or fuch a con-feffor to abfolve her ? ' Of what am I afraid, then ? Not ' my confcience, that's fafe enough ; my ghoftly father ' has given it a dofe of church opium to lull it. Well, ' for foothing fin, I'll fay that for him, he's a chaplain ' for any court in Chriftendom.'
Enter Lorenzo *and* Dominick.

Oh, Father Dominick, what news ? How, a companion with you ! What game have you in hand, that you hunt in couples ?

Lor. [*Lifting up his hood.*] I'll fhew you that im-mediately.

Elv. Oh, my love !

Lor. My life !

Elv. My foul !   [*They embrace.*

                          Dom.

Dom. I am taken on the fudden with a grievous fwim-ming in my head, and fuch a mift before my eyes, that I can neither hear nor fee.

Elv. Stay, and I'll fetch you fome comfortable water.

Dom. No, no, nothing but the open air will do me good. I'll take a turn in your garden ; but remember that I truft you both, and do not wrong my good opinion of you.   [*Exit.*

Elv. This is certainly the duft of gold which you have thrown in the good man's eyes, that on the fudden he can-not fee ; for my mind mifgives me, this ficknefs of his is but apocryphal.

Lor. 'Tis no qualm of confcience, I'll be fworn. You fee, Madam, 'tis intereft governs all the world. He preaches againft fin ; why ? Becaufe fo much more is bidden for his filence.

Elv. And fo much for the Fryar.

Lor. Oh, thofe eyes of yours reproach me juftly, that I negleft the fubjeft which brought me hither.

Elv. Do you confider the hazard I have run to fee you here ? If you do, methinks it fhould inform you, that I love not at a common rate.

Lor. Nay, if you talk of confidering, let us confider why we are alone. Do you think the Fryar left us to-gether to tell beads ? Love is a kind of penurious god, very niggardly of his opportunities : he muft be watched like a hard-hearted treafurer ; for he bolts out on the fud-den, and if you take him not in the nick, he vanifhes in a twinkling.

Elv. Why do you make fuch hafte to have done loving me ? ' You men are like watches, wound up for ftriking ' twelve immediately ; but, after, you are fatisfied, the ' very next that follows, is the folitary found of fingle ' one.

' *Lor.* How, Madam ! do you invite me to a feaft, and ' then preach abftinence ?

' *Elv.* No. I invite you to a feaft where the difhes are ' ferved up in order. You are for making a hafty meal, ' and for chopping up your entertainment like a hungry ' clown. Truft my management, good Colonel, and call ' not for your defert too foon.' Believe me, that which comes laft, as it is the fweeteft, fo it cloys the fooneft.

Lor.

Lor. I perceive, Madam, by your holding me at this distance, that there is somewhat you expect from me. What am I to undertake or suffer, ere I can be happy?

Elv. I muft firft be fatisfied that you love me.

Lor. By all that's holy, by thefe dear eyes ——

Elv. Spare your oaths and proteftations: I know you gallants of the time have a mint at your tongue's end, to coin them.

Lor. You know you cannot marry me; but, by heavens, if you were in a condition ——

Elv. Then you would not be fo prodigal of your promifes, but have the fear of matrimony before your eyes. In few words, if you love me, as you profefs, deliver me from this bondage, take me out of Egypt, and I'll wander with you as far as earth, and feas, and love can carry us.

Lor. I never was out at a mad frolic, though this is the maddeft I ever undertook. Have with you, lady mine, I take you at your word; and if you are for a merry jaunt, I'll try, for once, who can foot it fartheft. There are hedges in fummer, and barns in winter to be found: I with my knapfack, and you with your bottle at your back. We'll leave honour to madmen, and riches to knaves; and travel till we come to the ridge of the world, and then drop together into the next.

Elv. Give me your hand, and ftrike a bargain.

[He takes her hand, and kiffes it.

Lor. In fign and token whereof, the parties interchangeably, and fo forth —— When fhould I be weary of fealing upon this foft wax?

Elv. Oh, heavens, I hear my hufband's voice!

Enter Gomez.

Gom. Where are you, gentlewoman? There's fomething in the wind, I'm fure; becaufe your woman would have run up ftairs before me; but I have fecured her below, with a gag in her chops —— Now, in the devil's name, what makes this Fryar here again? I do not like thefe frequent conjunctions of the flefh and the fpirit; they are boding.

Elv. Go hence, good father; my hufband, you fee, is in an ill humour, and I would not have you witnefs of his folly.   *[Lorenzo *going.*

Gom. [*Running to the door.*] By your reverence's favour, hold a little ; I muſt examine you ſomething better before you go. Hey-day ! who have we here ? Father Dominick is ſhrunk in the wetting two yards and a half about the belly. What are become of thoſe two timber-logs, that he uſed to wear for legs, that ſtood ſtrutting like the two black poſts before a door ? I am afraid ſome bad body has been ſetting him over a fire in a great cauldron, and boiled him down half the quantity for a receipt. This is no Father Dominick, no huge over-grown abbey-lubber ; this is but a diminutive ſucking fryar. ' As ſure ' as a gun, now, Father Dominick has been ſpawning the ' young ſlender antichriſt.'

Elv. [*Aſide.*] He will be found out ; there's no prevention !

Gom. Why does he not ſpeak ? What, is the Fryar poſſeſſed with a dumb devil ? If he be, I ſhall make bold to conjure him.

Elv. He is but a novice in his order, and is enjoined ſilence for a penance.

Gom. A novice, quoth-a ! you would make a novice of me too, if you could.. But what is his buſineſs here ? Anſwer me that, gentlewoman, anſwer me that.

Elv. What ſhould it be, but to give me ſome ſpiritual inſtructions ?

Gom. Very good ! and you are like to edify much from a dumb preacher. This will not paſs ; I muſt examine the contents of him a little cloſer. Oh, thou confeſſor, confeſs who thou art, or thou art no fryar of this world !

[*He comes to* Lorenzo, *who ſtruggles with him ; his habit flies open, and diſcovers a ſword* ; Gomez *ſtarts back.*
As I live, this is a manifeſt member of the church militant !

Lor. [*Aſide.*] I am diſcovered—Now, impudence be my refuge—Yes, faith, 'tis I, honeſt Gomez. Thou ſeeſt I uſe thee like a friend. This is a familiar viſit.

Gom. What, Colonel Hernando turned fryar ! Who could have ſuſpected you of ſo much godlineſs ?

Lor. E'en as thou ſeeſt, I make bold here.

Gom. A very frank manner of proceeding ! But I do not wonder at your viſit, after ſo friendly an invitation as I made you. Marry, I hope you'll excuse the blunderbuffes for not being in readinefs to falute you; but let me know your hour, and all fhall be mended another time.

Lor. Hang it, I hate fuch ripping up old unkindnefs. I was upon the frolic this evening, and came to vifit thee in mafquerade.

Gom. Very likely; and not finding me at home, you were forced to toy away an hour with my wife, or fo.

Lor. Right; thou fpeakeft my very foul.

Gom. Why, am not I a friend, then, to help you out? you would have been fumbling half an hour for this excufe. But, as I remember, you promifed to ftorm my citadel, and bring your regiment of red locufts upon me, for free quarter: I find, Colonel, by your habit, there are black locufts in the world, as well as red.

Elv. [*Afide.*] When comes my fhare of the reckoning to be called for?

Lor. Give me thy hand; thou art the honefteft kind man—I was refolved I would not go out of the houfe till I had feen thee.

Gom. No, in my confcience, if I had ftaid abroad till midnight. But, Colonel, you and I fhall talk in another tone hereafter; I mean, in cold friendfhip, at a bar before a judge, by way of plaintiff and defendant. Your excufes want fome grains to make them current: hum and haw will not do the bufinefs. There's a modeft lady of your acquaintance; fhe has fo much grace to make none at all, but filently to confefs the power of dame Nature working in her body to youthful appetite.

Elv. How he got in I know not, unlefs it were by virtue of his habit.

Gom. Ay, ay, the virtues of that habit are known abundantly.

Elv. I could not hinder his entrance; for he took me unprovided.

Gom. To refift him.

Elv. I'm fure he has not been here above a quarter of an hour.

Gom. And a quarter of that time would have ferved thy turn. Oh, thou epitome of thy virtuous fex! Madam
Meffalina

Meſſalina the ſecond, retire to thy apartment; I have an aſſignation there to make with thee.

Elv. I'm all obedience.   [*Exit.*

Lor. I find, Gomez, you are not the man I thought you. We may meet before we come to the bar, we may; and our differences may be decided by other weapons than by lawyers tongues, In the mean time, no ill treatment of your wife, as you hope to die a natural death, and go to hell in your bed. Bilbo is the word; remember that, and tremble——   [*He is going out.*

Enter Dominick.

Dom. Where is this naughty couple ? Where are you, in the name of goodneſs ? My mind miſgave me, and I durſt truſt you no longer by yourſelves. Here will be fine work, I'm afraid, at your next confeſſion !

Lor. [*Aſide.*] The devil is punctual, I ſee : he has paid me the ſhame he owed me ; and now the Fryar is coming in for his part too.

Dom. [*Seeing* Gom.] Bleſs my eyes ! what do I ſee ?

Gom. Why, you ſee a cuckold of this honeſt gentleman's making, I thank him for his pains.

Dom. I confeſs, I am aſtoniſhed !

Gom. What, at a cuckoldom of your own contrivance ! your head-piece and his limbs have done my buſineſs—— Nay, do not look ſo ſtrangely : remember your own words, Here will be fine work at your next confeſſion ! What naughty couple were they, whom you durſt not truſt together any longer, when the hypocritical rogue had truſted them a full quarter of an hour ? And, by the way, horns will ſprout in leſs time than muſhrooms.

Dom. Beware how you accuſe one of my order upon light ſuſpicions. The naughty couple that I meant, were your wife and you, whom I left together with great animoſities on both ſides. Now, that was the occaſion, mark me, Gomez, that I thought it convenient to return again and not to truſt your enraged ſpirits too long together. You might have broken out into revilings and matrimonial warfare, which are ſins; and new ſins make work for new confeſſions.

Lor. [*Aſide.*] Well ſaid, i'faith, Fryar ; thou art come off thyſelf, but poor I am left in limbo.

Gom. Angle in ſome other ford, good father ; you
ſhall

shall catch no gudgeons here. Look upon the prisoner at the bar, Fryar, and inform the court what you know concerning him: he is arraigned here by the name of Colonel Hernando.

Dom. What Colonel do you mean, Gomez? I see no man, but a reverend brother of our order, whose profession I honour, but whose person I know not, as I hope for Paradise.

Gom. No, you are not acquainted with him; the more's the pity; you do not know him, under this disguise, for the greatest cuckold-maker in all Spain.

Dom. Oh, impudence! Oh, rogue! Oh, villain!——— Nay, if he be such a man, my righteous spirit rises at him! Does he put on holy garments, for a cover-shame of lewdness?

Gom. Yes, and he's in the right on't, father: when a swingeing sin is to be committed, nothing will cover it so close as a fryar's hood; for there the devil plays at bo-peep, puts out his horns to do a mischief, and then shrinks them back for safety, like a snail into her shell.

Lor. [*Aside.*] It's best marching off while I can retreat with honour. There's no trusting this fryar's conscience; he has renounced me already more heartily than he e'er did the devil, and is in a fair way of prosecuting me for putting on these holy robes. ' This is the old church-' trick: the clergy is ever at the bottom of the plot; ' but they are wise enough to slip their own necks out of ' the collar, and leave the laity to be fairly hanged for it.'

[*Exit* Lor.

Gom. Follow your leader, Fryar; your Colonel is trooped off; but he had not gone so easily, if I durst have trusted you in the house behind him. Gather up your gouty legs, I say, and rid my house of that huge body of divinity.

Dom. I expect some judgment should fall upon you, for your want of reverence to your spiritual director. Slander, covetousness, and jealousy will weigh thee down,

Gom. Put pride, hypocrify, and gluttony into your scale, father, and you shall weigh against me: nay, if sins come to be divided once, the clergy puts in for nine parts, and scarce leaves the laity a tithe.

Dom. How darest thou reproach the tribe of Levi?

Gom.

Gom. Marry, becaufe you make us laymen of the tribe of Iſſachar.   You make aſſes of us, to bear your burdens. When we are young, you put panniers upon us with your church-difcipline; and when we are grown up, you load us with a wife: after that, you procure for other men, and then you load our wives too.   A fine phrafe you have amongſt you to draw us into marriage: you call it ſettling of a man; juſt as when a fellow has got a found knock upon the head, you ſay he is ſettled—marriage is a ſettling blow indeed.   They ſay every thing in the world is good for fomething, as a toad, to fuck up the venom of the earth; but I never knew what a fryar was good for, till your pimping ſhewed me.

Dom. Thou ſhalt anſwer for this, thou flanderer! Thy offences be upon thy head.

Gom. I believe there are fome offences there of your planting.   [*Exit* Dom.
Lord, Lord, that men ſhould have fenfe enough to fet ſnares in their warrens to catch pole-cats and foxes! And yet———
   Want wit a prieſt-trap at their door to lay,
   For holy vermin that in houfes prey.   [*Exit.*

S C E N E, a Palace.

Queen and Tereſa.

Ter. You are not what you were fince yeſterday;
Your food forfakes you, and your needful reſt;
You pine, you languiſh, love to be alone;
Think much, fpeak little, and, in fpeaking, figh.
When you fee Torrifmond, you are unquiet;
But when you fee him not, you are in pain.

Qu. Oh, let them never love, who never try'd!
They brought a paper to me to be ſign'd;
Thinking on him, I quite forgot my name,
And writ, for Leonora, Torriſmond.
' I went to bed, and to myfelf I thought
' That I would think on Torrifmond no more;
' Then ſhut my eyes, but could not ſhut out him.
' I turn'd, and try'd each corner of my bed,
' To find if ſleep were there, but ſleep was loſt.
' Fev'riſh, for want of reſt, I rofe, and walk'd,
' And, by the moonſhine, to the windows went;
                                              ' There

‘ There thinking to exclude him from my thoughts.’
I caſt my eyes upon the neighbouring fields,
And, ere I was aware, ſigh’d to myſelf,
There ſought my Torriſmond.
    Ter. What hinders you to take the man you love ?
The people will be glad, the ſoldiers ſhout,
And Bertran, tho’ repining, will be aw’d.
  ‘ *Qu.* I fear to try new love ;
‘ As boys to venture on the unknown ice,
‘ That crackles underneath them while they ſlide.
‘ Oh, how ſhall I deſcribe this growing ill !
‘ Betwixt my doubt and love, methinks I ſtand
‘ Falt’ring, like one that waits an ague-fit :
‘ And yet, would this were all !
   ‘ *Ter.* What fear you more ?
   ‘ *Qu.* I am aſham’d to ſay ; ’tis but a fancy.
‘ At break of day, when dreams, they ſay, are true,
‘ A drowſy ſlumber, rather than a ſleep,
‘ Seiz’d on my ſenſes, with long watching worn.
‘ Methought I ſtood on a wide river’s bank,
‘ Which I muſt needs o’erpaſs, but knew not how ;
‘ When, on a ſudden, Torriſmond appear’d,
‘ Gave me his hand, and led me lightly o’er,
‘ Leaping and bounding on the billows heads,
‘ ’Till ſafely we had reach’d the farther ſhore.   [’ſcape.
  ‘ *Ter.* This dream portends ſome ill which you ſhall
‘ Would you ſee fairer viſions, take, this night,
‘ Your Torriſmond within your arms to ſleep :
‘ And, to that end, invent ſome apt pretence
‘ To break with Bertran. ’Twould be better yet,
‘ Could you provoke him to give you th’ occaſion,
‘ And then to throw him off.’
       Enter Bertran *at a diſtance.*
Qu. My ſtars have ſent him ;
For ſee, he comes. How gloomily he looks !
If he, as I ſuſpect, have found my love,
His jealouſy will furniſh him with fury,
And me with means to part.
   Bert, [*Aſide.*] Shall I upbraid her ? Shall I call her
If ſhe be falſe, ’tis what ſhe moſt deſires.   [falſe ?
My genius whiſpers me, Be cautious, Bertran ;
                  Thou

Thou walk'ſt as on a narrow mountain's neck,
A dreadful height, with ſcanty room to tread.
   Qu. Whaṭ bus'neſs have you at the court, my Lord?
   Bert. What bus'neſs, Madam!
   Qu. Yes, my Lord, what bus'neſs?
'Tis ſomewhat ſure of weighty conſequence
That brings you here ſo often, and unſent for.   [enough
   Bert. [*Aſide.*] 'Tis what I fear'd; her words are cold
To freeze a man to death——May I preſume
To ſpeak, and to complain?
   Qu. They who complain to princes, think them tame.
' What bull dares bellow, or what ſheep dares bleat,
' Within the lion's den?'
   Bert. Yet men are ſuffer'd to put Heav'n in mind
Of promis'd bleſſings; for they then are debts.   [give;
   Qu. My Lord, Heav'n knows its own time when to
But you, it ſeems, charge me with breach of faith.
   Bert. I hope I need not, Madam.
But as when men in ſickneſs ling'ring lie,
They count the tedious hours by months and years,
So every day deferr'd to dying lovers,
Is a whole age of pain.
   Qu. What if I ne'er conſent to make you mine?
My father's promiſe ties me not to time;
And bonds without a date, they ſay, are void.
   Bert. Far be it from me to believe you bound:
Love is the freeſt motion of our minds;
Oh, could you ſee into my ſecret ſoul,
There you might read your own dominion doubled,
Both as a queen and miſtreſs! If you leave me,
Know, I can die, but dare not be diſpleas'd.
   Qu. Sure you affect ſtupidity, my Lord,
Or give me cauſe to think, that when you loſt
Three battles to the Moors, you coldly ſtood
As unconcern'd as now.
   Bert. I did my beſt;
Fate was not in my power.
   Qu. And with the like tame gravity you ſaw
A raw young warrior take your baffled work,
And end it at a blow.
   Bert. I humbly take my leave; but they who blaſt
2
Your

Your good opinion of me, may have caufe
To know I am no coward.   [*He is going.*
  Qu. Bertran, ftay——
[*Afide,*] This may produce fome difmal confequence
To him whom dearer than my life I love.
[*To him.*] Have I not manag'd my contrivance well,
To try your love, and make you doubt of mine ?
  Bert. Then was it but a trial ?
Methinks I ftart as from fome dreadful dream,
And often afk myfelf if yet I wake.
[*Afide.*] This turn's too quick to be without defign :
I'll found the bottom of't, ere I believe.
  Qu. I fiud your love, and would reward it too ;
But anxious fears folicit my weak breaft.
I fear my people's faith,
That hot-mouth'd beaft that bears againft the curb,
Hard to be broken even by lawful kings,
But harder by ufurpers.
Judge, then, my Lord, with all thefe cares opprefs'd,
If I can think of love.
  Bert. Believe me, Madam,
Thefe jealoufies, however large they fpread,
Have but one root, the old imprifon'd King,
Whofe lenity firft pleas'd the gaping crowd ;
But when long try'd, and found fupinely good,
Like Æfop's log, they leap'd upon his back.
Your father knew them well, and when he mounted,
He rein'd them ftrongly, and he fpurr'd them hard ;
And, but he durft not do it all at once,
He had not left alive this patient faint,
This anvil of affronts, ' but fent him hence,
' To hold a peaceful branch of palm above,
' And hymn it in the choir.'
  Qu. You've hit upon the very ftring, which, touch'd,
Echo's the found, and jars within my foul :
There lies my grief.
  Bert. So long as there's a head,
Thither will all the mounting fpirits fly ;
Lop that but off, and then——
  Qu. My virtue fhrinks from fuch a horrid act.
  Bert. This 'tis to have a virtue out of feafon.
' Mercy is good, a very good dull virtue ;

E

' But

' But kings miſtake its timing, and are mild
' When manly courage bids them be ſevere.'
Better be cruel once, than anxious ever.
Remove this threat'ning danger from your crown,
And then ſecurely take the man you love.
    Qu. [*Walking aſide.*] Ha! let me think of that—the man
'Tis true, this murder is the only means   [I love!
That can ſecure my throne to Torriſmond;
Nay, more, this execution done by Bertran,
Makes him the object of the people's hate.
    Bert. [*Aſide.*] The more ſhe thinks, 'twill work the
        ſtronger in her.
    Qu. [*Aſide.*] How eloquent is miſchief to perſuade!
Few are ſo wicked as to take delight
In crimes unprofitable; nor do I.
If then I break divine and human laws,
No bribe but love could gain ſo bad a cauſe.
    Bert. You anſwer nothing.
    Qu. 'Tis of deep concernment,
And I a woman ignorant and weak.
I leave it all to you: think, what you do,
You do for him I love.
    Bert. [*Aſide.*] For him ſhe loves!
She nam'd not me; that may be Torriſmond,
Whom ſhe has thrice in private ſeen this day.
Then I am finely caught in my own ſnare——
I'll think again——Madam, it ſhall be done;
And mine be all the blame.   [*Exit.*
    Qu. Oh, that it were! I would not do this crime;
And yet, like Heaven, permit it to be done.
' The prieſthood groſsly cheat us with free-will;
' Will to do what, but what Heaven firſt decreed?
' Our actions then are neither good nor ill,
' Since from eternal cauſes they proceed:
' Our paſsions, fear and anger, love and hate,
' Mere ſenſeleſs engines that are mov'd by fate;
' Like ſhips on ſtormy ſeas without a guide,
' Toſt by the winds, are driven by the tide.'
                    Enter Torriſmond.
    Tor. Am I not rudely bold, and preſs too often
Into your preſence, Madam? If I am——
    Qu. No more, leſt I ſhould chide you for your ſtay.
                                            Where

Where have you been, and how could you fuppofe
That I could live thefe two long hours without you?
   Tor. Oh, words to charm an angel from his orb!
Welcome as kindly fhowers to long-parch'd earth!
But I have been in fuch a difmal place,
Where joy ne'er enters, which the fun ne'er cheers,
Bound in with darknefs, overfpread with damps;
Where I have feen (if I could fay I faw)
The good old king, majeftic in his bonds,
And midft his griefs moft venerably great;
By a dim winking lamp, which feebly broke
The gloomy vapours, he lay ftretch'd along
Upon th' unwholefome earth, his eyes fix'd upward;
And ever and anon a filent tear
Stole down and trickled from his hoary beard.
   Qu. Oh, Heaven! what have I done? My gentle love,
Here end thy fad difcourfe; and, for my fake,
Caft off thefe fearful melancholy thoughts.
   Tor. My heart is wither'd at that piteous fight,
As early bloffoms are with eaftern blafts.
He fent for me, and while I rais'd my head,
He threw his aged arms about my neck;
And, feeing that I wept, he prefs'd me clofe:
So, leaning cheek to cheek, and eyes to eyes,
We mingled tears in a dumb fcene of forrow.
   Qu. Forbear; you know not how you wound my foul.
   Tor. Can you have grief, and not have pity too?
He told me, when my father did return,
He had a wond'rous fecret to difclofe.
He kifs'd me, blefs'd me, nay, he call'd me fon;
He prais'd my courage; pray'd for my fuccefs;
He was fo true a father to his country,
To thank me for defending ev'n his foes,
Becaufe they were his fubjects.
   Qu. If they be, then what am I?
   Tor. The fovereign of my foul, my earthly Heaven.
   Qu. And not your Queen.
   Tor. You are fo beautiful,
So wond'rous fair, you juftify rebellion;
As if that faultlefs face could make no fin,
But Heaven, with looking on it, muft forgive.
   Qu. The King muft die, he muft, my Torrifmond:

E 2

Though

Though pity foftly plead within my foul,
Yet he muft die, that I may make you great,
And give a crown in dowry with my love.
    Tor. Perifh that crown, on any head but yours !
Oh, recollect your thoughts !
Shake not his hour-glafs, when his hafty fand
Is ebbing to the laft.
A little longer, yet a little longer,
And nature drops him down without your fin,
Like mellow fruit without a winter ftorm.
    Qu. ' Let me but do this one injuftice more :'
His doom is paft, and for your fake he dies.
    Tor. Would you for me have done fo ill an act,
And will not do a good one ?
Now, by your joys on earth, your hopes in heaven,
Oh, fpare this great, this good, this aged king,
And fpare your foul the crime !
    Qu. The crime's not mine ;
'Twas firft propos'd, and muft be done by Bertran,
Fed with falfe hopes to gain my crown and me.
I, to enhance his ruin, gave no leave ;
But barely bade him think, and then refolve.
    Tor. In not forbidding, you command the crime.
Think, timely think on the laft dreadful day ;
How will you tremble, there to ftand expos'd,
And foremoft in the rank of guilty ghofts,
That muft be doom'd for murder ! Think on murder :
That troop is plac'd apart from common crimes ;
The damn'd themfelves ftart wide, and fhun that band,
As far more black, and more forlorn than they.
    Qu. 'Tis terrible ; it fhakes, it ftaggers me.
' I knew this truth, but I repell'd that thought.
' Sure there is none but fears a future ftate :
' And when the moft obdurate fwear they do not,
' Their trembling hearts belie their boafting tongues.'
                    Enter Terefa.
Send fpeedily to Bertran ; charge him ftrictly
Not to proceed, but wait my further pleafure.
    Ter. Madam, he fends to tell you, 'tis perform'd. [*Exit.*
    Tor. Ten thoufand plagues confume him ! furies drag
Fiends tear him ! Blafted be the arm that ftruck,   [him !
The tongue that order'd ! only fhe be fpar'd,
                                That

That hinder'd not the deed! Oh, where was then
The power that guards the ſacred lives of kings?
Why ſlept the lightning and the thunder-bolts,
Or bent their idle rage on fields and trees,
When vengeance call'd them here?
  Qu. Sleep that thought too.
'Tis done; and ſince 'tis done, 'tis paſt recall;
And ſince 'tis paſt recall, muſt be forgotten.
  Tor. Oh, never, never ſhall it be forgotten!
High Heaven will not forget it; after ages
Shall with a fearful curſe remember ours,
And blood ſhall never leave the nation more.
  ' *Qu.* His body ſhall be royally interr'd,
' And the laſt funeral pomps adorn his herſe.
' I will myſelf (as I have cauſe too juſt)
' Be the chief mourner at his obſequies;
' And yearly fix, on the revolving day,
' The ſolemn mark of mourning, to atone,
' And expiate my offences.
  ' *Tor.* Nothing can,
' But bloody vengeance on that traitor's head,
' Which, dear departed ſpirit, here I vow.'
  Qu. Here end our ſorrows, and begin our joys.
' Love calls, my Torriſmond: though hate has rag'd,
' And rul'd the day, yet love will rule the night.
' The ſpiteful ſtars have ſhed their venom down,
' And now the peaceful planets take their turn.
' This deed of Bertran's has remov'd all fears,
' And giv'n me juſt occaſion to refuſe him.'
What hinders now, but that the holy prieſt
In ſecret join our mutual vows? ' And then
' This night, this happy night is yours and mine.'
  Tor. Be ſtill my ſorrows, and be loud my joys:
Fly to the utmoſt circles of the ſea,
Thou furious tempeſt, that hath toſs'd my mind,
And leave no thought but Leonora there——
What's this?—I feel a boding in my ſoul,
As if this day were fatal—Be it ſo.
Fate ſhall but have the leavings of my love.
My joys are gloomy, but withal are great.
The lion, though he ſees the toils are ſet,

E 3

Yet,

Yet, pinch'd with raging hunger, scow'rs away,
Hunts in the face of danger all the day,
At night, with sullen pleasure, grumbles o'er his prey.

[Exeunt.

END of the THIRD ACT.

ACT IV.

SCENE, *before* Gomez's *door.*

Enter Lorenzo, Dominick, *and two Soldiers at a distance.*

DOMINICK.

I'LL not wag an ace farther: the whole world will not bribe me to it; for my conscience will digest these grofs enormities no longer.

Lor. How, thy conscience not digest them! There's ne'er a fryar in Spain can shew a conscience that comes near it for digestion. It digested pimping, when I sent thee with my letter; and it digested perjury, when thou sworest thou didst not know me: I'm sure it has digested me fifty pound of as hard gold as is in all Barbary: pr'ythee, why should'st thou discourage fornication, when thou knowest thou lovest a sweet young girl?

Dom. Away; away; I do not love them;—phau; no,—[*Spits.*] I do not love a pretty girl——you are so waggish.   [*Spits again.*

Lor. Why thy mouth waters at the very mention of them.

Dom. You take a mighty pleasure in defamation, Colonel; but I wonder what you find in running restless up and down, breaking your brains, emptying your purse, and wearing out your body, with hunting after unlawful game.

Lor. Why there's the satisfaction on't.

Dom. This incontinency may proceed to adultery, and adultery to murder, and murder to hanging; and there's the satisfaction on't.

Lor. I'll not hang alone, fryar; I'm resolved to peach thee before thy superiors, for what thou hast done already.

Dom. I am resolved to forswear it if you do: let me

advife

advife you better, Colonel, than to accufe a church-man to churchmen : in the common caufe we are all of a piece ; we hang together.

Lor. [*Afide.*] If you don't, it were no matter if you did.

Dom. Nay, if you talk of peaching, I'll peach firft, and fee whofe oath will be believed ; I'll trounce you for offering to corrupt my honefty, and bribe my confcience ; you fhall be fummoned by an hoft of paritors ; you fhall be fentenced in the fpiritual court ; you fhall be excom-municated ; you fhall be out-lawed ;——and——[*Here* Lorenzo *takes a purfe, and plays with it, and at laft, lets the purfe fall chinking on the ground; which the fryar eyes.*] [*In another tone.*] I fay, a man might do this now, if he were malicioufly difpofed, and had a mind to bring mat-ters to extremity ; but, confidering, that you are my friend, a perfon of honour, and a worthy good charitable man, I would rather die a thoufand deaths than difoblige you. [Lorenzo *takes up the purfe, and pours it into the fry-ar's fleeve.*] Nay, good Sir ; nay, dear Colonel ; Oh, Lord, Sir, what are you doing now ! I profefs this muft not be : without this I would have ferved you to the ut-termoft ; pray command me. A jealous, foul-mouthed rogue this Gomez is : I faw how he ufed you, and you marked how he ufed me too : Oh, he's a bitter man ; but we'll join our forces ; ah, fhall we, Colonel? We'll be re-venged on him with a witnefs.

Lor. But how fhall I fend her word to be ready at the door, (for I muft reveal it in confeffion to you,) that I mean to carry her away this evening, by the help of thefe two foldiers ? I know Gomez fufpects you, and you will hardly gain admittance.

Dom. Let me alone ; I fear him not; I am armed with the authority of my cloathing ; yonder I fee him keeping centry at his door : ' have you never feen a ' citizen, in a cold morning, clapping his fides, and ' walking forward and backward, a mighty pace before ' his fhop? But I'll gain the pafs, in fpite of his fuf-' picion ;' ftand you afide, and do but mark how I ac-coft him.

Lor. If he meet with a repulfe, we muft throw off

I   the

the fox's skin, and put on the lion's: come, gentlemen, you'll stand by me.

Sold. Do not doubt us, Colonel.

[*They retire all three to a corner of the stage,* Domi-nick *goes to the door where* Gomez *stands.*

Dom. Good even, Gomez, how does your wife?

Gom. Just as you'd have her, thinking on nothing, but her dear Colonel, and conspiring cuckoldum against me.

Dom. I dare say, you wrong her, she is employing her thoughts how to cure you of your jealousy.

Gom. Yes, by certainty.

Dom. By your leave, Gomez; I have some spiritual advice to impart to her on that subject.

Gom. You may spare your instructions, if you please, father, she has no further need of them.

Dom. How, no need of them! Do you speak in riddles?

Gom. Since you will have me speak plainer; she has profited so well already by your counsel, that she can say her lesson, without your teaching: do you understand me now?

Dom. I must not neglect my duty, for all that; once again, Gomez, by your leave.

Gom. She's a little indisposed at present, and it will not be convenient to disturb her.

[Dominick *offers to go by him, but t'other stands be-fore him.*

Dom. Indisposed, say you? Oh, it is upon those occa-sions that a confessor is most necessary; I think, it was my good angel that sent me hither so opportunely.

Gom. Ay, whose good angel sent you hither, that you best know, father.

Dom. A word or two of devotion will do her no harm, I'm sure.

Gom. A little sleep will do her more good, I'm sure: you know she disburdened her conscience but this morn-ing to you.

Dom. But, if she be ill this afternoon, she may have new occasion to confess.

Gom. Indeed as you order matters with the Colonel, she may have occasion of confessing herself every hour.

Dom. Pray how long has she been sick?

Gom.

Gom. Lord, you will force a man to speak; why ever since your laſt defeat.

Dom. This can be but ſome light indiſpoſition, it will not laſt, and I may ſee her.

Gom. How, not laſt! I ſay, it will laſt, and it ſhall laſt; ſhe ſhall be ſick theſe ſeven or eight days, and perhaps longer, as I ſee occaſion. What! I know the mind of her ſickneſs, a little better than you do.

Dom. I find then, I muſt bring a doctor.

Gom. And he'll bring an apothecary, with a chargeable long bill of Ana's: thoſe of my family have the grace to die cheaper; in a word, Sir Dominick, we underſtand one another's buſineſs here: I am reſolved to ſtand like the Swiſs of my own family, to defend the entrance; you may mumble over your *pater noſters*, if you pleaſe, and try if you can make my doors fly open, and batter down my walls, with bell, book and candle; but I am not of opinion, that you are holy enough to commit miracles.

Dom. Men of my order are not to be treated after this manner.

Gom. I would treat the pope and his cardinals in the ſame manner, if they offered to ſee my wife, without my leave.

Dom. I excommunicate thee from the church, if thou doſt not open, there's promulgation coming out.

Gom. And I excommunicate you from my wife, if you go to that; there's promulgation for promulgation, and bull for bull; and ſo I leave you to recreate yourſelf with the end of an old ſong——" and ſorrow came to the old fryar."   [*Exit.*

Enter Lorenzo *and* Soldiers.

Lor. I will not aſk you your ſucceſs; for I overheard part of it, and ſaw the concluſion; I find we are now put upon our laſt trump; the fox is earthed, but I ſhall ſend my two terriers in after him.

Sold. I warrant you, Colonel, we'll unkennel him.

Lor. And make what haſte you can, to bring out the lady: what ſay you, father? Burglary is but a venial ſin among the ſoldiers.

Dom. I ſhall abſolve them, becauſe he is an enemy of

the

the church——There is a proverb, I confefs, which fays, that dead men tell no tales ; but let your foldiers apply it at their own perils.

Lor. What take away a man's wife, and kill him too ! The wickednefs of this old villain ftartles me, ' and gives ' me a twinge for my own fin, though it comes far fhort of ' his :' hark you, foldiers, be fure you ufe as little violence to him as poffible.

Dom. Hold, a little, I have thought better how to fecure him, with lefs danger to us.

Lor. Oh, miracle ! the fryar is grown confcientious !

Dam. The old king, you know, is juft murdered, and the perfons that did it are unknown ; let the foldiers feize him for one of the affaffinates, and let me alone to accufe him afterwards.

Lor. I cry thee mercy with all my heart, for fufpecting a fryar of the leaft good-nature ; what, would you accufe him wrongfully ?

Dom. I muft confefs, 'tis wrongful *quoad hoc* as to the fact itfelf ; but 'tis rightful *quoad hunc,* as to this heretical rogue, whom we muft difpatch : he has railed againft the church, which is a fouler crime than the murder of a thoufand kings ; *omne majus continet in fe minus :* he that is an enemy to the church, is an enemy unto heaven ; and he that is an enemy to heaven, would have killed the king if he had been in the circumftances of doing it ; fo it is not wrongful to accufe him.

Lor. I never knew a churchman, if he were perfonally offended, but he would bring in heaven by hook or crook into his quarrel. Soldiers, do as you were firft ordered.　　　　　　　　　　　　　　　　　*[Exeunt foldiers.*

Dom. What was't you ordered them ? Are you fure it is fafe, and not fcandalous ?

Lor. Somewhat near your own defign, but not altogether fo mifchievous ; the people are infinitely difcontented, as they have reafon ; and mutinies there are, or will be, againft the queen ; now I am content to put him thus far into the plot, that he fhould be fecured as a traitor ; but he fhall only be prifoner at the foldiers quarters ; and when I am out of reach, he fhall be releafed.

Dom:.

Dom. And what will become of me then ? For when he is free, he will infallibly accuse me.

Lor. Why then, father, you muft have recourfe to your infallible church-remedies, lie impudently, and fwear devoutly ; and, as you told me but now, let him try whofe oath will be firft believed. Retire, I hear them coming.   [*They withdraw.*

Enter the Soldiers with Gomez *ftruggling on their backs.*

Gom. Help, good Chriftians, help neighbours ; my houfe is broken open by force, and I am ravifhed, and am like to be affaffinated. What do you mean, villains ? Will you carry me away like a pedlar's pack upon your backs ? Will you murder a man in plain day-light.

1ft Sold. No ; but we'll fecure you for a traitor, and for being in a plot againft the ftate.

Gom. Who, I in a plot : Oh, Lord ! Oh, Lord ! I never durft be in a plot. Why, how can you in confcience fufpect a rich citizen of fo much wit as to make a plotter ? There are none but poor rogues, and thofe that can't live without it, that are in plots.

2d Sold. Away with him, away with him.

Gom. Oh, my gold ! my wife ! my wife ! my gold ! As I hope to be faved now, I know no more of the plot than they that made it.   [*They carry him off, and exeunt.*

Lor. Thus far have we failed with a merry gale, now we have the Cape of good Hope in fight ; the trade-wind is our own, if we can but double it. [*He looks out.*] [*Afide.*] Ah, my father and Pedro ftand at the corner of the ftreet with company, there's no ftirring 'till they are paft !

Enter Elvira *with a Cafket.*

Elv. Am I come at laft into your arms ?

Lor. Fear nothing ? the adventure's ended, and the knight may carry off the lady fafely.

Elv. I'm fo overjoyed, I can fcarce believe I am at liberty ; ' but ftand panting, like a bird that has often ' beaten her wings in vain againft her cage, and at laft ' dares hardly venture out, though fhe fees it open.'

Dom. Lofe no time, but make hafte while the way is free for you ; and thereupon I give you my benediction.

Lor. 'Tis not fo free as you fuppofe ; for there's an
old

old gentleman of my acquaintance that blocks up the paſſage at the corner of the ſtreet.

Dom. What have you gotten there under you arm, daughter? ſomewhat, I hope, that will bear your charges in your pilgrimage.

Lor. The fryar has an hawk's eye to gold and jewels.

Elv. Here's that will make you dance without a fiddle, and provide a better entertainment for us than hedges in ſummer and barns in winter. Here's the very heart, and ſoul, and life-blood of Gomez; pawns in abundance, old gold of widows, and new gold of prodigals; and pearls and diamonds of court ladies, till the next bribe helps their huſbands to redeem them.

Dom. They are the ſpoils of the wicked, and the church endows you with them.

Lor. And, faith, we'll drink the church's health out of them. But all this while I ſtand on thorns; pr'ythee, dear, look out, and ſee if the coaſt be free for our eſcape; for I dare not peep for fear of being known.

    [Elvira *goes to look out, and* Gomez *comes running in upon her: ſhe ſhrieks out.*

Gom. Thanks to my ſtars, I have recovered my own territorities——What do I ſee! I'm ruined! I'm undone! I'm betrayed!

' *Dom.* [*Aſide.*] What a hopeful enterprize is here ' ſpoiled!'

Gom. Oh, Colonel, are you there? and you, fryar? nay, then I find how the world goes.

Lor. Chear up, man, thou art out of jeopardy; I heard thee crying out juſt now, and came running in full ſpeed with the wings of an eagle and the feet of a tiger to thy reſcue.

Gom. Ay, you are always at hand to do me a courteſy with your eagle's feet and your tiger's wings; and, what, were you here for, friar?

Dom. To interpoſe my ſpiritual authority in your behalf.

Gom. And why did you ſhriek out, gentlewoman?

Elv. 'Twas for joy at your return.

Gom. And that caſket under your arm, for what end and purpoſe?

Elv. Only to preſerve it from the thieves.

Gom.

Gom. And you came running out of doors——

Elv. Only to meet you, fweet hufband.

Gom. A fine evidence fummed up among you: thank you heartily; you are all my friends. The Colonel was walking by accidentally, and hearing my voice, came in to fave me; the fryar, who was hobbling the fame way too, accidentally again, and not knowing of the Colonel, I warrant you he comes in to pray for me; and my faithful wife runs out of doors to meet me with all my jewels under her arm, and fhrieks out for joy at my return. But if my father-in-law had not met your foldiers, Colonel, and delivered me in the nick, I fhould neither have found a friend nor a fryar here, and might have fhrieked out for joy myfelf, for the lofs of my jewels and my wife.

Dom. Art thou an infidel? Wilt thou not believe us?

Gom. Such churchmen as you would make any man an infidel. Get you into your kennel, gentlewoman! I fhall thank you within doors for your fafe cuftody of my jewels, and your own. [*He thrufts his wife off the ftage.* [*Exit* Elvira.] As for you, Colonel Muff-cap, we fhall try before a civil magiftrate who's the greateft plotter of us two, I againft the ftate, or you againft the petticoat.

Lor. Nay, if you will complain, you fhall for fomething.   [*Beats him.*

Gom. Murder! murder! I give up the ghoft! I am deftroyed! Help! murder! murder!

Dom. Away, Colonel, let us fly for our lives: the neighbours are coming out with forks, and fire-fhovels, and fpits, and other domeftic weapons; the militia of a whole alley is raifed againft us.

Lor. This is but the intereft of my debt, mafter ufurer, the principal fhall be paid you at our next meeting.

Dom. Ah, if your foldiers had but difpatched him, his tongue had been laid afleep, Colonel; but this comes of not following good counfel; ah——

      [*Exeunt* Lor. *and Fryar feverally.*

Gom. I'll be revenged of him, if I dare; but he's fuch a terrible fellow, that my mind mifgives me; I fhall tremble when I have him before the judge: all my misfortunes come together: I have been robbed and cuckolded, and ravifhed, and beaten, in one quarter of an hour;

F

my

my poor limbs fmart, and my poor head achs; ay, do,
do, fmart limb, ach head, and fprout horns; but I'll be
hanged before I'll pity you: you muft needs be married,
muft ye? There's for that, [*Beats his own head.*] and to a
fine, young, modifh lady, muft ye? There's for that too;
and, at threefcore, you old, doting cuckold, take that remembrance——A fine time of day for a man to be bound
'prentice, when he is paft ufing his trade: to fet up an
equipage of noife, when he has moft need of quiet; inftead of her being under covert-baron to be under covert-
femme myfelf; to have my body difabled, and my head
fortified; and laftly, to be crowded into a narrow box
with a fhrill treble,
That with one blaft, through the whole houfe does bound,
And firft taught fpeaking-trumpets how to found. [*Exit.*

SCENE, the Court.

Enter Raymond, Alphonfo, *and* Pedro.
Ray. Are thefe, are thefe, ye Powers, the promis'd joys,
With which I flatter'd my long, tedious abfence,
To find, at my return, my mafter murder'd?
Oh, that I could but weep, to vent my paffion!
But this dry forrow burns up all my tears.
Alph. Mourn inward, brother; 'tis obferv'd at court,
Who weeps, and who wears black; and your return
Will fix all eyes on every act of yours,
To fee how you refent king Sancho's death.
Ray. What generous man can live with that conftraint
Upon his foul, to bear, much lefs to flatter
A court like this! can I footh tyranny!
Seem pleas'd, to fee my royal mafter murder'd,
His crown ufurp'd, a diftaff in a throne,
A council made of fuch as dare not fpeak,
And could not, if they durft; whence honeft men
Banifh themfelves, for fhame of being there:
A government, that, knowing not true wifdom,
Is fcorn'd abroad, and lives on tricks at home?
Alph. Virtue muft be thrown off, 'tis a coarfe garment,
Too heavy for the fun-fhine of a court.
Ray. Well then, I will diffemble for an end
So great, fo pious, as a juft revenge:
You'll join with me?

Alph

Alph. No honeſt man but muſt.

Ped. What title has this queen but lawleſs force ?
And force muſt pull her down.

Alph. Truth is, I pity Leonora's caſe ;
Forc'd, for her ſafety, to commit a crime
Which moſt her ſoul abhors.

Ray. All ſhe has done, or e'er can do, of good,
This one black deed has damn'd.

Ped. You'll hardly join your ſon to our deſign.

Ray. Your reaſon for't ?

Ped. I want time to unriddle it :
Put on your t'other face ; the Queen approaches.
    Enter the Queen, Bertran, *and Attendants.*

Ray. And that accurſed Bertran
Stalks cloſe behind her, like a witch's fiend,
Preſſing to be employ'd. Stand, and obſerve them.

Qu. [*To Ber.*] Bury'd in private, and ſo ſuddenly !
It croſſes my deſign, which was to allow
The rites of funeral fitting his degree,
With all the pomp of mourning.

Bert. It was not ſafe :
Objects of pity, when the cauſe is new,
Would work too fiercely on the giddy croud.
Had Cæſar's body never been expos'd,
Brutus had gain'd his cauſe.

Qu. Then was he lov'd ?

Bert. O, never man ſo much, for ſaint-like goodneſs.

‘ *Ped.* [*Aſide.*] Had bad men fear'd him but as good
‘ He had not yet been ſainted.   [men lov'd him,

‘ *Qu.* I wonder how the people bear his death.

‘ *Bert.* Some diſcontents there are ; ſome idle murmurs.

‘ *Ped.* How, idle murmurs ! let me plainly ſpeak :
‘ The doors are all ſhut up ; the wealthier ſort,
‘ With arms a-croſs, and hats upon their eyes,
‘ Walk to and fro before their ſilent ſhops :
‘ Whole droves of lenders crowd the bankers' doors,
‘ To call in money ; thoſe who have none, mark
‘ Where money goes ; for when they riſe, 'tis plunder :
‘ The rabble gather round the man of news,
‘ And liſten with their mouths ;

F 2

‘ Some

' Some tell, fome hear, fome judge of news, fome make
' And he who lies moft loud, is moft believ'd.'   [it :
   Qu. This may be dangerous.
   Ray. [*Afide.*] Pray Heaven it may.
   Bert. If one of you muft fall ;
Self-prefervation is the firft of laws ;.
And if, when fubjects are opprefs'd by kings,
They juftify rebellion by that law :
As well may monarchs turn the edge of right
To cut for them, when felf-defence requires it.
   Qu. You place fuch arbitrary power in kings,
That I much fear, if I fhould make you one,
You'll make yourfelf a tyrant.   Let thefe know
By what authority you did this act.
   Bert. You much furprife me to demand that queftion ;
But fince truth muft be told, 'twas by your own.
   Qu. Produce it ; or, by Heaven, your head fhall anfwer
The forfeit of your tongue.
   Ray. [*Afide.*] Brave mifchief towards.
   Bert. You bade me.
   Qu. When, and where ?
   Bert. No, I confefs, you bade me not in words,
—The dial fpoke not, but it made fhrew'd figns,
And pointed full upon the ftroke of murder :
Yet this you faid,
You were a woman ignorant and weak,
So left it to my care.
   Qu. What, if I faid,
I was a woman ignorant and weak,
Were you ro take th' advantage of my fex,
And play the devil to tempt me ? ' You contriv'd,
' You urg'd, you drove me headlong to your toils ;
' And if, much tir'd, and frighten'd more, I paus'd ;
' Were you to make my doubts your own commiffion ?
   ' *Bert.* This 'tis to ferve a prince too faithfully ;
' Who, free from laws himfelf, will have that done,
' Which, not perform'd, brings us to fure difgrace ;
' And, if perform'd, to ruin.
   ' *Qu.* This 'tis to counfel things that are unjuft ;
' Firft, to debauch a king to break his laws,
' (Which are his fafety) and then feek protection
' From him you have endanger'd ; but, juft Heaven,
                        Where

' Where fins are judg'd, will damn the tempting devil,
' More deep than thofe he tempted.'
   Bert. If princes not protect their minifters,
What man will dare to ferve them ?
   Qu. None will dare
To ferve them ill, when they are left to laws ;
But, when a counfellor, to fave himfelf,
Would lay mifcarriages upon his prince,
Expofing him to public rage and hate,
O, 'tis an act as infamoufly bafe,
As, fhould a common foldier fculk behind,
And thruft his general in the front of war :
It fhews, he only ferv'd himfelf before,
And had no fenfe of honour, country, king ;
But center'd on himfelf ; and us'd his mafter,
As guardians do their wards, with fhews of care,
But with intent to fell the public fafety,
And pocket up his prince.
   Ped. [*Afide.*] Well faid, i'faith.
This fpeech is e'en too good for an ufurper.
   Bert. I fee for whom I muft be facrific'd ;
And had I not been fotted with my zeal,
I might have found it fooner.
   Qu. From my fight !
The prince who bears an infolence like this,
Is fuch an image of the powers above,
As is the ftatue of the thundering god,
Whofe bolts the boys may play with.
   Bert. Unreveng'd
I will not fall, nor fingle,   [*Exit cum fuis.*
   Qu. [*To* Ray. *who kiffes her hand.*] Welcome, wel-
I faw you not before : one honeft lord   [come :
Is hid with eafe among a crowd of courtiers :
How can I be too grateful to the father
Of fuch a fon as Torrifmond ?
   Ray. His actions were but duty.
   Qu. Yet, my Lord,
All have not paid that debt, like noble Torrifmond.
You hear, how Bertran brands me with a crime,
Of which, your fon can witnefs, I am free ;
I fent to ftop the murder, but too late ;
' For crimes are fwift, but penitence is flow,'

F 3

The

The bloody Bertran, diligent in ill,
Flew to prevent the foft returns of pity.
   Ray. O curfed hafte, of making fure a fin !
Can you forgive the traitor ?
   Qu. Never, never :
'Tis written here in characters fo deep,
That feven years hence (till then fhould I not meet him)
And in the temple then, I'll drag him thence,
Ev'n from the holy altar to the block.
   Ray. [*Afide.*] She's fir'd, as I would wifh her. Aid me,
       Juftice,
As all my ends are thine, to gain this point ;
And ruin both at once.——It wounds indeed,   [*To her.*
To bear affronts, too great to be forgiven,
And not have power to punifh. Yet one way
There is to ruin Bertran.
   Qu. O, there's none ;
' Except an hoft from Heaven can make fuch hafte
' To fave my crown, as he will do to feize it.'
You faw, he came furrounded with his friends,
And krew befides, our army was remov'd
To quarters too remote for fudden ufe.
   Ray. Yet you may give commiffion
To fome bold man, whofe loyalty you truft,
And let him raife the train-bands of the city.
   Qu. Grofs feeders, lion-talkers, lamb-like fighters.
   Ray. You do not know the virtues of your city,
What pufhing force they have : fome popular chief,
More noify than the reft, but cries halloo,
And in a trice, the bellowing herd come out ;
The gates are barr'd, the ways are barricado'd,
And one and all's the word ; true cocks o'th' game,
That never afk, for what, or whom, they fight ;
But turn 'em out, and fhew 'em but a foe,
Cry liberty, and that's a caufe for quarrel.
   Qu. There may be danger, in that boift'rous rout :
Who knows, when fires are kindled for my foes,
But fome new blaft of wind may turn thofe flames
Againft my palace-walls ?
   Ray. But ftill their chief
Muft be fome one, whofe loyalty you truft.

Qu.

Qu. And who more proper for that truft than you,
Whofe interefts, though unknown to you, are mine ?
Alphonfo, Pedro, hafte to raife the rabble,
He fhall appear to head 'em.

   Ray. [*Afide to* Alph. *and* Ped.] Firft feize Bertran,
And then infinuate to them, that I bring
Their lawful prince to place upon the throne.

   Alph. Our lawful prince ?

   Ray. Fear not : I can produce him.

   ' *Ped.* [*To* Alph.] Now we want your fon Lorenzo :
          what a mighty faction
' Would he make for us of the city wives,
' With, O, dear hufband, my fweet honey hufband,
' Wo'n't you be for the Colonel ? If you love me,
' Be for the Colonel ? O, he's the fineft man !'   [*Exit.*

   Ray. [*Afide.*] So, now we have a plot behind the plot ;
She thinks, fhe's in the depth of my defign,
And that it's all for her ; but time fhall fhow,
She only lives to help me ruin others,
And laft, to fall herfelf.

   Qu. Now to you, Raymond : can you guefs no reafon
Why I repofe fuch confidence in you ?
You needs muft think,
There's fome more powerful caufe than loyalty :
Will you not fpeak, to fave a lady's blufh ?
Muft I inform you, 'tis for Torrifmond,
That all this grace is fhewn ?

   Ray. [*Afide.*] By all the powers, worfe, worfe than
          what I fear'd.

   Qu. And yet, what need I blufh at fuch a choice ?
I love a man whom I am proud to love,
And am well pleas'd my inclination gives
What gratitude would force.   ' O pardon me ;
' I ne'er was covetous of wealth before ;
' Yet think fo vaft a treafure as your fon,
' Too great for any private man's poffeffion ;
' And him too rich a jewel to be fet
' In vulgar metal, or for vulgar ufe.
   ' *Ray.* Arm me with patience, Heaven !
   ' *Qu.* How, patience, Raymond ?
' What exercife of patience have you here ?
' What find you in my crown to be contemn'd,

' Or in my perſon loath'd ? Have I, a queen,
' Paſs'd by my fellow-rulers of the world,
' Whoſe vying crowns lays glittering in my way,
' As if the world were pav'd with diadems ?
' Have I refus'd their blood, to mix with yours,
' And raiſe new kingdoms from ſo obſcure a race,
' Fate ſcarce knew where to find them when I call'd ?
' Have I heap'd on my perſon, crown and ſtate,
' To load the ſcale, and weigh'd myſelf with earth,
' For you to ſpurn the balance ?
   ' *Ray.* Bate the laſt, and 'tis what I would ſay:
' Can I, can any loyal ſubject, ſee
' With patience ſuch a ſloop from ſovereignty,
' An ocean pour'd upon a narrow brook ?
' My zeal for you muſt lay the father by,
' And plead my country's cauſe againſt my ſon.
' What tho' his heart be great, his actions gallant,
' He wants a crown to poiſe againſt a crown,
' Birth to match birth, and power to balance power.
   ' *Qu.* All theſe I have, and theſe I can beſtow.
' But he brings worth and virtue to my bed ;
' And virtue is the wealth which tyrants want.
' I ſtand in need of one whoſe glories may
' Redeem my crimes, ally me to his fame,
' Diſpel the factions of my foes on earth,
' Diſarm the juſtice of the powers above——'
   Ray. The people never will endure this choice.
   Qu. If I endure it, what imports it you ?
Go raiſe the miniſters of my revenge,
Guide with your breath this whirling tempeſt round,
And ſee its fury fall where I deſign ;
' At laſt a time for juſt revenge is given ;
' Revenge, the darling attribute of Heav'n :
' But man, unlike his Maker, bears too long ;
' Still more expos'd, the more he pardons wrong ;
' Great in forgiving, and in ſuffering brave,
' To be a ſaint, he makes himſelf a ſlave.'   [*Exit.*
   Ray. Marriage with Torriſmond ! it muſt not be ;
By Heaven, it muſt not be ; or, if it be,
Law, juſtice, honour bid farewel to earth,
For Heaven leaves all to tyrants.

2   *Enter*

Enter Torrifmond, *who kneels to him.*

Tor. O, ever welcome, Sir,
But doubly now ! You come in fuch a time,
As if propitious Fortune took a care,
To fwell my tide of joys to their full height,
And leave me nothing farther to defire.

Ray. I hope I come in time, if not to make,
At leaft, to fave your fortune and your honour :
Take heed you fteer your veffel right, my fon ;
This calm of Heaven, this mermaid's melody,
Into an unfeen whirlpool draws you faft,
And in a moment finks you.

Tor. Fortune cannot,
And Fate can fcarce ; I've made the port already,
And laugh fecurely at the lazy ftorm
That wanted wings to reach me in the deep.
Your pardon, Sir ; my duty calls me hence ;
I go to find my queen, my earthly goddefs,
To whom I owe my hopes, my life, my love.

Ray. You owe her more perhaps than you imagine ;
Stay, I command you ftay, and hear me firft.
This hour's the very crifis of your fate,
Your good or ill, your infamy or fame,
And all the colour of your life depends
On this important now.

Tor. I fee no danger ;
The city, army, court efpoufe my caufe,
And, more than all, the Queen, with public favour,
Indulges my pretenfions to her love.

' *Ray.* Nay, if poffeffing her can make you happy,
' 'Tis granted, nothing hinders your defign.

' *Tor.* If fhe can make me bleft ? fhe only can :
' Empire, wealth, and all fhe brings befide,
' Are but the train and trappings of her love :
' The fweeteft, kindeft, trueft of her fex,
' In whofe poffeffion years roll round on years,
' And joys in circles meet new joys again :
' Kiffes, embraces, languifhing, and death
' Still from each other to each other move,
' To crown the various feafons of our love :
' And doubt you if fuch love can make me happy ?

' *Ray.* Yes, for I think you love your honour more.

Tor.

' *Tor.* And what can fhock my honour in a queen?
' *Ray.* A tyrant, an ufurper!
' *Tor.* Grant fhe be.
' When from the conqueror we hold our lives,
' We yield ourfelves his fubjects from that hour:
' For mutual benefits make mutual ties.
    ' *Ray.* Why, can you think I owe a thief my life,
' Becaufe he took it not by lawlefs force?
' What if he did not all the ill he could?
' Am I oblig'd by that t' affift his rapines,
' And to maintain his murders?
    ' *Tor.* Not to maintain, but bear them unreveng'd.
' Kings titles commonly begin by force,
' Which time wears off, and mellows into right:
' So power, which in one age is tyranny,
' Is ripen'd in the next to true fucceffion:
' She's in poffeffion.
    ' *Ray.* So difeafes are: '
' Should not a ling'ring fever be remov'd,
' Becaufe it long has rag'd within my blood?
' Do I rebel when I would thruft it out?
' What, fhall I think the world was made for one,
' And men are born for kings, as beafts for men,
' Not for protection, but to be devour'd?
' Mark thofe who doat on arbitrary power,
' And you fhall find them either hot-brain'd youth,
' Or needy bankrupts, fervile in their greatnefs,
' And flaves to fome, to lord it o'er the reft.
' O bafenefs, to fupport a tyrant throne,
' And crufh your free-born brethren of the world!
' Nay, to become a part of ufurpation;
' T' efpoufe the tyrant's perfon and her crimes,
' And on a tyrant get a race of tyrants,
' To be your country's curfe in after-ages.
    ' *Tor.* I fee no crime in her whom I adore,
' Or if I do, her beauty makes it none:
' Look on me as a man abandon'd o'er
' To an eternal lethargy of love;
' To pull, and pinch, and wound me, cannot cure,
' And but difturb the quiet of my death.'
    Ray. Oh, Virtue, Virtue! what art thou become,
That man fhould leave thee for that toy, a woman,

' Made

‘ Made from the drofs and refufe of a man ?
‘ Heaven took him fleeping when he made her, too :
‘ Had man been waking, he had ne’er confented.’
Now, fon, fuppofe
Some brave confpiracy were ready-form’d,
To punifh tyrants and redeem the land,
Could you fo far belie your country’s hope,
As not to head the party ?

   Tor. How could my hand rebel againft my heart ?

   Raym. How could your heart rebel againft your reafon ?

   Tor. No honour bids me fight againft myfelf ;
The royal family is all extinct,
And fhe who reigns beftows her crown on me.
So, muft I be ungrateful to the living,
To be but vainly pious to the dead ;
While you defraud your offspring of their fate.

   Raym. Mark who defraud their offspring, you or I ;
For, know, there yet furvives the lawful heir
Of Sancho’s blood, whom, when I fhall produce,
I reft affur’d to fee you pale with fear,
And trembling at his name.

   Tor. He muft be more than man who makes me tremble :
I dare him to the field, with all the odds
Of juftice on his fide, againft my tyrant.
Produce your lawful prince, and you fhall fee
How brave a rebel love has made your fon.

   Raym. Read that ; ’tis with the royal fignet fign’d,
And given me by the King, when time fhould ferve,
To be perus’d by you.

   Tor. [*Reads.*] “ I the King :
My youngeft and alone furviving fon,
Reported dead t’ efcape rebellious rage,
’Till happier times fhall call his courage forth
To break my fetters, or revenge my fate,
I will that Raymond educate as his,
And call him ‘Torrifmond.”——
If I am he, that fon, that Torrifmond,
The world contains not fo forlorn a wretch..
Let never man believe he can be happy ;
For when I thought my fortune moft fecure,
One fatal moment tears me from my joys ;
And when two hearts were join’d by mutual love,

The

The fword of juſtice cuts upon the knot,
And fevers them for ever.
   Raym. True, it muſt.
   Tor. Oh, cruel man, to tell me that it muſt!
If you have any pity in your breaſt,
Redeem me from this labyrinth of fate,
And plunge me in my firſt obſcurity.
The ſecret is alone between us two;
And though you would not hide me from myſelf,
Oh, yet be kind, conceal me from the world,
And be my father ſtill.
   Raym. Your lot's too glorious, and the proof's too plain.
Now, in the name of honour, Sir, I beg you,
(Since I muſt uſe authority no more)
On theſe old knees I beg you, ere I die,
That I may ſee your father's death reveng'd.
   Tor. Why, 'tis the only buſ'neſs of my life;
My order's iſſu'd to recall the army,
And Bertran's death reſolv'd.   [der!
   Raym. And not the Queen's? Oh, ſhe's the chief offen-
Shall Juſtice turn her edge within your hand?
No, if ſhe 'ſcape, you are yourſelf the tyrant,
And murderer of your father.
   Tor. Cruel Fates,
To what have you reſerv'd me?
   Raym. Why that ſigh?
   Tor. Since you muſt know, (but break, Oh, break, my
Before I tell my fatal ſtory out!)   [heart,
Th' uſurper of my throne, my houſe's ruin,
The murderer of my father, is my wife.
   Raym. Oh, horror, horror!—After this alliance,
Let tigers match with hinds, and wolves with ſheep,
And every creature couple with his foe.
How vainly man deſigns, when Heav'n oppoſes!
I bred you up to arms, rais'd you to power,
Permitted you to fight for this uſurper,
Indeed, to ſave a crown, not her's, but yours;
All to make ſure the vengeance of this day,
Which even this day has ruin'd.   One more queſtion
Let me but aſk, and I have done for ever:
Do you yet love the cauſe of all your woes,

Or

Or is she grown (as sure she ought to be)
More odious to your sight than toads and adders?
  Tor. Oh, there's the utmost malice of my fate,
That I am bound to hate, and born to love!
  Raym. No more—Farewel, my much-lamented king!
' [*Aside.*] I dare not trust him with himself so far,
' To own him to the people as their king,
' Before their rage has finish'd my designs
' On Bertran and the Queen, But, in despite
' Ev'n of himself, I'll save him.'   [*Exit* Raym.
  Tor. 'Tis but a moment since I have been king,
And weary on't already. I'm a lover,
And lov'd, possess; yet all these make me wretched;
And Heav'n has giv'n me blessings for a curse.
With what a load of vengeance am I press'd!
Yet never, never can I hope for rest;
For when my heavy burden I remove,
The weight falls down, and crushes her I love.
                      [*Exeunt.*

END of the FOURTH ACT.

A C T V.

S C E N E, *a Bed-chamber.*

Enter Torrismond.

TORRISMOMD.

LOVE, justice, nature, pity, and revenge,
  Have kindled up a wild-fire in my breast,
And I am all a civil war within.
      Enter Queen *and* Teresa *at a distance.*
My Leonora there!
Mine! is she mine? My father's murderer mine?
Oh, that I could, with honour, love her more,
Or hate her less, with reason!—See, she weeps;
Thinks me unkind, or false, and knows not why
I thus estrange my person from her bed.
Shall I not tell her? No; 'twill break her heart:
She'll know too soon her own and my misfortunes. [*Exit.*
  Qu. He's gone, and I am lost! Didst thou not see
          G   His

His fullen eyes, how gloomily they glanc'd?
He look'd not like the Torrifmond I lov'd.　　　　[ceeds?
　‘ *Ter.* Can you not guefs from whence this change pro-
　‘ *Qu.* No, there's the grief, Terefa.　Oh, Terefa!
‘ Fain would I tell thee what I feel within,
‘ But fhame and modefty have ty'd my tongue!
‘ Yet I will tell, that thou may'ft weep with me,
‘ How dear, how fweet h's firft embraces were ;
‘ With what a zeal he join'd his lips to mine,
‘ And fuck'd my breath at every word I fpoke,
‘ As if he drew his infpiration thence ;
‘ While both our fouls came upward to our mouths,
‘ As neighbouring monarchs at their borders meet.
‘ I thought—Oh, no, 'tis falfe, I could not think !
‘ 'Twas neither life nor death, but both in one.
　‘ *Ter.* Then fure his tranfports were not lefs than yours.
　‘ *Qu.* More, more ! for by the high-hung tapers' light
‘ I could difcern his cheeks were glowing red,
‘ His very eye-balls trembled with his love,
‘ And fparkled through their cafements humid fires:
‘ He figh'd, and kifs'd, breath'd fhort, and would have
‘ But was too fierce to throw away the time ;　　[fpoke,
‘ All he could fay, was love and Leonora.
　‘ *Ter.* How then can you fufpect him loft fo foon ?
　‘ *Qu.* Laft night he flew not with a bridegroom's hafte,
‘ Which eagerly prevents th' appointed hour.
‘ I told the clocks, and watch'd the wafting light,
‘ And lift'ned to each foftly-treading ftep,
‘ In hope 'twas he ; but ftill it was not he.
‘ At laft he came, but with fuch alter'd looks,
‘ So wild, fo ghaftly, as if fome ghoft had met him.
‘ All pale, and fpeechlefs, he furvey'd me round ;
‘ Then with a groan, he threw himfelf in bed,
‘ But far from me, as far as he could move,
‘ And figh'd, and tofs'd, and turn'd, but ftill from me.
　‘ *Ter.* What, all the night ?
　‘ *Qu.* Ev'n all the live-long night.
‘ At laft (for, blufhing, I muft tell thee all)
‘ I prefs'd his hand, and laid me by his fide ;
‘ He pull'd it back, as if he touch'd a ferpent.
‘ With that I burft into a flood of tears,
‘ And afk'd him how I had offended him ?
‘ He anfwer'd nothing but with fighs and groans ;

‘ So

‘ So reſtleſs paſs’d the night; and at the dawn,
‘ Leap’d from the bed, and vaniſh’d.
  ‘ *Ter.* Sighs and groans,
‘ Paleneſs and trembling, all are ſigns of love.
‘ He only fears to make you ſhare his ſorrows.
  ‘ *Qu.* I wiſh ’twere ſo; but love ſtill doubts the worſt.
‘ My heavy heart, the propheteſs of woes,
‘ Forebodes ſome ill at hand.   To ſooth my ſadneſs,
‘ Sing me the ſong which poor Olympia made,
‘ When falſe Bireno left her.

‘ S O N G.

  ‘ Farewel, ungrateful traitor,
    ‘ Farewel, my perjur’d ſwain ;
  ‘ Let never injur’d creature
    ‘ Believe a man again.
  ‘ The pleaſure of poſſeſſing
  ‘ Surpaſſes all expreſſing,
  ‘ But ’tis too ſhort a bleſſing,
    ‘ And love too long a pain.

  ‘ ’Tis eaſy to deceive us,
    ‘ In pity of your pain ;
  ‘ But when we love you leave us
    ‘ To rail at you in vain.
  ‘ Before we have deſcry’d it,
  ‘ There is no bliſs beſide it ;
  ‘ But ſhe that once has try’d it,
    ‘ Will never love again.

  ‘ The paſſion you pretended,
    ‘ Was only to obtain ;
  ‘ But when the charm is ended,
    ‘ The charmer you diſdain.
  ‘ Your love by ours we meaſure,
  ‘ ’Till we have loſt our treaſure ;
  ‘ But dying is a pleaſure,
    ‘ When living is a pain.’

Re-enter Torriſmond.
Tor. Still ſhe is here, and ſtill I cannot ſpeak ;
But wander, like ſome diſcontented ghoſt,
That oft appears, but is forbid to talk.   [*Going again.*
G 2

Qu. Oh, Torrifmond, if you refolve my death,
You need no more but to go hence again !
Will you not fpeak ?
　Tor. I cannot.
　Qu. Speak, Oh, fpeak !
Your anger would be kinder than your filence.
　' *Tor.* Oh !
　' *Qu.* Do not figh, or tell me why you figh.
　' *Tor.* Why do I live ye powers ?
　' *Qu.* Why do I live to hear you fpeak that word ?
' Some black-mouth'd villain has defam'd my virtue.
　' *Tor.* No, no ! pray, let me go. '
　' *Qu.* [*Kneeling.*] You fhall not go.
' By all the pleafures of our nuptial bed,
' If ever I was lov'd, though now I'm not,
' By thefe true tears, which, from my wounded heart,
' Bleed at my eyes ————
　' *Tor.* Rife.
　' *Qu.* I will never rife ;
' I cannot chufe a better place to die.
　' *Tor.* Oh, I would fpeak, but cannot !　　　[me not.
　' *Qu.* [*Rifing.*] Guilt keeps you filent then ; you love
' What have I done ? Ye pow'rs, what have I done,
' To fee my youth, my beauty, and my love,
' No fooner gain'd, but flighted and betray'd ;
' And like a rofe juft gather'd from the ftalk,
' But only fmelt, and cheaply thrown afide,
' To wither on the ground ?　　　　　　　　　[paffion.
　' *Ter.* For Heav'n's fake, Madam, moderate your
　' *Qu.* Why nam'ft thou heav'n? There is no heav'n for
' Defpair, death, hell have feiz'd my tortur'd foul.　[me :
' When I had rais'd his groveling fate from ground,
' To pow'r and love, to empire and to me ;
' When each embrace was dearer than the firft ;
' Then, then to be contemn'd ! then, then thrown off !
' It calls me old, and wither'd, and deform'd,
' And loathfome: Oh, what woman can bear loathfome !
' The turtle flies not from his billing mate ;
' He bills the clofer: but ungrateful man,
' Bafe, barbarous man, the more we raife our love,
' The more we pall, and cool, and kill his ardour.
　　　　　　　　　　　　　　　　　　' Racks,

‘ Racks, poifons, daggers, rid me of my life;
‘ And any death is welcome.’
   Tor. Be witnefs, all ye pow’rs that know my heart,
I would have kept the fatal fecret hid,
But fhe has conquer’d, to her ruin conquer’d.
Here, take this paper; read our deftinies:
‘ Yet do not; but, in kindnefs to yourfelf,
‘ Be ignorantly fafe.
   ‘ *Qu.* No, give it me,
‘ Even though it be the fentence of my death.
   ‘ *Tor.* Then fee how much unhappy love has made us.
‘ Oh, Leonora! Oh!
‘ We two were born when fullen planets reign’d;
‘ When each the other’s influence oppos’d,
‘ And drew the ftars to factions at our birth.
‘ Oh, better, better had it been for us,
‘ That we had never feen, or never lov’d!
   ‘ *Qu.* There is no faith in Heav’n, if Heav’n fays fo.
‘ You dare not give it.
   ‘ *Tor.* As unwillingly,
‘ As I would reach out opium to a friend
‘ Who lay in torture, and defir’d to die.’ [*Gives the paper.*
But, now you have it, fpare my fight the pain
Of feeing what a world of tears it cofts you.
Go, filently enjoy your part of grief,
And fhare the fad inheritance with me.
   Qu. I have a thirfty fever in my foul;
Give me but prefent eafe, and let me die.
          [*Exeunt* Queen *and* Terefa.
       Enter Lorenzo.
   Lor. Arm, arm, my Lord; the city bands are up,
Drums beating, colours flying, fhouts confus’d,
All cluft’ring in a heap, like fwarming hives,
And rifing in a moment.
  Tor. With defign.
To punifh Bertran, and revenge the King;
’Twas order’d fo.
   Lor. Then you’re betray’d, my Lord.
’Tis true, they block the caftle kept by Bertran;
But now they cry, Down with the palace, fire it,
Pull out th’ ufurping Queen.
   Tor. The Queen, Lorenzo! durft they name the Queen!
        G 3   *Lor.*

Lor. If railing and reproaching be to name her.

Tor. Oh, facrilege! Say, quickly, who commands
This vile blafpheming rout?

Lor. I'm loth to tell you;
But both our fathers thruft them headlong on,
And bear down all before them.

Tor. Death and hell!
Somewhat muft be refolv'd, and fpeedily.
How fay'ft thou, my Lorenzo? Dar'ft thou be
A friend, and once forget thou art a fon,
To help me fave the Queen?

Lor. [*Afide.*] Let me confider——
Bear arms againft my father! He begat me;
That's true : but for whofe fake did he beget me?
For his own, fure enough; for me he knew not.
Oh, but, fays Confcience, fly in Nature's face!
But how if Nature fly in my face firft?
Then Nature's the aggreffor—Let her look to't——
He gave me life, and he may take it back——
No, that's boy's play, fay I.
'Tis policy for fon and father to take different fides;
For then lands and tenements commit no treafon.
[*To* Tor.] Sir, upon mature confideration, I have found
my father to be little better than a rebel; and therefore
I'll do my beft to fecure him for your fake, in hope you
may fecure him hereafter for my fake.

Tor. Put on thy utmoft fpeed to head the troops,
Which every moment I expect t' arrive.
Proclaim me, as I am, the lawful king.
I need not caution thee for Raymond's life,
Though I no more muft call him father now.

Lor. [*Afide.*] How, not call him father! I fee preferment alters a man ftrangely: this may ferve me for a ufe
of inftruction, to caft off my father, when I am great. Methought, too, he called himfelf the lawful king, intimating
fweetly, that he knows what's what with our fovereign
Lady. Well, if I rout my father, as I hope in Heaven
I fhall, I am in a fair way to be a prince of the blood—
Farewel, General; I'll bring up thofe that fhall try what
mettle there is in orange-tawny.   [*Exit.*

Tor. [*At the door.*] Hafte, there, command the guards
    be all drawn up

                                      Before

Before the palace gate.   By Heaven, I'll face
This tempest, and deserve the name of king.
' Oh, Leonora, beauteous in thy crimes,
' Never were hell and heaven so match'd before!
' Look upward, fair, but as thou look'st on me ;
' Then all the bless'd will beg that thou may'st live,
' And ev'n my father's ghost his death forgive.'   [*Exit.*

' SCENE, *the Palace-yard.   Drums and trumpets within.*

  ' *Enter* Raymond, Alphonso, Pedro, *and their Party.*
  ' *Ray.* Now, valiant citizens, the time is come,
' To show our courage, and your loyalty.
' You have a prince of Sancho's royal blood,
' The darling of the heav'ns, and joy of earth :
' When he's produc'd, as soon he shall among you,
' Speak, what will you adventure to re-seat him
' Upon his father's throne ?
  ' *Omnes.* Our lives and fortunes.
  ' *Ray.* What then remains to perfect our success,
' But o'er the tyrant's guards to force our way ?
  ' *Omnes.* Lead on, lead on.
                    ' [*Drums and trumpets on the other side.*
' *Enter* Torrismond *and his party.   As they are going to
                    fight, he speaks.*
  ' *Tor.* [*To his.*] Hold, hold your arms,
  ' *Raym.* Retire.   What means this pause ?
  ' *Ped.* Peace ; nature works within them.
                    ' [Tor. *and* Raym. *go apart.*
  ' *Tor.* How comes it, good old man, that we two meet
' On these harsh terms ? Thou very reverend rebel,
' Thou venerable traitor, in whose face
' And hoary hairs treason is sanctified,
' And sin's black dye seems blanch'd by age to virtue.
  ' *Raym.* What treason is it to redeem my king,
' And to reform the state ?
  ' *Tor.* That's a stale cheat ;
' The primitive rebel, Lucifer, first us'd it,
' And was the first reformer of the skies.
  ' *Raym.* What! if I see my prince mistake a poison,
' Call it a cordial, am I then a traitor,
' Because I hold his hand, or break the glass ?
  ' *Tor.* How dar'st thou serve thy king against his will ?
                              ' *Raym.*

' *Raym.* Becaufe 'tis then the only time to ferve him.
' *Tor.* I take the blame of all upon myfelf.
' Difcharge thy weight on me.
' *Raym.* Oh, never, never!
' Why, 'tis to leave a fhip tofs'd in a tempeft,
' Without the pilot's care.
' *Tor.* I'll punifh thee,
' By Heav'n, I will, as I would punifh rebels,
' Thou ftubborn loyal man.
' *Raym.* Firft let me fee
' Her punifh'd, who mifleads you from your fame;
' Then burn me, hack me, hew me into pieces,
' And I fhall die well pleas'd.
' *Tor.* Proclaim my title,   [ftill
' To fave th' effufion of my fubjects' blood, and thou fhalt
' Be as my fofter-father, near my breaft,
' And next my Leonora.
' *Raym.* That word ftabs me;
' You fhall be ftill plain Torrifmond with me,
' Th' abetter, partner, (if you like that name)
' The hufband of a tyrant; but no king,
' Till you deferve that title by your juftice.
' *Tor.* Then, farewel pity; I will be obey'd.
' [*To the people.*] Hear, you miftaken men, whofe loyalty
' Runs headlong into treafon; fee your prince;
' In me behold your murder'd Sancho's fon:
' Difmifs your arms, and I forgive your crimes.
' *Raym.* Believe him not; he raves: his words are loofe
' As heaps of fand, and fcattering, wide from fenfe.
' You fee he knows not me, his natural father;
' But, aiming to poffefs th' ufurping Queen,
' So high he's mounted in his airy hopes,
' That now the wind is got into his head,
' And turns his brains to frenzy.
' *Tor.* Hear me yet; I am——
' *Raym.* Fall on, and hear him not:
' But fpare his perfon for his father's fake.
' *Ped.* Let me come; if he be mad, I have that fhall
' cure him; there's not a furgeon in all Arragon has
' fo much dexterity as I have, at breathing of the tem-
' ple-vein.
' *Tor.* My right for me!

                                                    ' *Raym.*

' *Raym.* Our liberty for us !

' *Om.* Liberty, liberty !   [*As they are ready to fight,*
        '*Enter* Lorenzo *and his party.*

' *Lor.* On forfeit of your lives, lay down your arms.

' *Alph.* How, rebel ! art thou there ?

' *Lor.* Take your rebel back again, father mine. The
' beaten party are rebels to the conquerors.   I have been
' at hard-head with your butting citizens; I have routed
' your herd; I have difperfed them ; and now they are
' retreated quietly, from their extraordinary vocation of
' fighting in the ftreets, to their ordinary vocation of
' cozening in their fhops.

' *Tor.* [*To* Raym.] You fee 'tis vain contending with
' Acknowledge what I am.   [the truth.

' *Raym.* You are my king ; would you would be your
' But, by a fatal fondnefs, you betray   [own ;
' Your fame and glory to th' ufurper's bed ;
' Enjoy the fruits of blood and parricide.
' Take your own crown from Leonora's gift,
' And hug your father's murderer in your arms.
        ' *Enter* Queen, Terefa, *and Woman.*

' *Alph.* No more : behold the Queen.

' *Raym.* Behold the bafilifk of Torrifmond,
' That kills him with her eyes.   I will fpeak on.
' My life is of no further ufe to me :
' I would have chaffer'd it before for vengeance ;
' Now let it go for failing.

' *Tor.* [*Afide.*] My heart finks in me while I hear him
' And every flack'd fibre drops its hold,   [fpeak,
' Like nature letting down the fprings of life ;
' So much the name of father awes me ftill.
' Send off the crowd.   For you, now I have conquer'd,
' I can hear with honour your demands.

' *Lor.* [*To* Alph.] Now, Sir, who proves the traitor ?
' My confcience is true to me ; it always whifpers right
' when I have my regiment to back it.
        ' [*Exeunt all but* Tor. Raym. *and* Queen.

' *Tor.* Oh, Leonora ! what can love do more ?
' I have oppos'd your ill fate to the utmoft,
' Combated heav'n and earth to keep you mine ;
' And yet, at laft, that tyrant, Juftice—Oh !——

' *Qu.* 'Tis paft, 'tis paft, and love is ours no more.

                              ' Yet

' Yet I complain not of the pow'rs above;
' They made m' a mifer's feaft of happinefs,
' And could not furnifh out another meal.
' Now, by yon ftars, by heav'n, and earth, and men;
' By all my foes at once, I fwear, my Torrifmond,
' That to have had you mine for one fhort day,
' Has cancell'd half my mighty fum of woes.
' Say but you hate me not.
　' *Tor.* I cannot hate you.
　' *Raym.* Can you not? Say that once more,
' That all the faints may witnefs it againft you.
　' *Qu.* Cruel Raymond!
' Can he not punifh me, but he muft hate?
' Oh, 'tis not juftice, but a brutal rage,
' Which hates th' offender's perfon with his crimes!
' I have enough to overwhelm one woman;
' To lofe a crown and lover in a day.
' Let pity lend a tear when rigour ftrikes.
　' *Raym.* Then, then you fhould have thought of tears
' When virtue, majefty, and hoary age　　　　[and pity,
' Pleaded for Sancho's life.
　' *Qu.* My future days fhall be one whole contrition.
' A chapel will I build, with large endowment,
' Where every day an hundred aged men
' Shall all hold up their wither'd hands to Heav'n,
' To pardon Sancho's death.
　' *Tor.* See, Raymond, fee, fhe makes a large amends.
' Sancho is dead: no punifhment of her
' Can raife his cold ftiff limbs from the dark grave;
' Nor can his bleffed foul look down from heaven,
' Or break th' eternal fabbath of his reft,
' To fee, with joy, her miferies on earth.
　' *Raym.* Heaven may forgive a crime to penitence;
' For Heaven can judge if penitence be true;
' But man, who knows not hearts, fhould make examples;
' Which, like a warning-piece, muft be fhot off,
' To fright the reft from crimes.
　' *Qu.* Had I but known that Sancho was his father,
' I would have pour'd a deluge of my blood,
' To fave one drop of his.
　' *Tor.* Mark that, inexorable Raymond; mark,
' 'Twas fatal ignorance that caus'd his death.
　　　　　　　　　　　　　　　　　' *Raym.*

' *Raym.* What if she did not know he was your father?
' She knew he was a man, the best of men,
' Heaven's image double-stamp'd, as man and king.
   ' *Qu.* He was, he was, ev'n more than you can say;
' But yet——————
   ' *Raym.* But yet you barbarously murder'd him.
   ' *Qu.* He will not hear me out!
   ' *Tor.* Was ever criminal forbid to plead?
' Curb your ill-manner'd zeal.
   ' *Raym.* Sing to him, syren;
' For I shall stop my ears.   Now mince the sin,
' And mollify damnation with a phrase:
' Say, you consented not to Sancho's death;
' But barely not forbade it.
   ' *Qu.* Hard-hearted man! I yield my guilty cause;
' But all my guilt was caus'd by too much love.
' Had I for jealousy of empire sought
' Good Sancho's death, Sancho had dy'd before.
' 'Twas always in my power to take his life;
' But interest never could my conscience blind,
' 'Till love had cast a mist before my eyes,
' And made me think his death the only means
' Which could secure my throne to Torrismond.
   ' *Tor.* Never was fatal mischief meant so kind;
' For all she gave has taken all away.
' Malicious pow'rs! is this to be restor'd?
' 'Tis to be worse depos'd than Sancho was.
   ' *Raym.* Heav'n has restor'd you, you depose yourself.
' Oh, when young kings begin with scorn of justice,
' They make an omen to their after-reign,
' And blot their annals in the foremost page!
   ' *Tor.* No more; lest you be made the first example,
' To show how I can punish.
   ' *Raym.* Once again,
' Let her be made your father's sacrifice,
' And after make me her's.
   ' *Tor.* Condemn a wife!
' That were t' atone for parricide with murder.
   ' *Raym.* Then let her be divorc'd: we'll be content
' With that poor scanty justice.   Let her part.   [love.
   ' *Tor.* Divorce! that's worse than death; 'tis death of
  ' *Qu.* The soul and body part not with such pain,

                                        ' As

‘ As I from you : but yet 'tis juſt, my Lord :
‘ I am th' accurſt of Heav'n, the hate of earth,
‘ Your ſubjects' deteſtation, and your ruin :
‘ And therefore fix this doom upon myſelf.'
  ‘ *Tor.* Heav'n ! can you wiſh it ? to be mine no more ?
  ‘ *Qu.* Yes, I can wiſh it, as the deareſt proof,
‘ And laſt that I can make you of my love.
‘ To leave you bleſt, I would be more accurſt
‘ Than death can make me ; for death ends our woes,
‘ And the kind grave ſhuts up the mournful ſcene :
‘ But I would live without you ; to be wretched long ;
‘ And hoard up every moment of my life,
‘ To lengthen out the payment of my tears,
‘ Till ev'n fierce Raymond, at the laſt ſhall ſay,
‘ Now let her die for ſhe has griev'd enough,
  ‘ *Tor.* Hear this, hear this, thou tribune of the people :
‘ Thou zealous, public blood-hound, hear, and melt.
  ‘ *Ray.* [*Aſide.*] I could cry now, my eyes grow wo-
‘ But yet my heart holds out.   [maniſh,
  ‘ *Qu.* Some ſolitary cloyſter will I chuſe,
‘ And there with holy virgins live immur'd :
‘ Coarſe my attire, and ſhort ſhall be my ſleep,
‘ Broke by the melancholy midnight-bell :
‘ Now, Raymond, now be ſatisfy'd at laſt,
‘ Faſting and tears, and penitence and prayer,
‘ Shall do dead Sancho juſtice every hour.
  ‘ *Ray.* [*Aſide.*] By your leave, manhood !
                                                  ‘ [*Wipes his eyes.*
  ‘ *Tor.* He weeps, now he is vanquiſh'd.
  ‘ *Ray.* No ; 'tis a ſalt rheum that ſcalds my eyes.
  ‘ *Qu.* If he were vanquiſh'd, I am ſtill unconquer'd.
‘ I'll leave you in the height of all my love,
‘ Ev'n when my heart is beating out its way,
‘ And ſtruggles to you moſt.
‘ Farewel, a laſt farewel ! my dear, dear Lord,
‘ Remember me ; ſpeak, Raymond, will you let him ?
‘ Shall he remember Leonora's love,
‘ And ſhed a parting tear to her misfortunes ?
  ‘ *Ray.* [*Almoſt crying.*] Yes, yes, he ſhall ; pray go.
  ‘ *Tor.* Now, by my ſoul, ſhe ſhall not go : why, Ray-
‘ Her every tear is worth a father's life ;   [mond,
‘ Come to my arms ; come, my fair penitent,

3   ‘ Let

‘ Let us not think what future ills may fall,
‘ But drink deep draughts of love, and lose them all.
                              [*Exit* Tor. *with the Queen.*
  ‘ *Ray.* No matter yet, he has my hook within him.
‘ Now let him frisk and flounce, and run and roll,
‘ And think to break his hold : he toils in vain.
‘ This love, the bait he gorg’d so greedily,
‘ Will make him sick, and then I have him sure.
              ‘ *Enter* Alphonso *and* Pedro.
  ‘ *Alph.* Brother, there’s news from Bertran ; he desires
‘ Admittance to the King, and cries aloud,
‘ This day shall end our fears of civil war ;
‘ For his safe conduct he entreats your presence,
‘ And begs you would be speedy.
  ‘ *Ray.* Though I loath
‘ The traitor’s sight, I’ll go : attend us here.’ [*Exeunt.*
Enter Gomez, Elvira, Dominick, *with Officers, to make the
                stage as full as possible.*

Ped. Why, how now, Gomez ; what makest thou
here with a whole brotherhood of city-bailiffs ? Why,
thou lookest like Adam in Paradise, with his guard of
beasts about him.

Gom. Ay, and a man had need of them, Don Pedro ;
for here are the two old seducers, a wife and a priest,
that’s Eve and the serpent, at my elbow.

Dom. Take notice how uncharitably he talks of churchmen.

Gom. Indeed you are a charitable belswagger : my wife
cried out fire, fire ; and you brought out your church
buckets, and called for engines to play against it.

Alph. I am sorry you are come hither to accuse your
wife ; her education has been virtuous, her nature mild
and easy.

Gom. Yes ; she’s easy with a vengeance, there’s a certain Colonel has found her so.

Alph. She came a spotless virgin to your bed.

Gom. And she’s a spotless virgin still for me—she’s never the worse for my wearing, I’ll take my oath on’t : I
have lived with her with all the innocence of a man of
threescore ; like a peaceable bedfellow as I am.

Elv. Indeed, Sir, I have no reason to complain of him
for disturbing of my sleep.

Dom. A fine commendation you have given yourself; the church did not marry you for that.

Ped. Come, come, your grievances, your grievances.

Dom. Why, noble Sir, I'll tell you.

Gom. Peace, fryar! and let me speak first. I am the plaintiff. Sure you think you are in the pulpit, where you preach by hours.

Dom. And you edify by minutes.

Gom. Where you make doctrines for the people, and uses and applications for yourselves.

Ped. Gomez, give way to the old gentleman in black.

Gom. No! the t'other old gentleman in black shall take me if I do; I will speak first; nay, I will, fryar, for all your *verbum sacerdotis*, I'll speak truth in few words, and then you may come afterwards, and lie by the clock, as you use to do: for, let me tell you, gentlemen, he shall lie and forswear himself with any fryar in all Spain; that's a bold word now.

Dom. Let him alone; let him alone; I shall fetch him back with a *circum-bendibus*, I warrant him.

Alph. Well, what have you to say against your wife, Gomez?

Gom. Why, I say, in the first place, that I and all men are married for our sins, and that our wives are a judgment; that a bachelor-cobler is a happier man than a prince in wedlock; that we are all visited with a household plague, and, "Lord have mercy upon us" should be written on all our doors.

Dom. Now he reviles marriage, which is one of the seven blessed sacraments.

Gom. 'Tis liker one of the seven deadly sins: but make your best on't, I care not; 'tis but binding a man neck and heels for all that! But, as for my wife, that crocodile of Nilus, she has wickedly and traiterously conspired the cuckoldom of me her anointed sovereign lord; and with the help of the aforesaid fryar, whom heaven confound, and with the limbs of one Colonel Hernando, cuckold-maker of this city, devilishly contrived to steal herself away, and under her arm feloniously to bear one casket of diamonds, pearls and other jewels, to the value of thirty thousand pistoles. Guilty, or not guilty; how sayest thou, culprit?

3

Dom.

Dom. Falfe and fcandalous! Give me the book. I'll take my corporal oath point-blank againft every particular of this charge.

Elv. And fo will I.

Dom. As I was walking in the ftreets, telling my beads and praying to myfelf, according to my ufual cuftom, I heard a foul out-cry before Gomez's portal; and his wife, my penitent, making doleful lamentations; thereupon, making what hafte my limbs would fuffer me, that are crimpled with often kneeling, I faw him fpurning and fifting her moft unmercifully; whereupon, ufing Chriftian arguments with him to defift, he fell violently upon me, without refpect to my facerdotal orders, pufhed me from him, and turned me about with a finger and a thumb, juft as a man would fet up a top. Mercy, quoth I. Damme, quoth he. And ftill continued labouring me, 'till a good-minded Colonel came by, whom, as Heaven fhall fave me, I had never feen before.

Gom. Oh, Lord! Oh, Lord!

Dom. Ay, and, Oh, Lady! Oh, Lady too! I redouble my oath, I had never feen him. Well, this noble Colonel, like a true gentleman, was for taking the weaker part you may be fure—whereupon this Gomez flew upon him like a dragon, got him down, the devil being ftrong in him, and gave him baftinado upon baftinado, and buffet upon buffet, which the poor meek Colonel, being proftrate, fuffered with a moft Chriftian patience.

Gom. Who? he meek? I'm fure I quake at the very thought of him; why, he's as fierce as Rhodomont; he made affault and battery upon my perfon, beat me into all the colours of the rainbow; and every word this abominable prieft has uttered is as falfe as the Alcoran. But if you want a thorough-paced liar, that will fwear through thick and thin, commend me to a fryar.

Enter Lorenzo, *who comes behind the company, and ftands at his father's back unfeen, over againft* Gomez.

Lor. [*Afide.*] How now! What's here to do? My caufe a trying, as I live, and that before my own father: now fourfcore take him for an old bawdy magiftrate, ' that ' ftands like the picture of Madam Juftice, with a pair ' of fcales in his hand, to weigh lechery by ounces.'

H 2

Alph.

Alph. Well—but all this while, who is this Colonel Hernando?

Gom. He's the first begotten of Beelzebub, with a face as terrible as Demogorgon. [Lorenzo *peeps over* Alphonso's *head, and stares at* Gomez.] No; I lie, I lie; he's a very proper handsome fellow! well proportioned, and clean shaped, with a face like a cherubin.

Ped. What, backward and forward. Gomez, dost thou hunt counter?

Alph. Had this Colonel any former design upon your wife? for, if that be proved, you shall have justice.

Gom. [*Aside.*] Now I dare speak; let him look as dreadful as he will. I say, Sir, and will prove it, that he had a lewd design upon her body, and attempted to corrupted her honesty. [Lorenzo *lifts up his fist clenched at* him.] I confess, my wife was as willing—as himself; and, I believe, 'twas she corrupted him; for I have known him formerly, a very civil and modest person.

Elv. You see, Sir, he contradicts himself at every word: he's plainly mad.

Alph. Speak boldly, man! and say what thou wilt stand by: did he strike thee?

Gom. I will speak boldly: he struck me on the face before my own threshold, that the very walls cried shame on him. [Lorenzo *holds up again.*] 'Tis true, I gave him provocation, for the man's as peaceable a gentleman as any is in all Spain.

Dom. Now the truth comes out, in spite of him.

Ped. I believe the fryar has bewitched him.

Alph. For my part, I see no wrong that has been offered him.

Gom. How? no wrong? why, he ravished me with the help of two soldiers, carried me away *vi & armis*, and would have put me into a plot against the government. [Lorenzo *holds up again.*] I confess, I never could endure the government, because it was tyrannical: but my sides and shoulders are black and blue, as I can strip and shew the marks of them. [Lorenzo *again.*] But that might happen too by a fall that I got yesterday upon the pebbles. [*All laugh.*

Dom. Fresh straw, and a dark chamber: a most manifest judgment; there never comes better of railing against the church.

Gom.

Gom. Why, what will you have me fay? I think you'll make me mad: truth has been at my tongue's end this half hour, and I have not power to bring it out, for fear of this bloody-minded Colonel.

Alph. What Colonel?

Gom. Why, my Colonel: I mean, my wife's Colonel, that appears there to me like my *malus genius*, and terrifies me.

Alph. [*Turning.*] Now you are mad indeed, Gomez; this is my fon Lorenzo.

Gom. How? Your fon, Lorenzo! It is impoffible.

Alph. As true as your wife, Elvira, is my daughter.

Lor. What, have I taken all this pains about a fifter?

Gom. No, you have taken fome about me: I am fure, if you are her brother, my fides can fhew the tokens of our alliance.

Alph. [*To* Lor.] You know I put your fifter into a nunnery, with a ftrict command not to fee you, for fear you fhould have wrought upon her to have taken the habit, which was never my intention; and, confequently, I married her without your knowledge, that it might not be in your power to prevent it.

Elv. You fee, brother, I had a natural affection to you.

Lor. What a delicious harlot have I loft! Now, pox upon me, for being fo near a-kin to thee.

Elv. However, we are both beholden to fryar Dominick, ' the church is an indulgent mother, fhe never‐
' fails to do her part.'

Dom. Heaven! what will become of me?

Gom. Why, you are not alike to trouble Heaven; thofe fat guts were never made for mounting.

Lor. I fhall make bold to difburden him of my hundred piftoles, to make him the lighter for his journey; indeed 'tis partly out of confcience, that I may not be acceffary to his breaking his vow of poverty.

Alph. I have no fecular power to reward the pains you have taken with my daughter: but I fhall do it by proxy, fryar: your bifhop's my friend, and 'tis too honeft, to let fuch as you infect a cloyfter.

Gom. Ay, do, father-in-law, let him to be ftripped of his habit, and difordered—I would fain fee him walk in

H 3

quirpo,

quirpo, like a cafed rabbet, without his holy furr upon
his back, that the world may once behold the infide of a
fryar.

    ' *Dom.* Farewel, kind gentlemen: I give you all my
' bleffing before I go.——May your fifters, wives and
' daughters, be fo naturally lewd, that they may have
' no occafion for a devil to tempt, or a fryar to pimp for
' them.'   [*Exit, with a rabble pufhing him.*

    Enter Torrifmond, Leonora, Bertran, Raymond, Te-
refa, &c.

    Tor. He lives! he lives! my royal father lives!
Let every one partake the general joy.
Some angel with a golden trumpet found,
King Sancho lives! and let the echoing fkies
From pole to pole refound, king Sancho lives!
Oh, Bertran, Oh, no more my foe, but brother:
One act like this blots out a thoufand crimes.

    Bert. Bad men, when 'tis their intereft, may do good:
I muft confefs, I counfel'd Sancho's murder;
And urg'd the Queen by fpecious arguments;
But ftill, fufpecting that her love was chang'd,
I fpread abroad the rumour of his death,
To found the very foul of her defigns:
Th' event you know was anfwering to my fears:
She threw the odium of the fact on me,
And publickly avow'd her love to you.

    Ray. Heaven guided all to fave the innocent.

    Bert. I plead no merit, but a bare forgivenefs.

    Tor. Not only that, but favour: Sancho's life,
Whether by virtue or defign preferv'd,
Claims all within my power.

    Qu. My prayers are heard;
And I have nothing farther to defire,
But Sancho's leave to authorize our marriage.

    Tor. Oh, fear not him! pity and he are one;
So merciful a king did never live;
Loth to revenge, and eafy to forgive:
But let the bold confpirator beware,
For Heaven makes princes its peculiar care.   [*Exeunt.*

END of the **FIFTH ACT.**

E P I L O G U E.

By a Friend of the AUTHOR.

THERE's none, I'm sure, who is a friend to love,
But will our fryar's character approve :
The ablest spark among you sometimes needs
Such pious help, for charitable deeds.
Our church, alas ! (as Rome objects) does want
These ghostly comforts for the falling saint :
This gains them their whore-converts, and may be
One reason of the growth of Popery.
So Mahomet's religion came in fashion,
By the large leave it gave to fornication.
Fear not the guilt, if you can pay for't well ;
There is no Dives in the Roman hell.
Gold opens the straight gate, and lets him in :
But want of money is a mortal sin.
For all besides you may discount to heaven,
And drop a bead to keep the tallies even.
How are men cozen'd still with shows of good !
The bawd's best mask is the grave fryar's hood.
Though vice no more a clergyman displeases,
Than doctors can be thought to hate diseases.
'Tis by your living ill, that they live well.
By your debauches their fat paunches swell.
'Tis a mock war between the priest and devil ;
When they think fit, they can be very civil.
As some, who did French counsels most advance,
To blind the world, have rail'd in print at France.
Thus do the clergy at your vices bawl,
That with more ease they may engross them all.
By damning yours, they do their own maintain,
A churchman's godliness is always gain.
Hence to their prince they will superior be ;
And civil treason grows church loyalty :
They boast the gift of heaven is in their power ;
Well may they give the god they can devour.

                                               —*Still*

Still to the sick and dead their claims they lay;
For 'tis on carrion that the vermin prey.
Nor have they less dominion on our life,
They trot the husband, and they pace the wife.
Rouze up, you cuckolds of the northern climes,
And learn from Sweden to prevent such crimes.
Unman the fryar, and leave the holy drone
To hum in his forsaken hive alone;
He'll work no honey when his sting is gone.
Your wives and daughters soon will leave the cells,
When they have lost the sound of Aaron's bells.

DOUBLE GALLANT

THE
DOUBLE GALLANT:
OR, THE
SICK LADY's CURE.

A COMEDY,

As written by COLLEY CIBBER, Esq.

DISTINGUISHING ALSO THE

VARIATIONS OF THE THEATRE,

AS PERFORMED AT THE

Theatre-Royal in Drury-Lane.

Regulated from the Prompt-Book,

By PERMISSION of the MANAGERS,

By Mr. HOPKINS, Prompter.

LONDON:

Printed for JOHN BELL, near *Exeter-Exchange*, in the *Strand*.

MDCCLXXVII.

PROLOGUE.

COULD those, who never try'd, conceive the sweat,
  The toil requir'd, to make a play complete,
They'd pardon, or encourage all that could
Pretend to be but tolerably good.
Plot, wit, and humour's hard to meet in one,
And yet without them all—all's lamely done :
One wit, perhaps, another humour paints ;
A third designs you well, but genius wants ;
A fourth begins with fire——but, ah ! too weak to hold
      it, faints.
A modern bard, who late adorn'd the bays,
Whose muse advanc'd his fame to envy'd praise,
Was still observ'd to want his judgment most in plays.
Those, he too often found, requir'd the pain
And stronger forces of a vig'rous brain :
Nay, even alter'd plays, like old houses mended,
Cost little less than new, before they're ended ;
At least, our author finds the experience true,
For equal pains had made this wholly new :
And though the name seems old, the scenes will shew
That 'tis, in fact, no more the same, than now
Fam'd Chatsworth is, what 'twas some years ago.
Pardon the boldness, that a play should dare,
With works of so much wonder to compare :
But as that fabrick's ancient walls or wood
Were little worth, to make this new one good ;
So of this play, we hope, 'tis understood.
For though from former scenes some hints he draws,
The ground-plot's wholly chang'd from what it was :
Not but he hopes you'll find enough that's new,
In plot, in persons, wit and humour too :
Yet what's not his, he owns in others right,
Nor toils he now for fame, but your delight.
If that's attain'd, what matter's whose the play's ?
Applaud the scenes, and strip him of the praise.

                    DRA-

DRAMATIS PERSONÆ.

M E N.

Drury-Lane.

Sir Solomon Sadlife,	Mr. Parsons.
Clerimont,	Mr. Packer.
Careless,	Mr. Jefferson.
Atall,	Mr. King.
Old Mr. Wilful,	Mr. Baddeley.
Sir Harry Atall,	Mr. Hurst.
Supple,	Mr. Burton.
Dr. Blister,	Mr. Keen.
Rhubarb,	Mr. Wrighten.
Finder,	Mr. Wright.

W O M E N.

Lady Dainty,	Miss Young.
Lady Sadlife,	Mrs. Abington.
Clarinda,	Mrs. Greville.
Sylvia,	Mrs. Baddeley.
Wishwell,	Mrs. Davies.
Situp,	Mrs. Bradshaw.

THE

THE
DOUBLE GALLANT.

ACT I.

SCENE, *The Park.*

Enter Clerimont *and* Atall.

CLERIMONT.

MR. Atall, your very humble ſervant.

At. O, Clerimont, ſuch an adventure! I was juſt going to your lodgings, ſuch a tranſporting accident! in ſhort, I am now poſitively in love for altogether.

Cler. All the ſex together, I believe.

At. Nay, if thou doſt not believe me, and ſtand my friend, I am ruin'd paſt redemption.

' *Cler.* Dear Sir, if I ſtand your friend without believing you, won't that do as well? But why ſhould you think I don't believe you? I have ſeen you twice in love within this fortnight; and it would be hard indeed to ſuppoſe a heart of ſo much mettle could not hold out a third engagement.

At. Then, to be ſerious, in one word, I am honourably in love; and, if ſhe proves the woman I am ſure ſhe muſt, will poſitively marry her.

Cler. Marry! O degenerate virtue!

At. Now will you help me?

Cler. Sir, you may depend upon me. Pray give me leave firſt to aſk a queſtion or two: What is this honourable lady's name?

A 3

At.

At. Faith, I don't know.

Cler. What are her parents ?

At. I can't tell.

Cler. What fortune has she ?

At. I don't know.

Cler. Where does she live ?

At. I can't tell.

Cler. A very concise account of the person you design to marry. Pray, Sir, what is't you do know of her ?

At. That I'll tell you: Coming yesterday from Greenwich by water, I overtook a pair of oars, whose lovely freight was one single lady, and a fellow in a handsome livery in the stern. When I came up, I had at first resolved to use the privilege of the element, and bait her with waterman's wit, till I came to the bridge ; but, as soon as she saw me, she very prudently prevented my design ; and, as I passed, bow'd to me with an humble blush, that spoke at once such sense, so just a fear, and modesty, as put the loosest of my thoughts to rout. And when she found her fears had moved me into manners, the cautious gloom that sat upon her beauties disappeared ; her sparkling eyes resumed their native fire ; she looked, she smiled, she talked, while her diffusive charms new fired my heart, and gave my soul a softness it never felt before—To be brief, her conversation was as charming as her person, both easy, unconstrained, and sprightly: but then her limbs ! O rapturous thought ! The snowy down upon the wings of unfledged love, had never half that softness.

Cler. Raptures indeed. Pray, Sir, how came you so well acquainted with her limbs ?

At. By the most fortunate misfortune sure that ever was : for, as we were shooting the bridge, her boat, by the negligence of the waterman, running against the piles, was overset ; out jumps the footman to take care of a single rogue, and down went the poor lady to the bottom. My boat being before her, the stream drove her, by the help of her cloaths, toward me ; at sight of her I plunged in, caught her in my arms, and, with much ado, supported her till my waterman pulled in to save us. But the charming difficulty of her getting into the boat, gave me a transport that all the wide water in the Thames had not power to cool? for, Sir, while I was giving her a lift into the boat, I found the floating of her cloaths had left her lovely limbs beneath as bare as a new-born Venus rising from the sea.

Cler. What an impudent happiness art thou capable of!

At. When she was a little recovered from her fright she began to enquire my name, abode, and circumstances, that she might know to whom she owed her life and pre-servation. Now, to tell you the truth, I durst not trust her with my real name, lest she should from thence have discovered that my father was now actually under bonds to marry me to another woman; so faith I even told her my name was Freeman, a Gloucestershire gentleman, of a good estate, just come to town about a chancery suit. Besides, I was unwilling any accident should let my fa-ther know of my being yet in England, lest he should find me out, and force me to marry the woman I never saw (for which, you know, he commanded me home) before I have time to prevent it.

Cler. Well, but could you not learn the lady's name all this while?

At. No faith, she was inexorable to all intreaties; only told me in general terms, that if what I vowed to her was sincere, she would give me a proof in a few days what hazards she would run to requite my services; so after having told her where she might hear of me, I saw her into a chair, pressed her by the cold rosy fingers, kis-sed them warm, and parted.

Cler. What, then you are quite off with the lady, I suppose, that you made an acquaintance with in the Park last week.

At. No, no; not so neither: one's my Juno, all pride and beauty; but this my Venus, all life, love, and softness. Now, what I beg of thee, dear Clerimont, is this: Mrs. Juno, as I told you, having done me the ho-nour of a civil visit or two at my own lodgings, I must needs borrow thine to entertain Mrs. Venus in; for if the rival goddesses should meet and clash, you know there would be the devil to do between them.

Cler. Well, Sir, my lodgings are at your service: but you must be very private and sober, I can tell you; for

my

my landlady's a Prefbyterian ; if fhe fufpects your defign, you're blown up, depend upon't.

At. Don't fear ; I'll be as careful as a guilty confcience : but I want immediate poffeffion ; for I expect to
hear from her every moment, and have already directed
her to fend thither. Pr'ythee, come with me.

Cler. 'Faith you muft excufe me ; I expect fome ladies
in the Park that I would not mifs of for an empire : but
yonder's my fervant, he fhall conduct you.

At. Very good ! that will do as well then ; I'll fend
my man along with him to expect her commands, and
call me if fhe fends : and in the mean time I'll e'en go
home to my own lodgings ; for, to tell you the truth, I
expect a fmall meffage there from my goddefs imperial.
And I am not fo much in love with my new bird in the
bufh, as to let t'other fly out of my hand for her.

Cler. And pray, Sir, what name does your goddefs imperial, as you call her, know you by ?

At. O, Sir, with her I pafs for a man of arms, and am
called Colonel Standfaft ; with my new face, John Freeman, of Flatland-Hall, efq. But time flies ; I muft leave
you.

Cler. Well, dear Atall, I'm yours—— Good luck to
you. [*Exit* At.] What a happy fellow is this, that owes
his fuccefs with the women purely to his inconftancy ?
Here comes another too almoft as happy as he, a fellow
that's wife enough to be but half in love, and make his
whole life a ftudied idlenefs.

Enter Carelefs.

So, Carelefs ! you're conftant, I fee, to your morning's
faunter. Well, how ftand matters ? I hear ftrange things
of thee ; that after having railed at marriage all thy
life, thou haft refolved to fall into the noofe at laft.

Care. I don't fee any great terror in the noofe, as you
call it, when a man's weary of liberty : the liberty of
playing the fool, when one's turned of thirty, is not of
much value.

Cler. Hey-day ! Then you begin to have nothing in
your head now, but fettlements, children, and the main
chance ?

Care. Even fo faith ; but in hopes to come at 'em too,
I am forced very often to make my way through pills,
elixirs, bolus's, ptifans, and gallipots.

Cler. What, is your miſtreſs an apothecary's widow ?

Care. No, but ſhe is an apothecary's ſhop, and keeps as many drugs in her bed-chamber; ſhe has her phyſic for every hour of the day and night——for 'tis vulgar, ſhe ſays, to be a moment in ·rude and perfect health. Her bed lined with poppies; the black boys at the feet, that the healthy employ to bear flowers in their arms, ſhe loads with diaſcordium, and other ſleepy potions; her ſweet-bags, inſtead of the common and offenſive ſmells of muſk and amber, breathe nothing but the more modiſh and ſalubrious ſcents of hart's-horn, rue, and aſ-ſafœtida.

Cler. Why, at this rate, ſhe's only fit to be the conſort of Hippocrates. But pray what other charms has this extraordinary lady ?

Care. She has one, Tom, that a man may reliſh with-out being ſo deep a phyſician.

Cler. What's that ?

Care. Why, two thouſand pounds a year.

Cler. No vulgar beauty, I confeſs, Sir. But canſt thou for any conſideration throw thyſelf into this hoſ-pital, this box of phyſic, and lie all night like leaf-gold upon a pill ?

Care. O, dear Sir, this is not half the evil; her hu-mour is as fantaſtic as her diet ; nothing that is Engliſh muſt come near her; all her delight is in foreign imper-tinencies : her rooms are all of Japan or Perſia, her dreſs Indian, and her equipage are all monſters : the coachman came over with his horſes, both from ·Ruſſia, Flanders are too common ; the reſt of her trim are a mot-ley crowd of blacks, tawny, olives, feulamots, and pale blues : in ſhort, ſhe's for any thing that comes· from beyond ſea ; her greateſt monſters are thoſe of her own country ; and ſhe's in love with nothing o'this ſide the line, but the apothecaries.

Cler. Apothecaries quotha ! why your fine lady, for aught I ſee, is a perfect doſe of folly and phyſic ; in a month's time ſhe'll grow like an antimonial cup, and a kiſs will be able to work with you.

Care. But to prevent that, Tom, I deſign upon· the wedding-day to break all her gallipots, kick the doctor down ſtairs, and force her, inſtead of phyſic, to take a
hearty

hearty meal of a fwinging rump of boiled beef and car-rots, and fo 'faith I have told her.

Clor. That's fomething familiar: are you fo near man and wife?

Care. O nearer; for I fometimes plague her till fhe hates the very fight of me.

Cler. Ha! ha! very good! So being a very trouble-fome lover, you pretend to cure her of her phyfic by a counter poifon.

Care. Right; I intend to fee a doctor to prefcribe to her an hour of my converfation to be taken every night and morning; and this to be continued till her fever of aver-fion's over.

Cler. An admirable recipe!

Care. Well, Tom, but how ftands thy own affair? Is Clarinda kind yet?

Cler. Faith I can't fay fhe's abfolutely kind, but fhe's pretty near it; for fhe's grown fo ridiculoufly ill-hu-moured to me of late, that if fhe keeps the fame airs a week longer, I am in hopes to find as much eafe from her folly, as my conftancy would from her good-nature ——But to be plain, I'm afraid I have fome fecret ri-val in the cafe; for women's vanity feldom gives them courage enough to ufe an old lover heartily ill, till they are firft fure of a new one, that they intend to ufe bet-ter.

Care. What fays Sir Solomon? He is your friend, I prefume?

Cler. Yes; at leaft I can make him fo when I pleafe: there is an odd five hundred pound in her fortune, that he has a great mind fhould ftick to his fingers, when he pays in the reft on't; which I am afraid I muft comply with, for fhe can't eafily marry without his confent. And yet fhe's fo altered in her behaviour of late, that I fcarce know what to do—Pr'ythee take a turn and ad-vife me.

Care. With all my heart,   [*Exeunt.*

The SCENE *changes to Sir* Solomon Sadlife's *Houfe.*

Enter Sir Solomon, *and* Supple *his man.*

Sir Sol. Supple, doft not thou perceive I put a great confidence in thee? I truft thee with my bofom fecrets.

Sup.

Sup. Yes, Sir.

Sir Sol. Ah, Supple! I begin to hate my wife——— but be secret.

Sup. I'll never tell while I live, Sir.

Sir Sol. Nay, then I'll truft thee further. Between thee and I, Supple, I have reafon to believe my wife hates me too.

Sup. Ah! dear, Sir, I doubt that's no fecret; for to fay the truth, my lady's bitter young and gamefome.

Sir Sol. But can fhe have the impudence, think'ft thou, to make a cuckold of a knight, one that was dubbed by the royal fword?

Sup. Alas, Sir, I warrant fhe has the courage of a coun- tefs; if fhe's once provoked, fhe cares not what fhe does in her paffion, if you were ten times a knight, fhe'd give you dub for dub, Sir.

Sir Sol. Ah! Supple, when her blood's up, I confefs fhe's the devil; and I queftion if the whole conclave of cardinals could lay her. But fuppofe fhe fhould refolve to give me a fample of her fex, and make me a cuckold in cool blood?

Sup. Why, if fhe fhould, Sir, don't take it fo to heart, cuckolds are no fuch monfters now-a-days: in the city you know, Sir, it's fo many honeft men's fortune, that no body minds it there; and at this end of the town a cuckold has as much refpect as his wife, for aught I fee; for gentlemen don't know but it may be their own cafe another day, and fo people are willing to do as they would be done by.

Sir Sol. And yet I do not think but my fpoufe is ho- neft—and think fhe is not—would I were fatisfied.

Sup. Troth, Sir, I don't know what to think, but in my confcience I believe good looking after her can do her no harm.

Sir Sol. Right, Supple; and in order to it, I'll firft demolifh her vifiting days. For how do I know but they may be fo many private clubs for cuckoldom?

Sup. Ah, Sir! your worfhip knows I was always againft your coming to this end of the town.

Sir Sol. Thou wert indeed, my honeft Supple: but woman! fair and faithlefs woman, wormed and worked me to her wifhes; like fond Mark Anthony I let my em-

pire

pire moulder from my hands, and gave up all for love.——
I muſt have a young wife, with a murrain to me—I hate
her to—and yet the devil on't is, I'm ſtill jealous of her
—Stay! let me reckon up all the faſhionable virtues ſhe
has that can make a man happy. In the firſt place—I
think her very ugly.

Sup. Ah! that's becauſe you are married to her, Sir.

Sir Sol. As for her expences, no arithmetic can reach
them ; ſhe's always longing for ſomething dear and uſe-
leſs ; ſhe will certainly ruin me in china, ſilks, ribbands,
fans, laces, perfumes, waſhes, powder, patches, jeſſamine-
gloves, and ratifia.

Sup. Ah, Sir, that's a cruel liquor with them.

Sir Sol. To ſum up all would run me mad——The
only way to put a ſtop to her career, muſt be to put off
my coach, turn away her chairmen, lock out her Swiſs
porter, bar up the doors, keep out all viſitors, and then
ſhe'll be leſs expenſive.

Sup. Ay, Sir, for few women think it worth their
while to dreſs for their huſbands.

Sir Sol. Then we ſhan't be plagued with my old lady
Tittle Tattle's howd'ye's in a morning, nor my Lady
Dainty's ſpleen, or the ſudden indiſpoſition of that grim
beaſt her horrible Dutch maſtiff.

Sup. No, Sir, nor the impertinence of that great fat
creature, my Lady Swill-Tea.

Sir Sol. And her ſquinting daughter.——No, Supple,
after this night, nothing in petticoats ſhall come within
ten yards of my doors.

Sup. Nor in breeches neither.

Sir Sol. Only Mr. Clerimont ; for I expect him to ſign
articles with me for the five hundred pounds he is to give
me, for that ungovernable jade my niece Clarinda.——
But now to my own affairs. I'll ſtep into the park, and
ſee if I can meet with my hopeful ſpouſe there. I warrant, engaged in ſome innocent freedom, as ſhe calls it,
as walking in a maſk, to laugh at the impertinencies of
fops that don't know her ; but 'tis more likely, I'm afraid,
a plot to intrigue with thoſe that do. Oh, how many
torments lie in the ſmall circle of a wedding-ring.

[Exeunt.

ACT

ACT II.

SCENE, Clarinda's *Apartment.*

Enter Clarinda *and* Sylvia.

CLARINDA.

HA, ha! poor Sylvia!

Syl. Nay, pr'ythee, don't laugh at me. There's no accounting for inclination: for if there were, you know, why fhould it be a greater folly in me, to fall in love with a man I never faw but once in my life, than it is in you to refift an honeft gentleman, whofe fidelity has deferved your heart an hundred times over.

Clar. Ah, but an utter ftranger, coufin, and one that, for aught you know, may be no gentleman.

Syl. That's impoffible; his converfation could not be counterfeit. An elevated wit, and good breeding, have a natural luftre that's inimitable. Befide, he faved my life at the hazard of his own; fo that part of what I gave him, is but gratitude.

' *Clar.* Well; you are the firft woman that ever took ' fire in the middle of the Thames, fure.' But fuppofe now he is married, and has three or four children.

Syl. Pfha! pr'ythee don't teaze me with fo many ill-natured objections: I tell you he is not married; I am fure he is not: for I never faw a face look more in humour in my life.—Befide, he told me himfelf, he was a country gentleman, juft come to town upon bufinefs: and I'm refolved to believe him.

Clar. Well, well; I'll fuppofe you both as fit for one another as a couple of tallies. But, ftill, my dear, you know there's a furly old father's command againft you; he is in articles to marry you to another: and though I know love is a notable contriver, I can't fee how you'll get over that difficulty.

Syl. 'Tis a terrible one, I own; but with a little of your affiftance, dear Clarinda, I am ftill in hopes to bring it to an even wager, I prove as wife as my father.

Clar. Nay, you may be fure of me: you may fee by the management of my own amours, I have fo natural a compaffion for difobedience, I fha'n't be able to refufe

you

you any thing in diftrefs:—There's my hand; tell me how I can ferve you?

Syl. Why thus:——becaufe I would not wholly difcover myfelf to him at once, I have fent him a note to vifit me here, as if thefe lodgings were my own.

Clar. Hither! to my lodgings! 'Twas well I fent Colonel Standfaft word I fhould not be at home. [*Afide.*

Syl. I hope you'll pardon my freedom, fince one end of my taking it too, was to have your opinion of him before I engage any farther.

Clar. Oh, it needs no apology; any thing of mine is at your fervice.——I am only afraid, my troublefome, lover, Mr. Clerimont, fhould happen to fee him, who is of late fo impertinently jealous of a rival, though from what caufe I know not——not but I l'e too. [*Afide.*] I fay, fhould he fee him, your country gentleman would be in danger, I can tell you.

Syl. Oh, there's no fear of that; for I have ordered him to be brought in the back way : when I have talked with him a little alone, I'll find an occafion to leave him with you; and then we'll compare our opinions of him.

Enter Servant to Clarinda.

Serv. Madam, my Lady Sadlife.　　　　　[*Exit.*

Syl. Pfha! fhe here!

Clar. Don't be uneafy; fhe fhan't difturb you: I'll take care of her.

Enter Lady Sadlife.

Lady Sad. Oh, my dears, you have loft the fweeteft morning, fure, that ever peeped out of the firmament. The park never was in fuch perfection.

Clar. 'Tis always fo when your ladyfhip's there.

Lady Sad. 'Tis never fo without my dear Clarinda.

Syl. How civilly we women hate one another! [*Afide.*] Was there a good deal of company, Madam?

Lady Sad. Abundance! and the beft I have feen this feafon : for 'twas between twelve and one, the very hour you know when the mob are violently hun ry. Oh, the air was fo infpiring! fo amorous! And, to complete the pleafure, I was attacked in converfation by the moft charming, modeft, agreeably infinuating young fellow, fure, that ever woman played the fool with.

Clar.

Clar. Who was it?

Lady Sad. Nay, Heaven knows; his face is as entirely new as his conversation. What wretches our young fellows are to him?

Syl. What sort of a person?

Lady Sad. Tall, straight, well-limbed, walked firm; and a look as chearful as a May-day morning.

Syl. The picture's very like: pray Heaven it is not my gentleman's!   [*Aside.*

Clar. I wish this don't prove my Colonel.   [*Aside.*

Syl. How came you to part with him so soon?

Lady Sad. Oh, name it not! that eternal damper of all pleasure, my husband, Sir Soloman, came into the Mall in the very crisis of our conversation—I saw him at a distance, and complained that the air grew tainted, that I was sick o'th' sudden, and left him in such abruptness and confusion, as if he had been himself my husband.

Clar. A melancholy disappointment, indeed!

Lady Sad. Oh, 'tis a husband's nature to give them.

    A Servant enters and whispers Sylvia.

Syl. Desire him to walk in—Cousin, you'll be at hand.

Clar. In the next room—Come, Madam, Sylvia has a little business. I'll shew you some of the sweetest, prettiest figured china.

Lady Sad. My dear, I wait on you.

             [*Exeunt Lady* Sad. *and* Clar.

    Enter Atall, *as Mr.* Freeman.

Syl. You find, Sir, I have kept my word in seeing you; 'tis all you yet have asked of me; and when I know 'tis in my power to be more obliging, there's nothing you can command in honour I shall refuse you.

At. This generous offer, Madam, is so high an obligation, that it were almost mean in me to ask a farther favour. But 'tis a lover's merit to be a miser in his wishes, and grasp at all occasions to enrich them. I own I feel your charms too sensibly prevail, but dare not give a loose to my ambitious thoughts, 'till I have passed one dreadful doubt that shakes them.

Syl. If 'tis in my power to clear it, ask me freely.

At. I tremble at the trial; and yet methinks my fears are vain: but yet to kill or cure them once for ever, be just and tell me: are you married?

                     Syl.

Syl. If that can make you eafy, no.

At. 'Tis eafe indeed—nor are you promifed, nor your heart engaged?

Syl. That's hard to tell you : but to be juft, I own my father has engaged my perfon to one I never faw ; and my heart, I fear, is inclining to one he never faw.

At. Oh, yet be merciful, and eafe my doubt; tell me the happy man that has deferved fo exquifite a blefling.

Syl. That, Sir, requires fome paufe : firft tell me why you're fo inquifitive, without letting me know the condition of your own heart.

At. In every circumftance my heart's the fame with yours ; 'tis promifed to one I never faw, by a commanding father, who, by my firm hopes of happinefs, I am refolved to difobey, unlefs your cruelty prevents it.

Syl. But my difobedience would beggar me.

At. Banifh that fear. I'm heir to a fortune will fupport you like yourfelf—May I not know your family.

Syl. Yet you muft not.

At. Why that nicety? Is not it in my power to enquire whofe houfe this is when I am gone?

Syl. And be never the wifer: thefe lodgings are a friend's, and are only borrowed on this occafion : but to fave you the trouble of any further needlefs queftions, I will make you one propofal. I have a young lady here within, who is the only confident of my engagements to you : on her opinion I rely ; nor can you take it ill, if I make no farther fteps without it : 'twould be miferable indeed fhould we both meet beggars. I own your actions and appearance merit all you can defire ; let her be as well fatisfied of your pretenfions and condition, and you fhall find it fha'n't be a little fortune fhall make me ungrateful.

At. So generous an offer exceeds my hopes.

Syl. Who's there?

Enter Servant.

Defire my coufin Clarinda to walk in.

At. Ha! Clarinda! if it fhould be my Clarinda now, I'm in a fweet condition—by all that's terrible the very fhe ; this was finely contrived of fortune.

Enter Clarinda.

Clar. Defend me! Colonel Standfaft! fhe has certainly difcovered my affairs with him, and has a mind to infult

me

me by an affected resignation of her pretensions to him—
I'll disappoint her, I won't know him.

Syl. Cousin, pray, come forward; this is the gentleman I am so much obliged to—Sir, this lady is a relation of mine, and the person we are speaking of.

At. I shall be proud to be better known among any of
your friends.   [*Salutes her.*

Clar. Soh! he takes the hint, I see, and seems not to
know me neither: I know not what to think.—I am
confounded! I hate both him and her. How unconcerned he looks! Confusion! he addresses her before my
face.   [*Aside.*

Lady Sadlife peeping in.

Lady Sad. What do I see? The pleasant young fellow that talked with me in the park just now! This is
the luckiest accident! I must know a little more of him.
                                                [*Retires.*

Syl. Cousin, and Mr. Freeman, I think I need not
make any apology—you both know the occasion of my
leaving you together——in a quarter of an hour I'll wait
on you again.   [*Exit Syl.*

At. So, I'm in a hopeful way now, faith; but buff's
the word: I'll stand it.

Clar. Mr. Freeman! So, my gentleman has changed
his name too! How harmless he looks—I have my senses
sure, and yet the demureness of that face looks as if he
had a mind to persuade me out of them. I could find in
my heart to humour his assurance, and see how far he'll
carry it—Won't you please to sit, Sir?   [*They sit.*

At. What the devil can this mean?—Sure she has a
mind to counterface me, and not know me too—With all
my heart: if her ladyship won't know me, I'm sure 'tis
not my business at this time to know her.   [*Aside.*

Clar. Certainly that face is cannon proof.   [*Aside.*

At. Now for a formal speech, as if I had never seen
her in my life before. [*Aside.*] Madam—a hem! Madam,—I—a hem!

Clar. Curse of that steady face.   [*Aside.*

At. I say, Madam, since I am an utter stranger to you,
I am afraid it will be very difficult for me to offer you
more arguments than one to do me a friendship with your
cousin; but if you are, as she seems to own you, her real

B 3   friend,

friend, I prefume you can't give her a better proof of your being fo, than pleading the caufe of a fincere and humble lover, whofe tender wifhes never can propofe to tafte of peace in life without her.

Clar. Umph! I'm choaked.   [*Afide.*

At. She gave me hopes, that when I had fatisfied you of my birth and fortune, you would do me the honour to let me know her name and family.

Clar. Sir, I muft own you are the moft perfect mafter of your art, that ever entered the lifts of affurance.

At. Madam!

Clar. And I don't doubt but you'll find it a much eafier tafk to impofe upon my coufin, than me.

At. Impofe, Madam! I fhould be forry any thing I have faid could difoblige you into fuch hard thoughts of me. Sure, Madam, you are under fome mifinformation.

Clar. I was indeed, but now my eyes are open; for, 'till this minute, I never knew that the gay Colonel Standfaft, was the demure Mr. Freeman.

At. Col. Standfaft! This is extremely dark, Madam.

Clar. This jeft is tedious, Sir—impudence grows dull, when 'tis fo very extravagant.

At. Madam, I am a gentleman—but not yet wife enough, I find, to account for the humours of a fine lady.

Clar. Troth, Sir, on fecond thoughts I begin to be a little better reconciled to your affurance; 'tis in fome fort modefty to deny yourfelf; for to own your perjuries to my face, had been an infolence tranfcendently provoking.

At. Really, Madam, my not being able to apprehend one word of all this is a great inconvenience to my affair with your coufin: but if you will firft do me the honour to make me acquainted with her name and family, I don't much care if I do take a little pains afterwards to come to a right underftanding with you.

Clar. Come, come, fince you fee this affurance will do you no good, you had better put on a fimple look, and generoufly confefs your frailties: the fame flynefs that deceived me firft, will ftill find me woman enough to pardon you.

At. That bite won't do. [*Afide.*] Sure, Madam, you miftake me for fome other perfon.

Clar.

Clar. Infolent! audacious villain! I am not to have my fenfes then!

At. No.   [*Afide.*

Clar. And you are refolved to ftand it to the laft!

At. The laft extremity.   .   .   [*Afide.*

Clar. Well, Sir, fince you are fo much a ftranger to Colonel Standfaft, I'll tell you where to find him, and tell him this from me; I hate him, fcorn, deteft, and loath him : I never meant him but at beft for my diverfion, and fhould he ever renew his dull addreffes to me, I'll have him ufed as his vain infolence deferves. Now, Sir, I have no more to fay, and I defire you would leave the houfe immediately.

At. I would not willingly difoblige you, Madam, but 'tis impoffible to ftir 'till I have feen your coufin, and cleared myfelf of thefe ftrange afperfions.

Clar. Don't flatter yourfelf, Sir, with fo vain a hope, for I muft tell you, once for all, you've feen the laft of her ; and if you won't be gone, you'll oblige me to have you forced away.

At. I'll be even with you. [*Afide.*] Well, Madam, fince I find nothing can prevail upon your cruelty, I'll take my leave : but as you hope for juftice on the man that wrongs you, at leaft be faithful to your lovely friend. And when you have named to her my utmoft guilt, yet paint my paffion as it is, fincere. Tell her what tortures I endured in this fevere exclufion from her fight, that 'till my innocence is clear to her, and fhe again receives me into mercy,

A madman's frenzy's heav'n to what I feel;
The wounds you give 'tis fhe alone can heal.   [*Exit.*

Clar. Moft abandoned impudence! And yet I know not which vexes me moft, his out-facing my fenfes, or his infolent owning his paffion for my coufin to my face : 'tis impoffible fhe could put him upon this, it muft be all his own; but be it as it will, by all that's woman I'll have revenge.   [*Exit.*

Re-enter Atall *and Lady* Sadlife *at the other fide.*

At. Hey-day! is there no way down ftairs here? Death! I can't find my way out! This is the oddeft houfe——

Lady Sad. Here he is—I'll venture to pafs by him.

At. Pray, Madam, which is the neareft way out ?

Lady

Lady Sad. Sir, out——a——

At. Oh, my stars! is't you, Madam, this is fortunate indeed?—I beg you'll tell me, do you live here, Madam?

Lady Sad. Not very far off, Sir: but this is no place to talk with you alone—indeed I muſt beg your pardon.

At. By all thoſe kindling charms that fire my ſoul, no conſequence on earth ſhall make me quit my hold, till you've given me ſome kind aſſurance that I ſhall ſee you again, and ſpeedily: 'egad I'll have one out of the family at leaſt.

Lady Sad. Oh, good, here's company!

At. Oh, do not rack me with delays, but quick, before this dear ſhort-lived opportunity's loſt, inform me where you live, or kill me: to part with this ſoft white hand is ten thouſand daggers to my heart.

[*Kiſſing it eagerly.*

Lady Sad. Oh, lud! I am going home this minute; and if you ſhould offer to dog my chair, I proteſt I——was ever ſuch uſage——lord——ſure! Oh——follow me down then.   [*Exeunt.*

Re-enter Clarinda, *and* Sylvia.

Syl. Ha, ha, ha!

Clar. Nay, you may laugh, Madam, but what I tell you is true.

Syl. Ha, ha, ha!

Clar. You don't believe then?

Syl. I do believe, that when ſome women are inclined to like a man, nothing more palpably diſcovers it, than their railing at him; ha, ha!—Your pardon, couſin; you know you laughed at me juſt now upon the ſame occaſion.

Clar. The occaſion's quite different, Madam; I hate him. And, once more I tell you, he's a villain, you're impoſed on. He's a colonel of foot, his regiment's now in Spain, and his name's Standfaſt.

Syl. But pray, good couſin, whence had you this intelligence of him?

Clar. From the ſame place that you had your falſe account, Madam, his own mouth.

Syl. What was his buſineſs with you?

Clar. Much about the ſame, as his buſineſs with you——love.

Syl.

Syl. Love! to you!

Clar. Me, Madam! Lord, what am I? Old, or a monster! Is it so prodigious that a man should like me?

Syl. No! but I'm amazed to think, if he had liked you, he should leave you so soon, for me!

Clar. For you! leave me for you! No, Madam, I did not tell you that neither! ha, ha!

Syl. No! What made you so violently angry with him then? Indeed, cousin, you had better take some other fairer way; this artifice is much too weak to make me break with him. But, however, to let you see I can be still a friend; prove him to be what you say he is, and my engagements with him shall soon be over.

Clar. Look you, Madam, not but I slight the tenderest of his addresses; but to convince you that my vanity was not mistaken in him, I'll write to him by the name of Colonel Standfast, and do you the same by that of Freeman; and let's each appoint him to meet us at my Lady Sadlife's at the same time: if these appear two different men, I think our dispute's easily at an end; if but one, and he does not own all I've said of him to your face, I'll make you a very humble curt'sy, and beg your pardon.

Syl. And if he does own it, I'll make your ladyship the same reverence, and beg yours.

Enter Clerimont.

Clar. Psha! he here!

Cler. I am glad to find you in such good company, Madam.

Clar. One's seldom long in good company, Sir.

Cler. I am sorry mine has been so troublesome of late; but I value your ease at too high a rate, to disturb it.   [*Going.*

Syl. Nay, Mr. Clerimont, upon my word you shan't stir. Hark you—[*Whispers.*] Your pardon, cousin.

Clar. I must not lose him neither—Mr. Clerimont's way is, to be severe in his construction of people's meaning.

Syl. I'll write my letter, and be with you, cousin. [*Ex.*

Cler. It was always my principle, Madam, to have an humble opinion of my merit; when a woman of sense frowns upon me, I ought to think I deserve it.

Clar.

Clar. But to expect to be always received with a smile, I think, is having a very extraordinary opinion of one's merit.

Cler. We differ a little as to fact, Madam: for these ten days past, I have had no distinction, but a severe reservedness. You did not use to be so sparing of your good-humour; and while I see you gay to all the world ut me, I can't but be a little concerned at the change.

Clar. If he has discovered the Colonel now, I'm undone! he could not meet him, sure.——I must humour him a little. [*Aside.*] Men of your sincere temper, Mr. Clerimont, I own, don't always meet with the usage they deserve: but women are giddy things, and had we no errors to answer for, the use of good-nature in a lover would be lost. Vanity is our inherent weakness: you must not chide, if we are sometimes fonder of your passions than your prudence.

Cler. This friendly condescension makes me more your slave than ever. Oh, yet be kind, and tell me, have I been tortured with a groundless jealousy?

Clar. Let your own heart be judge——but don't take it ill if I leave you now—I have some earnest business with my cousin Sylvia: but to-night at my Lady Dainty's I'll make you amends; you'll be there.

Cler. I need not promise you.

Clar. Your servant.—Ah, how easily is poor sincerity imposed on! Now for the Colonel.   [*Aside. Exit.*

Cler. This unexpected change of humour more stirs my jealousy than all her late severity.——I'll watch her close;

For she that from a just reproach is kind,
Gives more suspicion of her guilty mind,
And throws her smiles, like dust, to strike the lover
    blind.   [*Exit.*

END of the SECOND ACT.

ACT

A C T III.

SCENE, *Lady Dainty's Apartment: a table, with phials, gallipots, glasses, &c.*

Lady Dainty, *and* Situp *her woman.*

LADY DAINTY.

SITUP! Situp!

Sit. Madam!

Lady D. Thou art strangely flow; I told thee the hartfhorn; I have the vapours to that degree!

Sit. If your Ladyfhip would take my advice you fhould e'en fling your phyfic out of the window; if you were not in perfect health in three days, I'd be bound to be fick for you.

Lady D. Peace, goody impertinence! I tell thee, no woman of quality is, or fhould be in perfect health—— Huh, huh! [*Coughs faintly.*] To be always in health is as vulgar as to be always in humour, and would equally betray one's want of wit and breeding:—— where are the fellows?

Sit. Here, Madam——

Enter two Footmen.

Lady D. Cæfar!—run to my Lady Roundfides; defire to know how fhe refted; and tell her the violence of my cold is abated: huh, huh! Pompey, ftep you to my Lady Killchairman's; give my fervice; fay, I have been fo embarraffed with the fpleen all this morning, that I am under the greateft uncertainty in the world, whether I fhall be able to ftir out, or no—And, d'ye hear; defire to know how my Lord does, and the new monkey——

[*Exeunt Footmen.*

Sit. In my confcience, thefe great ladies make themfelves fick to make themfelves bufinefs; and are well or ill, only in ceremony to one another. [*Afide.*

Lady D. Where's t'other fellow?

Sit. He is not returned yet, Madam.

Lady D. 'Tis indeed a ftrange lump, not fit to carry a difeafe to any body; I fent him t'other day to the duchefs of Diet-Drink with the colic, and the brute put it into his own tramontane language, and called it the belly-ach.

Sit. I wifh your Ladyfhip had not occafion to fend for any; for my part——

Lady

Lady D. Thy part!—pr'ythee, thou wert made of the rough masculine kind; 'tis betraying our sex not to be sickly and tender. All the families I visit have something derived to them from the elegant nice state of indisposition; you see, even in the men, a genteel, as it were, stagger, or twine of the bodies; as if they were not yet confirmed enough for the rough laborious exercise of walking, ' a lazy saunter in their motion, some-
' thing so quality! and their voices so soft and low, you'd
' think they were falling asleep, they are so very delicate.

' *Sit.* But, methinks, Madam, it would be better if
' the men were not altogether so tender.

' *Lady D.* Indeed, I have sometimes wished the crea-
' tures were not, but that the nicenefs of their frame so
' much distinguishes them from the herd of common
' people :' nay, even most of their diseases, you see, are not prophaned by the crowd : the apoplexy, the gout, and vapours, are all peculiar to the nobility.—Huh, huh ! and I could almost wish, that colds were only ours; —there's something in them so genteel, so agreeably disordering—huh, huh !

Sit. That, I hope, I shall never be fit for them——Your Ladyship forgot the spleen.

Lady D. Oh !——my dear spleen,——I grudge that even to some of us.

Sit. I knew an ironmonger's wife, in the city, that was mightily troubled with it.

Lady D. Foh ! What a creature hast thou named ! An ironmonger's wife have the spleen ! Thou mightest as well have said her husband was a fine gentleman—— Give me something.

Sit. Will your Ladyship please to take any of the steel drops ? or the bolus ? or the electary ? or——

Lady D. This wench will smother me with questions, —huh, huh ! bring any of them——these healthy sluts are so boisterous, they split one's brains : I fancy myself in an inn while she talks to me; I must have some decayed person of quality about me; for the commons of England are the strangest creatures——huh, huh !

Enter Servant.

Serv. Mrs. Sylvia, Madam, is come to wait upon your Ladyship.

Lady

Lady D. Defire her to walk in; let the phyfic alone: I'll take a little of her company; fhe's mighty good for the fpleen.

Enter Sylvia.

Syl. Dear Lady Dainty!

Lady D. My good creature, I'm overjoyed to fee you ——huh, huh!

Syl. I am forry to fee your Ladyfhip wrapt up thus; I was in hopes to have had your company to the Indian houfe.

Lady D. If any thing could tempt me abroad, 'twould be that place, and fuch agreeable company; but how came you, dear Sylvia, to be reconciled to any thing in an Indian houfe? you ufed to have a moft barbarous inclination for our own odious manufactures.

Syl. Nay, Madam, I am only going to recruit my teatable: as to the reft of their trumpery, I am as much out of humour with it as ever.

Lady D. Well thou art a pleafant creature, thy diftafte is fo diverting.

Syl. And your Ladyfhip is fo expenfive, that really I am not able to come into it.

Lady D. Now it is to me prodigious! how fome women can muddle away their money upon houfwifery, children, books, and charities, when there are fo many well-bred ways, and foreign curiofities, that more elegantly require it—I have every morning the rarities of all countries brought to me, and am in love with every new thing I fee.—Are the people come yet, Situp?

Sit. They have been below, Madam, this half hour.

Lady D. Difpofe them in the parlour, and we'll be there prefently.   [*Exit* Sit.

Syl. How can your Ladyfhip take fuch pleafure in being cheated with the bawbles of other countries?

Lady D. Thou art a very infidel to all finery.

Syl. And you are a very bigot——

Lady D. A perfon of all reafon, and no complaifance.

Syl. And your Ladyfhip all complaifance, and no reafon.

Lady D. Follow me, and be converted.   [*Exeunt.*

C   *Re-enter*

Re-enter Situp, *a Woman with china ware ; an* Indian man *with screens, tea, &c. a* Birdman *with a paroquet, monkey, &c.*

Sit. Come, come into this room.

Chi. I hope your Ladyship's lady won't be long in coming.

Sit. I don't care if she never comes to you.—It seems you trade with the ladies for old clothes, and give them china for their gowns and petticoats, I'm like to have a fine time on't with such creatures as you indeed !

Chi. Alas, Madam, I'm but a poor woman, and am forced to do any thing to live: will your Ladyship be pleafed to accept of a piece of china ?

Sit. Puh! no;—I don't care.—Though I muft needs fay you look like an honeft woman.   [*Looks on it.*

Chi. Thank you, good Madam.

Sit. Our places are like to come to a fine pafs indeed, if our ladies muft buy their china with our perquifites: at this rate, my lady fha'n't have an old fan, or a glove; but———

Chi. Pray, Madam, take it.

Sit. No, not I ; I won't have it, efpecially without a faucer to't.   Here, take it again.

Chi. Indeed you fhall accept of it.

Sit. Not I, truly—come, give it me, give it me ; here's my lady.

Enter Lady Dainty and Sylvia.

Lady D. Well, my dear, is not this a pretty fight now ?

Syl. It's better than fo many doctors and apothecaries, indeed.

Lady D. All trades muft live you know; and thofe no more than thefe could fubfift, if the world were all wife, or healthy.

Syl. I'm afraid our real difeafes are but few to our imaginary, and doctors get more by the found than the fickly.

Lady D. My dear, you're allowed to fay any thing— but now I muft talk with the people.——Have you got any thing new there ?

Chi.
Ind.   } Yes, an't pleafe your Ladyfhip.
Bird.

Lady

Lady D. One at once.——

Bird. I have brought your Ladyſhip the fineſt monkey——

Syl. What a filthy thing it is!

Lady D. Now I think he looks very humourous and agreeable—I vow, in a white periwig he might do miſchief. Could he but talk and take ſnuff, there's ne'er a fop in town would go beyond him.

Syl. Moſt fops would go farther if they did not ſpeak; but talking, indeed, makes them very often worſe company than monkies.

Lady D. Thou pretty little picture of man!——How very Indian he looks! I could kiſs the dear creature.

Syl. Ah, don't touch him! he'll bite!

Bird. No, Madam, he is the tameſt you ever ſaw, and the leaſt miſchievous.

Lady D. Then take him away, I won't have him; for miſchief is the wit of a monkey; and I would not give a farthing for one that would not break me three or four pounds worth of china in a morning. Oh, I am in love with theſe Indian figures!—Do but obſerve what an innocent natural ſimplicity there is in all the actions of them.

Chi. Theſe are pagods, Madam, that the Indians worſhip.

Lady D. So far I am an Indian.

Syl. Now, to me they are all monſters.

Lady D. Profane creature!

Chi. Is your Ladyſhip for a piece of right Flanders lace?

Lady D. Um—no; I don't care for it, now it is not prohibited.

Ind. Will your Ladyſhip be pleaſed to have a pound of fine tea?

Lady D. What, filthy, odious bohea, I ſuppoſe?

Ind. No, Madam, right Kappakawawa.

Lady D. Well, there's ſomething in the very ſound of that name, that makes it irreſiſtible——What is it a pound.

Ind. But ſix guineas, Madam.

Lady D. How infinitely cheap! I'll buy it all—Situp, take the man in and pay him, and let the reſt call again to-morrow.

Omnes. Blefs your Ladyfhip.

[Exeunt Sit. Chi. Ind. *and* Bird.

Lady D. Lord, how feverifh I am !—the leaft motion does fo diforder me—do but feel me.

Syl. No, really, I think you are in very good temper.

Lady D. Burning, indeed, child.

Enter Servant, Doctor, and Apothecary.

Serv. Madam, here's Doctor Bolus, and the Apothecary.   *[Exit.*

Lady D. Oh, Doctor, I'm glad you're come ! one is not fure of a moment's life without you.

Dr. How did your Ladyfhip reft, Madam ?

[Feels her pulfe.

Lady D. Never worfe, indeed, Doctor : I once fell into a little flumber, indeed; but then was difturbed by the moft odious, frightful dream, that if the fright had not wakened me, I had certainly perifhed in my fleep, with the apprehenfion.

Dr. A certain fign of a difordered brain, Madam ; but I'll order fomething that fhall compofe your Lady-fhip.

Lady D. Mr. Rhubarb, I muft quarrel with you—— you don't difguife your medicines enough ; they tafte all phyfic.

Rhub. To alter it more might offend the operation, Madam.

Lady D. I don't care what is offended, fo my tafte is not.

Dr. Hark you, Mr. Rhubarb, withdraw the medicine, rather than to make it pleafant : I'll find a reafon for the want of its operation.

Rhub. But, Sir, if we don't look about us, fhe'll grow well upon our hands.

Dr. Never fear that ; fhe's too much a woman of quality to dare to be well without her doctor's opinion.

Rhub. Sir, we have drained the whole catalogue of difeafes already ; there's not another left to put in her head.

Dr. Then I'll make her go them over again.

Enter Carelefs.

Care. So, here's the old levee, doctor and apothecary in clofe confultation ! Now will I demolifh the quack and his medicines before her face——Mr. Rhu-

barb,

barb, your fervant. Pray, what have you got in your hand there?

Rhub. Only a julep and compofing draught for my Lady, Sir.

Care. Have you fo, Sir? Pray, let me fee—I'll prefcribe to-day. Doctor, you may go—the lady fhall take no phyfic at prefent but me.

Dr. Sir——

Care. Nay, if you won't believe me——

[*Breaks the phials.*

Lady D. Ah!—— [*Frighted, and leaning upon* Syl.

Dr. Come away, Mr. Rhubarb—he'll certainly put her out of order, and then fhe'll fend for us again.

[*Ex. Doctor and Apoth.*

Care. You fee, Madam, what pains I take to come into your favour.

Lady D. You take a very prepofterous way, I can tell you, Sir.

Care. I can't tell how I fucceed; but I am fure I endeavour right; for I ftudy every morning new impertinence to entertain you: for fince I find nothing but dogs, doctors, and monkies are your favourites, it is very hard if your Ladyfhip won't admit me as one of the number.

Lady D. When I find you of an equal merit with my monkey, you fhall be in the fame ftate of favour. I confefs, as a proof of your wit, you have done me as much mifchief here. But you have not half Pug's judgment, nor his fpirit; for the creature will do a world of pleafant things, without caring whether one likes them or not.

Care. Why, truly, Madam, the little gentleman, my rival, I believe, is much in the right on't: and, if you obferve, I have taken as much pains of late to difoblige, as to pleafe you.

Lady D. You fucceed better in one than t'other, I can tell you, Sir.

Care. I am glad on't; for if you had not me now and then to plague you, what would you do for a pretence to be chagrine, to faint, have the fpleen, the vapours, and all thofe modifh diforders that fo nicely diftinguifh a woman of quality?

C 3

Lady

Lady D. I am perfectly confounded—Certainly there are some people too impudent for our resentment.

Care. Modesty's a starving virtue, Madam, an old threadbare fashion of the last age, and would fit as oddly upon a lover now, as a picked beard and mustachios.

Lady D. Most astonishing!

Care. I have tried sighing and looking silly a great while, but 'twould not do—nay, had you had as little wit as good-nature, should have proceeded to dance and sing. Tell me but how, what face or form can worship you, and behold your votary.

Lady D. Not, Sir, as the Persians do the sun, with your face towards me. The best proof you can give me of your horrid devotion, is never to see me more. Come, my dear.   [*Exit with* Sylvia.

Syl. I'm amazed so much assurance should not succeed.   [*Exit.*

Care. All this shan't make me out of love with my virtue—Impudence has ever been a successful quality, and 'twould be hard, indeed, if I should be the first that did not thrive by it.   [*Exit.*

S C E N E, Clerimont's Lodgings.

Enter Atall, and Finder, his Man.

At. You are sure you know the house again?

Fin. Ah, as well as I do the upper gallery, Sir!——'Tis Sir Solomon Sadlife's, at the two glass lanthorns, within three doors of my Lord Duke's.

At. Very well, Sir—then take this letter, enquire for my Lady Sadlife's woman, and stay for an answer.

Fin. Yes, Sir.   [*Exit.*

At. Well, I find 'tis as ridiculous to propose pleasure in love without variety of mistresses, as to pretend to be a keen sportsman without a good stable of horses. How this lady may prove I can't tell; but if she is not a deedy tit at the bottom, I'm no jockey.

Re-enter Finder.

Fin. Sir, here are two letters for you.

At. Who brought them?

Fin. A couple of footmen, and they both desire an answer.

At. Bid them stay, and do you make haste where I ordered you.

Fin.

Fin. Yes, Sir. [*Exit.*

At. To Col. Standfaſt—that's Clarinda's hand——To Mr. Freeman—that muſt be my incognita. Ah, I have moſt mind to open this firſt! but if t'other malicious creature ſhould have perverted her growing inclination to me, 'twould put my whole frame in a trembling—— Hold, I'll gueſs my fate by degrees—this may give me a glimpſe of it. [*Reads* Clar. *letter.*] Um—um—um— Ha! To meet her at my Lady Sadlife's at ſeven o'clock to-night, and take no manner of notice of my late diſowning myſelf to her—Something's at the bottom of all this—Now to ſolve the riddle. [*Reads t'other letter.*]—— " My couſin Clarinda has told ſome things of you that very much alarm me ; but I am willing to ſuſpend my belief of them till I ſee you, which I deſire may be at my Lady Sadlife's at ſeven this evening."—The devil! the ſame place !—" As you value the real friendſhip of your

Incognita."

So, now the riddle's out—the rival queens are fairly come to a reference, and one or both of them I muſt loſe, that's poſitive—Hard !

Enter Clerimont.

Hard fortune ! Now, poor Impudence, what will become of thee ? Oh, Clerimont, ſuch a complication of adventures ſince I ſaw thee ! ſuch ſweet hopes, fears, and unaccountable difficulties, ſure never poor dog was ſurrounded with.

Cler. Oh, you are an induſtrious perſon ! you'll get over them. But, pray, let's hear.

At. To begin, then, in the climax of my misfortunes : in the firſt place, the private lodgings that my *Incognita* appointed to receive me in, prove to be the very individual habitation of my other miſtreſs, whom (to complete the blunder of my ill luck) ſhe civilly introduced in perſon, to recommend me to her better acquaintance.

Cler. Ha, ha ! Death ! how could you ſtand them both together ?

At. The old way—buff—I ſtuck like a burr to my name of Freeman, addreſs'd my *incognita* before the other's face, and with a moſt unmov'd good-breeding, harmleſsly faced her down I had never ſeen her in my life before.

Cler.

Cler. The prettiest modesty I ever heard of! Well, but how did they discover you at last?

At. Why, faith, the matter's yet in suspense; and I find, by both their letters, that they don't yet well know what to think: (but, to go on with my luck) you must know, they have since both appointed me, by several names, to meet them at one and the same place, at seven o'clock this evening.

Cler. Ah!

At. And, lastly, to crown my fortune (as if the devil himself most triumphantly rode a straddle upon my ruin), the fatal place of their appointment happens to be the very house of a third lady, with whom I made an acquaintance since morning, and had just before sent word I would visit near the same hour this evening.

Cler. Oh, murder! Poor Atall, thou art really fallen under the last degree of compassion.

At. And yet, with a little of thy assistance, in the middle of their small-shot, I don't still despair of holding my head above water.

Cler. Death! but you can't meet them both; you must lose one of them, unless you can split yourself.

At. Pr'ythee, don't suspect my courage or my modesty; for I'm resolved to go on, if you will stand by me.

Cler. Faith, my very curiosity would make me do that. But what can I do?

At. You must appear for me upon occasion in person.

Cler. With all my heart. What else?

At. I shall want a Queen's messenger in my interest, or rather one that can personate one.

Cler. That's easily found—But what to do?

At. Come along, and I'll tell you; for first I must answer their letters.

Cler. Thou art an original, faith.   [*Exeunt.*

SCENE changes to Sir Solomon's.

Enter Sir Solomon, *leading* Lady Sadlife, *and* Wishwell, *her Woman.*

Sir Sol. There, Madam, let me have no more of these airings—No good, I am sure, can keep a woman five or six hours abroad in a morning.

Lady Sad. You deny me all the innocent freedoms of life.

Sir Sol. Ha! you have the modish cant of this end of
the

the town, I fee; intriguing, gaming, gadding, and party-quarries with a pox to them, are innocent freedoms, forfooth!

Lady Sad. I don't know what you mean; I'm fure I have not one acquaintance in the world that does an ill thing.

Sir Sol. They muft be better looked after than your Ladyfhip then; but I'll mend my hands as faft as I can. Do you look to your reputation henceforward, and I'll take care of your perfon.

Lady Sad. You wrong my virtue with thefe unjuft fufpicions.

Sir Sol. Ay, it's no matter for that; better I wrong it than you. I'll fecure my doors for this day at leaft. [*Ex.*

Lady Sad. Oh, Wifhwell! what fhall I do?

Wifh. What's the matter, Madam?

Lady Sad. I expect a letter from a gentleman every minute; and if it fhould fall into Sir Solomon's hands, I'm ruined paft redemption.

Wifh. He won't fufpect it, Madam, fure, if they are directed to me, as they ufed to be.

Lady Sad. But his jealoufy's grown fo violent of late, there's no trufting to it now. If he meets it, I fhall be locked up for ever.

Wifh. Oh, dear Madam! I vow your Ladyfhip frights me—Why, he'll kill me for keeping counfel.

Lady Sad. Run to the window, quick, and watch the meffenger. [*Exit* Wifh.] Ah, there's my ruin near!—I feel it—[*A knocking at the door.*]—What fhall I do? Be very infolent, or very humble, and cry?—I have known fome women, upon thefe occafions, outftrut their hufbands' jealoufy, and make them afk pardon for finding them out. Oh, lud, here he comes!—I can't do't; my courage fails me——I muft e'en ftick to my hadkerchief, and truft to nature.

Re-enter Sir Solomon, *taking a letter from* Finder.

Sir Sol. Sir, I fhall make bold to read this letter; and if you have a mind to fave your bones, there's your way out.

Fin. Oh, terrible! I fhan't have a whole one in my fkin, when I come home to my mafter. [*Exit.*

Lady Sad. [*Afide.*] I'm loft for ever!

Sir Sol. [*Reads.*] "Pardon, moft divine creature, the impatience of my heart,"—Very well! thefe are her inno-

cent

cent freedoms! Ah, cockatrice!—" which languishes for an opportunity to convince you of its sincerity;"—Oh, the tender son of a whore!—" which nothing could relieve, but the sweet hope of seeing you this evening."—Poor lady, whose virtue I have wronged with unjust suspicions!

Lady Sad. I'm ready to sink with apprehension.

Sir Sol. [*Reads.*] "To-night, at seven, expect your dying Strephon."—Die, and be damn'd; for I'll remove your comforter, by cutting her throat. I could find in my heart to ram his impudent letter into her windpipe——Ha! what's this!—" To Mrs. Wishwell, my Lady Sadlife's woman."——Ad, I'm glad of it, with all my heart! What a happy thing it is to have one's jealousy disappointed!—Now have I been cursing my poor wife for the mistaken wickedness of that trollop. 'Tis well I kept my thoughts to myself: for the virtue of a wife, when wrongfully accused, is most unmercifully insolent. Come, I'll do a great thing; I'll kiss her, and make her amends——What's the matter, my dear? Has any thing frighted you?

Lady Sad. Nothing but your hard usage.

Sir Sol. Come, come, dry thy tears; it shall be so no more. But, hark ye, I have made a discovery here—Your Wishwell, I'm afraid, is a slut; she has an intrigue.

Lady Sad. An intrigue! Heavens, in our family!

Sir Sol. Read there—I wish she be honest.

Lady Sad. How!—If there be the least ground to think it, Sir Solomon, positively she shan't stay a minute in the house—Impudent creature!—have an affair with a man!

Sir Sol. But hold, my dear; don't let your virtue censure too severely neither.

Lady Sad. I shudder at the thoughts of her.

Sir Sol. Patience, I say—How do we know but his courtship may be honourable?

Lady Sad. That, indeed, requires some pause.

Wish. [*Peeping in.*] So, all's safe, I see—He thinks the letter's to me——Oh, good Madam! that letter was to me, the fellow says. I wonder, Sir, how you could serve one so! If my sweetheart should hear you had opened it, I know he would not have me, so he would not.

Sir Sol. Never fear that; for if he is in love with you, he's too much a fool to value being laughed at.

Lady Sad.

Lady Sad. If it be yours, here, take your stuff; and next time, bid him take better care, than to send his letters so publicly.

Wish. Yes, Madam. But, now your Ladyship has read it, I'd fain beg the honour of Sir Solomon to answer it for me; for I can't write.

Lady Sad. Not write!

Sir Sol. Nay, he thinks she's above that, I suppose; for he calls her divine creature—A pretty piece of divinity, truly!—But come, my dear; 'egad, we'll answer it for her. Here's paper—you shall do it.

Lady Sad. I, Sir Solomon! Lard, I won't write to fellows, not I—I hope he won't take me at my word. [*Aside.*

Sir Sol. Nay, you shall do it. Come, 'twill get her a good husband.

Wish. Ay, pray, good Madam, do.

Sir Sol. Ah, how eager the jade is!

Lady Sad. I can't tell how to write to any body but you, my dear,

Sir Sol. Well, well, I'll dictate then. Come, begin.

Lady Sad. Lard, this is the oddest fancy!———

[*Sits to write.*

Sir Sol. Come, come—Dear Sir—(for we'll be as loving as he, for his ears.)

Wish. No, pray, Madam, begin, Dear honey, or, My dearest angel.

Lady Sad. Out, you fool! you must not be so fond—Dear Sir, is very well. [*Writes.*

Sir Sol. Ay, ay, so 'tis; but these young fillies are for setting out at the top of their speed. But, pr'ythee, Wishwell, what is thy lover; for the stile of his letter may serve for a countess?

Wish. Sir, he's but a butler at present: but he's a good schollard, as you may see by his hand-writing; and in time may come to be a steward; and then we shan't be long without a coach, Sir.

Lady Sad. Dear Sir——What must I write next?

Sir Sol. Why——— [*Musing.*

Wish. Hoping you are in good health, as I am at this present writing.

Sir Sol. You puppy, he'll laugh at you.

Wish. I'm sure my mother used to begin all her letters so.

I *Sir*

Sir Sol. And thou art every inch of thee her own daughter, that I'll say for thee.

Lady Sad. Come, I have done it. [*Reads.*] " Dear Sir, She muſt have very little merit that is infenſible of yours."

Sir Sol. Very well, faith ! Write all yourſelf.

Wiſh. Ay, good Madam, do ; that's better than mine. But, pray, dear Madam, let it end with, So I reſt your deareſt loving friend, till death us do part.

Lady Sad. [*Aſide.*] This abſurd ſlut will make me laugh out.

Sir Sol. But, hark you, huſſy ; ſuppoſe now you ſhould be a little ſcornful and inſolent to ſhew your breeding, and a little ill-natured in it to ſhew your wit.

Wiſh. Ay, Sir, that is, if I deſigned him for my gallant ; but ſince he is to be but my huſband, I muſt be very good-natured and civil before I have him, and huff him, and ſhew my wit after.

Sir Sol. Here's a jade for you ! [*Aſide.*] But why muſt you huff your huſband, huſſy ?

Wiſh. Oh, Sir, that's to give him a good opinion of my virtue ! for you know, Sir, a huſband can't think one could be ſo very domineering, if one were not very honeſt.

Sir Sol. 'Sbud, this fool, on my conſcience, ſpeaks the ſenſe of the whole ſex !   [*Aſide.*

Wiſh. Then, Sir, I have been told, that a huſband loves one the better, the more one hectors him ; as a ſpaniel does, the more one beats him.

Sir Sol. Ha ! thy huſband will have a bleſſed time on't.

Lady Sad. So—I have done.

Wiſh. Oh, pray, Madam, read it !

Lady Sad. [*Reads.*] " Dear Sir—She muſt have very little merit that is inſenſible of yours ; and while you continue to love, and tell me ſo, expect whatever you can hope from ſo much wit, and ſuch unfeigned ſincerity— At the hour you mention, you will be truly welcome to your paſſionate——"

Wiſh. Oh, Madam, it is not half kind enough ! Pray, put in ſome more dears.

Sir Sol. Ay, ay, ſweeten it well ; let it be all ſyrup, with a pox to her.

Wiſh. Every line ſhould have a dear ſweet Sir in it, ſo it ſhould—he'll think I don't love him elſe.

Sir.

Sir Sol. Poor moppet!

Lady Sad. No, no, 'tis better now—Well, what muſt be at the bottom, to anſwer Strephon?

Sir Sol. Pray, let her divine ladyſhip ſign Abigail.

Wiſh. No, pray, Madam, put down Lipſamintha.

Sir Sol. Lipſamintha!

Lady Sad. No, come, I'll write Celia. Here, go in and ſeal it.

Sir Sol. Ay, come, I'll lend you a wafer, that he mayn't wait for your divinityſhip.

Wiſh. Pſhaw! you always flout one ſo.

[Exeunt Sir Sol. and Wiſh.

Lady Sad. So, this is luckily over—Well, I ſee a woman ſhould never be diſcouraged from coming off at the greateſt plunge; for though I was half dead with the fright, yet, now I'm a little recovered, I find—

That apprehenſion does the bliſs endear;
The real danger's nothing to the fear.   [*Exit.*

END of the THIRD ACT.

ACT IV.

SCENE, Sir Solomon's.

Enter Lady Sadlife, Atall, *and* Wiſhwell *with lights.*

LADY SADLIFE.

THIS room, I think, is pleaſanter; if you pleaſe, we'll ſit here, Sir—Wiſhwell, ſhut the door, and take the key o'th' inſide, and ſet chairs.

Wiſh. Yes, Madam.

Lady Sad. Lard, Sir, what a ſtrange opinion you muſt have of me, for receiving your viſits upon ſo ſlender an acquaintance!

At. I have a much ſtranger opinion, Madam, of your ordering your ſervant to lock herſelf in with us.

Lady Sad. Oh, you would not have us wait upon ourſelves!

At. Really, Madam, I can't conceive that two lovers, alone, have much occaſion for attendance.   [*They ſit.*

Lady Sad. Lovers! Lard, how you talk! Can't people converſe without that ſtuff?

At. Um—Yes, Madam, people may; but without a

D

little

little of that stuff, conversation is generally very apt to be insipid.

Lady Sad. Pooh! why, we can say any thing without her hearing, you see.

At. Ay; but if we should talk ourselves up to an occasion of being without her, it would look worse to send her out, than to have let her wait without when she was out.

Lady Sad. You are pretty hard to please, I find, Sir. Some men, I believe, would think themselves well used in so free a reception as yours.

At. Ha! I see this is like to come to nothing this time; so I'll e'en put her out of humour, that I may get off in time to my incognita. [*Aside.*] Really, Madam, I can never think myself free, where my hand and my tongue are tied.   [*Pointing to* Wish.

Lady Sad. Your conversation, I find, is very different from what it was, Sir.

At. With submission, Madam, I think it very proper for the place we are in. If you had sent for me only to sip tea, to sit still, and be civil, with my hat under my arm, like a strange relation from Ireland, or so, why was I brought hither with so much caution and privacy?

[*Sir Solomon knocks at the door.*

Wish. Oh, heavens, my master, Madam!

Sir Sol. [*Within.*] Open the door there!

Lady Sad. What shall we do?

At. Nothing now, I'm sure.

Lady Sad. Open the door, and say the gentleman came to you.

Wish. Oh, lud, Madam, I shall never be able to manage it at so short a warning!—We had better shut the gentleman into the closet, and say he came to nobody at all.

Lady Sad. In, in then, for mercy's sake, quickly, Sir!

At. So—this is like to be a very pretty business!—Oh, success and impudence, thou hast quite forsaken me!

[*Enters the closet.*

Wish. Do you step into your bed-chamber, Madam, and leave my master to me.   [*Exit* Lady Sadlife.

Wishwell *opens the door, and* Sir Solomon *enters.*

Sir Sol. What's the reason, mistress, I am to be locked out of my wife's apartment?

Wish. My Lady was washing her—her—neck, Sir, and I could not come any sooner.

Sir

Sir Sol. I'm fure I heard a man's voice. [*Afide.*] Bid your Lady come hither. [*Exit* Wifhwell.]—He muft be hereabouts—'tis fo; all's out, all's over now: the devil has done his worft, and I am a cuckold in fpite of my wifdom. 'Sbud! now an Italian would poifon his wife for this, a Spaniard would ftab her, and a Turk would cut off her head with a fcimitar; but a poor dog of an Englifh cuckold now, can only fquabble and call names—Hold, here fhe comes—I muft fmother my jealoufy, that her guilt mayn't be upon its guard.

Enter Lady Sadlife *and* Wifhwell.

Sir Sol. My dear, how do you do? Come hither, and kifs me.

Lady Sad. I did not expect you home fo foon, my dear.

Sir Sol. Poor rogue!——I don't believe you did, with a pox to you. [*Afide.*] Wifhwell, go down; I have bufinefs with your Lady.

Wifh. Yes, Sir—but I'll watch you; for I am afraid this good-humour has mifchief at the bottom of it.   [*Retires.*

Lady Sad. I fcarce know whether he's jealous or not.

Sir Sol. Now dare not I go near that clofet door, left the murderous dog fhould poke a hole in my guts thro' the key-hole—Um—I have an old thought in my head—ay, and that will difcover the whole bottom of her affair. 'Tis better to feem not to know one's difhonour, when one has not courage enough to revenge it.

Lady Sad. I don't like his looks, methinks.

Sir Sol. Odfo! what have I forgot now? Pr'ythee, my dear, ftep into my ftudy; for I am fo weary! and in the uppermoft parcel of letters, you'll find one that I received from Yorkfhire to-day, in the fcrutoir; bring it down, and fome paper; I will anfwer it while I think on't.

Lady Sad. If you pleafe to lend me your key—But had you not better write in your ftudy, my dear?

Sir Sol. No, no; I tell you, I'm fo tired, I am not able to walk.   There, make hafte.

Lady Sad. Would all were well over!   [*Exit.*

Sir Sol. 'Tis fo, by her eagernefs to be rid of me. Well, fince 1 find I dare not behave myfelf like a man of honour in this bufinefs, I'll at leaft act like a perfon of prudence and penetration; for fay, fhould I clap a brace of flugs, now, in the very bowels of this rafcal, it may hang me;

                                        but

but if it does not, it can't divorce me.   No, I'll e'en put
out the candles, and in a soft, gentle whore's voice, defire the gentleman to walk about his bufinefs; and if I
can get him out before my wife returns, I'll fairly poft
myfelf in his room; and fo, when fhe comes to fet him
at liberty, in the dark, I'll humour the cheat, till I draw
her into fome cafual confeffion of the fact, and then this
injured front fhall bounce upon her like a thunderbolt.

[Puts out the candles.

Wifh. [*Behind.*] Say you fo, Sir? I'll take care my
Lady fhall be provided for you.   [*Exit.*
   Sir Sol. Hift, hift, Sir, Sir!
Enter Atall from the clofet.
   At. Is all clear? May I venture, Madam?
   Sir Sol. Ay, ay, quick, quick! make hafte, before Sir
Solomon returns.   A ftrait-back'd dog, I warrant him.
[*Afide.*] But when fhall I fee you again?
   At. Whenever you'll promife me to make a better ufe
of an opportunity.
   Sir Sol. Ha! then 'tis poffible he mayn't yet have put
the finifhing ftroke to me.
   At. Is this the door?
   Sir Sol. Ay, ay, away. [*Exit* Atall.] So—now the danger of being murdered is over, I find my courage returns:
and if I catch my wife but inclining to be no better than
fhe fhould be, I'm not fure that blood won't be the confequence.   [*He goes into the clofet, and* Wifhwell *enters.*
   Wifh. So—my Lady has her cue; and if my wife ma-
fter can give her no better proofs of his penetration than
this, fhe'd be a greater fool than he, if fhe fhould not do
what fhe has a mind to.   Sir, Sir, come, you may come
out now; Sir Solomon's gone.
Enter Sir Solomon from the clofet.
   Sir Sol. So, now for a foft fpeech, to fet her impudent
blood in a ferment, and then let it out with my penknife.
[*Afide.*] Come, dear creature, now let's make the kindeft
ufe of our opportunity.
   Wifh. Not for the world.   If Sir Solomon fhould come
again, I fhould be ruined.   Pray, begone—I'll fend to
you to-morrow.
   Sir Sol. Nay, now you love me not; you would not
let me part elfe thus unfatisfied.

Wifh.

Wish. Now you're unkind.   You know I love you, or I should not run such hazards for you.

 Sir Sol. Fond whore ! [*Aside.*] But I'm afraid you love Sir Solomon, and lay up all your tenderness for him.

Wish. Oh, ridiculous !——How can so sad a wretch give you the least uneasy thought ?——I loath the very sight of him.

Sir Sol. Damn'd infernal strumpet !——I can bear no longer——Lights, lights, within there !   [*Seizes her.*

Wish. Ah ! [*Shrieks.*] Who's this ? Help ! murder !

Sir Sol. No, traitress, don't think to 'scape me ; for, now I've trapped thee in thy guilt, I could find in my heart to have thee flead alive, thy skin stuffed, and hung up in the middle of Guildhall, as a terrible consequence of cuckoldom to the whole city——Lights there !

Enter Lady Sadlife *with a light.*

Lady Sad. Oh, Heavens ! what's the matter ?

[*Sir Solomon looks astonished.*

Ha ! what do I see ? My servant on the floor, and Sir Solomon offering rudeness to her ! Oh, I can't bear it ! Oh !   [*Falls into a chair.*

Sir Sol. What has the devil been doing here ?

Lady Sad. This the reward of all my virtue ! Oh, revenge, revenge !

Sir Sol. My dear, my good, virtuous, injured dear, be patient ; for here has been such wicked doings——

Lady Sad. Oh, torture ! Do you own it too ? 'Tis well my love protects you.   But for this wretch, this monster, this sword shall do me justice on her.

[*Runs at* Wishwell *with* Sir Solomon's *sword.*

 Sir Sol. Oh, hold, my poor mistaken dear ! This horrid jade, the gods can tell, is innocent for me ; but she has had, it seems a strong dog in the closet here ; which I suspecting, put myself into his place, and had almost trapped her in the very impudence of her iniquity.

Lady Sad. How ! I'm glad to find he dares not own 'twas his jealousy of me——   [*Aside.*

Wish. [*Kneeling.*] Dear Madam, I hope your Ladyship will pardon the liberty I took in your absence, in bringing my lover into your Ladyship's chamber ; but I did not think you would come home from prayers so soon ; and so I was forced to hide him in that closet : but my ma-

ster

ster suspecting the business, it seems, turned him out unknown to me, and then put himself there, and so had a mind to discover whether there was any harm between us; and so, because he fancied I had been naught with him——

Sir Sol. Ay, my dear; and the jade was so confoundedly fond of me, that I grew out of all patience, and fell upon her like a fury.

Lady Sad. Horrid creature!—And does she think to stay a minute in the family after such impudence?

Sir Sol. Hold, my dear——for if this should be the man that is to marry her, you know there may be no harm done yet.

Wish. Yes, it was he indeed, Madam.

Sir Sol. [*Aside.*] I must not let the jade be turned away, for fear she should put it in my wife's head, that I hid myself to discover her Ladyship, and then the devil would not be able to live in the house with her.

Wish. Now, Sir, you know what I can tell of you.

[*Aside to* Sir Solomon.

Sir Sol. Mum—that's a good girl; there's a guinea for you.

Lady Sad. Well, upon your intercession, my dear, I'll pardon her this fault. But, pray, mistress, let me hear of no more such doings. I am so disordered with this fright—Fetch my prayer-book; I'll endeavour to compose myself.   [*Exit* Lady Sad. *and* Wish.

Sir Sol. Ay, do so; that's my good dear——What two blessed escapes have I had! to find myself no cuckold at last, and, which had been equally terrible, my wife not know I wrongfully suspected her!—Well, at length I am fully convinced of her virtue—and now, if I can but cut off the abominable expence that attends some of her impertinent acquaintance, I shall shew myself a Machiavel.

Re-enter Wishwell.

Wish. Sir, here's my Lady Dainty come to wait upon my Lady.

Sir Sol. I'm sorry for't, with all my heart——Why did you say she was within?

Wish. Sir, she did not ask if she was; but she's never denied to her.

Sir

Sir Sol. Gadfo! why then, if you pleafe to leave her Ladyfhip to me, I'll begin with her now.

Wifhwell brings in Lady Dainty.

Lady D. Sir Solomon, your very humble fervant.

Sir Sol. Yours, yours, Madam.

Lady D. Where's my Lady?

Sir Sol. Where your Ladyfhip very feldom is————at prayers.

Enter Lady Sadlife.

Lady Sad. My dear Lady Dainty!

Lady D. Dear Madam, I am the happieft perfon alive in finding your Ladyfhip at home.

Sir Sol. So, now for a torrent of impertinence.

Lady Sad. Your Ladyfhip does me a great deal of ho-nour.

Lady D. I am fure I do myfelf a great deal of pleafure. I have made at leaft twenty vifits to-day. Oh, I'm quite dead! not but my coach is very eafy—yet fo much per-petual motion, you know————

Sir Sol. Ah, pox of your diforder !—If I had the pro-viding your equipage, ods-zooks, you fhould rumble to your vifits in a wheel-barrow.   [*Afide.*

Lady Sad. Was you at my Lady Duchefs's?

Lady D. A little while.

Lady Sad. Had fhe a great circle?

Lady D. Extreme—I was not able to bear the breath of fo much company.

Lady Sad. You did not dine there?

Lady D. Oh, I can't touch any body's dinner but my own !————and I have almoft killed myfelf this week, for want of my ufual glafs of Tokay, after my ortolans and Mufcovy duck-eggs.

Sir Sol. 'Sbud, if I had the feeding of you, I'd bring you, in a fortnight, to neck-beef, and a pot of plain bub.
                 [*Afide.*

Lady D. Then I have been fo furfeited with the fight of a hideous entertainment, to-day, at my Lady Cormo-rant's, who knows no other happinefs, or way of making one welcome, than eating or drinking; for though fhe faw I was juft fainting at her vaft limbs of butcher's meat, yet the civil favage forced me to fit down, and heaped enough upon my plate to victual a fleet for an Eaft-In-dia voyage.   *Lady*

Lady Sad. How could you bear it? Ha, ha!——Does your Ladyſhip never go to the play?

Lrdy D. Never, but when I beſpeak it myſelf; and then not to mind the actors; for it's common to love ſights. My great diverſion is, in a repoſed poſture, to turn my eyes upon the galleries, and bleſs myſelf to hear the happy ſavages laugh; or when an aukward citizen crowds herſelf in among us, 'tis an unſpeakable pleaſure to contemplate her airs and dreſs: and they never 'ſcape me; for I am as apprehenſive of ſuch a creature's coming near me, as ſome people are when a cat is in the room—— But the play is begun, I believe; and if your Ladyſhip has an inclination, I'll wait upon you.

Lady Sad. I think, Madam, we can't do better; and here comes Mr. Careleſs moſt opportunely to 'ſquire us.

Sir Sol. Careleſs! I don't know him; but my wife does, and that's as well.

Enter Careleſs.

Care. Ladies, your ſervant. Seeing your coach at the door, Madam, made me not able to reſiſt this opportuni-ty to——to——you know, Madam, there's no time to be loſt in love. Sir Solomon, your ſervant.

Sir Sol. Oh, yours, yours, Sir!——A very impudent fellow; and I'm in hopes will marry her. [*Aſide.*

Lady D. The aſſurance of this creature almoſt grows diverting: all one can do, can't make him the leaſt ſenſi-ble of a diſcouragement.

Lady Sad. Try what compliance will do; perhaps that may fright him.

Lady D. If it were not too dear a remedy—One would almoſt do any thing to get rid of his company.

Care. Which you never will, Madam, till you marry me, depend upon it. Do that, and I'll trouble you no more.

Sir Sol. This fellow's abominable! He'll certainly have her. [*Aſide.*

Lady D. There's no depending upon your word, or elſe I might; for the laſt time I ſaw you, you told me then, you would trouble me no more.

Care. Ay, that's true, Madam; but to keep one's word, you know, looks like a tradeſman.

Sir Sol. Impudent rogue! But he'll have her—[*Aſide.*

Care.

Care. And is as much below a gentleman as paying one's debts.

Sir Sol. If he is not hanged firſt. 				[*Aſide.*

Care. Beſides, Madam; I conſidered that my abſence might endanger your conſtiturion, which is ſo very tender, that nothing but love can ſave it, and ſo I would e'en adviſe you to throw away your juleps, your cordials, and ſlops, and take me all at once.

Lady D. No, Sir, bitter potions are not to be taken ſo ſuddenly.

Care. Oh, to chooſe, Madam; for if you ſtand making of faces, and kicking againſt it, you'll but increaſe your averſion, and delay the cure. Come, come, you muſt be adviſed. 				[*Preſſing her.*

Lady D. What mean you, Sir?

Care. To baniſh all your ails, and be myſelf your univerſal medicine.

Sir Sol. Well ſaid! he'll have her. 				[*Aſide.*

Lady D. Impudent, robuſt man; I proteſt, did not I know his family, I ſhould think his parents had not lived in chairs and coaches, but had uſed their limbs all their lives! Huh! huh! but I begin to be perſuaded health is a great bleſſing. 				[*Aſide.*

Care. My limbs, Madam, were conveyed to me before the uſe of chairs and coaches, and it might leſſen the dignity of my anceſtors, not to uſe them as they did.

Lady D. Was ever ſuch a rude underſtanding? to value himſelf upon the barbariſm of his fore-fathers.——— Indeed I have heard of kings that were bred to the plough, and, I fancy, you might deſcend from ſuch a race; for you court as if you were behind one—Huh! huh! huh! To treat a woman of quality like an Exchange-wench, and expreſs your paſſion with your arms; unpoliſhed man!

Care. I was willing, Madam, to take from the vulgar the only deſirable thing among them, and ſhew you—how they live ſo healthy—for they have no other remedy.

Lady D. A very rough medicine! huh! huh!

Care. To thoſe that never took it, it may ſeem ſo—

Lady D. Abandoned raviſher! Oh! 			[*Struggling.*

Sir Sol. He has her; he has her. 			[*Aſide.*

Lady D. Leave the room, and ſee my face no more.

Care. [*Bows and is going.*]

Lady

Lady D. And, hark ye, Sir, no bribe, no mediations to my woman.

Care. [*Bows and sighs.*]

Lady D. Thou profligate! to hug! to clasp! to embrace and throw your robust arms about me, like a vulgar, and indelicate—Oh, I faint with apprehension of so gross an address! [*She faints, and* Care. *catches her.*

Care. Oh, my offended fair!

Lady D. Inhuman! ravisher! Oh!

[Care. *carries her off.*

Sir Sol. He has her! she's undone! He has her. -

[*Exeunt Sir* Sol. *and Lady* Sad.

Enter Clarinda *and* Sylvia.

Clar. Well, cousin, what do you think of your gentleman now?

Syl. I fancy, Madam, that would be as proper a question to ask you: for really I don't see any great reason to alter my opinion of him yet——

Clar. Now I could dash her at once, and shew it her under his own hand that his name's Standfast, and he'll be here in a quarter of an hour. [*Aside.*] I vow I don't think I ought to refuse you any service in my power; therefore if you think it worth your while not to be out of countenance when the Colonel comes, I would advise you to withdraw now; for if you dare take his own word for it, he will be here in three minutes, as this may convince you. [*Gives a letter.*

Syl. What's here? a letter from Colonel Standfast?—Really, Cousin, I have nothing to say to him——Mr. Freeman's the person I'm concerned for, and I expect to see him here in a quarter of an hour.

Clar. Then you don't believe them both the same person?

Syl. Not by their hands or stile, I can assure you, as this may convince you. [*Gives a letter.*

Clar. Ha! The hand is different indeed——I scarce know what to think, and yet I'm sure my eyes were not deceived.

Syl. Come, cousin, let's be a little cooler; 'tis not impossible but we may have both laughed at one another to no purpose—for I am confident they are two persons.

Clar. I can't tell that, but I'm sure here comes one of them.

Enter

Enter Atall *as* Colonel Standfast.

Syl. Ha !

At. Hey ! Bombard, (there they are, faith !) bid the chariot fet up, and call again about one or two in the morning——You fee, Madam, what 'tis to give an impudent fellow the leaft encouragement: I'm refolved now to make a night on't with you.

Clar. I am afraid, Colonel, we fhall have much ado to be good company, for we are two women to one man, you fee; and if we fhould both have fancy to have you particular, I doubt you'd make but bungling work on't.

At. I warrant you we will pafs our time like gods: two ladies and one man; the prettieft fet for Ombre in the univerfe—Come, come ! Cards ! cards ! cards ! and tea, that I infift upon.

Clar. Well, Sir, if my coufin will make one, I won't balk your good-humour.   [*Turning* Syl. *to face him.*

At. Is the lady your relation, Madam ?——I beg the honour to be known to her.

Clar. Oh, Sir ! that I'm fure fhe can't refufe you—— Coufin, this is Colonel Standfaft. [*Laughs afide.*] I hope now fhe's convinced.

At. Your pardon, Madam, if I am a little particular in my defire to be known to any of this lady's relations.

                                        [*Salutes.*

Syl. You'll certainly deferve mine, Sir, by being always particular to that lady——

At. Oh, Madam ! Tall, lall.   [*Turns away, and fings.*

Syl. This affurance is beyond example.   [*Afide.*

Clar. How do you do, coufin ?

Syl. Beyond bearing—but not incurable.   [*Afide.*

Clar. [*Afide.*] Now can't I find in my heart to give him one angry word for his impudence to me this morning; the pleafure of feeing my rival mortified makes me ftrangely good-natured.

At. [*Turning familiarly to* Clar.] Upon my foul you are provokingly handfome to-day. Ay Gad ! why is not it high treafon for any beautiful woman to marry ?

Clar. What, would you have us lead apes ?

At. Not one of you by all that's lovely.——Do you think we could not find you better employment ? Death ! what a hand is here ?——Gad, I fhall grow foolifh !

                                        Clar.

Clar. Stick to your affurance, and you are in no danger.

At. Why then, in obedience to your commands, pr'y-thee anfwer me fincerely one queftion ? How long do you really defign to make me dangle thus ?

Clar. Why really I can't juft fet you a time ; but when you are weary of your fervice, come to me with a fix-pence and modefty, and I'll give you a difcharge.

At. Thou infolent, provoking, handfome tyrant !

Clar. Come, let me go——this is not a very civil way of entertaining my coufin, methinks.

At. I beg her pardon indeed. [*Bowing to* Sylv.] But lovers you know, Madam, may plead a fort of excufe for being fingular when the favourite fair's in company. ——But we were talking of cards, ladies.

Clar. Coufin, what fay you ?

Syl. I had rather you would excufe me, I am a little unfit for play at this time.

At. What a valuable virtue is affurance ! Now am I as intrepid as a lawyer at the bar.   [*Afide.*

Clar. Blefs me ! you are not well.

Syl. I fhall be prefently——Pray, Sir, give me leave to afk you a queftion.

At. So, now it's coming. [*Afide.*] Freely, Madam.

Syl. Look on me well : have you never feen my face before ?

At. Upon my word, Madam, I can't recolleʇt that I have.

Syl. I am fatisfied.

At. But pray, Madam, why may you afk ?

Syl. I am too much difordered now to tell you——But if I'm not deceived, I'm miferable.   [*Weeps.*

At. This is ftrange—How her concern tranfports me !

Clar. Her fears have touched me, and half perfuade me to revenge them——Come, coufin, be eafy : I fee you are convinced he is the fame, and now I'll prove myfelf a friend.

Syl. I know not what to think——my fenfes are con-founded : their features are indeed the fame ; and yet there's fomething in their air, their drefs, and manner, ftrangely different : but be it as it will, all right to him in prefence I difclaim, and yield to you for ever.

At. Oh, charming ! joyful grief !   [*Afide.*

1

Clar.

Clar. No, coufin, believe it, both our fenfes cannot be deceived, he's individually the fame ; and fince he dares be bafe to you, he's miferable indeed, if flattered with a diftant hope of me ; I know his perfon and his falfehood both too well ; and you fhall fee will, as becomes your friend, refent it.

At. What means this ftrangenefs, Madam ?

Clar. I'll tell you, Sir ; and to ufe few words, know then, this lady and myfelf have borne your faithlefs infolence and artifice too long : but that you may not think to impofe on me, at leaft, I defire you would leave the houfe, and from this moment never fee me more.

At. Madam ! What ! what is all this ? Riddle me riddle me re,

> For the devil take me,
> For ever from thee,
> If I can divine what this riddle can be !

Syl. Not moved ! I'm more amazed.

At. Pray, Madam, in the name of common fenfe, let me know in two words what the real meaning of your laft terrible fpeech was ; and if I don't make you a plain, honeft, reafonable anfwer to it, be pleafed the next minute to blot my name out of your table-book, never more to be inrolled in the fenfelefs catalogue of thofe vain coxcombs, that impudently hope to come into your favour.

Clar. This infolence grows tedious : what end can you propofe by this affurance ?

At. Hey-dey !

Syl. Hold, coufin——one moment's patience : I'll fend this minute again to Mr. Freeman, and if he does not immediately appear, the difpute will need no farther argument.

At. Mr. Freeman ! Who the devil's he ? What have I to do with him ?

Syl. I'll foon inform you, Sir.

　　　　　　　　[*Going, meets* Wifhwell *entering.*

Wifh. Madam, here's a footman mightily out of breath, fays he belongs to Mr. Freeman, and defires very earneftly to fpeak with you.

Syl. Mr. Freeman ! Pray bid him come in——What can this mean ?

At. You'll fee prefently.　　　　　　　[*Afide.*

　　　　　　E　　　　　　　　　　*Re-enter*

Re-enter Wishwell *with* Finder.

Clar. Ha!

Syl. Come hither, friend: do you belong to Mr. Freeman?

Fin. Yes, Madam, and my poor master gives his humble service to your Ladyship, and begs your pardon for not waiting on you according to his promise; which he would certainly have done, but for an unfortunate accident.

Syl. What's the matter?

Fin. As he was coming out of his lodgings to pay his duty to you, Madam, a parcel of fellows set upon him, and said they had a warrant against him; and so, because the rascals began to be saucy with him, and my master knowing that he did not owe a shilling in the world, he drew to defend himself, and in the scuffle the bloody villains run one of their swords quite through his arm; but the best of the jest was, Madam, that as soon as they got him into a house, and sent for a surgeon, he proved to be the wrong person; for their warrant, it seems, was against a poor scoundrel, that happens, they say, to be very like him, one Colonel Standfast.

At. Say you so, Mr. Dog——if your master had been here I would have given him as much.

[*Gives him a box on the ear.*

Fin. Oh, Lord! pray, Madam, save me—I did not speak a word to the gentleman——Oh, the devil! this must be the devil in the likeness of my master.

Syl. Is this gentleman so very like him, say you?

Fin. Like, Madam! ay, as one box of the ear is like to another; only I think, Madam, my master's nose is a little, little higher.

At. Now, ladies, I presume the riddle's solved—Hark you, where is your master, rascal?

Fin. Master, rascal! Sir, my master's name's Freeman, and I'm a free-born Englishman; and I must tell you, Sir, that I don't use to take such arbitrary socks of the face from any man that does not pay me wages; and so my master will tell you too when he comes, Sir.

Syl. Will he be here then?

Fin. This minute, Madam, he only stays to have his wound dressed.

At.

At. I'm resolved I'll stay that minute out, if he does not come till midnight.

Fin. A pox of his mettle—when his hand's in, he makes no difference between jest and earnest, I find—If he does not pay me well for this, 'egad he shall tell the next for himself. [*Aside.*] Has your Ladyship any commands to my master, Madam?

Syl. Yes; pray give him my humble service, say I'm sorry for his misfortune; and if he thinks 'twill do his wound no harm, I beg, by all means, he may be brought hither immediately.

Fin. 'Shah! his wound, Madam, I know he does not value it of a rush; for he'll have the devil 'and all of actions against the rogues for false imprisonment, and smart-money——Ladies, I kiss your hands——Sir, I ——nothing at all—— [*Exit.*

At. [*Aside.*] The dog has done it rarely; for a lie upon the stretch I don't know a better rascal in Europe.

Enter an Officer.

Off. Ay! now I'm sure I'm right—Is not your name Colonel Standfast, Sir?

At. Yes, Sir; what then?

Off. Then you are my prisoner, Sir——

At. Your prisoner! who the devil are you? a bailiff? I don't owe a shilling.

Off. I don't care if you don't, Sir; I have a warrant against you for high treason, and I must have you away this minute.

At. Look you, Sir, depend upon't, this is but some impertinent malicious prosecution: you may venture to stay a quarter of an hour, I'm sure; I have some business here till then, that concerns me nearer than my life.

Clar. Have but so much patience, and I'll satisfy you for your civility.

Off. I could not stay a quarter of an hour, Madam, if you'd give me five hundred pounds.

Syl. Can't you take bail, Sir?

Off. Bail! no, no,

Clar. Whither must he be carried?

Off. To my house, 'till he's examined before the council.

Clar. Where is your house?

E 2

Off.

Off. Just by the secretary's office; every body knows Mr. Lockum the messenger—Come, Sir.

At. I can't stir yet, indeed, Sir.

          [Lays his hand on his sword.

Off. Nay, look you, if you are for that play—Come, in, gentlemen, away with him.

    Enter Musqueteers, and force him off.

Syl. This is the strangest accident: I am extremely sorry for the Colonel's misfortune, but I am heartily glad, he is not Mr. Freeman.

Clar. I'm afraid you'll find him so——I shall never change my opinion of him 'till I see them face to face.

Syl. Well, cousin, let them be two or one, I'm resolved to stick to Mr. Freeman; for to tell you the truth, this last spark has too much of the confident rake in him to please me, but there is a modest sincerity in t'other's conversation that's irresistible.

Clar. For my part I'm almost tired with his impertinence either way, and could find in my heart to trouble myself no more about him; and yet methinks it provokes me to have a fellow outface my senses.

Syl. Nay, they are strangely alike, I own; but yet, if you observe nicely, Mr. Freeman's features are more pale and pensive than the Colonel's.

Clar. When Mr. Freeman comes, I'll be closer in my observation of him—in the mean time let me confider, what I really propose by all this rout I make about him: suppose (which I can never believe) they should prove two several men at last, I don't find that I'm fool enough to think of marrying either of them; nor (whatever airs I give myself) am I yet mad enough to do worse with them—Well, since I don't design to come to a close engagement myself, then why should I not generously stand out of the way, and make room for one that would? No, I can't do that neither—I want methinks to convict him first of being one and the same person, and then to have him convince my cousin that he likes me better than her—Ay, that would do! and to confess my infirmity, I still find (though I don't care for this fellow) while she has assurance to nourish the least hope of getting him from me, I shall never be heartily easy 'till she's heartily mortified.

              [Aside.

               Syl.

Syl. You feem very much concerned for the Colonel's misfortune, coufin.

Clar. His misfortunes feldom hold him long, as you may fee; for here he comes.

Enter Atall, *as Mr.* Freeman.

Syl. Blefs me!

At. I am forry, Madam, I could not be more punctual to your obliging commands: but the accident that prevented my coming fooner, will, I hope, now give me a pretence to a better welcome than my laft; for now, Madam, [*To* Clar.] your miftake's fet right, I prefume, and, I hope, you won't expect Mr. Freeman to anfwer for all the mifcarriages of Colonel Standfaft.

Clar. Not in the leaft, Sir: the Colonel's able to anfwer for himfelf, I find! ha, ha!

At. Was not my fervant with you, Madam? [*To* Syl.

Syl. Yes, yes, Sir, he has told us all. [*Afide.*] And I am forry you have paid fo dear for a proof of your innocence. Come, come, I'd advife you to fet your heart at reft; for what I defign, you'll find, I fhall come to a fpeedy refolution in.

At. Oh, generous refolution!

Clar. Well, Madam, fince you are fo tenacious of your conqueft, I hope you'll give me the fame liberty: and not expect, the next time you fall a crying at the Colonel's gallantry to me, that my good-nature fhould give you up my pretenfions to him. And for you, Sir, I fhall only tell you, this laft plot was not fo clofely laid, but that a woman of a very flender capacity, you'll find, has wit enough to difcover it.   [*Exit* Clar.

At. So! fhe's gone to the meffenger's, I fuppofe—but, poor foul, her intelligence there will be extremely fmall. [*Afide.*] Well, Madam, I hope at laft your fcruples are over.

Syl. You can't blame me, Sir, if, now we are alone, I I own myfelf a little more furprifed at her pofitivenefs, than my woman's pride would let me confefs before her face; and yet methinks there's a native honefty in your look, that tells me I am not miftaken, and may truft you with my heart.

At. Oh, for pity ftill preferve that tender thought, and fave me from defpair.

Enter Clerimont.

Cler. Ha! Freeman again! Is it poffible?

At. How now, Clerimont, what are you furprized at?

Cler. Why to fee thee almoft in two places at one time; 'tis but this minute, I met the very image of thee with the mob about a coach, in the hands of a mef-fenger, whom I had the curiofity to ftop and call to; and had no other proof of his not being thee, but that the fpark would not know me!

Syl. Strange! I almoft think I'm really not deceived.

Cler. 'Twas certainly Clarinda I faw go out in a chair juft now —— it muft be fl.e——the circumftances are too ftrong for a miftake.   [*Afide.*

Syl. Well, Sir, to eafe you of your fears, now I dare own to you, that mine are over.   [*To* Atall.

Cler. What a coxcomb have I made myfelf, to ferve my rival e'en with my own miftrefs? But 'tis at leaft fome eafe to know him: all I have to hope is, that he does not know the afs he has made of me—that might indeed be fatal to him.   [*Afide.*

Enter Sylvia's *Maid.*

Maid. Oh, Madam, I'm glad I've found you: your father and I have been hunting you all the town over.

Syl. My father in town?

Maid. He waits below in the coach for you: he muft needs have you come away this minute; and talks of having you married this very night to the fine gentleman he fpoke to you of.

Syl. What do I hear?

At. If ever foft compaffion touched your foul, give me a word of comfort in this laft diftrefs, to fave me from the horrors that furround me.

Syl. You fee we are obferved——but yet depend upon my faith, as on my life—in the mean time, I'll ufe my utmoft power to avoid my father's hafty will: in two hours you fhall know my fortune and my family—Now don't follow me, as you'd preferve my friendfhip. Come——
                                      [*Exit with Maid.*

At. Death! how this news alarms me! I never felt the pains of love before.

Cler. Now then to eafe, or to revenge my fears—This fudden change of your countenance, Mr. Atall, looks as
                                                          if

you had a mind to banter your friend into a belief of your being really in love with the lady that juſt now left you.

At. Faith, Clerimont, I have too much concern upon me at this time, to be capable of a banter.

Cler. Ha! he ſeems really touched, and I begin now only to fear Clarinda's conduct——Well, Sir, if it be ſo, I'm glad to ſee a convert of you ; and now, in return to the little ſervices I have done you, in helping you to carry on your affair with both theſe ladies at one time, give me leave to aſk a favour of you——Be ſtill ſincere, and we may ſtill be friends. ..

At. You ſurprize me—but uſe me as you find me.

Cler. Have you no acquaintance with a certain lady whom you have lately heard me own I was unfortunately in love with ?

At. Not that I know of, I'm ſure not as the lady you are in love with : but, pray, why do you aſk ?

Cler. Come, I'll be ſincere with you too: becauſe I have ſtrong circumſtances, that convince me 'tis one of thoſe two you have been ſo buſy about.

At. Not ſhe you ſaw with me, I hope ?

Cler. No ; I mean the other—But to clear the doubt at once, is her name Clarinda ?

At. I own it is : but had I the leaſt been warned of your pretences——

Cler. Sir, I dare believe you ; and though you may have prevailed even againſt her honour, your ignorance of my paſſion for her makes you ſtand at leaſt excuſed to me.

At. No ; by all the ſolemn proteſtations tongue can utter, her honour is untainted yet for me ; nay, even un-attempted : ' nor had I ever an opportunity, that could ' encourage the moſt diſtant thought againſt it.'

Cler. You own ſhe has received your gallantries at leaſt.

At. Faith, not to be vain, ſhe has indeed taken ſome pains to pique her couſin about me ; and if her beautiful couſin had not fallen in my way at the ſame time, I muſt own, 'tis very poſſible, I might have endeavoured to puſh my fortune with her ; but ſince I now know your heart, put my friendſhip to a trial.

Cler. Only this—If I ſhould be reduced to aſk it of

you, promise to confess your imposture, and your passion to her cousin, before her face.

At. There's my hand,—I'll do't, to right my friend and mistress. But, dear Clerimont, you'll pardon me, if I leave you here; for my poor incognita's affairs at this time are in a very critical condition.

Cler. No ceremony—I release you.—

At. Adieu. *{Exeunt.*

END of the FOURTH ACT.

ACT V.

Enter Clerimont *and* Careless.

CLERIMONT.

AND so you took the opportunity of her fainting to carry her off! Pray, how long did her fit last?

Care. Why, faith, I so humoured her affectation, that 'tis hardly over yet; for I told her, her life was in danger, and swore, if she would not let me send for a parson to marry her before she died, I'd that minute send for a shroud, and be buried alive with her in the same coffin: but at the apprehension of so terrible a thought, she pretended to be frightened into her right senses again; and forbid me her sight for ever.—So that in short, my impudence is almost exhausted, her affectation is as unsurmountable as another's real virtue, and I must e'en catch her that away, or die without her at last.

Cler. How do you mean?

Care. Why, if I find I can't impose upon her by humility, which I'll try, I'll e'en turn rival to myself in a very fantastical figure, that I'm sure she won't be able to resist. You must know she has of late been flattered that the Muscovite Prince Alexander is dying for her, though he never spoke to her in his life.

Cler. I understand you : so you'd first venture to pique her against you, and then let her marry you in another person, to be revenged of you.

Care. One of the two ways I am pretty sure to succeed.

Cler. Extravagant enough ! Pr'ythee, is Sir Solomon in the next room?

Care.

Care. What, you want his affiftance? Clarinda's in her
airs again!

Clcr. Faith, Carelefs, I am almoft afhamed to tell you,
but I muft needs fpeak with him.

Care. Come along then.   [*Exeunt.*

Enter Lady Dainty, *Lady* Sadlife, *and* Carelefs.

Lady D. This rude boifterous man has given me a
thoufand diforders; the colic, the fpleen, the palpitation
of the heart, and convulfions all over—Huh! huh!—I
muft fend for the doctor.

Lady Sad. Come, come, Madam, e'en pardon him,
and let him be your phyfician—do but obferve his penitence, fo humble he dares not fpeak to you.

Care. [*Folds his arms and fighs.*] Oh!

Lady Sad. How can you hear him figh fo?

Lady D. Nay, let him groan—for nothing but his
pangs can eafe me.

Care. [*Kneels and prefents her his drawn fword; opening
his breaft.*] Be then at once moft barbaroufly juft, and
take your vengeance here.

Lady D. No, I give thee life to make thee miferable;
live, that my refenting eyes may kill thee every hour.

Care. Nay then, there's no relief——but this——

                 [*Offering at his fword, Lady* Sadlife *holds him.*

Lady Sad. Ah! for mercy's fake—Barbarous creature,
how can you fee him thus?

Lady D. Why, I did not bid him kill himfelf: but do
you really think he would have don't?

Lady Sad. Certainly, if I had not prevented it.

Lady D. Strange paffion! But 'tis its nature to be violent, when one makes it defpair.

Lady Sad. Won't you fpeak to him?

Lady D. No, but if your—is enough concerned to be
his friend, you may tell him—not that it really is fo—
but you may fay—you believe I pity him.

Lady D. Sure love was never more ridiculous on both
fides.

Enter Wifhwell.

Wifh. Madam, here's a page from Prince Alexander,
defires to give a letter into your Ladyfhip's own hands.

Lady D. Prince Alexander! what means my heart? I
come to him.

Lady

Lady Sad. By no means, Madam, pray let him come in.

Care. Ha ! Prince Alexander ! nay, then I have found out the secret of this coldnefs, Madam.

Enter Page.

Page. Madam, his Royal Highnefs Prince Alexander, my mafter, has commanded me, on pain of death, thus [*Kneeling.*] to deliver this, the burning fecret of his heart.

Lady D. Where is the Prince ?

Page. Repofed in private on a mourning pallat, 'till your commands vouchfafe to raife him.

Lady Sad. By all means, receive him here immediately. I have the honour to be a little known to his highnefs.

Lady D. The favour, Madam, is too great to be re-fifted : pray tell his highnefs then, the honour of the vifit he defigns me, makes me thankful and impatient ! huh ! huh !   [*Exit Page.*

Care. Are my fufferings, Madam, fo foon forgot then ! Was I but flattered with the hope of pity ?

Lady D. The happy have whole days, and thofe they choofe. [*Refenting.*] The unhappy have but hours, and thofe they lofe.   [*Exit repeating.*

Lady Sad. Don't you lofe a minute then.

Care. I'll warrant you—ten thoufand thanks, dear Madam, I'll be transformed in a fecond——

[*Exeunt feverally.*

Enter Clarinda *in a man's habit.*

Clar. So ! I'm in for't now ! how I fhall come off I can't tell : 'twas but a bare faving game I made with Clerimont ; his refentment had brought my pride to its laft legs, diffembling ; and if the poor man had not loved me too well, I had made but a difmal humble figure—I have ufed him ill, that's certain, and he may e'en thank himfelf for't—he would be fincere.—Well, (begging my fex's pardon) we do make the fillieft tyrants—we had bet-ter be reafonable ; for (to do them right) we don't run half the hazard in obeying the good-fenfe of a lover ; at leaft, I'm reduced now to make the experiment—Here they come.

Enter Sir Solomon *and* Clerimont.

Sir Sol. What have we here ! another captain ? If I

were

were fure he were a coward now, I'd kick him before he
fpeaks——Is your bufinefs with me, Sir?

Clar. If your name be Sir Solomon Sadlife.

Sir Sol. Yes, Sir, it is; and I'll maintain it as ancient
as any, and related to moft of the families in England.

Clar. My bufinefs will convince you, Sir, that I think
well of it.

Sir Sol. And what is your bufinefs, Sir?

Clar. Why, Sir—you have a pretty kinfwoman, called
Clarinda.

Cler. Ha!

Sir Sol. And what then, Sir?————Such a rogue as
t'other.   [*Afide.*

Clar. Now, Sir, I have feen her, and am in love
with her.

Cler. Say you fo, Sir?——I may chance to cure you
of it.   [*Afide.*

Clar. And to back my pretenfions, Sir, I have a good
fifteen hundred pounds a year eftate, and am, as you fee,
a pretty fellow into the bargain.

Sir Sol. She that marries you, Sir, will have a choice
bargain indeed.

Clar. In fhort, Sir, I'll give you a thoufand guineas to
make up the match.

Sir Sol. Hum—[*Afide.*]—But, Sir, my niece is provided for.

Cler. That's well!   [*Afide.*

Sir Sol. But if fhe were not, Sir, I muft tell you, fhe is
not to be caught with a fmock-face and a feather, Sir——
And——and——let me fee you an hour hence.   [*Afide.*

Clar. Well faid, uncle! [*Afide.*]——But, Sir, I'm in
love with her, and pofitively will have her.

Sir Sol. Whether fhe likes you or no, Sir?

Clar. Like me! ha, ha! I'd fain fee a woman that
diflikes a pretty fellow, with fifteen hundred pounds a
year, a white wig, and black eye-brows.

Cler. Hark you, young gentleman, there muft go more
than all this to the gaining of that lady.

[*Takes* Clarinda *afide.*

Sir Sol. [*Afide.*] A thoufand guineas—that's five hundred more than I propofed to get of Mr. Clerimont——
But my honour is engaged——Ay, but then here's a
                                                thoufand

thoufand pounds to releafe it——Now, fhall I take the money ?——It muft be fo——Coin will carry it.

Clar. Oh, Sir, if that be all, I'll foon remove your doubts and pretenfions ! Come, Sir, I'll try your courage.

Cler. I'm afraid you won't, young gentleman.

Clar. As young as I am, Sir, you fhall find I fcorn to turn my back to any man.

[*Exeunt* Clarinda *and* Clerimont.

Sir Sol. Ha ! they are gone to fight——with all my heart—a fair chance, at leaft, for a better bargain ; for if the young fpark fhould let the air into my friend Clerimont's midriff now, it may poffibly cool his love too, and then there's my honour fafe, and a thoufand guineas fnug. [*Exit.*

' *Enter* Lady Dainty, Lady Sadlife, *and* Carelefs, *as*
' Prince Alexander.

' *Lady D.* Your Highnefs, Sir, has done me honour
' in this vifit.

' *Care.* Madam—— [*Salutes her.*

' *Lady D.* A captivating perfon !

' *Care.* May the days be taken from my life, and added
' to yours, moft incomparable beauty, whiter than the
' fnow that-lies throughout the year unmelted on our
' Ruffian mountains !

' *Lady D.* How manly his expreffions are !——We are
' extremely obliged to the Czar, for not taking your
' Highnefs home with him.

' *Care.* He left me, Madam, to learn to be a fhip car-
' penter.

' *Lady Sad.* A very polite accomplifhment !

' *Lady D.* And in a prince entirely new.

' *Care.* All his nobles, Madam, are mafters of fome
' ufeful fcience ; and moft of our arms are quartered with
' mechanical inftruments, as hatchers, hammers, pick-
' axes, and hand-faws.

' *Lady D.* I admire the manly manners of your court.

' *Lady Sad.* Oh, fo infinitely beyond the foft idlenefs
' of ours !

' *Care.* 'Tis the fafhion, ladies, for the eaftern princes
' to profefs fome trade or other. The laft Grand Signior
' was a lockfmith.

' *Lady D.* How new his converfation is !

' *Care.*

' *Care.* Too rude, I fear, Madam, for so tender a com-
' position as your divine Ladyship's.

' *Lady D.* Courtly to a softness too !

' *Care.* Were it possible, Madam, that so much deli-
' cacy could endure the martial roughness of our manners
' and our country, I cannot boast ; but if a province at
' your feet could make you mine, that province and its
' master should be yours.

' *Lady D.* Ay, here's grandeur with address——An
' odious native lover, now, would have complained of the
' taxes, perhaps, and have haggled with one for a scanty
' jointure out of his horrid lead-mines, in some uninha-
' bitable mountains, about an hundred and four-score
' miles from unheard-of London.

' *Care.* I am informed, Madam, there is a certain poor,
' distracted English fellow, that refused to quit his saucy
' pretensions to your all-conquering beauty, though he
' had heard I had myself resolved to adore you. Careless,
' I think they call him.

' *Lady D.* Your Highness wrongs your merit, to give
' yourself the least concern for one so much below your
' fear.

' *Care.* When I first heard of him, I on the instant
' ordered one of my retinue to strike off his head with a
' scimitar ; but they told me the free laws of England al-
' lowed of no such power: so that, though I am a prince
' of the blood, Madam, I am obliged only to murder him
' privately.

' *Lady D.* 'Tis indeed a reproach to the ill-breeding
' of our constitution, not to admit your power with your
' person. But if the pain of my entire neglect can end
' him, pray, be easy.

' *Care.* Madam, I'm not revengeful ; make him but
' miserable, I'm satisfied.

' *Lady D.* You may depend upon't.

' *Care.* I'm in strange favour with her. [*Aside.*]——
' Please you, ladies, to make your fragrant fingers fami-
' liar with this box.

' *Lady D.* Sweet or plain, Sir ?

' *Care.* Right Mosco, Madam, made of the sculls of
' conquered enemies.

' *Lady Sad.* Gunpowder, as I live !   [*Exeunt.*'

The SCENE *changes to a Field.*

Enter Clarinda *and* Clerimont.

Cler. Come, Sir, we are far enough.

Clar. I only wish the lady were by, Sir, that the conqueror might carry her off the spot——I warrant she'd be mine.

Cler. That, my talking hero, we shall soon determine.

Clar. Not that I think her handfome, or care a rufh for her.

Cler. You are very mettled, Sir, to fight for a woman you don't value.

Clar. Sir, I value the reputation of a gentleman; and I don't think any young fellow ought to pretend to it, till he has talked himfelf into a lampoon, loft his two or three thoufand pounds at play, kept his mifs, and killed his man.

Cler. Very gallant, indeed, Sir! but if you pleafe to handle your fword, you'll foon go through your courfe.

Clar. Come on, Sir——I believe I fhall give your miftrefs a truer account of your heart than you have done. I have had her heart long enough, and now will have yours.

Cler. Ha! does fhe love you, then?

[Endeavouring to draw.

Clar. I leave you to judge that, Sir. But I have lain with her a thoufand times; in fhort, fo long, till I'm tired of it.

Cler. Villain, thou lieft! Draw, or I'll ufe you as you deferve, and ftab you.

Clar. Take this with you firft, Clarinda will never marry him that murders me.

Cler. She may the man that vindicates her honour—— therefore be quick, or I'il keep my word——I find your fword is not for doing things in hafte.

Clar. It fticks to the fcabbard fo, I believe I did not wipe off the blood of the laft man I fought with.

Cler. Come, Sir, this trifling fhan't ferve your turn— Here, give me yours, and take mine.

Clar. With all my heart, Sir—Now have at you.

[Cler. draws, and finds only a hilt in his hand.

Cler. Death! you villain, do you ferve me fo?

Clar.

Clar. In love and war, Sir, all advantages are fair: fo we conquer, no matter whether by force or ftratagem— Come, quick, Sir—Your life or miftrefs.

Cler. Neither. Death! you fhall have both or none! Here drive your fword; for only through this heart you reach Clarinda.

Clar. Death, Sir! can you be mad enough to die for a woman that hates you?

Cler. If that were true, 'twere greater madnefs, then, to live.

Clar. Why, to my knowledge, Sir, fhe has ufed you bafely, falfly, ill, and for no reafon.

Cler. No matter; no ufage can be worfe than the con- tempt of poorly, tamely parting with her. She may abufe her heart by happy infidelities; but 'tis the pride of mine to be even miferably conftant.

Clar. Generous paffion! You almoft tempt me to re- fign her to you.

Cler. You cannot, if you would. I would indeed have won her fairly from you with my fword; but fcorn to take her as your gift. Be quick, and end your infolence.

Clar. Yes, thus—Moft generous Clerimont, you now, indeed, have fairly vanquifhed me! [*Runs to him.*] My woman's follies and my fhame be buried ever here.

Cler. Ha, Clarinda! Is it poffible? My wonder rifes with my joy!—How came you in this habit?

Clar. Now you indeed recall my blufhes; but I had no other veil to hide them, while I confefs'd the injuries I had done your heart, in fooling with a man I never meant on any terms to engage with. Befide, I knew, from our late parting, your fear of lofing me would reduce you to comply with Sir Solomon's demands, for his intereft in your favour. Therefore, as you faw, I was refolved to ruin his market, by feeming to raife it; for he fecretly took the offer I made him.

Cler. 'Twas generoufly and timely offered; for it really prevented my figning articles to him. But if you would heartily convince me that I fhall never more have need of his intereft, e'en let ut fteal to the next prieft, and ho- neftly put it out of his power ever to part us.

Clar. Why, truly, confidering the trufts I have made you, 'twould be ridiculous now, I think, to deny you any

thing: and if you should grow weary of me after such
usage, I can't blame you.

Cler. Banish that fear; my flame can never waste,
For love sincere refines upon the taste.   [*Exeunt.*

Enter Sir Solomon, *with old* Mr. Wilful; Lady Sadlife,
        and Sylvia *weeping.*

Sir Sol. Troth, my old friend, this is a bad business indeed; you have bound yourself in a thousand pounds
bond, you say, to marry your daughter to a fine gentleman, and she, in the mean time, it seems, is fallen in love
with a stranger.

Wilf. Look you, Sir Solomon, it does not trouble me
o' this; for I'll make her do as I please, or I'll starve her.

Lady Sad. But, Sir, your daughter tells me that the
gentleman she loves is in every degree in as good circumstances as the person you design her for; and if he does
not prove himself so before to-morrow morning, she will
chearfully submit to whatever you'll impose on her.

Wilf. All sham! all sham! only to gain time. I expect my friend and his son here immediately, to demand
performance of articles; and if her Ladyship's nice stomach does not immediately comply with them, as I told
you before, I'll starve her.

Lady Sad. But, consider, Sir, what a perpetual discord
must a forced marriage probably produce.

Wilf. Discord! pshaw, waw! One man makes as good
a husband as another. A month's marriage will set all to
rights, I warrant you. You know the old saying, Sir
Solomon, lying together makes pigs love.

Lady Sad. [*To* Syl.] What shall we do for you?
There's no altering him. Did not your lover promise to
come to your assistance?

Syl. I expect him every minute; but can't foresee from
him the least hope of my redemption——This is he.

Enter Atall *undisguised.*

At. My Sylvia, dry those tender eyes; for while
there's life there's hope.

Lady Sad. Ha! is't he? but I must smother my confusion.   [*Aside.*

Wilf. How now, Sir! Pray, who gave you commission
to be so familiar with my daughter?

At. Your pardon, Sir; but when you know me right,
                                          you'll

you'll neither think my freedom or my pretenfions familiar or difhonourable.

Wilf. Why, Sir, what pretenfions have you to her?

At. Sir, I fav'd her life at the hazard of my own: that
gave me a pretence to know her; knowing her made me
love, and gratitude made her receive it.

Wilf. Ay, Sir! and fome very good reafons, beft known
to myfelf, make me refufe it.   Now, what will you do?

At. I can't tell yet, Sir; but if you'll do me the favour to let me know thofe reafons——

Wilf. Sir, I don't think myfelf obliged to do either;
but I'll tell you what I'll do for you: fince you fay you
love my daughter, and fhe loves you, I'll put you in the
neareft way to get her.

At. Don't flatter me, I beg you, Sir.

Wilf. Not I, upon my foul, Sir; for, look you, 'tis only this——get my confent, and you fhall have her.

At. I beg your pardon, Sir, for endeavouring to talk
reafon to you.   But, to return your raillery, give me
leave to tell you, when any man marries her but myfelf,
he muft extremely afk my confent.

Wilf. Before George, thou art a very pretty impudent
fellow; and I'm forry I can't punifh her difobedience, by
throwing her away upon thee.

At. You'll have a great deal of plague about this bufinefs, Sir; for I fhall be mighty difficult to give up my
pretenfions to her.

Wilf. Ha! 'tis a thoufand pities I can't comply with
thee.   Thou wilt certainly be a thriving fellow; for thou
doft really fet the beft face upon a bad caufe, that ever I
faw fince I was born.

At. Come, Sir, once more, raillery apart, fuppofe I
prove myfelf of equal birth and fortune to deferve her?

Wilf. Sir, if you were eldeft fon to the Cham of Tar-
tary, and had the dominions of the Great Mogul entailed
upon you and your heirs for ever, it would fignify no
more than the bite of my thumb.   The girl's difpofed of;
I have matched her already, upon a thoufand pounds
forfeit; and faith fhe fhall fairly run for't, though fhe's
yerk'd and flead from the creft to the crupper.

At. Confufion!

Syl. What will become of me?

Wilf. And if you don't think me in earneſt now, here comes one that will convince you of my ſincerity.

At. My father! Nay, then, my ruin is inevitable.

Enter Sir Harry Atall.

Sir Har. [*To* At.] Oh, ſweet Sir! have I found you at laſt? Your very humble ſervant. What's the reaſon pray, that you have had the aſſurance to be almoſt a fort-night in town, and never come near me, eſpecially when I ſent you word I had buſineſs of ſuch conſequence with you?

At. I underſtood your buſineſs was to marry me, Sir, to a woman I never ſaw: and to confeſs the truth, I durſt not come near you, becauſe I was at the ſame time in love with one you never ſaw.

Sir Har. Was you ſo, Sir? Why, then, Sir, I'll find a ſpeedy cure for your paſſion——Brother Wilful—Hey, fiddles there!

At. Sir, you may treat me with what ſeverity you pleaſe; but my engagements to that lady are too power-ful and fixed, to let the utmoſt miſery diſſolve them.

Sir Har. What does the fool mean?

At. That I can ſooner die than part with her.

Wilf. Hey!—Why, is this your ſon, Sir Harry?

Sir Har. Hey-day!——Why, did not you know that before?

At. Oh, earth, and all you ſtars! is this the lady you deſigned me, Sir?

Syl. Oh, fortune! is it poſſible?

Sir Har. And is this the lady, Sir, you have been ma-king ſuch a buſtle about?

At. Not life, health, or happineſs are half ſo dear to me.

Sir Sol. [*Joining* At. *and* Sylvia's *bands.*]—Loll, loll, leroll!

At. Oh, tranſporting joy!   [*Embracing* Sylvia.
Sir Har. ⎤   [*Joining in the tune, and dancing about them.*]
Wilf.   ⎦   Loll! loll!

Sir Sol. Hey! within, there! [*Calls the fiddles.*] By jingo, we'll make a night on't!

Enter Clarinda *and* Clerimont.

Clar. Save you, ſave you, good people——I'm glad, uncle,

uncle, to hear you call so chearfully for the fiddles; it
looks as if you had a husband ready for me.

Sir Sol. Why, that I may have by to-morrow night,
Madam; but, in the mean time, if you please, you may
wish your friends joy.

Clar. Dear Sylvia!

Syl. Clarinda!

At. Oh, Clerimont, such a deliverance!

Cler. Give you joy, joy, Sir.

Clar. I congratulate your happiness, and am pleased
our little jealousies are over; Mr. Clerimont has told me
all, and cured me of curiosity for ever.

Syl. What, married?

Clar. You'll see presently. But, Sir Solomon, what
do you mean by to-morrow? Why, do you fancy I have
any more patience than the rest of my neighbours?

Sir Sol. Why, truly, Madam, I don't suppose you
have; but I believe to-morrow will be as soon as their
business can be done, by which time I expect a jolly fox-
hunter from Yorkshire; and if you are resolved not to
have patience till next day, why, the same parson may
toss you up all four in a dish together.

Clar. A filthy fox-hunter!

Sir Sol. Odzooks, a mettled fellow, that will ride you
from day-break to sun-set! none of our flimsy London
rascals, that must have a chair to carry them to their
coach, and a coach to carry them to a trapes, and a con-
stable to carry both to the round-house.

Clar. Ay, but this fox-hunter, Sir Solomon, will come
home dirty and tired as one of his hounds; he'll be always asleep before he's a-bed, and on horseback before
he's awake; he must rise early to follow his sport, and I
sit up late at cards for want of better diversion. Put
this together, my wise uncle.

Sir Sol. Are you so high fed, Madam, that a country
gentleman of fifteen hundred pounds a year won't go
down with you?

Clar. Not so, Sir; but you really kept me so sharp,
that I was e'en forced to provide for myself; and here
stands the fox-hunter for my money.

[Claps Cler. on the shoulder.

Sir Sol. How!

Cler.

Cler. Even fo, Sir Solomon—Hark in your ear, Sir— You really held your confent at fo high a price, that, to give you a proof of my good hufbandry, I was refolved to fave charges, and e'en marry her without it.

Sir Sol. Hell and——

Clar. And hark you in t'other ear, Sir——Becaufe I would not have you expofe your reverend age by a mif-take, know, Sir, I was the young fpark with a fmooth face and a feather, that offered you a thoufand guineas for your confent, which you would have been glad to have taken.

Sir Sol. The devil!—If ever I traffic in women's flefh again, may all the bank ftocks fall when I have bought them, and rife when I have fold them—Hey-day! what have we here! More cheats?

Cler. Not unlikely, Sir; for I fancy they are married.

Enter Lady Dainty *and* Carelefs.

Lady Sad. That they are, I can affure you——I give your Highnefs joy, Madam.

Lady D. Lard, that people of any rank fhould ufe fuch vulgar falutations! though, methinks, highnefs has fome-thing of grandeur in the found. But I was in hopes, good people, that confident fellow, Carelefs, had been among you.

Care. What fay you, Madam, (to divert the good company) fhall we fend for him by way of mortification?

Lady D. By all means; for your fake, methinks, I ought to give him full defpair.

Care. Why, then, to let you fee, that 'tis a much ea-fier thing to cure a fine lady of her fickly tafte, than a lover of his impudence—there's Carelefs for you, without the leaft tincture of defpair about him. [*Difcovers himfelf.*

All. Ha, Carelefs!

Lady D. Abufed! undone!

All. Ha, ha!

Cler. Nay, now, Madam, we wifh you a fuperior joy; for you have married a man inftead of a monfter.

Care. Come, come, Madam; fince you find you were in the power of fuch a cheat, you may be glad it was no greater: you might have fallen into a rafcal's hands; but you know I am a gentleman, my fortune no fmall one, and, if your temper will give me leave, will deferve you.

Lady

Lady Sad. Come, e'en make the beſt of your fortune for, take my word, if the cheat had not been a very agreeable one, I would never have had a hand in't—You muſt pardon me, if I can't help laughing.

Lady D. Well, ſince it muſt be ſo, I pardon all; only one thing let me beg of you, Sir; that is, your promiſe to wear this habit one month for my ſatisfaction.

Care. Oh, Madam, that's a trifle! I'll lie in the ſun a whole ſummer for an olive complexion, to oblige you.

Lady D. Well, Mr. Careleſs, I begin now to think better of my fortune, and look back with apprehenſion of the eſcape I have had; you have already cured my folly, and were but my health recoverable, I ſhould think myſelf completely happy.

Care. For that, Madam, we'll venture to ſave you doctor's fees,

And truſt to nature : time will ſoon diſcover,

Your beſt phyſician is a favour'd lover.

[Exeunt.

END of the FIFTH ACT.

E P I L O G U E.

WELL, Sirs, I know not how the play may pass,
 But, in my humble sense.—our bard's an ass;
For had he ever known the least of nature,
H' had found his double spark a dismal creature:
To please two ladies he two forms puts on,
As if the thing in shadows could be done;
The women really two, and he, poor soul! but one.
Had he revers'd the hint, h' had done the feat,
Had made th' impostor credibly complete;
A single mistress might have stood the cheat.
She might to several lovers have been kind,
Nor strain'd your faith, to think both pleas'd and blind.
Plain sense had known, the fair can love receive,
With half the pains your warmest vows can give.
 But, hold!—I'm thinking I mistake the matter——
On second thoughts—The hint's but honest satire,
And only meant t'expose their modish sense,
Who think the fire of love's but impudence.
Our spark was really modest: when he found
Two female claims at once, he one disown'd;
Wisely presuming, though in ne'er such haste,
One would be found enough for him at last.
So that, to sum the whole, I think the play
Deserves the usual favours on his day;
If not, he swears he'll write the next to music,
In doggrel rhimes would make or him or you sick.
His groveling sense Italian airs shall crown,
And then he's sure ev'n nohsense will go down.
But if you'd have the world, suppose the stage
Not quite forsaken in this airy age,
Let your glad votes our needless fears confound,
And speak in claps as loud for sense as sound.